TOM AND KAREN HORTON are former residents of Hawaii now living in San Francisco. They are the authors of three Dolphin travel guides to San Francisco, Los Angeles, and Hawaii and write frequently about the Islands. They are the editorial consultants for this guidebook.

RICK CARROLL, an author, journalist, and photographer, lives on Oahu. He has written for the *Honolulu Advertiser* and the *San Francisco Chronicle* and is the author of *From Mauka to Makai* and is writing *Tropical Style: The Architecture of Paradise.*

THELMA CHANG is a Honolulu-based writer specializing in travel and human-interest stories. Her articles have appeared in such publications as *Westways, Essence,* and the Smithsonian's *Air and Space* magazine.

BETTY FULLARD-LEO, the associate editor of *Aloha* magazine, writes and edits the *Aloha Travelers' Newsletter,* a bimonthly guide for visitors to Hawaii. She has lived in Hawaii since 1962.

JOHN HECKATHORN, a former professor of English at the University of Hawaii, is now associate editor of *Honolulu* magazine, for which he also writes a monthly dining column. He has lived in Honolulu for more than a dozen years.

LINDA KEPHART, the editor of *Discover Hawaii* magazine for three years and associate editor of *Hawaii Business* before that, has contributed articles on Hawaii to magazines such as *Pleasant Hawaii* and *Manulani.* She lives in Honolulu.

JOHN W. PERRY, a longtime resident of the Pacific area, is a contributor to several North American and Asia-Pacific magazines. He lives in Honolulu and often travels in the South Seas on magazine assignments.

THE PENGUIN TRAVEL GUIDES

AUSTRALIA

CANADA

THE CARIBBEAN

ENGLAND & WALES

FRANCE

GERMANY

GREECE

HAWAII

IRELAND

ITALY

MEXICO

NEW YORK CITY

PORTUGAL

SPAIN

THE PENGUIN GUIDE TO HAWAII 1990

ALAN TUCKER

General Editor

PENGUIN BOOKS

PENGUIN BOOKS

Published by the Penguin Group
Viking Penguin, a division of Penguin Books USA Inc.,
40 West 23rd Street, New York, New York 10010, U.S.A.
Penguin Books Ltd, 27 Wrights Lane,
London W8 5TZ, England
Penguin Books Australia Ltd, Ringwood,
Victoria, Australia
Penguin Books Canada Ltd, 2801 John Street,
Markham, Ontario, Canada L3R 1B4
Penguin Books (N.Z.) Ltd, 182-190 Wairau Road,
Auckland 10, New Zealand

Penguin Books Ltd, Registered Offices:
Harmondsworth, Middlesex, England

First published in Penguin Books 1989

1   3   5   7   9   10   8   6   4   2

Copyright © Viking Penguin,
a division of Penguin Books USA Inc., 1989
All rights reserved

ISBN 0 14 019.909 8
ISSN 1043-4569

Printed in the United States of America

Set in ITC Garamond Light
Designed by Beth Tondreau Design
Maps by David Lindroth
Illustrations by Bill Russell
Copy Edited by Amy Hughes
Fact-checked in Hawaii by Robert Mon

THIS GUIDEBOOK

The Penguin Travel Guides are designed for people who are experienced travellers in search of exceptional information that will help them sharpen and deepen their enjoyment of the trips they take.

Where, for example, are the interesting, isolated, fun, charming, or romantic places within your budget to stay? The hotels and resorts described by our writers (each of whom is an experienced travel writer who either lives on or regularly tours the island of Hawaii he or she covers) are some of the special places, in all price ranges except for the lowest—not the run-of-the-mill, heavily marketed places on every travel agent's CRT display and in advertised airline and travel-agency packages. We indicate the approximate price level of each accommodation in our description of it (no indication means it is moderate), and at the end of every chapter we supply contact information so that you can get precise, up-to-the-minute rates and make reservations.

The Penguin Guide to Hawaii 1990 highlights the more rewarding parts of Hawaii so that you can quickly and efficiently home in on a good itinerary.

Of course, the guides do far more than just help you choose a hotel and plan your trip. *The Penguin Guide to Hawaii 1990* is designed for use *in* Hawaii. Our Penguin Hawaii writers tell you what you really need to know, what you can't find out so easily on your own. They identify and describe the truly out-of-the-ordinary restaurants, shops, activities, sights, and beaches, and tell you the best way to "do" your destination.

Our writers are highly selective. They bring out the significance of the places they cover, capturing the personality and the underlying cultural resonances of a town or region—making clear its special appeal. For exhaustive detailed coverage of local attractions, we suggest that you

also use one of the locally available reference-type guidebooks along with the Penguin Guide.

   The Penguin Guide to Hawaii 1990 is full of reliable
and timely information, revised each year. We would like
to know if you think we've left out some very special
place.

Alan Tucker
General Editor
Penguin Travel Guides

40 West 23rd Street
New York, New York 10010
or
27 Wrights Lane
London W8 5TZ

CONTENTS

MAPS

THE
PENGUIN
GUIDE
TO
HAWAII
1990

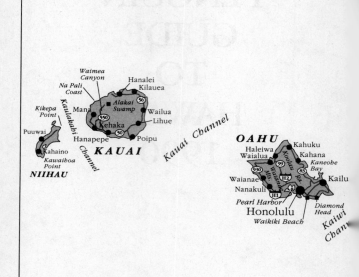

Waimea
Canyon

Hanalei
Kilauea

Na Pali
Coast

Mana

Alakai
Swamp

Kikepa
Point

Wailua
Lihue

550

Puuwai

Kehaka

Hanapepe

56

50

Poipu

Kahaino

KAUAI

Kauai Channel

Kawaihoa
Point

NIIHAU

OAHU

Kahuku

Haleiwa
Waialua

Kahana

99

Kaneobe
Bay

Waianae

H2

85

Kailu

Nanakuli

H1

Pearl Harbor

Diamond
Head

Honolulu

Waikiki Beach

Kaiwi
Chan

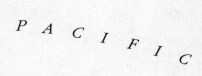

P A C I F I C

N

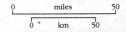

State of Hawaii
(main islands)

0   miles   50

0   km   50

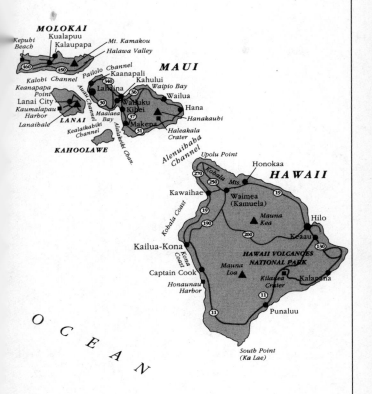

MOLOKAI

Kepuhi
Beach

Kualapuu
Kalaupapa

Mt. Kamakou
Halawa Valley

M A U I

Kalobi Channel

450

Keanapapa
Point

Kaanapali
Kahului
Lahaina   Waipio Bay
Wailua

Patiolo Channel

340

460

Lanai City

Kaumalapau
Harbor

LANAI

Lanaihale

Wailuku
Kihei
Makena

37

30

36

31

*Maalaea
Bay*

Hana

Hanakaubi

Auau Channel

Alalakiki Chan.

*Kealaikabiki
Channel*

*Haleakala
Crater*

KAHOOLAWE

*Alenuihaha
Channel*

Upolu Point

Honokaa

HAWAII

270

*Kobala
Mts*

250

Kawaihae

Waimea
(Kamuela)

19

Kohala Coast

19

190

Kailua-Kona

*Mauna
Kea*

200

Hilo

Keaau

130

*Kona
Coast*

Captain Cook

*Mauna
Loa*

*HAWAII VOLCANOES
NATIONAL PARK*

*Honaunau
Harbor*

11

*Kilauea
Crater*

Kalapana

11

Punaluu

*South Point
(Ka Lae)*

O C E A N

OVERVIEW

By Tom and Karen Horton

Tom and Karen Horton are former residents of Hawaii now living in San Francisco. They are the authors of three Dolphin travel guides to San Francisco, Los Angeles, and Hawaii and write frequently about the Islands for other publications. They return to all the major Hawaiian islands regularly.

There is little need to parade evidence here in support of Hawaii as an estimable destination for a break from the world of the ordinary. Despite everything that Western civilization has done to them in 200 years, the Hawaiian Islands remain one of the most naturally beautiful places on earth. There is, however, a need to help the traveller who is destined for Hawaii without knowing *which* Hawaii he wants. There are, as connoisseurs of the Islands have learned, many Hawaiis from which to choose. Disappointment sets in when visitors arrive in Hawaii for the right reasons, then head off in all the wrong directions. The beauty of Hawaii is clearly visible and reasonably accessible—it is the true Hawaii *experience* that can be elusive.

It is not hidden, however, and it is not a well-kept secret, and it is not something available only to the highest bidder. Hawaii is too small, and the tourists too great in number, for anything even remotely appealing to be kept out of the public grasp. The best way to experience Hawaii is simply to understand in advance the choices that must be made, so you can improve the odds of making the right choice.

The process begins with deciding which island—or how many islands—you are going to visit. There are six choices: *Oahu, Maui, Molokai, Lanai, Kauai,* and the island of *Hawaii* (commonly referred to as the *Big Island*). Two other islands can be seen and not touched: **Niihau**, a small, arid island off the coast of Kauai that is privately owned by a Kauai family and populated entirely by a tiny community of Hawaiians who work the island as a ranch and live in something of a time warp, removed as they are from most forms of 20th-century progress (for the first time, helicopter tours are now allowed to land on an unpopulated part of Niihau); and **Kahoolawe**, an even smaller and even dryer island off the coast of Maui that the U.S. Navy kept for itself as a convenient place to practice dropping bombs.

In truth, the average visitor narrows the choice to four islands, ignoring Molokai because its tourism facilities are severely limited (so, for that matter, are the reasons for going there), and Lanai for the same reasons—although this little island that's been used purely as a Dole pineapple plantation is now venturing into tourism with its first seaside resorts. The most popular islands are, in order: Oahu, Maui, Kauai, and the Big Island of Hawaii. These are where you will find most of the six million people who visit Hawaii during the year. It follows that these four islands are also where you find the greatest concentration of hotels, condominiums, restaurants, tourist shops, tour buses, rental cars, and traffic jams. So if you want to go to a Hawaiian island completely removed from all that, go to Molokai or Lanai. Or you could go to the êast side of Maui, or the north side of Kauai, or.... And here we begin to get a glimpse of all those different Hawaiis.

Waikiki and Oahu
versus the Neighbor Islands

If you are going to be in Hawaii for only one week, it is a mistake to book accommodations on more than two islands. At least two weeks are needed to extend your visit to three or four islands and leave with anything more than a cursory view of what each of those islands is all about. Don't be misled by the flying time between islands, which is 20 to 30 minutes by jet, the hop from Oahu to Kauai being the shortest and the flight from Kauai to the Big Island the longest. Island airports are crowded, baggage service is slow, renting cars is a tedious procedure, and then you may have to drive for a half-hour or longer to reach your hotel or condominium, unless you take a shuttle van, which will move even more slowly. Add the inevitable delays of checking in and checking out of hotels and condominiums, returning rental cars, and packing and unpacking and you will find yourself exhausted if you try island-hopping without allowing three or more nights on each island. More important, you are sure to form an incomplete opinion, or a completely unfair one, of an island based on a hurried visit—and you simply won't have as good a time as you should.

A wise choice for the first-time visitor is to spend one part of the vacation in Waikiki, and the rest on a Neighbor Island, as the islands beyond Oahu are collectively known. Maui is the favored Neighbor Island by a wide margin, and was the first island to begin drawing its own exclusive clientele, visitors who chose to skip Waikiki entirely and go directly to Maui. Before Maui became a magical name, *all* tourists went to Waikiki, and then some went on to the Neighbor Islands. Now there are direct flights from the West Coast of the United States to Kauai and to the Big Island as well as to Maui.

Still, you are shortchanging yourself if, on an inaugural visit, you listen to the travel snobs who tell you to skip Oahu because Waikiki is an overcrowded, overbuilt, overly commercialized, concrete, high-rise mess. It *is* all that. It is also one square mile of around-the-clock, international-flavored energy, fun, and excitement that is worth the price of congestion. And nowhere else in the Islands is there such a wide range of prices. Waikiki has a more extensive choice of hotel rooms, dining, shopping, and entertainment than all the other islands combined. You can also just turn your back on high-rise Waikiki and, with your feet in the sand and your face in the sun, contemplate the balmy view from Waikiki Beach, a beach that may be elbow-to-elbow in people but is still a clean, safe beach massaged by cool-but-never-cold surf rolling out of an unpolluted sea and breaking in mild-mannered waves over coral reefs.

Beyond Waikiki are historic palaces and tombs containing the fascinating history of the kings and queens of 19th-century Hawaii; the military history of Pearl Harbor; and the less-than-flattering history of American merchants who stole the Islands from the Hawaiian monarchy so they could harvest fortunes in sugar and pineapple. Beyond the pineapple fields that still cover the plains of central Oahu there are the beaches of the **North Shore**, where the only high-rises are the monstrous waves of Waimea, Sunset, and Pipeline, which provide a stage for some of the most spectacular surfing on earth.

The quality of life in Waikiki, it should be noted, *has* improved lately, although the tiny area is unquestionably congested to the point of choking on its own vehicular traffic—but then this is true of the whole island of Oahu and its resident population of approximately one million. Millions in public funds have been spent on a Waikiki face-lift that widened the sidewalks and generally improved the appearance of the two main thoroughfares, Kalakaua and Kuhio avenues, that have carried traffic through the heart of Hawaii's tourism ever since streetcars were hauling people from Honolulu to Waikiki Beach's first luxury hotel, The Moana, in 1901. Even more millions in private dollars have been spent upgrading the look and the quality of some of Waikiki's most venerable hostelries, including the vintage Moana. The result has not provided Waikiki with anything close to a country-club atmosphere, but it has improved the look of Waikiki, and made its disfigurements seem just a little less obtrusive.

So unless you are a stress victim from an inner city who truly needs to escape any semblance of urbanization, include Waikiki in your introduction to Hawaii.

Maui

There is no secret to Maui's magic. It has the state's best combination of weather, beaches, mountain greenery, luxury resorts, budget-oriented condominiums, indoor, outdoor, and in-the-ocean activities, wide-open spaces where you can drink in the view, and plenty of places where you can eat and drink with a view. Maui has some of Hawaii's best golf courses, the absolute best windsurfing, the most prolific choices in sailing, scuba diving, and snorkeling, and the only dining and nightlife scene of any real substance and variety beyond Oahu. Even the migrating humpback whales choose the waters off Maui for mating and birthing, making whale-watching cruises a major tourist activity here from January to April. Maui has **Lahaina**, a bawdy old whaling port reborn as the most colorful little two-story, wooden-sidewalk, waterfront town ever to tempt a tourist with endless rows of souvenir tee-shirts, overpriced jewelry, and food and grog priced to pay for the view. Of the big four, only on Maui does the view include other islands clearly: From a

Lahaina restaurant deck or a Kaanapali Resort beach you can gaze across glassy waters where the sun is dancing and study the sloping profiles of Lanai and Molokai.

Maui has Haleakala, a 10,023-foot volcano you can drive to the top of, hike down into, or coast all the way down the side of on bicycles. Maui also has **Hana**, a heavenly place close to the sea but protected by no-growth gods who keep it almost out of reach on the other side of Haleakala at the end of a long, crooked road. If you are dead serious about getting away from it all, get yourself to Hana, where you have to fall in love with the raw beauty of the land because there is nothing else to do in Hana except look at the scenery.

Maui may seem to have it all, but be forewarned that the island also has severe traffic problems, high prices, and two of Hawaii's worst strips of concrete pollution, the condominium corridors of Kahana and Kihei. None of this has deterred the trendy traveller, who knows it's nothing special to explain a winter tan with, "I went to Hawaii," and so much more chic to say, "I just came back from Maui."

The Big Island versus Kauai

This brings us to Kauai and to the Big Island of Hawaii. They could not be more opposite in every sense. Kauai is at the northwest end of the gentle curve of Islands, 72 miles from the shores of Oahu; the Big Island holds the southeast end of the chain, putting its northwest coastline a scant 26 miles across the water from the east side of Maui. Kauai is small (553 square miles), easygoing, and as green as an Irish spring—a condition created by very wet weather. The Big Island is, by comparison, enormous (4,038 square miles, three times the size of Rhode Island), rough around the edges, full of fire in the belly, drenched with rain on one side *and* bone-dry on the other. Here is a perfect example of the need to choose between the different Hawaiis. At the risk of oversimplifying to make the point, it's reasonable to suggest that anyone who loves Kauai would not be attracted by the Big Island, and vice versa. Each has ardent admirers, although neither island draws visitors in numbers anywhere near those pulled in by Oahu and Maui.

That, in fact, is one attraction Kauai and the Big Island share: Repeat visitors who long ago gave up Oahu and now find Maui too crowded are beginning to choose the

Big Island or Kauai. The two islands have responded with a splurge of impressive new resort hotels and attendant amenities such as golf courses.

Kauai is the only island that has embraced tourism and nonetheless avoided high-rises. By law nothing on the island can be built higher than four stories. (A grandiose exception is the new Westin Kauai; the original ten-story structure predated the height limitations.) The personal style of the so-called Garden Isle is also low-profile. This island has a way of making you slow down, quiet down, stay put. True, there aren't a lot of choices on Kauai, where the road only goes part of the way around the island and the bulk of the land mass is inaccessible except to helicopters and hikers. And maybe you have to slow down because traffic on Kauai's limited roadways is often bumper-to-bumper. A line heard often on Oahu is, "Kauai is beautiful, but what do you do the second day?" Actually, many choose Kauai precisely because they don't want to do much of anything even on the first day.

Visitors to Kauai who want the sun and safe swimming beaches choose the **Poipu Beach Resort** hotels and condominiums in the south. Serious golfers stay at the North-Shore **Princeville Resort**, along with the nongolfers who enjoy the cooler, greener (and thus wetter) wide-open spaces and the accessibility to the bucolic Hanalei Valley and the awesome Na Pali Coast. In between the moist North Shore and the sunny South Shore is the east shore, where a woman in a gift shop once stripped Kauai to its basics by asking the clerk as she faced west, "Have I got this straight? If I want sunshine I go to the left and if I don't I go to the right?"

Kauai is also known for the most adventurous hiking in Hawaii, mainly into ancient Kalalau Valley; some of the most gorgeous, uncrowded beaches anywhere; thrilling Zodiac boat tours along the rugged **Na Pali Coast**; breath-taking "flight-seeing" helicopter tours of the little island's remarkably large natural wonders, such as Waimea Canyon, the Na Pali sea cliffs, and the 5,148-foot peak of Mount Waialeale, the mountain the Kauai Visitors Bureau hates because tour guides always point it out as the wettest spot on earth. Kauai is also known for Hawaii's only navigable rivers and for the almost nothing that goes on after dark.

Of all the islands, the **Big Island** of Hawaii is the most difficult for the casual visitor to understand, appreciate, and enjoy. It's more than that the Big Island has very few good beaches of the white-sand quality found on the other islands. It's a problem of size, time, and diversity: The Big Island is so large, and its qualities so diverse, that there is not enough time to see and experience it all in one visit.

Maui and Kauai can be love at first sight. The Big Island is often fright at first sight. Visitors leave the airport and travel through a flat, black, treeless, lifeless landscape composed of mile after mile of hard, mean-looking lava, and the same unspoken question is on every nervous mind: "My God, this is Hawaii?"

Nothing could be more Hawaii. This is the way all the islands began, smoldering volcanoes forcing themselves out of the earth's crust and exploding above the ocean in showers of fire that spilled over like burning rivers, cooled, and hardened into lava, a process repeated over and over through hundreds of years until permanent land masses were formed as islands in the sea. That process can still be seen on the Big Island, where Hawaii's only active volcanoes are found—and which happen to be some of the most active volcanoes in the world.

The volcanoes, however, have brought more discredit than credit to the Big Island's reputation among the world of discriminating travellers. Many shun the island on the assumption it is nothing but one large lava field. They never see the rain forests, the waterfalls, the lineup of nice beaches along the western shoreline, the high country where white-faced cattle graze in the tall grass, the snow-capped mountains, the verdant valleys, the calm seas teeming with giant marlin, the famous Kona sunsets. But it takes time to see all that. It takes much more time before you begin to *feel* the power of the Big Island, the island of Kamehameha and a place where the physical evidence of ancient Hawaii is better preserved and the haunting memory of the Hawaiians who lived and died here is more strongly felt than on any other island.

But it is also an island full of *fun*. The volcanoes, even while erupting—and Kilauea is almost always erupting in one form or another—are fun. Only on the Big Island are volcanic eruptions a spectator sport, and a safe one be-cause the lava flows slowly out of shield volcanoes, which do not explode with the dangerous violence of a cone-type volcano. Hawaii Volcanoes National Park is one of the natural wonders of the world, as well as a dramatic place for long hikes through dense forests, across lava deserts, around crater rims, and even onto the floor of the lunarlike craters.

Unfortunately, the volcanoes are on one side of the island and the vast majority of the tourist facilities, and every other attraction except the volcanoes, are on the opposite, or west, side of the island. This has added to the confusion over the Big Island. Simply put, the west side is where the **Kona Coast**, the village of **Kailua-Kona**, and the **Kohala Coast** are located, and this is where the sun shines and the resorts and hotels, condominiums, and golf courses bask in its persistent rays. The east side, a two- to three-hour drive from West Hawaii, has the **Hawaii Volcanoes National Park**, the island's largest town and seat of island government, **Hilo**, and a lot of rain. Additionally, the Big Island has sprawling cattle ranches (Parker Ranch is the largest privately owned ranch in the United States), macadamia-nut orchards, America's only commercial coffee farms, papaya farms, enough orchid growers to qualify the Big Island as the Orchid Isle, and enough hidden marijuana fields to require a periodic "green harvest" by both local and national park authorities, who try to prevent the illegal crop from taking over the landscape and competing with tourism as the dominant economy.

There is more to the Big Island—but that's the island's blessing and its burden: There's always more here than you can get to, which is why those who have found the time to recognize it keep coming back to what they feel is not just the biggest but the best of the Islands.

Hotels versus Condominiums versus Condominium-Hotels versus the Mega-Resorts

Hawaii's choice in accommodations, once limited to the traditional hotel or the up-and-coming condominium, has now been complicated by a third choice: the up-and-coming condominium-hotel. While the resort hotels have become larger and more spectacular, the condominiums have become more like small hotels.

Billing themselves as all-suite hotels or full-service condominium-hotels, these are usually high-rises divided into studios and one- and two-bedroom apartments, all with kitchens. They appeal to the budget-minded couple or family that prefers the space and the privacy of a condo-minium, where they can prepare snacks or full meals, to the expense of a hotel where all meals are taken in restaurants or through room service, and the tipping can kill you. The new configuration, the condo-hotel, offers many of the same services as a traditional hotel—front desk, restaurant, daily maid service, guest activities—combined with rooms that are larger than hotel rooms, that include kitchens, and that are reasonably priced by Hawaii standards.

While there are choices in hotels and condominiums at various levels of luxury and price on every island, some basic differences characterize each island. Oahu, of course, has the greatest variety of accommodations, packed into Waikiki, where the average room rate is still under $100 a night. The Neighbor Islands, on the other hand, have been setting their sights more and more on the upscale traveller, meaning $200 and up for a hotel room.

Maui is generally considered the most expensive, especially West Maui where the popular Kaanapali Beach Resort and the silk-purse Kapalua Bay Resort are located. Wailea Resort, a half-hour away on the sunny southwestern shoreline, is a lovely and considerably quieter alternative to West Maui, and the beaches are even better. Maui has far more choices in condominiums than all the other islands, even including Oahu, where the Waikiki hotels are still dominant. There are first-rate—and high-priced—condominiums at Kaanapali Beach Resort and Wailea Resort, and some luxury villas at Kapalua Bay Resort. Careful research can yield some comfortable, reasonably priced condos in the Na Pali area north of Kaanapali—but beware the condo ghettos of Kahana and Kihei, where you might save a buck but wreck a vacation.

You may already have heard of a new kind of resort taking hold in Hawaii: the mega-resort. This is the sprawling, super-spectacular, action-oriented, deep-pockets kind of resort hotel introduced by flamboyant Honolulu developer Chris Hemmeter. His first entry in this category was something of a mini-mega-resort, the highly successful Hyatt Regency Maui at Kaanapali. Since then he has dwarfed that project with the massive Kauai Lagoons, site of the opulent Westin Kauai, and the stunning Hyatt Regency Waikoloa on the South Kohala Coast of the Big Island. These are not hotels by any ordinary definition of the word. Although all his Neighbor Island hotels are oceanfront, Hemmeter has an incredible fascination for filling his properties with water. At Westin Maui, Westin Kauai, and Hyatt Regency Waikoloa there are multiple swimming pools the size of football fields, and water everywhere you turn: shooting upward from fountains, cascading as waterfalls, gushing out of the mouths of stone animals, and forming lagoons for dolphins, swans, and exotic fish. Before long, probably, there will be a humpback whale swimming in a Hemmeter hotel lobby.

These hotels, often described as Disneylands for adults, are not for everyone. But they are exciting; kids love them, adults who want to act like kids on vacation love them, and people who like to spend a whole vacation just hanging out around the pool absolutely adore them. They are actually an extension of the ongoing trend on the Neighbor Islands toward "complete destination resort hotels," meaning hotels that provide such an attractive variety of activities, shopping, dining, and entertainment within the confines of the resort that there is no need ever to go anywhere else.

Indeed, this is where Hawaii is becoming divided into two kinds of visitors: the type who come to experience the Islands in all their beauty, history, culture, and available outdoor activity; and the type who come to stay at the very best hotel with the best amenities, and rarely leave it. There are sufficient accommodations in Hawaii to satisfy both desires.

The Other Hawaii

People searching for the real Hawaii should look in the heart of Waikiki and along every sunny, easily accessible western coastline of every Neighbor Island, where the luxury resorts and the manicured golf courses cover the shorelines. *This* is the real Hawaii of today, a state completely and totally dominated by tourism as the number-one industry, with no viable alternative in sight. Sugar is nearly dead, pineapple is weak, other crops are minimal in importance, and there has been no industry to come along to replace King Cane, as sugar was once known, except tourism. Mass tourism anchors and propels the economy of the state of Hawaii.

Do not despair, however. There are still sides to Hawaii that have nothing to do with resorts and guided tours and all the other facilities and attractions designed specifically for the transient visitor. You can easily experience the other Hawaii, the one beyond the tourist track, if you are interested enough to search for it and energetic enough to pursue it. No guidebook can tell you exactly where to look, and certainly can't guarantee you'll find it, but you have to start by backing away from the centers of tourism and the well-marked destinations and let serendipity be your guide.

No more open space in Hawaii? Barely 5 percent of Hawaii's land is in urban use. On every island there is a wealth of natural splendor to be explored, from ancient valleys that once held large communities of Hawaiians to mountain trails that are as silent now as when precontact Hawaiians hurried along them. On every island there are still golden beaches that are hard to reach, and if you go to the trouble to get there, your footprints may be the only ones made in the sand all day. Travel slowly through the Islands, taking the time to follow different roads, stopping in the country stores, talking to the people who work and live far from the shadow of construction cranes, and you will be surprised at how easy it is to find the kind of Hawaii experiences that can't be packaged and sold.

USEFUL FACTS

When to Go
The standard weather forecast in Hawaii is, "Another beautiful day in paradise." Most of the time it's true. Because climatic variations are so slight throughout the year, with sunshine and mild temperatures the norm, Hawaii is always a vacation destination, no matter the season. There are some subtleties to consider, however, if you want sunshine to the max. Summer in the Islands runs from May to mid-October, with plenty of sunshine and gusty trade winds. Winter, from late October through April, is when the weather is cooler and there is more likely to be rain. August and September are usually the hottest and most humid months, with temperatures in the high 80s Fahrenheit and sometimes above 90. The coolest and often the wettest months are February and March, when evening temperatures can dip into the low 70s.

Hawaii's peak tourist traffic is launched with the Christmas season and runs through April, neatly coinciding with the worst elements of winter in the Northern Hemisphere. Some hotels raise their room rates during these months, but others don't. Another busy period is July and August, before children have to return to school in North

America. Good times to visit Hawaii are just before these two saturation periods begin. Rooms, rental cars, flights, and even restaurant reservations are easier to come by then.

Entry Requirements
Non–U.S. citizens must have a passport and visa. For Canadians, a document proving citizenship is required, such as a passport or birth certificate. There are no vaccination requirements.

Flying to Hawaii
There are daily direct nonstop flights to Honolulu from several major U.S. cities, most of them on or close to the West Coast. United Airlines offers the greatest number of flights from the most cities. Other U.S. carriers serving the Islands include Alaska, American, Continental, Delta, Northwest, Pan Am, TWA, and Hawaiian Airlines.

It is possible to bypass Honolulu completely with direct flights to three Neighbor Islands. United, American, and Delta have direct flights to Maui. United also has direct flights to Kauai and to the Big Island of Hawaii.

Foreign carriers landing in Honolulu include Canadian Airlines International, China Airlines, Qantas, Air New Zealand, Japan Airlines, Korean Air, and Philippine Airlines.

Flying from Island to Island
Jet aircraft and smaller planes offer regular interisland service. Aloha Airlines and Hawaiian Airlines are the jet carriers serving the major airports on Oahu, Maui, Kauai, and the Big Island. Aloha IslandAir, a subsidiary of Aloha Airlines, flies 18-passenger propeller-driven planes to the Princeville Resort on the North Shore of Kauai, to the Kapalua–West Maui Airport, and to Hana on the far east side of Maui, to Waimea on the Big Island, and to the islands of Lanai and Molokai. Hawaiian Air flies 50-passenger de Havilland DASH-7 turboprops to Lanai, Molokai, and Kapalua–West Maui. Air Molokai's nine-passenger, twin-engine Cessnas fly to Lanai, Molokai, and Kahului in central Maui. Niihau Helicopter (Tel: 808-335-3500) departs from Port Allen Airport on Kauai daily at 9:00 A.M., 12:00 P.M., and 3:00 P.M. for a two-hour flight with two stops on Niihau, for $185 per person (four to seven passengers).

Cruising Hawaii

An attractive alternative to negotiating air terminals in order to see the Neighbor Islands is to take a seven-day cruise aboard a 900-passenger ocean liner. American Hawaii Cruises' SS *Constitution* and SS *Independence* depart Honolulu Harbor from Piers 9 and 10 each Saturday for a week-long swing through the Islands, each one following an itinerary that is the reverse of the other's. They visit four ports on three islands (Hilo and Kailua-Kona on the Big Island, Kahului on Maui, and Nawiliwili, near Lihue, on Kauai), with optional shore excursions available at each stop. The two transatlantic veterans, built in the 1950s, were refurbished for the cruise line's Hawaii program, which was launched in 1980. While their comfort and convenience are generally lauded, food and service aboard these vessels have been subject to criticism over the years. Tel: (800) 227-3666.

Renting a Car

Before arriving on any island, it is best to make a rental-car reservation in advance, especially during peak seasons. There are dozens of rental-car companies in the Islands, and the competition is very aggressive, with most firms offering flat per-day rates with unlimited mileage. When shopping for the best price, however, confirm that the rate is for unlimited mileage, and use caution on quotes for low daily rates: Some are linked to a three-day minimum rental; if you want the car that long, fine. A valid driver's license is required to rent a car. A major credit card avoids the need to pay a deposit. Because shuttle service is generally the rule between rental offices and their car lots, allow sufficient time for returning a car in order to make a flight.

What to Wear

This is easy. Light sportswear, bathing suits, sandals, sunglasses, and a hat are the daytime rule in Hawaii. So is sunscreen. Better restaurants expect the female clientele to be in dressier attire at night. Men can leave their ties at home. A jacket is advisable, however, since a few of Hawaii's premier restaurants do require a jacket for dinner (it is preferable to be wearing one's own under these circumstances, rather than an ill-fitting loaner provided by the restaurant). Retail clothing options in the Islands have improved dramatically in recent years; if you need more Benettons or Polo/Ralph Laurens during the trip, there will be opportunities to buy them.

Local Time
Hawaii is 5 hours behind New York and the non-Maritime east coast of Canada, and 2 hours behind California and western Canada. It is 10 hours behind the United Kingdom. And when it is 10:00 A.M. in Honolulu, it is 8:00 A.M. the next day in Sydney, Australia, for a time difference of 20 hours. When daylight saving time is in effect elsewhere, add one hour to the time difference (Hawaii does not have daylight saving time).

Telephoning
The area code for all of the state of Hawaii is 808. Each island has its own telephone directory. The information operator will ask you for which island you are requesting a number. Most of the major hotels in Hawaii, as well as many of the condominium chains, have toll-free 800 numbers to be used for making reservations.

Electric Current
The state of Hawaii uses standard North American current: 110 volts, 60 cycles.

Business Hours and Holidays
Most businesses open early in Hawaii, with offices on an 8:00 A.M. to 5 P.M. weekday schedule, and banks are open from 8:30 A.M. to 3 P.M., later on Fridays. Big retail locations at shopping malls are open from 9:30 A.M. until 9 P.M., closing earlier on Saturdays and open for reduced hours on Sundays. Hawaii's major holidays are similar to those on the U.S. Mainland, with two important additions: Prince Kuhio Day on March 26 and Kamehameha Day on June 11. Aloha Week is an annual statewide event that is celebrated island by island from mid-September through mid-October.

Cautions
Don't swim at untended beaches, especially during winter months, without first checking with knowledgeable local people; undertows and other strong currents can surprise and kill even the strongest swimmers.

Also, avoid trekking on unmarked trails, or alone into

wilderness areas anywhere. The dangers here can come from nature or from human beings with bad intent.

For Further Information
The main office of the Hawaii Visitors Bureau (HVB) is at 2270 Kalakaua Avenue, Honolulu, HI 96815; Tel: (808) 923-1811. There are branch offices in Kahului, Maui; Lihue, Kauai; and in Hilo and Kailua-Kona on the Big Island of Hawaii. HVB also maintains offices in New York, Chicago, Los Angeles, and San Francisco. Their addresses are: 441 Lexington Avenue, Suite 1407, New York, NY 10017; 180 North Michigan Avenue, Suite 1031, Chicago, IL 60601; 3440 Wilshire Boulevard, Suite 502, Los Angeles, CA 90010; 50 California Street, Suite 450, San Francisco, CA 94111.

—*Tom and Karen Horton*

BIBLIOGRAPHY
Some of the volumes listed below are available only in Hawaii. Check with bookshops in Honolulu and on the islands you visit for titles about individual islands and their culture and history.

MARTHA WARREN BECKWITH, *Hawaiian Mythology* (1940; reprinted, 1982). Classic work of Hawaiiana based on oral and written narratives. Beckwith focuses on gods, chiefs, heroes, and lovers to highlight a culture where religion and mythology are interwoven.

ISABELLA L. BIRD (BISHOP), *Six Months in the Sandwich Islands* (1890; reprinted, 1985). In letters to her sister, this Victorian lady traveller records her tomboyish escapades in 1873 Hawaii, including a descent into Kilauea volcano and an excursion around Hilo on a horse.

OSWALD BUSHNELL, *Ka`a`awa: A Novel About Hawaii in the 1850's* (1972; reprinted, 1980). Historical fiction depicting social conflict in 19th-century Hawaii, by a writer with a strong knowledge of Hawaiian culture and history. Other Bushnell fiction includes *The Return of Lono* (1971), about Captain Cook's ill-fated visit to Hawaii, and *The Stone of Kannon* (1979), a saga of the first Japanese to work on Hawaii's sugar plantations.

SHERWIN JOHN CARLQUIST, *Hawaii: A Natural History* (1970). A comprehensive study of Hawaii's fascinating animal and plant life, useful as an aid in understanding and identifying hundreds of species.

JOHN CHARLOT, *Chanting the Universe: Hawaiian Religious Culture* (1983). This slim volume is a personal insight into the Hawaiian perception of life through place chants and songs.

CRAIG CHISHOLM, *Hawaiian Hiking Trails* (1985; reprinted, 1986). The best trails of all the Islands for the trekker at heart. Includes a short description of each trail and a tiny topographical map.

JOHN R. K. CLARK, *The Beaches of O`ahu* (1977; reprinted, 1982). A must read for beach-goers interested in the cultural history of Oahu sand. Clark has written companion beach volumes for Maui and the Big island, Hawaii.

VIRGINIA COWAN-SMITH AND BONNIE DOMROSE STONE, *Aloha Cowboy* (1988). A short, entertaining glimpse of horsemanship in Hawaii, from the introduction of the horse in 1803 to modern-day parades, rodeos, and polo matches.

JOHN L. CULLINEY, *Islands in a Far Sea: Nature and Man in Hawaii* (1988). This readable overview of nature's uneasy relationship with *Homo sapiens* explores the environmental impact of human settlement on wildlife and evolution. The author is a marine biologist.

GAVAN DAWS, *Shoal of Time: A History of the Hawaiian Islands* (1968, reprinted, 1974). Written by a former University of Hawaii professor of history, this reliable and entertaining book traces the Islands' history from Western discovery and the missionary and whaling periods to annexation and statehood.

———, *Holy Man: Father Damien of Molokai* (1973; reprinted, 1984). A popular, yet scholarly, biography of the famous leper-priest martyred on Molokai's Kalaupapa Peninsula.

A. GROVE DAY AND CARL STROVEN, EDS., *A Hawaiian Reader* (1959; reprinted, 1984). A selection of writings from the last hundred years, featuring both obscure and big-name writers (Mark Twain, Robert Louis Stevenson, James Jones). A companion volume is the same editors' *The Spell of Hawaii* (1968; reprinted, 1985).

A. GROVE DAY, *Books about Hawaii: Fifty Basic Authors* (1977). An annotated guide to the writers and books that have contributed to Hawaii's literary history.

MARNIE HAGMANN, *Hawaii Parklands* (1988). Thumbnail sketches of the Islands' national, state, and county parks illustrated with fine photography. Includes a parklands directory for each island.

HAWAII AUDUBON SOCIETY, *Hawaii's Birds* (1967; reprinted, 1988). This easy-to-use, pocket-size guide for novice bird watchers covers the common birds seen in Waikiki as well as the rarer high-country birds, such as the Kauai *oo,* a native of the high country.

JERRY HOPKINS, HANS HOEFER, LEONARD LUERAS, AND REBECCA CROCKETT-HOPKINS, *The Hula* (1982). A well-written introduction to Hawaii's traditional dance, complete with historical illustrations and a hall of fame of hula greats.

EDWARD JOESTING, *Kauai: The Separate Kingdom* (1984; reprinted, 1988). A history of the Garden Isle from precontact to the close of the 19th century, by a past president of the Hawaiian Historical Society and author of *Hawaii: An Uncommon History* (1972; reprinted, 1978).

JAMES JONES, *From Here to Eternity* (1951; reprinted, 1980). Wartime fiction about army life in Hawaii before and during the 1941 Japanese attack on Pearl Harbor. Jones, a soldier stationed on Oahu during the war, dedicated the novel to the U.S. Army.

RALPH S. KUYKENDALL, *The Hawaiian Kingdom, 1778–1893.* A detailed trilogy—*Foundation and Transformation* (1938), *Twenty Critical Years* (1953), *The Kalakaua Dynasty* (1967)—dryly written, but considered a definitive history of 19th-century Hawaii.

JACK LONDON, *Stories of Hawaii* (1965). Reprinted short stories by a master of the genre, who visited the islands in 1907. The American people, said London about Hawaii, "don't know what they've got! Just watch this land in the future, when once Americans wake up!"

GORDON A. MACDONALD, AGATIN T. ABBOTT, AND FRANK L. PETERSON, *Volcanoes in the Sea: The Geology of Hawaii* (1970; reprinted, 1983). Millions of years in the making, the Hawaiian Islands are geological masterpieces created and shaped by volcanoes and erosion. This is the

most detailed book available on the processes that have
formed the Islands.

JAMES A. MICHENER, *Hawaii* (1959; reprinted, 1982). The
"big book" of Hawaii fiction by a Pulitzer Prize–winning
author, this novel ranges from the Islands' geological
birth to modern times. The film version was shot on
Oahu's Waianae Coast.

LINDA PAIK MORIARTY, *Niihau Shell Leis* (1986). An illustrated introduction to the Forbidden Isle's shell leis—
history, shell species, lei making—written by a shell en-
thusiast of Hawaiian ancestry.

THE NATURE CONSERVANCY OF HAWAII AND GAVAN DAWS, *Hawaii: The Islands of Life* (1988). Strong on photographs,
with a short text by Gavan Daws, this book showcases
Hawaii's fascinating, yet fragile, environment. The spon-
sor is an organization dedicated to protecting Hawaii's
endangered ecosystems.

GORDON W. PRANGE, DONALD M. GOLDSTEIN, AND KATHERINE
DILLON, *At Dawn We Slept: The Untold Story of Pearl
Harbor* (1981; reprinted, 1982). A massive account (873
pages) of that famous Sunday in December 1941, exam-
ined from both the American and Japanese sides. Prange
spent 37 years preparing this book.

MARY K. PUKUI, SAMUEL H. ELBERT, AND ESTHER T. MOOKINI,
Place Names of Hawaii (1974). A scholarly guide to the
curious meanings of the Islands' place-names. A question
frequently asked at Hawaii's public libraries is "What
book will tell me the meaning of a Hawaii name?" This is
it.

RONN RONCK, *Ronck's Hawaii Almanac* (1984). Hawaii in
a nutshell, packaged in a pocket-size fact book; dated, but
still useful.

MICHAEL SLACKMAN, *Remembering Pearl Harbor: The Story
of the USS* Arizona *Memorial* (1984). Short chapters highlight the ship; the attack; the fund raising for (Elvis Presley
helped), and construction of, the memorial; and the
ship's underwater archaeology. Sponsored by the *Arizona* Memorial Museum Association.

JOHN J. STEPHAN, *Hawaii under the Rising Sun* (1984).
Subtitled *Japan's Plans for Conquest after Pearl Harbor,*
this is a fascinating account of the Imperial Navy's schemes

to invade and occupy Hawaii prior to the disastrous defeat at Midway.

AUDREY SUTHERLAND, *Paddling My Own Canoe* (1978). Adventures of a woman and her inflatable canoe on Molokai's northern seacoast, one of Hawaii's most isolated areas.

RUTH M. TABRAH, *Ni`ihau: The Last Hawaiian Island*(1987). Homely history of Hawaii's privately owned island, purchased by a Scottish family in 1864.

RICHARD WILLIAM TREGASKIS, *The Warrior King: Hawaii's Kamehameha the Great* (1973; reprinted, 1984). Fictional biography of the Islands' best-known historical personage, who united and ruled all Hawaii. Kamehameha and Tregaskis share common characteristics: One was a warrior-king, the other a war correspondent (*Guadalcanal Diary*), and both stood six foot six.

MARK TWAIN, *Mark Twain's Letters from Hawaii* (1966; reprinted, 1975). For four months in 1866 Twain roamed the Islands as a reporter for a California newspaper. These reprinted letters, first published in the Sacramento *Union,* helped launch his literary career.

UNIVERSITY OF HAWAII, *Atlas of Hawaii* (1973; reprinted, 1983). A godsend for the cartographic-minded traveller, this collection of easy-to-interpret maps and data is presented in a colorful format, with special emphasis on Hawaii's ecology.

—*John W. Perry*

HONOLULU

By Rick Carroll

Rick Carroll, an author, journalist, and photographer, lives on Oahu. He has written for the Honolulu Advertiser *and the* San Francisco Chronicle *and is the author of* From Mauka to Makai *and is writing* Tropical Style: The Architecture of Paradise.

With its polyglot population, Honolulu is America's first true multinational city, and its only metropolis to be declared a city by a king. Not even old Kamehameha III, however, could have guessed that his mud-and-thatch seaport on a tiny volcanic island in the middle of the sea would become one of the prime destinations of sun lovers everywhere.

MAJOR INTEREST

Tropical scenery in an urban setting
East-West cultural and historical mix
The waterfront
Waikiki and Diamond Head (see separate chapter below)
Iolani Palace and the Capitol District
National Memorial Cemetery of the Pacific (Punchbowl)
The neighborhoods
Nuuanu Pali Lookout
Chinatown
The Bishop Museum (Hawaiiana)
Fishing-boat charters
Shopping
Restaurants and nightlife

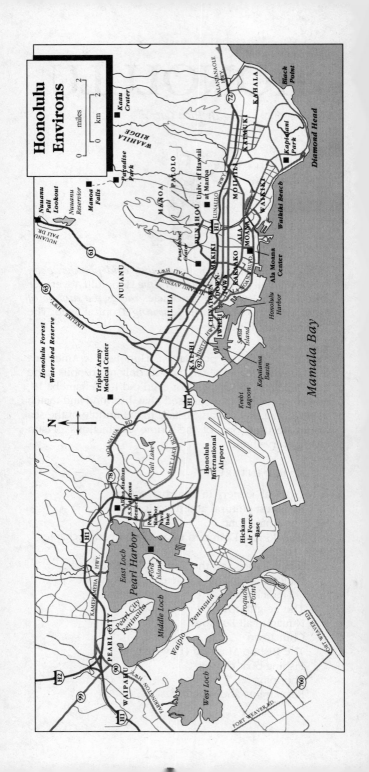

Honolulu is more than just a port of entry to a vacation; it's also a major urban center of the Pacific, the westernmost American state capital, and the nation's 11th largest—and most exotic—city. Most visitors to Honolulu are headed exclusively to Waikiki—to which we devote its own chapter, following this one—and never veer off the path into the rest of this splendid city of 800,000 that is more Asian than American, and where none of a score of ethnic groups is a majority. The people here are as varied as their many points of origin, and each nationality contributes to the Amerasian mosaic that is modern Honolulu. "Half the world's races seem to be represented and interbred here," Jan Morris wrote in the London *Sunday Times*, "and between them they have created an improbable microcosm of human society as a whole."

(Few visitors may discover the good things that Honolulu outside Waikiki holds, but the island of Oahu outside the urban center of Honolulu is overwhelmingly Hawaii's best-kept secret, overlooked by tourists who never venture into the open country, and whose scenery can be compared to that of Tahiti. We cover the island itself in a separate chapter, even though the legal boundaries of Oahu and Honolulu are contiguous.)

Honolulu is a beautiful, cosmopolitan city, blessed by temperatures that seldom achieve more than 90 or less than 70 degrees Fahrenheit, with nearly 300 days of sunshine a year. Although technically in the North Pacific, Honolulu enjoys nearly the same climate as Acapulco and Havana, and is just high enough in the tropic band to dodge the steaminess of her southern Polynesian sisters, yet blessed again by trade winds that refresh the city and keep it from simmering in tropical heat.

"Hawaii has the weather California thinks it has," wrote Earl Derr Biggers, creator of Charlie Chan, the fictional Honolulu detective, and he wasn't wrong. There are only two seasons—wet and dry—and when it rains, it's considered a blessing.

An ancient natural harbor, Honolulu has survived a great deal: first, "discovery" in the late 1700s by the British, who introduced venereal disease; then, stern New England missionaries who banned hula and dressed women in long, loose dresses called muumuu; then, the loss of everything—land, language, and the monarchy—at the hands of an oligarchy of prospering traders, merchants, and missionaries who seized the kingdom. Sugar and pineapple profits became king.

In 1959, Hawaii—before then only a U.S. territory—
was admitted to the Union as the 50th, and last, state, and
the same year, the first jet landed, a Qantas Boeing 707. It
was a big year for Honolulu, which became a state capital
and a major tourist destination. Soon, high-rises dwarfed
Aloha Tower, and a five-o'clock rush became an evening
ritual—yet the small port town that became a big city
stayed nice and friendly, with its own peculiar social
graces. It is considered rude, for example, to honk in
traffic. And nearly everyone—*haole* (HOW-lee; Hawaiian
for "white man," generally used in a neutral, nonderog-
atory way) too—takes their shoes off when entering a
house. People indicate enthusiastic approval by waving
the *shaka* sign: little finger and thumb extended, and
index, middle, and ring fingers down.

Nearly everyone in Honolulu knows or speaks a little
pidgin, the popular local patois, and gives directions local
style: *mauka* and *makai* (toward the mountains and toward the sea), Diamond Head (east toward the volcano),
and Ewa (toward the westerly suburb of that name). Daily
in Honolulu's courts, author Joan Didion once noted,
police officers testify that the traffic accident occurred "in
the *mauka*-most lane"—and the judge, jurors, and lawyers all know exactly what that means.

There is more than linguistic anomaly in Honolulu,
though. There are no billboards in Hawaii, no pay toilets
or motor homes, no snakes or rabies, and no daylight
savings time—not with 12 hours of sunshine daily. People, like the climate, tend to be kind, and the year-round
balmy air results in a sense of well-being that is a mix of
the Asian ethos and the California laid-back (Hawaii
style). This is, after all, America's last frontier, where East
and West meet daily over a bowl of chili-rice, a popular
local dish.

While many aspects of the old kingdom still run through
life in Honolulu, the city has nonetheless become one of
the most progressive in the Pacific Basin—only to be
condemned by those who see traffic snarls under swaying
palms as deleterious. Whatever, Honolulu remains just far
enough from the continent to possess its own smug, pro-
vincial style. Even at its urban heart, the city manages to
conjure up Conradian images and South Seas fantasies, but
the truth is greater than all the fiction. Honolulu is like a
hardware store: Whatever you're looking for is probably
there.

Downtown Honolulu rises from the waterfront along

the curve of Ala Moana Boulevard, between the airport and Waikiki. Built first as a seaport, downtown is smaller than Waikiki—but far more cosmopolitan—and has a nautical flair. The tall ship–tall building contrast is often startling, especially when the cruise ships nose into town. Waikiki, which is where all the hotels are, is east of Honolulu, and Diamond Head stands on the far (east) side of Waikiki. The Ala Wai Canal separates Honolulu and Waikiki, but Waikiki is connected to the "real world" at its western end by Ala Moana Boulevard, Kalakaua Avenue, and McCully Street. It's easy to get into Waikiki, but many have problems getting out—probably because they prefer to stay. The easiest exit is via McCully Street, *mauka* off Ala Wai Boulevard. The best way to downtown and back is TheBus.

DOWNTOWN HONOLULU

The jagged skyline set at the foot of mountains gives downtown Honolulu a look of tropical urbanity, with mynah birds, palm trees, and tropical fruit dangling from roadside trees to contrast with the high-rise buildings. The bustling downtown is graced by parks, fountains, and public sculpture by Benny Bufano, Henry Moore, and Isamu Noguchi. Most people who arrive on Oahu never see any of this as they roll into Waikiki from Honolulu International Airport.

The best way to see Honolulu is on foot downtown, starting on the waterfront, where it all began with European "contact" in the 18th century when liberty sailors swaggered ashore to swap nails (which were bent into fishhooks) for sex, a rite that continues with a different commodity now when ships are in port.

The landmark **Aloha Tower**, built in 1926 as a lighthouse, was the city's tallest structure until 1959. After the December 7, 1941, raid on Pearl Harbor, the 184-foot clock tower was painted regulation GI camouflage color in hopes of disguising it in the event of further enemy attack. Now humbled by skyscraper office buildings, it still offers a grand view up **Fort Street Mall** to the cloud-wreathed, emerald green volcanic peaks of the 3,000-foot Koolau Range to the northeast.

Ride the tower's poky elevator to the tenth-floor lookout for the best free view in town. The observation deck, posted with the official Schedule of Passenger Cruise

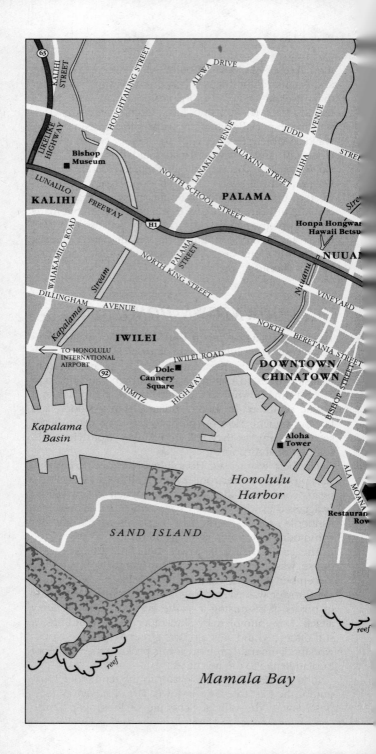

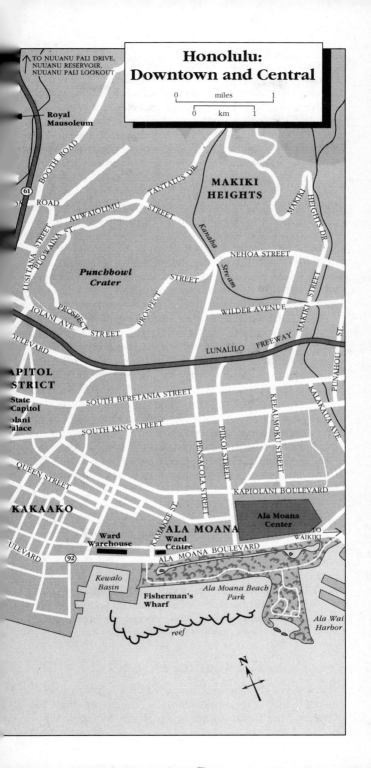

Vessels, is decorated with 20 sun-faded color photos of famous ships entering Honolulu Harbor, from the world-cruising *QE2* to the outrigger *Hokulea*, which reenacted the ancient Polynesian canoe voyages between Hawaii and Tahiti in 1976. You can see some of this action yourself if you go before sundown on any Saturday night when the interisland cruise ships, SS *Independence* and SS *Constitution*, are berthed at Pier 9. From the tower you'll see the shoreside lei sellers, in a pale imitation of the old "Boat Days" when *everyone* came by ship. The 360-degree view also takes in all the ships at sea; Honolulu Harbor, the largest of seven in Hawaii; the distant Waianae Mountains; the two-mile-long reef runway, which doubles as a Space Shuttle emergency-landing strip; the cherry-blossom pink Tripler Army Medical Center Hospital on the hill; downtown Honolulu; and a peek at Diamond Head and Waikiki through the skyscrapers.

Walk "Diamond Head" (i.e., east) along the waterfront, past the 100-year-old *Falls of Clyde*, the only four-masted, square-rigged ship afloat, and you will be at **Hawaii Maritime Museum**'s new Kalakaua Boat House on Pier 7. This artifact-packed museum right on the waterfront has 30 exhibits on such nautical themes as surfing, Matson ships, seaplanes, and whaling (the Calley O'Neill mural is Hawaii's best). A new open-air restaurant on the pier, **Coasters**, has turned out to be a culinary surprise, offering such local favorites as smoked fish salad and shellfish sausage. The inexpensive, local-style food is served with a close-up view of passing tugboats, sampans (Hawaiian fishing boats), and cruise ships.

To gain a sense of downtown Honolulu's center, walk up either Fort Street Mall or Bishop Street, still the home of two of the historic Big Five ruling companies, where business is conducted by executives in aloha shirts, who count coin on both abacus and computer. The last houses of the Big Five, Alexander & Baldwin, for example, and the Big Sixth, Dillingham, stand like memorials to the oligarchy on Bishop Street. Bishop intersects Hotel Street five blocks *mauka* (as we said, toward the mountains), then offers a choice to the Capitol District or Chinatown.

The Capitol District

The jewel of the Capitol District is **Iolani Palace**, a stone, Italian Renaissance remnant of the monarchy, built in 1882 by King David Kalakaua, the Merrie Monarch, who filled the royal house with European period furniture shipped round the Horn. The king lived and entertained here until his death in 1891. His sister, Queen Liliuo-kalani, lived in the palace until the monarchy was overthrown in 1893. The word *iolani* means "royal hawk."

The king's **Coronation Pavilion**, the green-domed, gazebo-like octagon on the palace grounds, is now used for the governor's inaugural and for free public concerts of Hawaiian, pop, and classical music at 12:15 P.M. every Friday by the Royal Hawaiian Band. The Friends of Iolani Palace, which supervised a restoration of America's only palace, conducts tours Wednesdays through Saturdays by reservation only (Tel: 522-0832).

The most photographed statue in Hawaii, the **statue of King Kamehameha the Great**, across South King Street from Iolani Palace, is a replica. The original was lost at sea off the Falkland Islands, but it was later found, and now stands in the Big Island coast town of Kapaau. (A third version of the statue stands in Washington, D.C., 4,829 miles and five time zones from Honolulu.) None of this artful dodge bothers the busloads of tourists who disembark to photograph and all but worship the life-size, nearly seven-foot-tall, black-and-gold statue, which is draped with 18-foot-long leis on King Kamehameha Day, June 11, a state holiday.

The statue stands in front of the State Judiciary Building, known as **Alliolani Hale** (House of the Heavenly Chief) in Hawaiian. More grandiose than the Iolani Palace, it was built in 1872 for Kamehameha V, but he died before it was completed.

Downhill South King Street at Punchbowl Street stands the coral-block **Kawaiahao Church**, often called the "Westminster Abbey of the Pacific." There are hundreds of churches in Honolulu, but Kawaiahao, and the Honpa Hongwanji Betsuin on the Pali Highway are most eye-catching because of their unique architecture and their historic significance.

Dedicated in 1842 by the missionary Hiram Bingham, Kawaiahao Church was a five-year effort, begun in 1836, involving hundreds of workers, who quarried 1,000-pound blocks from the reef and cut massive timbers to erect the church. Christmas services are held here in the Hawaiian language.

Early Hawaiians worshipped the sun and the gods Lono and Maui, among others. Now there are 35 Christian denominations here, 22 Buddhist denominations, 2

Jewish, 1 Muslim, 5 Shinto, 7 New Religious movements, and 4 other movements, including Scientologists and Moonies. Some deeds of the first among these post-contact arrivals, the fire-and-brimstone New England missionaries, who arrived in 1820 on the brigantine *Thaddeus,* are told at **Mission Houses Museum** (Diamond Head of Kawaiahao Church, at 553 South King Street), a tract of their "proper" clapboard houses shipped around the Horn.

Honolulu City and County stretches 1,500 miles west beyond **Honolulu Hale** (City Hall), the California Mission–style building with a red tile roof on the corner of South King and Punchbowl streets, and encompasses all the northwestern Hawaiian Islands except Midway. Some of the Honolulu County islets, such as French Frigate Shoals and Pearl and Hermes Atoll, are populated only by seabirds and monk seals, while others are underwater, emerging only at high tide.

Under Queen Kapiolani's giant banyan (she planted the seedling) between the palace and the state capitol is a drab, modern government building that contains one of Hawaii's best-kept secrets. The **State Archives** has 40,000 historic prints by photographers James Williams, A. Montano, Menzie Dickson, and Rice and Perkins. The Hawaiian category, featuring hula girls, beach boys, and lei sellers, is the most popular. Go here to order blowup photos of early Hawaii at bargain prices.

Hawaii's **State Capitol**, at South Beretania and Punchbowl streets, mimics the elements of air, land, and sea in its volcano-shaped chambers that are surrounded by carp ponds and supported by graceful palm-tree-like columns. A bronze Marisol Escobar statue of Father Damien de Veuster, the "leper priest" of Molokai, greets mauka-side visitors. Inside the Senate Chamber, 620 pearlized nautilus shells from the Philippines form the elaborate shell-craft chandelier, devised by German artist Otto Piene—who fitted the shells with lights. Also of interest are giant tapestries by Ruthadell Anderson and a mosaic by Tadashi Sato in the center of the courtyard.

The governor of Hawaii lives downtown in **Washington Place** (South Beretania Street, across the street from the capitol), a New England Colonial designed by Isaac Hart for John Dominis, a New England sea captain who was lost at sea and never took occupancy. The deposed Queen Liliuokalani took refuge here until her death in 1917. The house has served as the governor's mansion since 1921, and is the oldest continuously occupied dwelling in Honolulu.

The downtown Bishop Street crowd goes to Tamarind Square for lunch, where Marc Cohen's **Café Che Pasta**, an art-filled, San Francisco–style bar and grill, serves fresh clams and pasta with California Chardonnay by the glass. Or it grazes dim sum around the corner at **Yong Sing** on Alakea Street, or munches tuna melts at **The Croissanterie**, a sidewalk café on Merchant Street.

Near Downtown

Overlooking downtown Honolulu and often confused for Diamond Head by first-timers, the ironically named **Punchbowl**, a graveyard in a dead volcano that was once used for human sacrifices, is the number one tourist attraction in Hawaii. Here, in the National Memorial Cemetery of the Pacific, lie almost 35,000 dead, many of them casualties of three American wars in Asia and the Pacific, as well as other heroes such as World War II correspondent Ernie Pyle and Hawaiian astronaut Ellison Onizuka, a victim of the *Challenger* explosion. The 112-acre Punchbowl is an almost perfect bowl-shaped crater that is, after all these years, nearly full.

Like something out of *The Arabian Nights,* the **Honpa Hongwanji Hawaii Betsuin,** up the Pali Highway, is a whitewashed fantasy of minarets, built in 1918 to commemorate the 700th anniversary of the founding of the Shin sect of Buddhism. The sect's island headquarters, this Buddhist temple combines Japanese and Indian architectural features.

THE NEIGHBORHOODS

Politically, the city and county of Honolulu extends over the entire island of Oahu. The city itself is a diverse collection of neighborhoods and people, with oddly juxtaposed architectural styles, from plantation shacks and New England bungalows to hard-edged International high-rises, scattered over hills and clefts between mountains and sea. The 22-mile-long residential corridor from the man-made lagoons of Hawaii Kai in the east to the "new town" sprawl of Mililani above Pearl Harbor in the west is divided lengthwise by the H-1, an east-west, eight-lane "interstate" freeway that goes island-wide. Along the

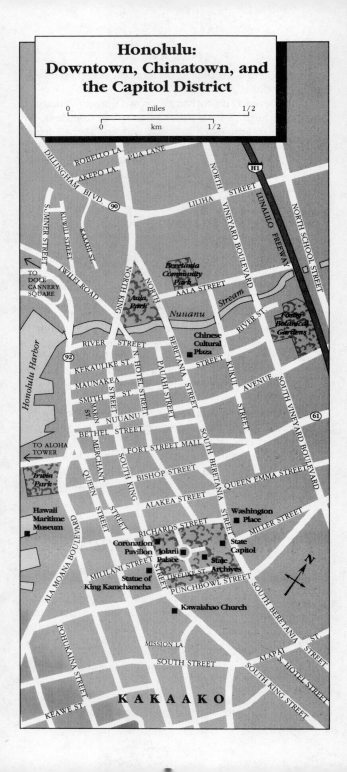

Honolulu:
Downtown, Chinatown, and
the Capitol District

0   miles   1/2

0   km   1/2

ROBELLO LA.
AKEPO LA.   PUA LANE
DILLINGHAM BLVD.
90
H1
NORTH SCHOOL STREET
LUNALILO FREEWAY
LILIHA STREET
NORTH VINEYARD BOULEVARD
S.JMNER STREET
KUWILI STREET
KAAHI ST.
IWILEI ROAD
NORTH KING STREET
Beretania Community Park
AALA STREET
Foster Botanical Gardens
Aala Park
Nuuanu   Stream
RIVER STREET
RIVER ST.
Honolulu Harbor
92
N. HOTEL STREET
BERETANIA STREET
PAUAHI STREET
Chinese Cultural Plaza
KUKUI STREET
SOUTH VINEYARD BOULEVARD
KEKAULIKE ST.
MAUNAKEA
SMITH ST.
MARIN ST.
NUUANU
AVENUE
61
TO DOLE CANNERY SQUARE
BETHEL STREET
MERCHANT
FORT STREET MALL
SOUTH BERETANIA STREET
TO ALOHA TOWER
Irwin Park
QUEEN STREET
SOUTH KING STREET
BISHOP STREET
ALAKEA STREET
QUEEN EMMA STREETVARD
Hawaii Maritime Museum
ALA MOANA BOULEVARD
RICHARDS STREET
Washington Place
MILLER STREET
Coronation Pavilion
Iolani Palace
State Capitol
MILILANI STREET
State Archives
Statue of King Kamehameha
LIKELIKE ST.
PUNCHBOWL STREET
SOUTH BERETANIA ST.
N
Kawaiahao Church
POHUKAINA STREET
MISSION LA.
SOUTH STREET
ALAPAI STREET
S. HOTEL STREET
SOUTH KING STREET

KAKAAKO

KEAWE ST.

corridor are a number of Honolulu neighborhoods that often go unexplored. Those that happen to have places of strong interest are:

- Nuuanu
- Chinatown
- Iwilei
- Kalihi
- Kakaako
- Ala Moana
- Kaimuki
- Manoa
- Kapahulu

Nuuanu

Under the Hawaiian flag, on high, sacred ground above Honolulu near the Pali Highway (61) running up into the Koolau Range from H-1, stands the **Royal Mausoleum**, where six Hawaiian rulers are interred. Take Nuuanu Avenue mauka to the Gothic Revival mausoleum, built in 1863 in the shape of a Greek cross by Theodore Heuck, Honolulu's first architect. The Royal Mausoleum is one of the few places open on Kuhio Day, March 26; Kamehameha Day, June 11; and Memorial Day. Only the Kalakaua Crypt is open to visitors. The royal remains are guarded by curator Lydia Namahana Maioho, a descendant of Kamehameha I, who lives in a small house nearby.

You can drive through a tropical rain forest by taking the Nuuanu Pali Drive, off Pali Highway. A refreshing detour under many-trunked banyan trees and giant bamboo, the drive takes you past old *kamaaina* (longtime residents') estates and the catfish-filled Nuuanu Reservoir and back again to the Pali Highway. Be alert, because the **Nuuanu Pali Lookout** is the next—and well-marked— exit. Most scenic lookouts don't live up to expectations, but the Nuuanu Pali Lookout (Nuuanu means "cool heights," Pali means "steep cliffs") really does—especially on windy days, when updrafts strike the Pali, those corrugated volcanic peaks separating Honolulu from Oahu's Windward side, and make waterfalls run uphill. This is where Kamehameha the Great vanquished his enemies by driving them off the cliff in 1795 (see also the Oahu outside Honolulu chapter).

Back down in town, east of downtown and south of the Punchbowl, is the **Honolulu Academy of Arts**, 900

South Beretania Street, a small but important institution founded in 1929, housing not just one collection but highly distinguished groups of objects, including van Gogh's *Wheatfield,* Tang dynasty porcelain, the James Michener collection of *ukiyo-e* prints, an unrivaled Korean cup collection, a rare Hubert Vos painting of an early Hawaiian fisherman's catch of the day, and a statue of Kwan Yin, the Chinese goddess of mercy, circa 1025. Admission is free; there's also the delightful garden café with a modest lunch menu.

Chinatown

In Honolulu's Chinatown, the barber at Sunday Barber Shop catnaps in her chair while yawning transvestites stroll on Hotel Street, but this always evolving, mostly Vietnamese/Filipino neighborhood that lives under a misnomer is awakening to a new look every day. High-rises now loom over old coral-block buildings with tin roofs. Hotel Street these days is wide and handsome (but still a tricky place to visit at night). The Maunakea Marketplace is a new development here. Already infiltrated by Japanese, Koreans, Laotians, and Pacific islanders as well as Vietnamese and Filipinos, the ramshackle 15-block Chinatown, where only 5 percent of Hawaii's Chinese live, is becoming gentrified, turned into a grab bag of artists' lofts, bistros, and boutiques. Aphrodisiacs such as deer antlers and ginseng root still appear in herbalists' windows, but this 130-year-old hangout of immigrant Asians between Nuuanu Stream and Bethel Street is attracting artists amid the lei stands.

The pagoda of Wo Fat, the oldest chop suey house in Honolulu, founded in 1882 by the baker Wat Ging, sports a new coat of paint, but the menu needs rejuvenation. This showplace has a long history, but locals go to **Sea Fortune**, at 111 North King Street, or **Doong Kong Lau-Hakka** in the **Chinese Cultural Plaza**, a retail arcade housing primarily Chinese shops and restaurants at Beretania and Maunakea streets, when they want good Chinese seafood in Chinatown. There's "plenny local kine" fish at the open-air **Oahu Market**, 145 North King Street, saved from the wrecker's ball by 17 stall keepers who pooled their money to buy it, then kept it just the way it was—a thriving native market full of "catch-of-the-day" fish stands and other stands that attracts hundreds of Saturday morning shoppers. Fresh-baked, flaky croissants and French coffee can be found just across the street at **Ba-Le**, run by refugees from Saigon.

The **Tak Wah Tong Chinese Herb Shop**, across from the Moon Gate (a large, round, wooden gate), next to the video-game parlor at the Chinese Cultural Plaza is the biggest of 17 in Chinatown. Alan Lau, a direct descendant of a Ching dynasty emperor's very own herbal doctor, sells 14 herbs that are, he claims, the Chinese cure for the common cold.

In the mauka corner of the same complex, at Phil Lau's **Royal Kitchen**, you will find what locals claim are Honolulu's best baked *manapua*—baked dim sum stuffed with fresh *char siu* pork—for only 55 cents each.

Chinatown is attracting a cluster of art galleries worth browsing. **Ramsay**, a pen-and-ink artist, creates sketches of historical Hawaiian buildings in the 1923 Tan Sing Building on Smith Street. On Nuuanu Avenue, William Waterfall's coral-block **Waterfall Gallery** offers Balinese objects and vivid Pacific photographs, including rare, archival photographs of Easter Island statues. Next door, artist **Pegge Hopper**, painter of colorful Polynesian women in the tradition of Madge Tennent, works in her studio by day, while Hong Kong artist **Ka-Ning Fong** paints moody oils of urban Honolulu at dusk in his second-floor loft at King and River streets, just Ewa of Oahu Market.

Aviation buffs must see the lobby of Kramer and Kennedy Graphic Design, 1128 Nuuanu Avenue, Suite DC-3, which visitors enter through the fuselage of a 1944 Air Molokai DC-3 plane, complete with piped-in Frank Sinatra music and original 1944 *Life* magazines.

On King Street, old Filipino men play nine-ball daylong at the Cebu Pool Hall; don't try to join them, it's a closed game. There's little else for the old-timers to do since the closure of Chinatown's last taxi dance hall, where bachelor Filipino plantation workers two-stepped with young Chinese girls for a dollar a dance. Hookers still work the streets of Chinatown, and Michael Malone, at the China Sea Tattoo Parlor, 1033 Smith Street, founded in 1952, still needles sailors' arms (the tattoo "Remember Pearl Harbor" is seldom requested now). Hotel Street, widened and lined with malls, serves as a major transit artery for TheBus, and hardly resembles its sleazy former self when World War II GIs stood on line outside the hotels reading comics, waiting for girls.

Even old taverns fade away in Chinatown—the 1883 Pantheon, once the oldest bar in Honolulu, is closed now—but **Murphy's Bar & Grill**, a sociable, glass-and-brass, San Francisco–style bar that evolved out of the old Royal Saloon on Merchant Street, does a big business, especially in football season, when it beams in Monday Night Football "live," on Monday afternoon because of the time difference, via satellite dish, unlike the local network television affiliates, which delay the telecast until evening. Other, less toney Chinatown taverns that pour an honest shot include **Smith's Union Bar** (19 North Hotel Street), an early-day wateringhole for sailors, so called because the seaman's union used to be upstairs, and **Tommy's**, where the Wurlitzer jukebox still gives seven plays for a buck—and where some of the girls may be boys. (A recent Honolulu Police Department census revealed that half of Chinatown's 40 hookers are men.)

The best time to be in Chinatown, of course, is Chinese New Year's (January or February, depending on the lunar calendar), when lions dance, firecrackers explode, and thousands celebrate at the Maunakea Street party where special foods like *jai* and *jong* bring good luck.

Iwilei

In the old red-light district of Iwilei (Ewa from Chinatown, toward the airport) under the landmark Dole pineapple tower is **Dole Cannery Square**, a new attraction that venerates the Hawaiian pineapple, the second-largest cash crop in the Islands. A 35-minute tour takes 1,000 people daily through James Dole's cannery, founded in 1903. Visitors see the unique Ginaca device core and peel 98 pineapples a minute, then get a free sample at the juice bar. The 199-foot-tall, 100,000-gallon, 30-ton, pineapple-shaped tank, erected in 1928, doesn't hold pineapple juice; it's a gravity-feed water tank and Honolulu's most visible advertising symbol. (The first marketable pineapple, the Smooth Cayenne, was imported to Hawaii from Jamaica in 1886 by Captain John Kidwell, an Englishman. The Spanish called it *piña* because it's shaped like a pinecone, and the English name, pineapple, resulted.)

Just across the street, the many-paned **Gentry Pacific Center**, the old pineapple-can factory, has been restored and converted by world-champion speedboat racer Tom Gentry into an assemblage of shops, including Leslie Mow's Oriental Bedding, selling futons and *zabutons,* and a new Continental restaurant, **Angelica's**, serving good, affordable food in a gardenlike setting. Around the corner, on 806 Iwilei Road, is the Salvation Army Thrift Shop, a likely source of old aloha shirts.

Kalihi

There are only two reasons to go to Kalihi (north of Iwilei): One is a museum, the other is a fish market. Get to both on H-1, head Ewa until exit 20A (also known as the Likelike offramp) for the **Bernice Pauahi Bishop Museum**, a forbidding, four-story, cut-stone structure on a hill that looks like something out of a Charles Addams cartoon and houses the premier collection of things Hawaiian and things Pacific. The Bishop is stuffed with 20 million acquisitions (there are 12 million insect specimens alone), from ceremonial spears to calabashes and old photos of hula girls of the past. A bas-relief sea map of the Islands makes keen visual sense of the 1,500-mile-long archipelago that points like a crooked finger across the Pacific at Japan.

A 50-foot sperm whale, mounted in 1901 with a papier-mâché skin, soars overhead in the Great Hawaiian Hall, where the last little grass shack in Hawaii still stands. The *pili hale* (grass house) was built in the museum in 1902 using rafters and posts from a *pili hale* built before 1800 in Miloli'i Valley on Kauai. Local fire and safety codes now prohibit anyone in Hawaii from actually residing in a grass shack, although a number of popular tourist attractions, like the Tahitian Lanai restaurant in Waikiki and the Waioli Tea Room in Manoa Valley are made of thatched grass.

The museum owes its existence to real-life Hawaiian princess Bernice Pauahi, who once owned 12 percent of Hawaii, and collected Hawaiian artifacts now considered priceless. Her will instructed her husband, Charles Reed Bishop, to establish a Hawaiian museum "to enrich and delight," which it has for nearly a century. A world-renowned center for South Pacific studies, the Bishop Museum is the home of such legendary South Pacific archaeologists as Dr. Kenneth Emory and Dr. Yosihiko Sinoto, who have explored more Oceanic real estate than Captain Cook; excavated the remains of "lost" civilizations in Huahine, one of the Society Islands; traced the history of Hawaii through its fishhooks; and are helping restore Easter Island's fallen statues. The museum has the best collection of Polynesian artifacts, with seashells, historic photos, and relics such as koa-wood bowls, nose flutes, and war clubs. (The Easter Island statue in the front yard is a replica.) The museum's copper-roofed, 100-seat planetarium and observatory offers an imaginary "Journey by Starlight" look at the Pacific skies at 1:00 and 3:00 P.M. daily. **Shop Pacifica**, in the museum's lobby, has authentic souvenirs and a good selection of books on Hawaii.

Elsewhere in the Kalihi neighborhood, **Tamashiro's Fish Market**, corner of North King and Palama streets, is a two-story, New Orleans–style building with a giant orange crab out front. Inside are more than 100 varieties of fresh local seafood—some still kicking—including fish such as *ahi, aku, mahimahi, au, ono, opakapaka;* shellfish such as live abalone from the Big Island's Keahole aquaculture farm, *opihi,* geoducks; and live Kahuku prawns, eels, and even live Maine lobster flown from the Mainland. If you don't have facilities to cook, take out some *poke,* Hawaii's version of Tahiti's *poisson cru*—marinated fish, usually *ahi* (tuna), with *ugu* (seaweed) and sesame-seed oil. It's the perfect Hawaiian *pupu* (hors d'oeuvre) with a cold beer, sold singly at Tamashiro's.

Kakaako

As tin-roof shanties topple in Honolulu's new wave of urban redevelopment to make way for a thicket of 45-story luxury condo towers, the old waterfront district of Kakaako, that last undeveloped chunk of land between downtown and Waikiki, is fast disappearing. First to go was the old Honolulu Iron Works on Ala Moana Boulevard between South and Punchbowl streets, which reconstituted itself as a vertical mall of 13 bars and restaurants and 11 specialty shops in a twin-tower complex known as **Restaurant Row**. Here you will find a collection of moderate to expensive restaurants, from Tom Selleck's **Black Orchid** to the smoky **Sunset Grill**, a see-and-be-seen, L.A.–style bistro offering grilled fish and meat, and the 1950s-inspired, doo-wop **Rose City Diner**, open 24 hours on weekends.

Take the elevator to the skymall (a favorite spot for weddings and private parties) just for a look at Kakaako, the last low-rent district in Honolulu, where body and fender shops jostle Korean girlie bars and take-out restaurants, the latter like those in the decrepit Caesar J. Lopez Building, Queen and Cooke streets, that serve teriyaki chicken, macaroni salad, and two scoops of rice, wrapped in foil on a paper plate, for under $4—*the* Honolulu noontime treat.

The last ukulele factory in Hawaii is at 550 South Street, where Sam Kamaka started making the four-stringed instruments in 1916. His sons, Sam junior and Frederick, who run **Kamaka Hawaii, Inc.**, now turn out 5,000 ukuleles a year, including the rare pineapple-shaped uke, at prices from $150 to $500. Their instruments have been owned and played by Arthur Godfrey, Hilo Hattie, and Neil Armstrong, who ordered a baritone from outer space and picked it up in person after splashing down in the Pacific and going ashore here from the pick-up ship in 1969. Brought to Hawaii in 1897 from the island of Madeira by Portuguese, the ukulele caught the ear of King Kalakaua, the Merrie Monarch, and became an Island favorite. The word *ukulele* is Hawaiian for jumping flea, as in nimble fingers on the strings.

A few blocks away, at 831 Queen Street, stop by the **Lion's Coffee** roasting house for a cappuccino made with fresh roasted Kona coffee, and take home a sampler of Hawaii's own at the lowest prices in the Islands. A historical site marker should be placed at 753B Halekauwila Street in Kakaako, because on that spot in 1978 former New Yorker Stephen Gelson baked the first bagel in the Pacific, and sold it for 35 cents at his **Hawaiian Bagel Inc**. Gelson, who imported the bagel maker from the Big Apple, still sells his bagels—the onion are to die for—at 35 cents each. Now there's a bagel shop on Maui, and that's progress.

Savvy anglers seek out **K. Kida Fishing Supplies**, 212 Kamani Street, where trophy-winning *ono* and *ahi* are hung on the wall, and exotic lures like eels, frogs, and hula-skirted psychedelics are snapped up by resident and visitor fishermen alike. Pick up K. Kida's annual Hawaiian Tide Calendar and the latest issue of *Hawaiian Fishing News.* Now head for Slip E at **Kewalo Basin**, where Captain Dudley Worthy goes out daily on his luxury, 50-foot troller, *Kahuna Kai,* to catch marlin, mahimahi, ahi, ono, aku, and *kawakawa* in the Molokai channel. This popular captain lets you keep your catch of the day—other captains don't—and there's nothing finer than a freshly caught mahimahi grilled in butter, garlic, and wine by your hotel chef, or done your way on an Ala Moana Park grill. Reservations recommended; Tel: 235-6236.

When rental cars get towed, and it happens day and night to scores of tourists, they usually end up in Kakaako at Waimanu Street's impound lot, the limbo for the mis-parked, where it costs $45 and up to get out of hock. A cab ride from Waikiki runs about $6. Avoid Waimanu Street by observing official No Parking signs.

Saber-toothed tiger skulls, Ionic columns, Thai pup-pets, and jade from China are the stock in trade at **The Consignment Center**, 1219 Hopaka Street, a most un-usual shop full of stuff too good for Goodwill. On the edge of Kakaako, on Auahi Street, is **The Ultimate You**, "the Bergdorf Goodman of consignment shops," one of those discount stores that sells designer castoffs of the rich and famous for ten cents on the dollar. Nearby, bargain-priced Hawaiian music on records, cassettes, and compact disks may be found at **Jelly's Comics and Books**, 404 Piikoi Street, one of several good used-book and record shops. (Other are Froggies and Interlude Books, both on South King Street.)

The two barn-sized structures on Ala Moana Boulevard near Kewalo Basin that look like the packing crates the Ala Moana Center (see below) came in are **Ward Centre** and **Ward Warehouse**, informal specialty shopping (Pan-ama hats, Polo shirts, and local art) and restaurant clus-ters. At Ward Centre, Sandee Garcia's **Mocha Java** is one of those European-style coffee bars that everyone in Ho-nolulu walks by—or stops in, for a cup of Hawaii's own Maui Mocha Java with a fresh pastry and the morning paper. Ward Centre also distinguishes itself with the nou-velle California cuisine restaurant, **Il Fresco**, and **An-drew's Italian Restaurant**, which spotlights Mahi Beamer singing real Hawaiian songs in the pitch-black piano bar while waiters in black tie serve a nice garlicky Caesar salad and good cheesy Roman cannellone. At Ward Ware-house, **Dynasty II** is a very good Chinese restaurant (but Dynasty I, in the Dynasty Hotel in Waikiki, is also very good, and cheaper).

Ala Moana

A favorite pastime in Hawaii is people-watching, and one of the best places to do it is the **Ala Moana Center**, a 180-shop, tri-level mall at the gateway to Waikiki near the eastern end of Ala Moana Boulevard that claims to attract 37 million people a year—more than Disneyland—and awaits only the long-rumored opening of Neiman-Marcus. Everybody's favorite attraction at the center is **Makai Mar-ket Food Court**, an assemblage of 20 fast-food restaurants

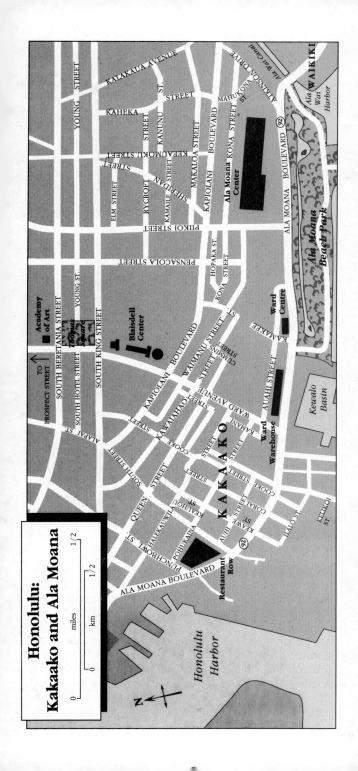

Honolulu: Kakaako and Ala Moana

miles

0   1/2

km

0   1/2

N

■ Academy of Art

TO PROSPECT STREET

SOUTH BERETANIA STREET

YOUNG ST.

SOUTH HOTEL STREET

SOUTH KING STREET

ALAPAI ST.

SOUTH STREET

Thomas Square

Blaisdell Center

YOUNG STREET

KALAKAUA AVENUE

KAHEKA STREET

ELM STREET

RYCROFT STREET

STREET

SHERIDAN

KANUNU STREET

KEEAUMOKU STREET

MAKALOA STREET

KAMAILE STREET

KAPIOLANI

MAHUKONA ST.

KONA STREET

Ala Moana KONA STREET Center

Ala Wai Canal

WAIKIKI

Ala Wai Harbor

ATKINSON DRIVE

BOULEVARD

ALA MOANA BOULEVARD

(92)

Ala Moana Beach Park

PIIKOI STREET

PENSACOLA STREET

HOPAKA ST.

KAPIOLANI BOULEVARD

WAIMANU STREET

CUMMINS STREET

KAMAKEE

Ward Centre

WARD AVENUE

KAMANI STREET

AUAHI STREET

Ward Warehouse

Kewalo Basin

KAWAIAHAO STREET

COOKE STREET

QUEEN STREET

KEAWE ST.

CORAL STREET

COOKE STREET

ILALO ST.

KEAWE ST.

AUAHI STREET

HALEKAUWILA ST.

POHUKAINA

KEAWE ST.

PUNCHBOWL ST.

ALA MOANA BOULEVARD

KAKAAKO

Restaurant Row

(92)

KEWALO ST.

Honolulu Harbor

N

under one roof, on the center's makai side. Don't look for the Kentucky colonel here; this is fast food Hawaii style: inexpensive ethnic foods like *manapua, kim chee, poke, lumpia,* Japanese *soba* noodles, Thai *sateh,* and Hawaii's own shave ice.

Directly across from Ala Moana Center is **Ala Moana Park**, a 118-acre beach park popular with Island families and visitors alike. The beach isn't the sole attraction here; there are ten tennis courts, three softball fields, a bowling green, facilities for kayak and canoe paddling, walking and jogging paths, and picnic areas—good fun in the busy city, and away from the Waikiki hotel zone.

Many Honolulu residents have never pushed through the giant double doors to **Treasures of the East** (1320 Makaloa Street, one block mauka from Ala Moana Center, off Keeaumoku Street), one of the largest private collections of Asian art objects, antiques, and collectibles. It's a museum-size antiques shop full of irresistible treasures gathered on regular expeditions by the staff, for sale to hotels and restaurants as well as individuals.

Between Keeaumoku and Piikoi streets on South Beretania Street is **Asian Food Trading Co.**, Honolulu's only complete Asian grocery, with Thai, Malay, Singaporean, and Indonesian spices and unidentified dried objects, including crack seed, the local Chinese treat (it's really dried fruit).

On Keeaumoku Street, between Ala Moana Center and H-1, so-called Korean bars with names like Crystal Palace and Butterfly Lounge, offering "free pupus and exotic dancers," proliferate like black holes for the unwary, who are soon parted from their cash by skilled hustlers. Skip these joints.

Kaimuki

The local restaurant district of Kaimuki is a short taxi ride from Waikiki, on Waialae Avenue, between 11th and 12th streets. In this one area are a chic pasta café, **Iroha Jaya**, the best *kaiseki* Japanese restaurant in Honolulu (across from the Kaimuki Public Library on Koko Head Avenue), a Mexican restaurant, a Chinese restaurant called **Red Rooster Chop Suey**, a nine-seat sushi bar, a Vietnamese restaurant as well as Thai, Italian, and Korean—but, alas, no place for ethnically mixed creations such as blackened Thai sushi, *limu*-dressed fettuccine with salt-and-pepper Kahuku prawns, or even tempura-style Maui onion rings.

(Go to Avalon on Lahaina's Front Street in Maui for such avant-garde fare.)

More traditional fare, however, such as *saimin,* can be readily found in the Kaimuki area. Saimin is a restorative, uniquely Hawaiian soup of questionable ethnic derivation, made with noodles, sliced green onion, and usually Spam in a clear broth. (The saimin at Chicken Alice's on Kapiolani Boulevard near Ala Moana Center is *ono*— delicious—and an excellent hangover cure.)

Manoa

You didn't come to Hawaii to go to college, and the odd lot of architecture on the campus of the **University of Hawaii,** at Dole Street and University Avenue, is hardly worth seeing, but the campus itself is set in misty Manoa Valley, often streaked by rainbows, and *is* worth visiting, if only for the view of Waikiki and Diamond Head from the parking garage (or "structure," as it's known here). The **East-West Center,** founded in 1960 to promote transpacific understanding, and the Korean Studies Center adjoin the campus on East-West Road. On up University Avenue and Manoa Road, past bungalows built by early *haole* settlers, the road ends at **Paradise Park,** an exotic-bird theme park that also is the trail head to **Manoa Falls,** a popular hike. It's about an hour's walk 800 feet up a muddy trail past wild guava and natural pools to the falls in their lush green setting. Go weekdays to avoid crowds, and bring along mosquito repellant.

Kapahulu

On the Diamond Head border of Waikiki, Kapahulu Avenue is a funky adjunct to Waikiki's neon glitz, a district of shops, restaurants, and bars that is fun to explore. A variety of retail merchandise displays itself here in typical, mile-long strip zoning, anchored by Hale Niu Formal Wear on one end and **Hee Hing's,** where the lemon chicken isn't what it used to be, on the other. In between there's a plethora of good restaurants, such as locally popular **J.R's Upstairs,** a mom-and-pop bistro that's like being invited over for dinner; **Irifune,** a serene Japanese restaurant with *joto miso;* and **Keo's Thai Cuisine,** an orchid-filled celebrity hangout where everyone from Tina Turner to Jimmy Carter has chopsticked through the *mee krob.*

After dinner go to **Dave's Ice Cream** for two scoops of home-style mango, *lilikoi,* or *poha* ice cream, voted Hawaii's best in *Honolulu* magazine reader surveys. Along this avenue you may find one of those threadbare swimsuits that girls sort of wear on Waikiki, or you can continue the search for the perfect aloha shirt at the new, bigger **Bailey's Antique and Thrift Shop**, which claims to have the largest collection—imported mostly from California now that local closets have been depleted. Vintage silkies go for as much as $1,000 each. There's a skateboard shop, a diving-gear shop, a Chinese drive-through restaurant, and a nightclub that advertises a singular "exotic dancer." Of all the restaurants, only **Harpo's Pizza**, which delivers free to Waikiki, stays open after 10:00 P.M.

GETTING AROUND

Honolulu International is one of the busiest jetports in the nation, yet one of the easiest to get around—big, clear, international graphics are the secret, and everyone here has "plenny aloha" for visitors. Arriving travellers may catch the free WikiWiki van to the baggage carousels on the street level, where taxis are available. Taxi is the best and fastest way to Waikiki, about $15 for the nearly 8-mile trip. All the major rental-car agencies are on the airport's street level.

The best way to explore Waikiki is on foot. The popular pedicabs (and skateboards) are now banned in Waikiki, and traffic is too intense for bicycling with any comfort. Mopeds are available for rent.

Exploring Oahu is easy on TheBus, Honolulu's excellent municipal transit system, which will take you almost anywhere on the island for 60 cents, exact change. The most popular route is the number 8, which shuttles between Waikiki and Ala Moana and back about every ten minutes. TheBus goes to all the fun places, including Sea Life Park (number 57 or 58) and the Bishop Museum (number 2). On weekends and holidays, there's the special Beach Bus (number 22) from Waikiki to Hanauma Bay, east near Koko Head. Every day of the week the number 52 or 55 Circle Island bus goes around the island, from Ala Moana Center and back; it takes almost all day. The 57 or 58 swings around the southeastern loop of Oahu via Kailua, Waimanalo, Sea Life Park, and Hawaii Kai. Many attractions offer free shuttles to and from destinations. One of these, Windward Expeditions, runs vans from Waikiki to Oahu's Windward side, where visitors then cruise among migrating whales (migration season is January through April) to uninhabited islands; Tel: 263-3899. The Dole Pineapple Transit minibus leaves every five minutes from 12 Waikiki locations between 8:30 A.M. and 3:30 P.M., for 50 cents, and travels through downtown and Chinatown and on to Cannery Square. The newest way to get around is on a motorized replica of a San Francisco cable car that loops out of Waikiki to a variety of destinations. For the $7 pass you are free to get off and on the trolley all day; Tel: 941-6608.

DINING IN HONOLULU
OUTSIDE WAIKIKI
Most of the hotel rooms on Oahu are in Waikiki, but many of the interesting restaurants are in Honolulu proper. It's worth it—both in time and money—to rent a car or grab a cab to get out of Waikiki to eat. The Hawaiian street names may seem disorienting at first, but a map or a helpful concierge should set you on the right path. It's difficult to get seriously lost; Honolulu is a compact city, squeezed between the mountains and the ocean. Even in heavy traffic there are plenty of restaurants within 15 minutes of most Waikiki hotels.

For the past 25 years it has been the custom here to put restaurants in shopping centers—freestanding locations are simply too expensive. Many of the major centers are dotted like loosely strung beads along Ala Moana Boulevard, one of the arteries leading out of Waikiki: Ala Moana Center, Ward Centre, Ward Warehouse, and Restaurant Row. All are easy to find and have ample parking.

For a city of 800,000, Honolulu is singularly blessed with restaurants. The successive waves of immigrants have each brought their own cuisine with them. Several kinds of cooking—Asian, Polynesian, European—exist side by side here and occasionally meld together. The problem is deciding which kind of food you want to eat on any given night. Local residents eat early, visitors tend to eat later. Outside Waikiki, therefore, where there are fewer visitors, it's much easier to get an 8:30 or 9:00 dinner reservation than one at 7:30, especially on weekends.

The telephone area code for Hawaii is 808.

Fine Dining
The Black Orchid (Restaurant Row, 500 Ala Moana Boulevard) is the flagship restaurant of the newly developed Restaurant Row. The restaurant got off to a fast start because TV and movie star Tom Selleck is a part owner.

Don't go expecting Selleck. If he's there (unlikely), he's in a private dining room. You may wish to go instead for the first-rate food, the elegance of the service, or the Art Deco decor. The Black Orchid does a Cajun-style, seared yellowfin tuna (called black and blue *ahi*) with a soy-mustard sauce that will wake any taste buds, as will the red-hot shrimp with 15 spices. Desserts are out of the ordinary here; there's one that looks like the cross section of a giant Snickers bar, served with caramel sauce. The cocktail lounge sees lots of action at night, and offers a limited menu. Tel: 521-3111.

Byron II Steak House (Ala Moana Center, 1450 Ala Moana Boulevard) is a haven for those who long for old-fashioned restaurants. The menu is familiar, portions are ample, the veteran waiters are courteous, the tablecloths are white linen, and the whole atmosphere is calm. Byron II will do a Chateaubriand for one, finishing it off tableside and serving it with a forest of fresh vegetables. Massive portions of French onion soup, avocado salads with jumbo shrimp, and fresh fish in a variety of preparations are some of the other things offered here—all at moderate prices. The wine selection is limited, but you can't have everything. Tel: 949-8855.

The **Maile Restaurant** (5000 Kahala Avenue) is the top-of-the-line dining room at the Kahala Hilton, which is not in Waikiki, but sits in splendid isolation between a swank residential district and the ocean, east of Waikiki, about 2 miles past Diamond Head. The Maile has always maintained a high standard with its food, but in recent years prices have skyrocketed. Now the Maile is holding down prices by allowing its patrons to assemble a fixed-price dinner out of virtually any of the menu items: for example, ragout of escargot and shrimp on puff pastry, Hawaiian sunfish fillet and lobster dumplings on black linguine, roast duckling cooked tableside with lychees, peaches, banana, and mandarin oranges. There's always beluga caviar and it's always extra. The wine list is excellent and expensive. Dancing is offered during dinner in the adjoining lounge. The Maile only does dinner, so those planning a daytime visit to see the Kahala Hilton's tame dolphins and penguins might try the open-air **Hala Terrace**, offering extensive breakfast and lunch menus. Reservations for both restaurants; Tel: 734-2211.

Roy's (6600 Kalanianaole Highway, in Hawaii Kai Corporate Plaza shopping center) is by far the hottest of Honolulu's new restaurants. Located in residential East Honolulu (don't try to drive there until rush hour ends, about 6:30 P.M.), with a sweeping second-story view of Maunalua Bay, this is more than the latest trendy eatery. Young chef Ray Yamaguchi works alongside his crew in a large display kitchen, turning out food that combines his French training with his Asian heritage. The appetizers alone show off Yamaguchi's cuisine: perfect grilled shrimp with *wasabi* cocktail sauce, rich seafood pot stickers with sesame-seed butter sauce, and steamed pork *shu mai* with mustard-soy vinaigrette. Among the entrées, the star is a slightly sweet, remarkably low-fat, mesquite-smoked crispy duck—a dish that owes its inspiration to both China and California. The duck arrives taken off the bone and beautifully arranged on top of a passion-fruit and ginger sauce. Another good choice is the seared scallops swimming in Cabernet butter. The food is memorable, and there's another reward for driving 20 minutes out of town: Prices here are about half what you would expect in Waikiki. Tel: 396-ROYS.

The Swiss Inn (5730 Kalanianaole Highway), located in Niu Valley Shopping Center in East Honolulu, is one of Honolulu's best-kept secrets. Owner-chef Martin Wyss cooks every meal personally, and his wife, Jeanie, presides over the unpretentious little dining room as if it were her own home. A whole range of wonderful veal dishes tops the menu, including, when Wyss feels like it, osso buco. There is good fresh fish, roasted chicken redolent of rosemary, heartwarming *rösti* potatoes (with bacon and onions), and fresh fruit tarts and coupes for dessert. The Swiss Inn is always packed—reservations a must; Tel: 377-5447.

Seafood

A few minutes out of Waikiki toward downtown, in a warehouse district near the wholesale fish auction, sits **John Dominis** (43 Ahui Street), with a sweeping view of the ocean and Kewalo Basin. You enter the large dining room on a bridge over an artificial pond full of live local lobsters. There's no question about the quality of seafood here—especially the tiger prawns and the wide variety of fresh local fish, prepared virtually any way you'd like it, including *en papillote*. But there are some who grumble that no matter how high the quality of the food, it's never as high as the check. Unpretentious, but attentive, service; adequate wine list. Reserve ahead, especially on weekends; Tel: 523-0955.

There's no such thing as an inexpensive seafood restaurant in Honolulu, but **Horatio's** (Ward Warehouse, 1050 Ala Moana Boulevard) does an excellent job at moderate prices. A stark, gray interior gives way to a relaxed, comfortable atmosphere once you're inside. The restaurant always has an assortment of fresh local fish, done in interesting preparations (Szechwan chili butter, for instance). There is a wider menu for those who aren't crazy about fish. The signature dessert here is burnt cream. Expect a lot of business talk at neighboring tables at lunch. Service is informal, but reasonably good. Tel: 521-5002.

Chinese

With its art collection, vases, folding screens, and carved furniture, **Dynasty II** (Ward Warehouse, 1050 Ala Moana Boulevard) is as attractive and upscale a Chinese restaurant as you could hope to find anywhere. Stay away from the lunch buffet, but you can make a wonderful meal from the Cantonese menu: Peking duck, tofu pillows with broccoli, crystal shrimp on candied walnuts. Tel: 531-0208.

On the other end of the scale, **The New Golden Duck** (930 McCully Street, just a few blocks over the McCully Street overpass from Waikiki) has a cement floor, vinyl booths, and boxes stacked in corners. But it's close to Waikiki, has plenty of parking, and it's cheap. The ample portions of spicy beef *chow fun* and the billowy shrimp Canton may make you forget the surroundings. No liquor served, but there is no charge for bringing your own wine or beer. Honolulu is full of neighborhood "greasy chopsticks"; this one is the best. Reservations taken, but not necessary; Tel: 947-9755.

King Tsin (1110 McCully Street, a block or two past the Golden Duck, above) was once a stylish small restaurant packed by devotees of Szechwan cuisine. It has since moved to larger, far less attractive quarters, but it now has parking and is located a few blocks from the McCully Street bridge, one of Waikiki's main gateways. The kitchen still turns out marvels, including beggar's chicken and steamed whole fish with ginger and onion. Call ahead for a whole fish; Tel: 946-3273.

Also close to Waikiki is **Maple Garden** (909 Isenberg Street, just off Kapiolani Boulevard). Maple Garden has a conventional, vinyl-booth interior that is far from dazzling, but this small restaurant has attracted the attention of a number of West Coast food writers. There is a good selection of Szechwan and Mandarin dishes, but the star here is the smoked tea duck made on the premises, which is always available, and is served with small rice-flour buns. Supplement the duck with the braised spinach and the meal will be praiseworthy. Tel: 941-6641.

All things considered, Howard Co's **Yen King** (Kahala Mall, 4211 Waialae Avenue) may be Honolulu's best everyday Chinese restaurant. The decor is more comfortable than most shopping-center restaurants: wooden tables, nicely papered walls. The kitchen reliably cooks more than 100 Szechwan, Hong Kong, and vegetarian dishes, including excellent hot-and-sour soup, pot stickers, *kung pao* shrimp, and Mongolian beef. Sometimes the service is wonderful; other times it's hard to figure which of the young staff bustling through the dining room is your waiter. Unpretentious and reasonably priced, Yen King is also the right place to arrange a ten-course banquet if you can raise a large party. Tel: 732-5505.

Over a century old, **Wo Fat** (115 North Hotel Street, downtown) was Hawaii's first restaurant. Originally a cooking shack set up by a group of Chinese immigrants, Wo Fat has prospered for generations, despite being burned down twice in Chinatown fires. Its present landmark building, which combines Chinese motifs with Western construction, was a sensation when it first opened in the 1930s. The high-ceilinged upstairs dining room is painted in a riot of red, green, and gold. The food is not the attraction here: It is pallid, cornstarchy Cantonese. This is a historic spot—thousands of visiting servicemen ate here during the war. If you ask the dining-room hostess if she remembers you from the war years, she always says, "Yes, and you were a handsome young man then." She didn't work at the restaurant during the war; she was with the police department.

Thai

Celebrities from Jimmy Carter to Tina Turner have eaten in the plant- and orchid-filled dining room of **Keo's Thai Cuisine** (625 Kapahulu Avenue, a few blocks up from the zoo). This reasonably priced restaurant is a big favorite when local residents take Waikiki guests to dinner. The food, while certainly adequate, is not as impressive as the restaurant's reputation. It's the atmosphere and not the Evil Jungle Prince (a Keo invention made with chicken, beef, shrimp, or fish in a sauce of coconut milk, fresh basil, and Thai spices) that keeps the tables full. Keo owns most of Honolulu's other Thai restaurants, so you may as well try the flagship. Tel: 737-8240.

Vietnamese

Vietnamese refugees make up the latest wave of immigrants to the Islands, and tiny Vietnamese restaurants are springing up all over town. Most might as well be in Saigon; they make few concessions to English-speaking clientele. But the freshness of the cuisine, the spicy sauces, and the profusion of fresh basil and mint are worth the trouble. The best of these restaurants, especially if you do not speak Vietnamese, is **Hale Vietnam** (1140 12th Avenue, in Kaimuki). The building, next to a bowling alley, is not without its charms—brass ceiling fans and 1920s modernist touches—but it's also a bit dingy, and the service can sometimes be outright rude. The food, however, is first-rate: rich *pho* (a beef soup with noodles and fresh vegetables), translucent shrimp rolls, shaking beef, and shrimp on sugarcane. Tel: 735-7581.

Korean

Highly spiced Korean food has become a permanent part of Island cuisine, but Honolulu still lacks an elegant Korean restaurant. Most are fast-food or take-out places. In the absence of a more glittering establishment, the reigning champ is Henry Chun's **Kim Chee II** (3569 Waialae Avenue, along Kaimuki's main commercial strip; ample parking in the rear). Kim Chee II is the best of a small family chain. It's a red-vinyl-booth establishment, with some uninspired oil paintings on the wall. The specialty of the house is ample portions of beef, short ribs, and chicken marinated in sesame oil, green onion, garlic, ginger, and red pepper. Also excellent are the small pork pastries called *mandoo*. Prices are unbelievably low here. No liquor, but you can bring your own (beer is probably the beverage of choice with food of this fervor).

Japanese

You're likely to see three generations of the same family seated at the next table in **Kamigata** (Manoa Marketplace, 2756 Woodlawn Drive), located in a neighborhood shopping center near the University of Hawaii. Although it looks attractively Japanese—full of fans, kimonos, masks, and shoji partitions—Kamigata, like much of Hawaii, is solidly Japanese-American. You keep your shoes on, and the seating is Western chairs and tables. Even the tatami rooms have wells under the low tables in which you can dangle your legs. The small sushi bar, with its tiny artificial stream, is often full, but sushi is also available in the dining room, as are excellent sashimi, tempura, *tonkatsu, udon,* and so forth, all moderately priced. The combination dinners, served in *bento* boxes, are often the best of the menu. The signature dessert here is an Island favorite, shave ice (flavored syrup poured over shaved ice, often called a snow cone on the Mainland). The reservation policy is inconsistent; call ahead for a large party, at least. Tel: 988-2107.

Restaurant Sada, on a crowded wide street near Ala Moana Center (1432 Makaloa Street), has some of the freshest seafood in town. The sushi bar here is large enough that you can usually get a seat; the sushi chefs are easy to deal with and often make you little extras if you eat enough. The informal dining room serves a full line of Japanese food, with an emphasis on seafood items. The help often doesn't speak enough English to sustain a conversation, but they can be counted on to get your order. Tel: 949-0646.

The best sushi bar in Honolulu is **Sushi Hirota** (3435 Waialae Avenue, in Kaimuki). Hirota-*san* himself works behind the nine-seat counter, and if it is a duty of a sushi chef to strike up a rapport with the customer, then Hirota is a master. He'll explain what you should eat and how you should eat it. Hirota is a purist; he'll pull a live freshwater prawn from a tank, kill it, and serve it to you wriggling on a finger of rice. But don't ask him to make a California roll; avocado and mayonnaise are simply not Japanese enough. This is such a small place, you may have to beg for a reservation; Tel: 735-5694.

Hawaiian

Hawaiian restaurants are surprisingly difficult to find in Hawaii, even though Hawaiian food is a staple at parties and catered affairs. The Hawaiian food offered to visitors at commercial luaus is often supplemented by pseudo-Hawaiian touches such as batter-dipped *mahimahi* (a white-fleshed fish nowadays often imported frozen from Taiwan) and "Polynesian" chicken. But if you want real Hawaiian food, short of finding a community luau, you have to go looking for little hole-in-the-wall restaurants. Of these, the best is **Ono Hawaiian Foods** (726 Kapahulu Avenue, a few blocks up from Keo's Thai Cuisine, above), which is run—in one of those twists typical of Hawaii—by a family of Okinawans. Ono is so small there is often a line on the sidewalk outside, prospective patrons with six-packs of beer tucked under their arms (Ono does not serve liquor). Once inside, you find yourself jammed into a small wooden booth to eat excellent *kalua* pig (shreds of pork with the smoky taste of an underground barbecue), *lomilomi* salmon (rubbed salmon in tomatoes and green onion), *laulau* (pork or fish and taro leaves, steamed inside a green ti leaf), or *pipi kaula* (a local beef jerky). You have your choice of rice or poi, and all meals come with raw onions and coarse Hawaiian salt. Prices are commensurate with the decor, which features trophies, faded pictures, and baseball hats. Despite the crush, the atmosphere is friendly. Don't dress up.

Slightly larger, but no more expensive, is **People's Café** (1310 Pali Highway). People's is more attractive than Ono—it looks like a standard coffee shop—and draws a crowd of downtown office workers at lunchtime. The usual Hawaiian offerings here are supplemented by a tasty chicken luau, a soupy dish with cooked taro leaves and bean thread noodles. For some reason, beef stew is now thought of as Hawaiian food, and that too is a popular item.

It is not exclusively a Hawaiian restaurant, but **The Willows** (901 Hausten Street, a small street near University Avenue that runs between South King Street and Kapiolani Boulevard—once you find Hausten Street you can't miss the restaurant) does offer a Hawaiian plate as part of its extensive international menu, which includes wok cooking and curries as well as more conventional shrimp, steak, chicken, and veal dishes. But the food at The Willows pales beside the splendor of its setting: five and a half acres of landscaped grounds with a winding carp pond spanned by footbridges. Walking into The Willows is like turning the clock back 40 years, before the Islands discovered high-rises and concrete. The food here will not knock your socks off, but the restaurant very well might. Tel: 946-4808.

Mexican

Honolulu is not rich in Mexican restaurants. The best of them, **Compadres** (Ward Centre, 1200 Ala Moana Boulevard), was designed to serve not Mexican food, but fresh California cuisine with a Mexican accent. Still, all the standard Mexican specialties are available in this bright, cheerful, bustling restaurant: rich carnitas and fajitas with plenty of fresh salsa, for example, and excellent grilled chicken and shrimp. The margaritas here are large and potent. The open lanai is a popular gathering spot for drinks after work or for whiling away a hot afternoon. The waiters and waitresses are largely young and enthusiastic. No reservations, but the dining room is quite large and there's usually a table.

For those who expect Mexican restaurants to be small, dark, and unpretentious, there's **Mama's Mexican Kitchen** (378 North School Street, near the School Street exit off the H-1, northwest of downtown), with a neighborhood feel and low prices. Standard combination plates are available with beans and rice, as are fajitas and large "gorilla" burritos. Bring your own liquor. Tel: 537-3200.

Italian
A decade ago the only Italian food in Honolulu was in Waikiki. Suddenly, small Italian restaurants have sprung up all over town, offering creative Italian food at reasonable prices. One favorite is **Andrew's** (Ward Centre, 1200 Ala Moana Boulevard), which was deliberately designed to look like a San Francisco restaurant, to the point of bricking up one wall that would otherwise have a pleasant view of the fishing-boat harbor. Whatever the wisdom of that, this is a dignified, hushed atmosphere in which to sample some excellent spaghetti carbonara, made with *pancetta*, or *linguine tutto mare* with shrimp, crab, scallops, and squid. There are veal, seafood, and fish dishes, and daily specials; everything comes in large portions. Although not inexpensive, Andrew's is a bargain compared to the Waikiki places, and provides much of the same kind of formal dining experience. Tel: 523-8677.

On the other end of the scale from the formal Andrew's is the newest of Honolulu's new Italian restaurants, **Café Cambio** (1680 Kapiolani Boulevard, near Ala Moana Center). Owner Sergio Mitroti presides over his kitchen, turning out pastas flavored with espresso or wild mushrooms, as well as veal, fresh fish, and pizzas. Mitroti and his wife were both designers before plunging into the restaurant business, and they have turned a storefront restaurant into a dazzler: walls covered with graphics, and long stretches of marble along the bar and pizza oven.

Always full is **Castagnola's** (Manoa Marketplace, 2752 Woodlawn Drive, near the University of Hawaii). Cass

Castagnola prides himself on using the freshest local ingredients, and imports much of what his kitchen uses from Italy—buffalo mozzarella from Naples, extra virgin first-press olive oil, plum tomatoes for his sauces. The traditional Italian fare is solid here, especially the home-made pork sausage with peppers and onion. This is an-other small storefront restaurant. Customers are plentiful here, the tables are jammed together, and sometimes the service is less than friendly. But you're likely to find Castagnola himself wandering the dining room, spread-ing good cheer. Reservations necessary; Tel: 988-2969.

The two **Che Pasta** branches (Che Pasta, 3571 Waialae Avenue, in Kaimuki, and Café Che Pasta, Pacific Tower, 1001 Bishop Street, downtown) are very similar: mini-malist gray interiors dressed up by the works of local artists who display their paintings for sale. It's hard to predict the look here—it depends on what's on the wall—but the effect always seems casually elegant. The downtown Café Che Pasta covers the tables with paper, and should inspiration strike, there are crayons on the table to doodle with. The *cucina nuova* kitchen sets itself high standards: fresh ingredients, pasta made on the premises, and sauces based on careful reductions, individually prepared for each dish. Ravioli stuffed with herbed chicken, with lobster, or with four cheeses, a rich lasagna, and cannelloni are all available at reason-able prices. The downtown location does more grilled items, including an excellent hamburger topped with mozzarella. There is a good wine selection for such small restaurants, with an emphasis on value. Many wines may be ordered by the glass. Tel: 735-1777 for Che Pasta; 524-0004 for Café Che Pasta.

In a remodeled mansion that's more quaint than stylish is **Phillip Paolo's** (2312 South Beretania Street, near Isenberg Street). Phillip Paolo is his own chef, and seems to put a great deal of energy into every plate. The por-tions are large, with an emphasis on seafood dishes: *opakapaka* (a local snapper) with capers, scallops with linguine, stuffed Dungeness crab, and so forth. The whole atmosphere is casual, but far from amateurish. If you are without your own transportation, not to worry: Phillip Paolo has put together a package deal with a limousine company. You can be transported to dinner in style (and not take up any of the restaurant's limited parking). Tel: 946-1163.

The chef at **Salerno** (McCully Shopping Center, 1960

Kapiolani Boulevard, just over the McCully Street over-pass), Khubo Luu, is Vietnamese. That often doesn't show: His pesto is the best in town. But sometimes it does, to good effect: His linguine with calamari and vegetables is as rich, hot, and garlicky as Southeast Asian food. The dining room is spare here, decorated with Asian knock-offs of clichéd Western paintings. But Salerno pulls in a crowd because the food is first-rate and moderately priced. On the second floor of a small shopping center, so close to Waikiki you could walk. Tel: 942-5273.

Fun

California Pizza Kitchen (Kahala Mall, a major shopping center on Waialae Avenue) is a bright, noisy establish-ment done up in white, yellow, and black tile. This is the fourth restaurant in a small Beverly Hills chain designed to bring California pizza to the masses. The pizzas come out of the wood-burning oven topped with Peking duck; Thai chicken; bacon, lettuce, and tomato; even traditional sausage and pepperoni.

There's a similarly irreverent attitude toward pastas: angel hair topped with black-bean sauce, fettuccine with chicken-tequila sauce. But stick to the pizzas. They're not as strange as they might sound. In fact, they tend to be as cheerful and accessible as the decor. There is a reason-able selection of California wines, with an emphasis on value. If you're alone or in a hurry, there's a counter in front of the display kitchen. No reservations, and some-times a wait for a table.

Murphy's Bar & Grill (2 Merchant Street) is a favorite downtown wateringhole and lunch spot, in a historic building that once housed the Royal Tavern, frequented by King Kalakaua. The food is casual but surprisingly good: salads, pastas, sandwiches, fresh fish, and hamburg-ers with homemade cottage fries. Packed at lunch, far less busy at dinner. Tel: 531-0422.

Rose City Diner (Restaurant Row, 500 Ala Moana Boule-vard) is a re-creation of a 1950s diner, complete with a jukebox playing old-time rock 'n' roll in each gray and pink booth. Although a bit cluttered with memorabilia, the diner manages to avoid being precious. The atmo-sphere is invigorating, and the food remarkable for its genre: fresh vegetables with the entrées, lumpy home-made mashed potatoes with gravy, meat loaf, chicken-fried steak, burgers, chili, and shakes. Rose City Diner is open 24 hours on weekends.

Ryan's Parkplace Bar & Grill (Ward Centre, 1200 Ala Moana Boulevard) draws a large bar crowd, attracted by the open, airy seating, the huge back bar with its vast collection of single-malt scotches and imported beers, the free happy-hour *pupu* (Hawaiian for hors d'oeuvres or snacks), and the informal atmosphere. The dining room is large and the menu eclectic—everything from mesquite-grilled fish to Japanese noodles with shrimp. The appetizer choices are vast, and you are welcome to assemble a meal in any fashion you like. Tel: 523-9132.

—*John Heckathorn*

HONOLULU NIGHTLIFE AND ENTERTAINMENT

Out there on the outskirts of Waikiki, in the great beyond of Oahu, the nightlife is diverse, traditional, spontaneous, corny, sometimes sophisticated, sometimes illegal—and always fun.

The best place to start in Honolulu may be the tourist show at the Kahala Hilton, where Danny Kaleikini holds the endurance record as Hawaii's longest-running act in show business, second only to New York's Bobby Short, who never played the *ohe hano ihu* (Hawaiian nose flute) or the ukulele or the slack key guitar, and doesn't sing in 12 languages. The Kahala star, who makes Kyoto honeymooners giggle as easily as their Kansas counterparts, has logged 22 years as the **Hala Terrace** headliner, and has sung the *haole* version of "The Hawaiian Wedding Song" more than 10,000 times in the three decades that he has performed his 75-minute, Hawaiian-Polynesian variety show. He sings in Spanish, Italian, Chinese, Korean, and Japanese, and cracks jokes in pidgin. But he'd rather be playing golf at nearby Waialae Country Club, where he hosts the annual Hawaiian Open.

Downhill from the University of Hawaii across from Moiliili baseball field at 2440 South Beretania Street is a classic college hangout, **Anna Bannanas**, home of Pagan Babies, one of Honolulu's most creative bands, with musical roots in Third World rhythms of reggae, *soca,* Antillean *zouk,* and African *soukous.* Not just another boogie band, Pagan Babies is an Afro-Caribbean band of Asian musicians that often seems far ahead of its usually beery audience until the itchy rhythms kick in and everybody dances. This is the Afro-Asian split Duke Ellington first discovered, crossed with Hawaii's own ethnomusical undercurrents. And great fun to dance to. The band's name refers to those poster waifs that Christian charities used to solicit money to convert. The band's black tee-shirt bears the painted red and yellow face of a Papua New Guinea highlander from Malcolm Kirk's book *Man as Art in New Guinea.*

A more traditional Hawaiian sound is captured by Mahi Beamer, a smooth-voiced singer who accompanies himself on piano in the inky black lounge at **Andrew's Italian Restaurant**, a popular hula *halau* (school) hangout at Ward Centre, 1200 Ala Moana Boulevard.

When Billie Holiday sang Ellington's "It's Always Swingtime in Honolulu," she probably had in mind **The Swing Club** down on Chinatown's North Hotel Street between Nuuanu Avenue and Smith Street, the cradle of jazz in Hawaii. The joint's still jumping after all these years, only with a soul sound now, and this dark and smoky landmark club is still fun on a Friday night. (And this is still a somewhat seedy neighborhood at night, so if you do go, exercise some caution.)

The newest jazz notes in Honolulu emanate from a classic 1950s, New York–style cellar club in Chinatown, the **AWM Club**, on the site of the first Chinese-language newspaper office at 1128 Smith Street. AWM stands for artists, writers, and musicians, which is apropos, because the club is the latest venture of artist–jazz patron Ramsay. It's downstairs of Ramsay's Chinatown Gallery, on Smith Street between Pauahi and North Hotel streets.

Around the island, look for local players, such as pianists Ed Moody and Rich Crandall, the Bob Klem Jazz Quartet, or Rolando Sanchez & Friends at various clubs.

Out in Pearl City, in a light industrial district, **Reni's Back Room**, founded by Roger Mosley (he flew the helicopter on the TV show "Magnum, P.I."), features Island fusion favorite Nueva Vida and various other rock and jazz groups on a regular basis.

Performance Venues

Highbrow entertainment may be found in Chinatown at the Neoclassical-style Hawaii Theater (1130 Bethel Street between Hotel and Beretania streets), the first movie palace in the Islands, which opened in September 1922. The only remaining theater in downtown Honolulu, the Hawaii Theater is open in a limited way for special local events, such as the Chinese Opera of Canton, the Hawaii

State Ballet, and the International East-West Film Festival. A restoration project, scheduled to begin in mid-1990, may cause the theater to go dark for a year.

Neal Blaisdell Center, named for a former mayor of Honolulu, is the spiky building that looks like a fallen star on Ward Avenue at Kapiolani Boulevard. It serves as the city's star arena for main events and road shows from the San Francisco Ballet, which plays annually, to the latest pop sensations. The touring entertainers, like all visitors, appear briefly, but nevertheless do keep Honolulu from becoming "Racine, Wisconsin, Saturday night," as author Joan Didion once wrote, perhaps too harshly. The best thing about any Honolulu concert is the proximity to the performer that spectators enjoy; the aloha spirit seems to relax even security goons.

In the nearby Neal Blaisdell Center Concert Hall (Ward Avenue at South King Street), the small, spirited Honolulu Symphony performs a 127-concert season. The symphony often features guest soloists like Vladimir Ashkenazy, Peter Nero, and Seiji Ozawa.

Hawaiian Music

Out on Dillingham Avenue, across from Honolulu Community College, the **Jubilee** (closed Mondays) is the last true bastion of live Hawaiian music, where most weeknights and every weekend aficionados of slack key, steel guitar, and falsetto may find the Peter Moon Band, the Makaha Sons of Niihau, Ledward Kalapana, Olomana with Jerry Santos, Wally Suenaga, Haunani Apoliona and Willy Paikuli IV, the Kamalamalama Brothers, Kipapa Rush, the Nuuanu Brothers, Kalani Okalani, and Island Magic. Host Richard Kashimoto is "holding on," keeping the endangered Hawaiian music live in Honolulu at this small, intimate nightclub that stays open until 4:00 A.M. on weekends. So there's no excuse to go to the Islands and not see or hear *real* Hawaiian music.

A favorite expression in Hawaii is *pau hana* (work finished). **Pau hana parties** usually are impromptu, local-style affairs, a few friends getting together after work with some *tako poke* (marinated bits of octopus) and a six-pack of Bud. But canny barkeeps now offer more organized pau hana parties, with food, drink, and live entertainment, usually after work on Aloha Friday, and, boy, are they fun. (For Aloha Week, see "Business Hours and Holidays" in the Useful Facts section, above.)

The best pau hana happens almost every Aloha Friday on Merchant Street on the makai edge of Chinatown. The street is barricaded between Bethel and Smith streets, outside **Murphy's Bar & Grill**, so an old-fashioned block party may commence with live music, maybe Eddie Kamae and the Sons of Hawaii and sometimes surprise guest artists such as Herbie Mann.

Some of the best indoor pau hana parties are at **Rumours** at the Ala Moana Hotel and **Studebaker's** at Restaurant Row, in Kakaako between downtown Honolulu and Waikiki.

Restaurant Row

Restaurant Row (a square block at 500 Ala Moana Boulevard, near downtown, bordered by Punchbowl, South, and Pohu Kaina streets) is the catchy name of an urban entertainment center that comprises a collection of theme bistros and leftover attractions that worked somewhere else, some time ago, including a world's fair clock from Vancouver. The "nice," sociable bars of Honolulu may be found at Restaurant Row, which is still unfolding and is attracting mostly local crowds (because it is fun, but mainly because it is just about the only game in town). The open-air **Row Bar** offers free, live entertainment by local bands such as Nueva Vida and Rolando Sanchez & Friends. Several other trendy bars and restaurants in the complex, such as Studebaker's and **Rose City Diner**, attract great crowds of local folks out on the town on the weekends, but there's nothing in this sterile food condo that says Hawaii, not even a Trader Vic's. The main attractions at Restaurant Row are Studebaker's pau hana party, a wall-to-wall jumble of bodies; singer Azure McCall at the **Black Orchid**; and the expensive **Sunset Grill** (which has no great sunset view).

Hula

Looking for authentic Hawaiian hula? Hawaii's best hula *halau* (schools) compete in modern and ancient hula categories at the **King Kamehameha Hula Competition**, held for two nights on the third weekend in June at Neal Blaisdell Center. The big international competition, sponsored by the State Council of Hawaiian Heritage, attracts dancers from New Zealand to Texas. Devotees claim it's bigger and more exciting than Hilo's Merrie Monarch

Festival. A $5 ticket in the balcony is the best way to see
and hear hula the way it's supposed to be.

Korean Hostess Bars

There are 400 Korean "hostess" bars in Honolulu, with
names like Crystal Palace and Club By You, featuring
"naked Penthouse" dancers and free *pupu*—usually fried
chicken wings. Inside, young, attractive Asian women
hover like flies to hustle $20 drinks with promises of
sexual favors. These clip joints, periodically raided by
Honolulu Vice, are designed to empty your wallet, and
should be entered only at your own risk.

These bars are called Korean bars because Korean
refugees started them in the 1950s; most now are owned
by Vietnamese refugees, who hire blue-eyed, blonde California girls to dance totally naked to the delight of Japanese tourists, men and women. It may sound kinky, but
it's great fun to watch the Japanese tourists watch the
California girls.

If you must attend any of these nudity night spots—for
purely sociological reasons, of course—these are more
or less safe: The Classic Cat on Sheridan Street, Dirty Dan
on Sand Island, and The Lolli-Pop Club in Waikiki.

—*Rick Carroll*

SHOPS AND SHOPPING
IN HONOLULU

Central Honolulu is small compared to other major
cities, but what it lacks in size, it makes up for in
character. Certain streets have their own distinct flavor.
By day on Honolulu's Bishop Street (unlike in Waikiki,
where the dress code says anything goes) you'll see
secretaries and receptionists clipping along in high
heels, and lawyers carrying briefcases and wearing
honest-to-goodness shoes—not thong slippers (though
they only wear suits on the days they go to court). Two
blocks away, a short section of Hotel Street is the only
downtown area where there is any after-dark action, and
it seems to appeal mostly to curious sailors or rough
types who enjoy peep shows, gyrating topless waitresses,
and blaring music. Contrary to the popular song, downtown in Honolulu is not "where all the lights are bright."

Ala Moana Boulevard separates the downtown area
from Honolulu Harbor. Directly inland from Aloha Tower
(the spire with the big clock on the waterfront) is **Fort**

Street Mall, the walk-and-shop center of the city. A fort of coral stone built in 1816, King Kamehameha's palace, and hundreds of grass houses were pictured in the first sketch of the port of Honolulu drawn shortly after 1816—the year Russian explorers built the fort that Kamehameha I later took as his own. When the first white men visited the small fishing village in 1793, Nuuanu Stream emptied into the harbor (then called Kou); inland the explorers found a small village headed by a native chief named Honoruru (Honolulu). (Honolulu has been variously translated: "where the back of the neck is sheltered from the wind," "place of abundant calm," "sheltered cove," and "fair haven.")

Today the major streets that run mauka to makai (mountains to sea) are Bishop Street (the financial center), Fort Street Mall, Nuuanu Avenue, and Maunakea Street (the Chinatown district). Chinatown is the area that furnishes the most interesting shopping diversions.

The shops along Fort Street Mall, for the most part, carry the same merchandise as Anytown, USA. There's a branch of Longs Drugs, a Woolworth variety store, a few dress shops, and shoe stores anchored by one of the Liberty House department stores. Bargain-hunting office workers head for the **Penthouse** on King Street and Nuuanu Avenue, where merchandise is 50 percent off the price originally charged in the Liberty House stores, and on the first Monday of every month is marked down another 35 percent. In addition to discounted clothing and shoes, attractive gift items, silver-plated bowls, wine glasses, and fine china can often be found here.

Antiques and Art

In the last few years the lower (waterfront) end of Maunakea Street has become a collectors' heaven frequented by antiques and gallery lovers. In talking to the proprietors of these interesting little shops you'll discover there's a bit of rivalry among Honolulu's antiques dealers. One will tell you that his neighbor doesn't carry authentic antiques; another will gossip about the outrageous prices of the dealer next door. **Robyn Buntin of Honolulu** (900-A Maunakea Street) is actually three shops in a row, plus an upstairs framing gallery. All are housed in a historic building dating from 1911, which was originally used for smoking beef. In Buntin's **Honolulu Gallery** are works by popular contemporary Western and

Hawaii artists such as Elly Tepper and the whimsical Guy Buffet, as well as by fine European artists. When artwork by earlier renowned artists of Hawaii, such as David Hitchcock and Madge Tennent, finds its way to the gallery, it seldom remains for long, but mounted lithographs of Hawaiian fish dating from 1903 are normally in stock for about $30 or less. A connecting gallery carries fine Oriental antiques—a ladle from the Han dynasty dating back 2,000 years, a Tang dynasty camel, and fine pieces of Chinese jade. A third room, run by Buntin's wife, features sterling, crystal, Art Nouveau, and Art Deco glass and jewelry.

Next door, at 926 Maunakea, **Aloha Antiques and Collectibles** is a marvelous jumble of "stuff" perhaps not quite so authentically antique, but a prowl through the overcrowded basement, main floor, and loft is intriguing. Amid the river jade from China, the cobalt glass, and the figurines from occupied Japan are dusty pieces of Hawaiiana— old stone bowls, *ulu maika* (polished stones used in a Hawaiian game similar to bowling), poi pounders, pig boards, koa ukuleles, and 1940s koa furniture (the beautifully grained koa wood was also used by early Hawaiians for their canoes). The store is a thrift-shopper's paradise, though not exactly at thrift prices—but proprietor George Kurisu has been known to deal, so don't hesitate to negotiate if you really want something.

Take another step up the street to browse through **Ailana** (930 Maunakea), with its lovely porcelain, glass, artwork, pottery, and some furnishings and paintings. Also, don't miss the upstairs loft where **Watters O. Martin** displays a little cache of Hawaiiana: paintings, engravings, and rare books (you can leave your name on file and ask him to look for any special book you have in mind). In one display case might be silver spoons from 1959 commemorating statehood, buttons from the 1880s, a decorative dog's-tooth pin, and a letter written by Queen Liliuokalani.

Finally, sword collectors can cut a wide swath through all the sword paraphernalia and head right for the basement of **Bushido** at 936 Maunakea Street, where antique Japanese swords are priced from $500 to $150,000. Proprietor Robert Benson, who for years actually studied traditional sword polishing in Japan, is an expert in this field. At street level the shop displays more variety: old jade buttons for $5 each, antique Korean ceramics, and obis and kimonos.

Hawaii's largest selection of blackwood furniture, Japanese *tansu,* scrolls, screens, baskets, and other treasures from the Orient is several blocks away at **Mills Gallery** (701 Bishop Street). Tucked way back in one corner of the shop is another gem, **Past Era**. Owner Marion Glober collects only the goodies in antique and estate jewelry that she personally likes. Typical treasures include a flower pin with leaves of yellow agate and a diamond center, a gold salamander pin inset with rare green rubies, a collection of gleaming cameos, and a little perfume vial with an etched 14-karat-gold top resting in a coffinlike case. Walking canes topped with carved ivory figures and silver handles lean in a corner. She accepts credit cards.

Chinatown

Back on Maunakea Street, turn left onto King Street to find the **Oahu Market**, where, if you trust your senses, you'll think you're in another country. Ducks hang on display hooks, and pigs' heads lie in butcher cases; the butcher will slice off a taste of red pork if you intend to buy. The chatter is in Japanese, Chinese, Vietnamese, and pidgin along the crowded aisle that leads past the fresh produce—Chinese cabbage, kale, lemon cress, and daikon.

In the last few years the end of King Street near Nuuanu Stream has become a dynamic, bustling stretch of small shops operated by recent Vietnamese immigrants. Stop for lunch at **Ba-Le**, an inexpensive Vietnamese sandwich shop where the fresh bread and flaky croissants rival those baked in a French *boulangerie*. Returning to Maunakea Street, you'll find the **Lee and Young Mall**, a conglomeration of stalls under one roof where the freshwater-pearl necklaces are cheap enough that you can take home several for friends.

As you continue inland, Maunakea Street goes through the heart of Chinatown. This historic district has prospered despite two fires, the first of which, in 1886, destroyed eight blocks. The second was set deliberately by the board of health in 1900 to halt the spread of bubonic plague, but it raged out of control when wind blew burning embers to other rooftops. The buildings standing in Chinatown today were therefore built after 1900. Recently, private developers, with help from government agencies, have been restoring the original buildings. The newest addition, which opened during the fall of 1989 on Hotel and Maunakea streets, is **Maunakea Marketplace**, featuring 70 shops and stalls in a huge open market.

All along Maunakea Street are bakeries, lei stands, herb shops, noodle factories, and restaurants. Almond cookies and candied ginger, or the salty *li hing mui* (preserved plum) that local children suck on like jawbreakers, are tasty treats to buy at **Shung Chong Yuen**. Incense burns at an altar in the **Fook Sau Tong** herb shop, where you can describe your ailment and receive a mixture of ginseng, herbs, powdered deer horn, and the like from tiny drawers that line the back wall. You can watch or buy from the ladies stringing fragrant *pikake,* crown flower, or ginger leis at **Cindy's Lei Shoppe** or **Sweetheart's Lei Shop**— prices are lower here than at airport lei stands. At Hawaii's oldest Chinese restaurant, Wo Fat, a pink building with a distinctive, Oriental, green-tile roof right around the corner on North Hotel Street, a plate lunch in the upstairs dining room is about five dollars. At the top of Maunakea Street, across King Street and bordered by Nuuanu Stream, is the **Chinese Cultural Plaza**, with more shops and restaurants, which by now may be an anticlimax—except for the statue of Sun Yat-sen, which stands as a reminder of his years as a student in Hawaii.

The Chinese Chamber of Commerce, Tel: (808) 533-3181, and the Hawaii Heritage Center, Tel: (808) 521-2749, conduct inexpensive walking tours of Chinatown with lunch as an optional added attraction. The area can also be reached by catching TheBus (number 2) on Kuhio Avenue in Waikiki.

Galleries

Just a block or two away from Chinatown, artists' galleries and studios proliferate. At 1128 Smith Street, the artist **Ramsay** (best known for her detailed drawings of buildings) displays the works of many other Hawaii artists as well. (While you're in the neighborhood, peek into **Young's Noodle Factory** across the street to see the bakers up to their arms in flour and dough making fresh chow mein noodles.) On Nuuanu Avenue's Gallery Row, photographer William Waterfall (1160-A Nuuanu Avenue) may have, for example, a vivid series of volcano pictures on one wall of his **Waterfall Gallery**. He also sells such things as jewelry, Burmese baskets, and Philippine backpacks in other nooks and crannies. Next door, **Pegge Hopper** displays her ever-popular paintings of Hawaiian women in soft shades of rose, green, and beige. Down the street, the **Gateway Gallery** at 1050 Nuuanu Avenue specializes in romantic fine art. Anchoring Gallery Row at 928 Nuuanu Avenue is the **Bakkus Gallery**, which adds interesting fashion and jewelry pieces to its selection of art offerings.

One of the nicest little galleries for gift shopping is **Pauahi Nuuanu Gallery** (1 North Pauahi Street, at the corner of Nuuanu Avenue), where pillows, appliquéd and quilted with Hawaiian patterns of leaves and plants, are $85 to $100; mirrors and hairbrushes have satiny-smooth koa handles; and stone poi pounders and mortars and pestles are for sale. Carver Richard Howell markets his intriguing wooden fish, turtles, and other Hawaiian figures through the Pauahi Nuuanu Gallery exclusively.

Back on Nuuanu at number 1118 is **Lai Fong Department Store**, not a gallery, but anyway a long-standing tradition. The name is deceiving, as the store is a sort of glorified secondhand emporium of Chinese teak and rosewood furniture, ivory and jade jewelry, dishes, clothing, and other artifacts. You can even order a custom-made, figure-fitting, silk-brocade, Chinese *cheong sam* with a high collar and frog fastenings. Lai Fong also carries Niihau-shell necklaces—one beauty was recently priced at $7,000.

Special Hawaiiana

If you want an authentic made-in-Hawaii remembrance of your trip, you might consider watercolors, pastels, or oil paintings by local artists; 14-karat-gold engraved heirloom jewelry; Niihau-shell leis; resort wear (including bathing suits, muumuu, and aloha shirts); beautifully crafted and finished bowls, boxes, and hand mirrors of koa, milo, or monkeypod wood; perfumes with Island scents such as *pikake,* tuberose, and ginger; and grown-in-the-Islands food items: macadamia nuts and candies, Kona coffee, guava, passion fruit, *poha* (wild cape gooseberry) jams and jellies, and fresh pineapples and other fruit.

Hawaii residents themselves purchase from **Pacific Handcrafters Guild**. The guild sponsors four major sales a year—spring, summer, fall, and before Christmas—at either Thomas Square (a park bounded by King, Be-

retania, and Ward streets near the Honolulu Academy of
Arts and Blaisdell Center) or Ala Moana Park. Stringent
requirements ensure the amount of handwork done on
an item, the quality of the work, and so on. Call or write
the main office for specific dates and locations: 1121
Nuuanu Avenue, Suite 204, Honolulu, HI 96817; Tel: (808)
538-1600.

For a large selection of rare Niihau-shell necklaces as
well as other Hawaiian jewelry, the place to go is **Hildgund**,
at 119 Merchant Street downtown.

Hawaii Wear

If you're looking for just the perfect muumuu or aloha
shirt, you will want to strike out from Waikiki. To the
uninitiated, the styles and incumbent status of these casual
pieces of tropical fashion might be indistinguishable. To a
resident, however, a muumuu can place its wearer precisely at a certain economic level, and it definitely reveals
something about style and taste. No local couples, unless
they are 80-year-old new arrivals, would walk arm-in-arm
dressed alike in bold prints from **Hilo Hattie's Fashion
Center** (700 North Nimitz Highway; if your aim *is* to look
like a tourist, however, a free bus will take you there from
Waikiki). A middle-income housewife would be much
more likely to find her muumuu at **Island Muumuu
Works**. Catch the Pineapple Transit for 50 cents from many
Waikiki hotels or the Waikiki Trolley (a $7 city tour allows
you to hop on and off the trolley all day) to Dole Cannery
Square, where Island Muumuu Works is located among
the newly completed shops on the second floor. These
muumuu with the Hilda of Hawaii label cost about $40.

If you are status conscious, like many Island career
women, you might choose instead a designer muumuu
by Princess Kaiulani, Mamo, or Roselyn Petrus. The **Princess Kaiulani** outlet is at 1222 Kaumualii Street; **Mamo
Howell, Inc.**, is at Ward Warehouse on Ala Moana Boulevard (see below) and at Dole Cannery Square; and all
three brands are carried by Liberty House. Designer muumuu range from $90 to $200.

Middle- and upper-income men, on the other hand,
will undoubtedly buy their inside-out-print aloha shirt
from **Reyn's** or **Andrade & Company** (two clothing stores
with branches at Ala Moana Center, see below), or perhaps they'll choose a Tori Richard shirt from Liberty
House. Those whose tastes lean to Art Deco or who

fondly remember their days as flower children will find their way to **Bailey's Antique and Thrift Shop** (764 Kapahulu Avenue) to buy a "silkie," the wildly colorful, early rayon shirts that now run from $40 to $600. These oldies but goodies never seem to fade—neither out nor away. Bailey's carries all kinds of collectibles from the 1940s and 1950s—hula-girl figurines, barefoot ashtrays, scenic old Matson menu covers, ukuleles, and more.

Across town, behind Ward Centre (see below), is a secondhand store of another ilk. Kelsey Sears, a vibrant former flight attendant, opened **The Ultimate You** (1112 Auahi Street) six years ago when she realized Hawaii had nothing like it. Honolulu's society folks bring in their designer clothing on consignment for resale. A $500 Dior evening dress might be priced at $90. Slacks, dresses, suits, muumuu—all must pass Kelsey's critical eye. She carries jewelry, too.

When you feel as if you've shopped till you're ready to drop, it's time to head for the beach. **Ann Tongg Swimwear** (1128 Nuuanu Avenue, Room 270, Honolulu, HI 96817; Tel: 537-6255) will custom design a new suit from your favorite old one in any combination of prints or solids you choose from among her lycra swatches. She actually charges less than ready-made (from $25 to $30). She can whip up a two-piece suit to cover the female form with some degree of modesty yet not make the wearer look like an old fossil—and on request she will even sneak a little fiberfill lining in the top. For visitors who want to wear their new suits when they get to Hawaii, Tongg works by mail order; simply send her an old bathing suit and list your color preferences; she'll send you swatches and have the suit ready for a fitting when you arrive. Otherwise, it might take about ten days and two visits to have a custom suit completed.

Shopping Malls

Honolulu's major shopping mall, **Ala Moana Center** (from Waikiki catch TheBus [number 18, 19, or 20] for 60 cents on Kuhio Avenue and take it to 1450 Ala Moana Boulevard), located on the way into Waikiki from the airport, is open Monday through Friday from 9:30 A.M. to 9:00 P.M., Saturday from 9:30 to 5:30, and Sunday from 10:00 to 5:00. It houses Honolulu's leading department store, Liberty House, as well as Mainland standbys JC Penney and Sears Roebuck. In the last few years, Ala

Moana has been undergoing remodeling, and numerous trendy, upscale boutiques have been added. The shops and restaurants on the lower level (near the stage where Hawaiian entertainment is regularly featured) seem more interesting than the standard mall shops on the upper level. **Iida's** has Japanese goods: cups with covers to keep your tea steaming, elegant fans for a couple of dollars, lacquer trays, trinket boxes, and coasters; while on the opposite (ocean) side, **Irene's Hawaiian Gifts** carries made-in-Hawaii everything, from key chains to etched glass. For lunch, stop in the **Makai Market Food Court**, a complex that dishes out every kind of fast food you can possibly crave—*saimin* (a noodle soup), pizza, plate lunches with rice and teriyaki beef, hamburgers—or make your way back upstairs to order something exotic from **Shirokiya's** sushi bar. Ala Moana is well worth a stop if you have the time; it resembles a modern Mainland mall, but it has a definite Hawaiian flavor, with colorful *koi* (carp) in the center ponds, blue skies overhead, and local shoppers in shorts and thong slippers.

Three other shopping malls along Ala Moana Boulevard rate acknowledgment for in-depth visitors: **Ward Centre** (1200 Ala Moana Boulevard), **Ward Warehouse** (1050 Ala Moana Boulevard), and, closer to downtown, **Restaurant Row** (500 Ala Moana Boulevard). Ride TheBus (number 19 or 20) from Kuhio Avenue, or catch the Waikiki Trolley—$7 for a daily pass—which will take you to all three shopping malls (10 to 20 minutes from Waikiki), as well as to Chinatown. Much of the success of Ward Centre and the new Restaurant Row has come about because of the innumerable restaurants located in each. Both attract the upwardly mobile crowd. Ward Centre has a Polo/Ralph Lauren shop and a **Lady Judith** for gorgeous and dear evening gowns and sweaters. Everybody loves the gadgets at Restaurant Row's ingenious little shop called **Nothing You Need**, which carries just that. The **Row Bar** in the center of the complex is becoming an after-work meeting place, and on Sunday afternoons live local entertainment is often featured there. At Ward Warehouse, the **Artist Guild** presents the most elegant of Hawaiian gifts. Look for translucent-thin wooden bowls by Ron Kent or Jack Strakka, but be prepared for the $400 price tag. Wood-block prints depicting Hawaiian legends by Big Island artist Dietrich Varez are more affordable, from $6.50 to $18.00, unframed.

Bargain Hunting

It's the excursions to the world of shopping beyond Waikiki that result in real finds. Wear comfortable walking shoes and cool clothing. Some shoppers even take umbrellas to shade themselves from the tropical sun at the year-round shopping phenomenon called the **Aloha Flea Market**, where more than 1,500 merchants rim Aloha Stadium every Wednesday, Saturday, and Sunday from 7:30 A.M. to 3:00 P.M., selling new and used goods from every corner of the earth. In the last few years commercial sellers with new merchandise have come to predominate the "swap meet," but if you go during the cooler early-morning hours, especially on weekends, you might find a real deal among the few sellers who have cleaned their cupboards and closets of grandma and grandpa's heirlooms. But even if you don't find an English bone-china cup for 50 cents, or a Baccarat bowl for $10, it's great fun to browse for an hour or two, and the entry fee is only 35 cents; parking is free. The inevitable tee-shirts are here in heaping piles, and the sweat shirts are actually a good buy. You'll find a wider variety of Hawaiian-print cotton material than in the fabric stores—and it will cost less, too. Eel-skin purses, wallets, and briefcases are a deal here.

You can get to Aloha Stadium from Kuhio Avenue in Waikiki aboard TheBus (number 20) for 60 cents (exact fare required). If you expect to make many purchases, Eastmark Enterprises, with large baggage compartments on its buses, will shuttle you to the stadium in air-conditioned comfort for $6 round trip; Tel: 955-4050 for boarding schedules.

Maybe they're not uniquely Hawaiian, but **garage sales** in Hawaii are a marvelous Saturday morning diversion. Though you might find a few Sunday sales, the best hunting is on Saturday mornings from eight to noon during June, July, and August. To find the best locale, look through the ads in the newspaper. Adventurous types who don't give in to disappointment might simply head for a well-populated suburb like Hawaii Kai, Enchanted Lake, or Lanikai on the windward side, and look for Garage Sale signs tacked on mailboxes and lampposts. Handymen are bound to find old monkeypod bowls sorely in need of rescuing and refinishing—but even if you find nothing of interest, it's a great way to get out and talk with some local people. They'll tell you about the high cost of living and the low rate of pay, and you won't feel so bad about going back to sub-zero temperatures.

Shopping in Honolulu takes time and stamina, but the variety and quality of goods rank right up there with shopping capitals of the world. The possibility for super-shopping is one of Hawaii's best-kept secrets, but you have to look beyond the obvious tinsel of Waikiki.

—*Betty Fullard-Leo*

WAIKIKI

by Rick Carroll

The Oahu coast covers 112 miles, elbowroom enough to surf, snorkle, or sunbathe, but a thin crescent of white sand on the Pacific doorstep of mostly Japanese-owned high-rise hotels is where everybody gathers daily. Waikiki is the statistical first choice of vacationers in Hawaii. Honolulu imports the white sand of Waikiki from Australia to replenish the beach and keep it fresh. Just before sunset, when the coast is usually clear, Waikiki Beach is swept by beach "bums" with metal detectors in search of lost coins, then later groomed by special raking machines that comb out all litter.

Once a duck pond and royal playground, this two-mile-long urban beach is the magnet for nearly seven million annual sun-absorbing guests to a never-ending beach party that begins each sunrise when surfers catch the day's first wave. The king of the beach resorts has 89 hotels and 61 condos, with a total of 33,661 units; 240 restaurants; 279 drinking establishments; only four churches (one for sale); and a tree house where a couple can dine tête-à-tête above milling crowds.

People-watching is the best show in town. There's nothing like a Waikiki crowd; it's 100,000-strong daily from all over the world, and also changes daily—like hotel sheets. Chances are you will see almost everything under the sun here, especially on the beach.

Waikiki is actually just a part of Honolulu, of course, but it is such a singular part that to cover it well we have had to treat it separately.

MAJOR INTEREST

The beach and the surf
People-watching

75

Shopping for Hawaiiana
Kalakaua Avenue strip
Sunset views
The Moana and other luxury hotels
Restaurants and nightlife
Diamond Head

At Waikiki, ancient kings worshipped the sun, played in the surf, and generally set the tone for what would go on here for years to come: having a good time, all the time. The seat of power for King Kahuhihewa in the 1500s, Waikiki sits between the Pacific and the Ala Wai Canal under the brow of ancient Diamond Head, one of the world's best-known landmarks (which early Hawaiians called Leahi—tuna nose—because it resembles the tuna's profile).

Hire a taxi at Honolulu International Airport and head for Waikiki (about $15). You'll only need a car for day trips—to the North Shore's Banzai Pipeline or Lanikai Beach, for example—and parking in Waikiki is a hassle even if your hotel validates. You can rent a car from one of the agencies near your hotel when you are ready to venture out. Tell the cab driver to cruise Kalakaua Avenue, which goes one-way Diamond Head, as locals say. You will wonder what all the fuss is about as you traverse this canyon of high-rises that blocks all beach views—until you clear the newly restored Moana Hotel and the last surfboard racks. Then look right and catch that first dazzling view of the sunlit Pacific with its bright shades of jade green, dark blue, and turquoise. The sweet scent is coconut oil wafting off the basting bodies on **Kuhio Beach**, that great open strand on the Diamond Head side of the Moana Hotel.

Check into your hotel, hit the beach, and take the plunge. Go anytime day or night and the water will be warm (average: 77 degrees Fahrenheit) and wonderful, the best cure for jet lag. In the morning, go early to stake out a spot; on any day there are about 16,000 people on the beach at Waikiki, according to lifeguards' head counts.

WAIKIKI BEACH

Waikiki Beach consists largely of a splendid collection of prone, semi-naked bodies that covers nearly every square inch of sand until sundown, then vanishes. When it rains,

it's hell; everyone sits in traffic or sits in their hotel
room—people get cabin fever and tempers get short.
Some big hotels, for example the Halekulani, give out
rain checks good for free drinks to keep everyone mel-
low at such times. Not to worry, almost every day is
perfect year round—temperatures in the low 80s, light
and variable trade winds, average relative humidity 66
percent, and water temperatures in the mid-70s, except
on August afternoons when they can hit 82 degrees.

Waikiki is actually many beaches on Oahu's Mamala
Bay, which extends from Diamond Head west to Barbers
Point; the best at Waikiki are Sans Souci, Royal-Moana,
and Queen's Surf. Away from the crowd, **Sans Souci**, a
quiet strip of fine sand on gentle water, is also known as
"Dig Me" beach because of all the young sunbathers in
skimpy suits. The beach is out near the end of Kalakaua
Avenue opposite Kapiolani Park, in the front yard of the
New Otani Kaimana Beach Hotel near the Natatorium War
Memorial (once the biggest salt water pool in the United
States; its façade is now a ruin).

Royal-Moana Beach. No elbowroom here. This is Action Central on Waikiki Beach, where the beautiful bodies
go to see and be seen. Inside the rope are Royal Hawaiian
guests, outside are not, but the sun strikes each with
equanimity. This beach, from the Royal Hawaiian Hotel to
the Moana, is perfectly sited for viewing the graceful
seacoast curve to Diamond Head and all the beach action.
The late afternoon sun is better here than at Sans Souci.

If all the men look too good to be true, and they're
lounging around in Band-Aid-size *cache-sexe,* you've
probably just found **Queen's Surf Beach**, across the street
from Kapiolani Beach Park on the *ewa* side of Waikiki
Aquarium. It is so-called because royal ladies used to take
the waters here. Now it's a gay hangout—though you'll be
perfectly comfortable here if you're not gay.

Kapiolani Park, the green, open space just past the end
of the built-up part of Waikiki, close to Sans Souci Beach
and Diamond Head, is 200 acres of high-energy, seaside
fun, where there's always something going on—a luau,
joggers, soccer matches, stunt kite-flying, jugglers, and
flocks of pigeons. The park's Waikiki Shell grounds is the
home of the **Kodak Hula Show**, Hawaii's longest running
song-and-dance act (since 1937; the show goes on at
10:00 A.M. every Tuesday, Wednesday, and Thursday). It's
free, family-style entertainment by ukulele-plinking hula
dancers of the Royal Hawaiian Girls Glee Club. A great

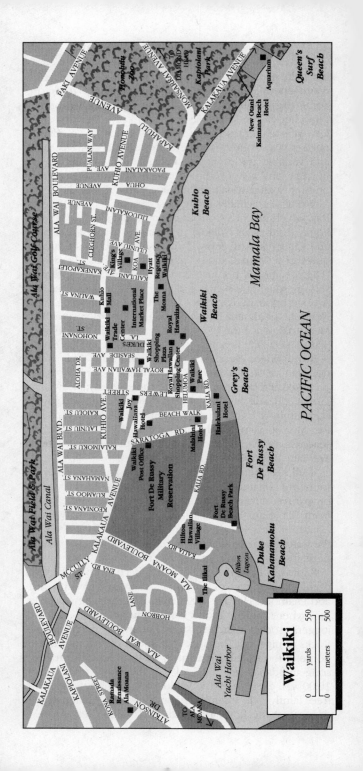

Waikiki

| 0 | yards | 550 |
| 0 | meters | 500 |

grassy plain, ideal for those who like the beach but hate the sand, the beach park is also the home of the **Honolulu Zoo**, **Waikiki Aquarium**, and the Honolulu Marathon finish line.

Waikiki is, first and last, a great surfing beach. The perfect surf that rolls ashore has been ridden since at least the 1500s, when, according to Hawaiian chants, chiefs held *hee nalu* (wave sliding) contests and bet on the outcome. Surfing is how Waikiki really got its start; it was happening when Captain Cook first cruised around Diamond Head, and it seemed to be even more popular 100 years later when the straitlaced missionaries arrived—and tried to stop it as a frivolous pastime involving seminudity and having a sexual connotation.

"The appearance of destitution, degradation, and barbarism, among the chattering and almost naked savages, whose heads and feet and much of their sunburnt skins were bare, was appalling," wrote the missionary leader Hiram Bingham in 1820, upon seeing Hawaiians on surfboards. "Some of our number, with gushing tears, turned away from the spectacle. Others, with firmer nerve, continued their gaze, but were ready to exclaim, 'Can these be human beings?'"

Ancient Hawaiians regarded surfing as vital to their social and spiritual life, in fact, something of a courtship ritual, and they carved that message in stone above Kaunolu Bay on Lanai, where the petroglyph of a tandem surfer may still be seen.

Old-time beach boys such as Duke Kahanamoku, Splash Lyons, Fat Kala, and Panama Dave are gone, and the legendary "golden man," Kelly Kanakoa, existed only in James Michener's best seller *Hawaii,* but the tradition continues. Rabbit Kekai and his brother Jammer, Blue Mauka, Jr., Manong, and Mr. Rosa still give surfing lessons to *malahini.* Once you're up on a long board, beach boy–photographer Bobby Achoy will snap the classic shot of you surfing the "beeg wahns" at Waikiki with your choice of Diamond Head or the Royal Hawaiian in the background. It's about seven dollars, the all-time deal. Go early, around 7:00 A.M., to Kuhio Beach, near the surfboard racks.

Offshore, the surfing lanes all bear colorful, self-explanatory names, according to use, coastal landmarks, or what's underwater. There are Canoes, The Wall, and Rock Pile (there's also Shark's Hole, but it's near Point Panic at Kewalo Basin on the Honolulu side of Ala

Moana Park). Good for beginners are Paradise or Canoes, just off the Pink Lady (the Royal Hawaiian Hotel).

It's always perfect surf at Waikiki in the summertime, when the south swells run and the trades blow offshore against the waves to lift their faces and send spindrift trailing behind the crest. Waikiki pumps in mid- to late summer with easy rollers most of the time. Of Oahu's 594 surfing sites, Waikiki is the ideal place to experience what devotees call "the ultimate pleasure."

Gearing up for Waikiki

The best surfboard shop in Hawaii is like the perfect aloha shirt—always being sought—but surf pioneer Barry Morrison's **Wave Riding Vehicles**, east of Waikiki at 1148 Koko Head Avenue in the Kaimuki district about two miles from Waikiki, is where locals go for new and used boards and to "talk story" about their rides.

Sunburned? Rub Hawaii's own soothing aloe vera lotion on your red shoulders to ease the sting and get ready for more sun. Most people will by this time have kicked off their hard shoes in favor of rubber *zori,* otherwise known as flip-flops. The best deals on postcards, beach mats, suntan lotion, and such may be found at the Woolworth on Kalakaua Avenue, the only variety store in America that sells sushi, *saimin,* and macadamia nut brittle. Their aisle of *zori,* however, is especially worth perusing, because it has a full range of sizes and classic styles, including the best-selling black-rubber numbers with chrome toe grab and all the Islands brightly painted on the insteps.

Only steps away is **Cherry Blossom**, the last dry-goods store in Waikiki, with hundreds of bolts of bright tropical prints—the best place to buy a Polynesian *pareu* (sarong), which amounts to three yards of body wrapping tied loosely about the neck.

If you don't already own an aloha shirt, one of the gaudy, loose-fitting, tail-out jobs with a hula girl–outrigger canoe–hibiscus flower print, or a muumuu, the floral-printed Mother Hubbard, now's the time. When it comes to Hawaiian shirts, "more is more," according to Ellery Chun, who created them in 1931 to save his father's sagging garment business after coming home from Yale. The brighter the better, and the best place in Waikiki to find aloha shirts and muumuu is **Linda's Vintage Isle**, the antique haberdashery specializing in "silkies" in the $250 to $350 range; the cotton shirts start at $25. A collector for 12 years, owner Linda Sheehan has between 200 and 300 shirts, Hawaiian quilts, muumuu, and other Hawaiiana.

Shoppers outnumber surfers ten to one in Waikiki, even though almost everything in Waikiki is marked up 15 to 30 percent, including cheeseburgers at the Golden Arches. Gimcrack vies with designer labels, and canned pearls and *tiki* gods sell beside Louis Vuitton bags, Cartier watches, and Armani suits, even at the **Royal Hawaiian Shopping Center** along Kalakaua Avenue.

The recreational shopper will find the most satisfaction, sometimes even bargains, at the **International Market Place**, an open-air bazaar under banyan trees up the other side of Kalakaua Avenue toward Diamond Head, where Koreans vend trinkets from pushcarts and prices are negotiable.

Hawaii's most unusual souvenir may be the coconut, which can be mailed anywhere in the world from the Waikiki post offices, or any post office in Hawaii for that matter. The best way to get a coconut is to find one lying on the ground or pick one out for about a buck at any grocery store—they're cheaper outside Waikiki. Coconuts weigh three or four pounds, and the flat rate, airmail, is $2.40 for up to two pounds, $4.32 for three pounds, and $5.33 for four pounds. Duke Gum of the U.S. Postal Service, which mails nearly 2,000 a year from here, says the coconut's own plain brown wrapper meets postal shipping requirements. Just ink on the address, add the stamps, and mail a coconut to someone anywhere on the Mainland.

WAIKIKI OFF THE BEACH

There's almost too much to see and do in this tourist quarter, which sits like an island between the **Ala Wai Canal** and the Pacific Ocean, with Diamond Head to the east and the Ala Wai Yacht Harbor at the west. Ala Wai means "waterway," and that's what it is: a three-mile-long canal built in the 1920s to drain the swamp that Waikiki once was. The canal, earlier a harbor for Honolulu's fishing fleet, is now used for training by outrigger canoe clubs; it serves as a sort of moat for Waikiki. On the mauka (toward the mountains) banks, the 18-hole municipal Ala Wai Golf Course is the nation's busiest, with more than 600 players daily.

Ala Wai Boulevard, a backside exit route from Waikiki, runs along the Waikiki side of the canal. Parallel to it is **Kuhio Avenue**, the mid-Waikiki thoroughfare. Kuhio Avenue is home to many less-than-posh accommodations and restaurants. And more or less parallel to Kuhio to the south is the center of it all, the main drag parallel to the beachfront, Kalakaua Avenue.

Kalakaua Avenue

Waikiki's main drag, named for Hawaii's Merrie Monarch, who ruled like a party host from 1874 to 1891, is by day an eastbound, one-way street of cars, intersected by beach-bound pedestrians in various stages of undress, with rolled-up bamboo mats under their arms, seeking their place in the sun.

It's a street of shops, where fast-food joints and tacky souvenir shops stand chockablock with French designer boutiques and parfumeries, a schizo, eclectic collection of goods at jacked-up prices.

Not everyone likes Waikiki. Some locals brag that they haven't been on Kalakaua Avenue in years, but that's like missing life itself, and critics who say it's another Miami should take another look.

The Kalakaua neighborhood sports a new international look today, with an extensive recent face-lift that introduced wide brick sidewalks, manicured palms, and Italianate streetlights. Pedicabs, daytime delivery vans, skateboards, and roller skates have been banned.

The fun zone may never develop the "fashionable urban resort" image Honolulu burghers yearned for in the 1920s, but Waikiki is what it is: a dynamic cross section of the world at the beach. While some may grumble about the good old days, Waikiki's hip gaudiness only contributes to its festive airs.

The Sunset

Come sundown, everyone finds a favorite spot from which to watch it, and the two best vantage points are outdoors, on two special hotel lanais: **House without a Key** at the Halekulani Hotel, where Sonny Kamahele and the Sunset Serenaders sing *hapa-haole* (those pseudo-Hawaiian classics like "Yacka Hula Hickey Dula" cranked out by Tin Pan Alley from 1915 to 1925) songs, and **Hau Tree Lanai** at the New Otani Kaimana Beach Hotel, on the spot where Robert Louis Stevenson wrote poems to Kaiulani, a real Hawaiian princess. (Other bars with a sunset vantage point are at the Moana and Royal Hawaiian hotels.)

The best way to see any island is by sea, and if surfboards or outrigger canoes seem too small a craft, ships come in all different sizes and shapes at Waikiki. There are booze cruises, glass-bottom cruises, Pearl Harbor cruises, sport-fishing cruises, snorkeling cruises, sunset cruises, dinner cruises, all-day cruises, and seven-day, around-the-Islands cruises on the newly outfitted, 600-passenger luxury cruise ship SS *Monterey,* a grand old Matson liner that crossed the Pacific for three decades and is now back in service, as are the SS *Independence* and SS *Constitution*. These ships call on ports of the Big Island of Hawaii, Maui, and Kauai. Ask at your hotel's front desk for details on these cruises.

The best choice is also one of the least expensive, a sunset cocktail cruise aboard the 45-foot racing catamaran **Leahi**, a sleek, green-sailed craft that departs from Waikiki Beach five times daily. The last cruise is the best, a 90-minute sail on Mamala Bay at just the right time in the evening.

There's no such thing as the best dinner cruise anywhere (unless it's your own yacht), but the food aboard the Hilton's 72-foot catamaran, **Rainbow I**, is decent: bay shrimp salad, teriyaki beef skewers, barbecued chicken, a pineapple boat full of fresh fruits—and Waikiki's skyline and sunset views, straight out of postcards.

Waikiki After Sundown

Kalakaua Avenue really comes alive in the evening, as thousands of solar-powered people go in search of food and drink in Waikiki's 240 restaurants. After sunbathing, the major Waikiki pastime is eating. There's something about salt air that stirs the appetite, and while Honolulu is only developing its *nouvelle tropicale* cuisine, it already ranks second in the nation, after San Francisco, for dollars spent on dining out. There are thousands of restaurants in Waikiki, from *bento*-to-go to five-star award winners, but La Mer, The Third Floor, Bagwells 2424, and Guy

Banal's Bon Appetit consistently top the Best-of-Hawaii lists by local, national, and international wine and food writers.

In the sudden tropical darkness highlighted by neon, Waikiki takes on a new look, as afternoon card players fold their hands and pocket their penny-ante pots, while teenage "boom cruisers" in garishly painted Volkswagen Bugs start to cruise the avenue.

Out at the Kalakaua street party, jet-lagged people from all over the world sleepwalk in neon brightness, pushing past handbill distributors, street musicians, and local kids selling seaweed as *pakalolo* (marijuana). Then come the miniskirted streetwalkers, motor-scooter cops, sidewalk Bible thumpers, and bad saxophone players. The Waikiki night is in gear. (See Waikiki Nightlife, below.)

DIAMOND HEAD

Hawaii's most famous landmark calls to those who want the big view. Thousands have climbed to the crater's summit, a rite of passage like climbing Japan's Mount Fuji.

To get to the crater, drive east along Monsarrat Avenue (or take the number 8 bus to the entrance) and look for the sign. A narrow, 90-year-old tunnel penetrates the crater wall, and across the wide, flat valley the first set of 99 steps awaits you on the three-quarter-mile hike to the summit of the rim. Bring a flashlight for the tunnels.

This dormant (don't say extinct; you never know) volcano is twice named. Early Hawaiians called it Leahi (which means "brow of tuna"), and British sailors who thought they saw crystals sparkling on its steep flanks called it Diamond Head. Since it's only 760 feet high at the south rim, this hike is for everyone; it takes less than an hour to see the 360-degree view.

Beyond Diamond Head

After Kapiolani Park, a real-people neighborhood appears as Kalakaua Avenue becomes Diamond Head Road and winds along the coast past **Diamond Head Beach Park** and the Diamond Head Lighthouse.

A wide scenic turnout on the high bluff here enables you to gain a big Pacific view and a real closeup of Diamond Head. You may also watch the windsurfers here smash waves head-on and go airborne to gain "hang time."

The **Maunalua Bay** panorama to the east takes in Black Point, a small peninsula where such notables as actor Tom Selleck and tobacco heiress Doris Duke have homes behind guarded gates, and Koko Head in the distance.

Just down Diamond Head's eastern slope lies the "gold coast" of **Kahala**, where Japanese speculators have luxed up an already ritzy neighborhood of multi-million-dollar seaside estates. This ultra-rich enclave (homes here sell for up to $21 million) has included such neighbors as Saudi Arabian arms dealer Adnan Khashoggi and the late Clare Boothe Luce.

On Kahala Avenue, look for sand alleys between the mansions that access the beach, but be prepared for disappointment—the beaches are thin and gnarly, the water shallow, and there are no waves. The beach at the end of Hunakai Street is as good as it gets in Kahala.

At the beach end of Kahala Avenue stands the **Kahala Hilton Hotel**, the home away from home for presidents and kings, with pools full of porpoises and a private beach.

Inland from Kahala Avenue the homes diminish in size and value until they more resemble a suburban California neighborhood clustered around the very L.A. Kahala Shopping Center, which offers valet parking at peak shopping seasons. This enclosed mall contains all the usual shops and two restaurants worth a visit: the **California Pizza Kitchen**, started by two ex-Los Angeles lawyers who concoct innovative pizzas such as Thai chicken and ginger, and **Yen King**, considered one of Honolulu's best Chinese restaurants.

Out on trafficky Kalanianaole Highway 72 (you're a *kamaaina* when you can pronounce it: kah-la-knee-ah-nah-OH-lee), head east for Honolulu's first commuter suburb, the 6,000-acre **Hawaii Kai** tract, created out of ancient fishponds by California industrialist Henry J. Kaiser, who built houses and a marina here along canals that access Maunalua Bay.

Up the adjacent slope of ancient **Koko Head**, the suburban world of east Honolulu falls away as the land becomes arid and barren with an occasional cactus. Ahead, in the caldera of an extinct volcano whose side facing the sea has broken down, is one of Oahu's major attractions, a fishpond like no other, **Hanauma Bay**, where Hawaii's

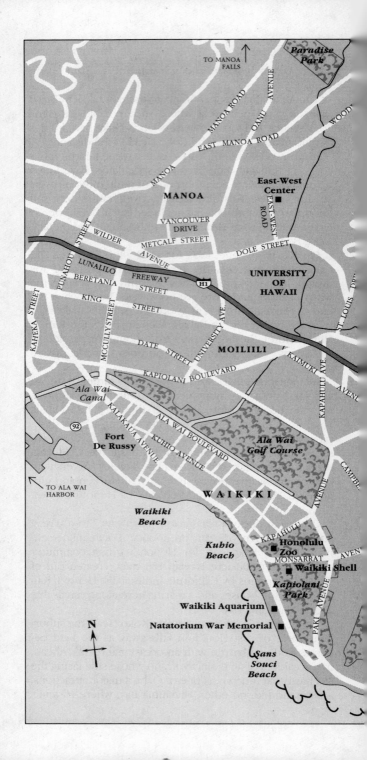

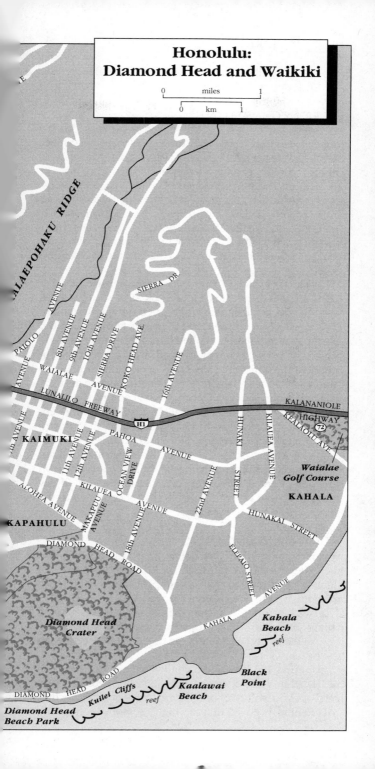

Honolulu:
Diamond Head and Waikiki

KALAEPOHAKU RIDGE

SIERRA DR.

PAIOLO AVENUE
8th AVENUE
9th AVENUE
10th AVENUE
SIERRA DRIVE
KOKO HEAD AVE.
16th AVENUE

WAIALAE AVENUE

LUNALILO FREEWAY

H1

KALANANIOLE HIGHWAY
72

KEALAOLU AVE.

AVENUE
11th AVENUE
12th AVENUE
PAHOA AVENUE
OCEAN VIEW DRIVE

KAIMUKI

HUNAKI
KILAUEA AVENUE

Waialae Golf Course

ALOHEA AVENUE
KILAUEA AVENUE
MAKAPUU AVENUE
18th AVENUE
22nd AVENUE
HUNAKAI STREET

KAHALA

KAPAHULU

DIAMOND HEAD ROAD

ELEPAIO STREET

AVENUE

Diamond Head Crater

KAHALA

Kabala Beach
reef

DIAMOND HEAD ROAD

Kuilei Cliffs
reef
Kaalawai Beach

Black Point

Diamond Head Beach Park

tropical fish still outnumber visitors to the Beach Park and Underwater Park here.

GETTING AROUND

The ideal way to get around Waikiki is on foot, but for longer excursions catch TheBus; it's the best way to meet people and learn pidgin, the local patois. A ticket costs 60 cents, and exact change please, but if you don't have it, ask around. TheBus, which is spelled likethat, goes everywhere, including a three-and-a-half-hour ride around the entire island—for 60 cents. There's even a special Beach Bus (22) on weekends and holidays that runs from Waikiki to Hanauma Bay, Sandy Beach, and Sea Life Park. You can also catch TheBus (8) to the volcano at Diamond Head.

Or take the Waikiki Trolley, a new, inexpensive ride that loops out into the world beyond Waikiki, to such places as Ward Centre, a collection of high-priced shops; Restaurant Row, a collection of mid-range theme restaurants; and the Dole Cannery Square, a collection of pineapple-canning artifacts. The 34-passenger, open-air trolley goes on a 90-minute tour of historic sites, hotels, parks, and beaches. It runs from about 8:45 A.M. to 5:45 P.M. and follows part of the original route of Hawaii's turn-of-the-century streetcars. The route originates at the Royal Hawaiian Shopping Center and goes to the Hilton Hawaiian Village, then downtown along Bishop Street to Honolulu Harbor, on to Hilo Hattie's garment factory, and then Dole Pineapple's Cannery Square before returning to Waikiki via Chinatown and Ward Centre. Passengers may get on and off all day along the route to explore, eat lunch, shop, or go to the beach. Tel: 599-2561 for tickets.

ACCOMMODATIONS

Waikiki's landmark luxury hotels are on the beach, while the others are back between the sand and the Ala Wai Canal. Room rates vary in direct proportion to distance from the beach. The choices are vast.

A two-bedroom Alii Tower beachfront suite at the new Hilton Hawaiian Village tops out at $2,500 a night; the opposite end of the scale is a can of Raid and directions to the beach.

Oahu has 183 hotels and condos with 37,841 rooms—nearly all in Waikiki, where occupancy averages 86.7 percent. As you will see, our list below is *highly* selective.

Hoteliers used to define "high" season as that time

between the first snowfall in New England and the first day of spring, but now that Japan, Canada, Australia, Great Britain, West Germany, and the rest of Europe have discovered Waikiki there is really no such thing as "high" or "low" season; it's always busy here.

Accommodations in Waikiki are changing, becoming luxurious and expensive. (The average daily room rate is $79.95, plus Honolulu's new 5 percent hotel tax. We consider anything under $75 to be "inexpensive.")

Many Waikiki hoteliers have upgraded their establishments, then bumped up rates, but new, small "boutique" hotels, like the Waikiki Joy and the Waikiki Parc, offer affordable alternatives. And special little "finds" may still be found on side streets.

The rate ranges given here are projections for winter 1989 through summer 1990. Unless otherwise indicated, rates are for double room, double occupancy. Hawaii's telephone area code is 808. For all Waikiki accommodations, the city and zip code are: Honolulu, Hawaii 96815.

Luxury

The Moana. The floor squeaks and the name has been corporately revised (it's officially "Sheraton Moana Surfrider" now) but she'll always be The Moana to her fans. And they're going to love her new "old" look. This grand old beach hotel, on the Diamond Head end of the hotel row at Kuhio Beach, is all dressed up for the new century with a multi-million-dollar make-over that once again makes her the First Lady of Waikiki. The open, airy, triple-wing, Victorian beach resort has been restored to its original simple elegance with an Ionic-columned lobby facing onto the Pacific, a grand staircase, birdcage elevator, and Hawaii's only three-story porte cochère.

The first major hotel in Waikiki, designed by architect Oliver G. Traphagen in the Beaux Arts style, and built for $150,000, the Moana opened March 11, 1901, "the costliest, most elaborate hotel building in the Hawaiian Islands," according to a journalist of the day. Now she's the fairest of them all. Newly air-conditioned rooms are furnished in period pieces, with koa armoires and bedside computer command centers. The Victorian treasure is wedded to the Sheraton Surfrider's bland concrete tower on the Ewa side. The best rooms are on the sixth floor of the newly restored Diamond Head wing, about $260, with ocean and Diamond Head views. This jewel box is once again a first-class luxury hotel, right down to the royal palms. The hotel's famous banyan tree still stands in the beachside courtyard, but in place of the late, unlamented Polynesian show a white-suited piano stylist now plays Hawaiian melodies on a white baby grand from the veranda—so you may drink under the spreading tree at sunset in relative peace. A new period-piece restaurant, **W. C. Peacock & Co., Ltd.** (after the original developers), features fresh Hawaiian seafood and produce. The lady's back in town, and, as before, she's still "a sight to behold."

2365 Kalakaua Avenue Tel: 922-3111; elsewhere in U.S., (800) 334-8484. $170–$375.

Halekulani. A marbled oasis in Waikiki, this contemporary seafront hotel is the only one to meet Asian standards (it's in league with Hong Kong's Regent, Singapore's Raffles, and The Manila Hotel), even though it has no beach, only a pool. The hotel is sited just so, to catch the perfect postcard view of Diamond Head. Built in 1917 but completely rebuilt as a high-rise in 1983, the Halekulani has a high-pitched roof and an indoor-outdoor design that exemplify modern Hawaiian architecture. The hotel became famous as "The House Without a Key" in Earl Derr Biggers's 1925 Charlie Chan detective classic. The lanai is still unrivaled at sundown when Sonny Kamahele's Sunset Serenaders play and sing *hapa-haole* steel-guitar favorites such as "Farewell Malahini" and "Sweet Leilani." The open, airy, expensive **La Mer**, one of Honolulu's finest restaurants, is redefining Honolulu's *nouvelle tropicale* cuisine, while **Orchids**, the lower-priced version downstairs, makes an unforgettable seaside lunch. And for a dark, clubby bar (with no view), drop into **Lewers Lounge**, which features singer-guitarist Melinda "Road to Paradise" Caroll.

2199 Kalia Road, Tel: 923-2311; elsewhere in U.S., (800) 367-2343. $190–$325; after 12/20/89 add $25–$30.

Kahala Hilton. The guest register reads like a who's who of the world at this genteel retreat in a toney residential neighborhood, not in Waikiki but east of Diamond Head between the blue Pacific and the manicured greens of Waialae Golf Course, a fully private course that is the home of the Hawaiian Open. The starkly elegant hotel, at the head of an avenue of multi-million-dollar beachfront estates, recently celebrated its 25th birthday with a tasteful renovation that gilded the lily—it cost $40,000 to remodel each room, which originally cost only $30,000 to build. Everything else is the same—wonderful. There are dolphins, penguins, and turtles in the garden pools; a white-sand beach and a palm-fringed island offshore; nearby tennis courts that are lit at night; tropical gardens; and Honolulu's best oceanfront Sunday brunch at the **Hala Terrace**. The few changes in the menu at the **Maile Restaurant** include the addition of veal fillet with lobster ravioli and chanterelles, and, in a nod to New Orleans, blackened *opakapaka* fillets on fresh tomato *coulis* with linguine *al pesto*. Singer Danny Kaleikini, a 20-year fixture, offers his vintage Polynesian revue at the Hala Terrace, while Kit Samson and orchestra play old favorites in the **Maile Lounge** for dancing. May some good things never change.

5000 Kahala Avenue, Tel: 734-2211; elsewhere in U.S., (800) 367-2525. $180–$295; after 12/15/89, $195–$325.

Expensive

Hilton Hawaiian Village. A mega-resort in Waikiki, this 20-acre beachfront park between Fort De Russy and the Ala Wai Yacht Harbor is a destination all its own, a vacation resort that includes the new, exclusive **Alii Tower**, right on the beautiful beach, with its $2,000-a-night two-bedroom suites. A three-year remodeling has transformed Waikiki's biggest resort (2,524 rooms) into a showplace, full of gardens, pools, exotic birds, and works of art, with ten restaurants (including the **Golden Dragon**, one of Honolulu's only Chinese restaurants with an ocean view); the **Paradise Lounge** jazz club, featuring Jimmy Borges; curio shops on Hong Kong Alley; designer shops such as Adrienne Vittadini, Lancel, Esprit, Benetton, Guess, and Polo; the state's biggest swimming pool, a 10,000-square-foot plunge; and the 5,000-seat ballroom. The Hilton Hawaiian Village boasts two beaches: the one that encircles the man-made lagoon and Duke Kahanamoku Beach, which honors Hawaii's Olympic gold medalist beach-boy/surfer/swimmer. A 150-passenger twin-hulled catamaran and nearby helicopter are at the ready for scenic tours by sea or air. Singer Don "Tiny Bubbles" Ho anchors the show at Hilton Hawaiian Village's Dome.

2005 Kalia Road, Tel: 949-4321; elsewhere in U.S., (800) HILTONS. $139–$235; suites $375–$2,500.

Hyatt Regency Waikiki. This 40-story, twin-towered hotel on Kalakaua Avenue across the street from Waikiki Beach—but on a part of the avenue where there are no buildings blocking out the beach—has views, both beachy and urban, and a village of shops and restaurants at its feet.

The hotel has completed a renovation of its 1,230 rooms, now done in soft pastels with Oriental rattan and white-washed oak furniture. A three-ton sculpture dangles over Harry's Bar & Café, where the roar of a man-made waterfall drowns out the soft Hawaiian music. Japanophiles swarm over **Musashi**, one of the Islands' best Japanese restaurants; and **Bagwells 2424**, a chic supper club with a wine cellar, is adored by critics. The Hyatt Regency is big-city hotel with international excitement.

2424 Kalakaua Avenue, Tel: 923-1234; elsewhere in U.S., (800) 228-9000. $130–$275; suites $490–$1,600.

The Royal Hawaiian. Dwarfed by high-rises, this pink, Spanish Baroque palace with Alice-in-Wonderland gardens and colonnaded walkways right on the middle of the main beach in Waikiki is worth a visit if only for nostalgia's sake. Now owned by Japanese tycoon Kenji Osano, the Royal has received a fresh coat of paint, but needs to improve service. The **Surf Room** is still a dramatic beachside setting for lunch, with the blue-green water a vivid contrast to the pink paint, but the food is unimpressive. The **Surf Bar** is one of the few on-the-beach, open-air bars on Waikiki. The romantic **Mai Tai Bar** offers free Hawaiian song and dance by Keith and Carmen Haugen; the 3,000-seat Monarch Room show-cases the Brothers Cazimero at $50 a ticket. Opened in 1927, the "Pink Palace" was the choice of all who came by steamship to stay in luxury's lap. Eclipsed now by newer, fancier hotels, the Royal lives on its laurels, but nostalgia buffs, old-hotel freaks, and honeymooners check in year after year. Stay in the old wing or a $1,500-a-day suite if you want the full Royal experience.

2259 Kalakaua Avenue, Tel: 923-7311; elsewhere in U.S., (800) 325-3535. $160–$280; suites $340–$1,650.

Ramada Renaissance Ala Moana. In midtown Hono-lulu next door to Ala Moana Center is Honolulu's newly remodeled and newly named Ramada Renaissance Ala Moana. The best location in town for businessmen, the Ala Moana sits at Waikiki's gateway, minutes to down-town Bishop Street banks and offices and only a five-mile taxi ride to the airport. The top choice of Asia-Pacific flight crews, this Japanese-owned hotel has under-gone an extensive makeover that created a lobby the size of a football field, improved all rooms, and rewired the disco, **Rumours**, into a high-tech lounge with flash-ing lights and walls of video panels. The **Royal Garden** Chinese restaurant escaped renovation and still serves the city's best Hong Kong dim sum from 11:00 A.M., and **Nicholas Nickolas**, the skyroom restaurant on the 36th floor, provides a glittering nightscape along with dining and dancing.

410 Atkinson Drive, Tel: 955-4811; elsewhere in U.S., (800) 367-6025. $90–$160; suites $200–$1,300.

Moderate

New Otani Kaimana Beach Hotel. It's small, private, and wonderful, just enough off Waikiki's center stage to be sophisticated, yet not too far away to miss the carnival. The choice of writers, artists, and jazz musicians, the Kaimana, as it's called, is right on Sans Souci Beach opposite Kapiolani Park, with the high-rises of central Waikiki in walking distance. **The Hau Tree Lanai**, on the site where Robert Louis Stevenson wrote poems, is a romantic beachside restaurant, one of the very few in Waikiki. Upstairs, **Miyako** is a *kaiseki*-style restaurant in a Tokyo teahouse setting, with a big Pacific view from the white pine *tatami* rooms. There's an easy, personal feeling at the low-rise Kaimana, generated by hotelier Steve Boyle, who runs this small hotel on a first-name basis as if a few hundred close friends were popping over for a glass of Chardonnay, a little fish dinner, and a good night's sleep at his house.

2863 Kalakaua Avenue, Tel: 923-1555; elsewhere in U.S. and in Canada, (800) 421-8795. $78–$92; suites $120–$315.

Waikiki Parc Hotel. It's got the right address—just across the street from the Halekulani—at the right price, albeit in one of the most built-up, congested areas of Waikiki. The Waikiki Parc Hotel's rooms even seem identical to those of its neighbor, except for the price—a mere $85 a night compared to the Halekulani's $165 and up. Owned, built, and operated by its ritzy neighbor. the Parc isn't on the beach, but it's nearby. It features well-appointed rooms, upscale amenities, a free *Wall Street Journal* daily, and remote-control cable television. Each room has a lanai with either ocean, mountain, or city view. Eight rooms are wheelchair accessible. There are two excellent restaurants that cater to both Japanese and *haole* visitors: **Kacho**, a 40-seat sushi bar serving *bento* (braised vegetables, pickled vegetables, soup, rice, and fruit in a box) and California rolls, and the **Parc Café**, a garden-terrace Continental restaurant offering Island specialties, with an outstanding wine list.

2233 Helumoa Road, Tel: 921-7272; elsewhere in U.S., (800) 422-0450. $90–$165.

Waikiki Joy Hotel. Its airy, bright lobby and marble floors give this new, small, boutique hotel an uptown look. On a quiet Waikiki side street at the edge of the gay district, the Joy only *looks* expensive. It has unusual amenities, like Jacuzzi baths and Bose stereo systems in rooms, and a courtyard pool. This is the best of the new boutique hotels popping up on Waikiki's side streets between Kuhio Avenue and the Ala Wai Canal. The trade-off here is the eight-block hike to Waikiki Beach.

Surfer's Corner, a tropical bistro under banana leaves with a French chef in the kitchen, and **New Orleans Bistro**, a Bourbon Street transplant with spicy seafood on the menu and spicy singer Andrea Young on stage, are just around the corner from the Waikiki Joy—so a daily stroll to the beach may be necessary exercise.

320 Lewers Street, Tel: 923-2300; elsewhere in U.S., (800) 367-8047. $110–$235.

Inexpensive

The Hawaiiana Hotel. Nestled in lush tropical gardens, a half block from the beach between Kalakaua Avenue and the Halekulani, this charming, three-story hotel is a relic from Waikiki's past, a comfortable lodge with an all-Hawaiian staff that embraces its loyal guests like family. Everyone gets a flower lei upon arrival, with fresh pineapple juice and Kona coffee served poolside every morning. The modern rooms are air-conditioned, but windows open to catch the trade winds. The tranquil surroundings and warm hospitality really will take you back in time.

260 Beach Walk, Tel: 923-3811; elsewhere in U.S. and in Canada, (800) 367-5122. $70–$80; suites $105.

Malahini Hotel. There's no television, no air conditioning, no restaurant (but Buzz's Steak House is next door), not even a Coke machine—and legions of Malahini Hotel loyalists like it that way. If this cozy little 35-year-old hotel, owned by a Stanford University lawyer, changed a thing, there probably would be complaints. It's nothing fancy, just a small, cheap, tidy hotel facing Fort De Russy near the beach, with the lowest rates in Waikiki—about $45 to $65 a night, depending on the season and the mood of night clerk Janet Clark, who came here in 1933 from Portland, Oregon, and runs the open-air front desk in the shade of a coconut tree.

217 Saratoga Road, Tel: 923-9644.

Special

The Manoa Valley Inn. Out of the way, on a hill in the misty Manoa Valley, about 3 miles back from Waikiki Beach, this charming, antique-filled, 75-year-old plantation-style mansion has seven bedrooms and a common lanai with an unobstructed view of Diamond Head, which seems to change by morning light. Mornings here bring a free full breakfast, not just a muffin and coffee; evening begins at five o'clock with port and cheese on the lanai. A separate cottage also is available. The former John Guild Inn was restored to old-world opulence in 1984, and attracts those who like to be surrounded by wonderful old curiosity pieces.

2001 Vancouver Drive, Tel: 947-6019; elsewhere in U.S., (800) 634-5115. $80–$140.

The Honolulu Airport Mini Hotel. Airport seats are never big enough to stretch out on between flights, but Honolulu International has something better—eight hours' sleep and a shower in a private room for $22.75 a person. One of Hawaii's most popular hotels, it is at the airport's center lobby, across from the cocktail lounge. Rooms also rent for $4 an hour; showers are $7.50, including towels, soap, shampoo, all toilet articles, and use of a hair drier. Call ahead; beds are limited.

Honolulu International Airport Center Lobby, Tel: 836-3044; or write Terminal Box 42, Honolulu, HI 96819, for reservations.

The Intrepid Dragon II. It's not in Waikiki; it's not even *on* the island of Oahu. The Intrepid Dragon II, a hand-carved Hong Kong junk, serves as a floating bed-and-breakfast in Honolulu's Keehi Lagoon, east of the airport. The luxury junk, owned by a Honolulu architect, sleeps four for less than a Waikiki suite.

Keehi Lagoon, Tel: 737-2780; or write David Hoe, 1750 Kalakaua Avenue, Suite 3583, Honolulu, HI 96826. $150 for two people; can accommodate up to six.

—*Rick Carroll*

DINING IN WAIKIKI

Waikiki has some of the best restaurants in the Islands and some of the worst—with scores of stunningly mediocre eateries in between. The key to dining well in Waikiki is to focus on top-of-the-line establishments.

With only a few exceptions, expensive Waikiki restaurants provide better value than those that are moderately priced. The simple reason is rent. Waikiki is among the most expensive real estate on the planet. Decent restaurant space can now run as high as $150 to $200 per square foot a year. So a restaurant with a mid-range menu probably combines some overpricing with skimping on food costs or service, or both, to pay the landlord.

In addition, few Honolulu residents are willing to venture into the congestion of Waikiki except for a special occasion or a memorable meal. For an average restaurant, they won't bother. And why should they? The city itself outside Waikiki has plenty of restaurants that are both cheaper and better. So an unexceptional Waikiki restaurant depends almost entirely on tourist business. And too great a reliance on transient rather than repeat customers is never good for a restaurant: It breeds cynicism and slackness even in a well-intentioned establishment.

If you wish to dine at moderate cost while staying in Waikiki, your best bet is to rent a car or catch a cab. Travelling just a few blocks out of Waikiki can cut your dinner tab in half—and probably guarantee a more interesting evening, or at least more interesting food (see Dining in Honolulu above).

Inside Waikiki, the best restaurants are top-rank hotel dining rooms where service is formal, the wine list extensive, and dinner costs $40 to $90 a person, not including wine. Most travellers are rightfully wary of hotel restaurants, but the best half-dozen Waikiki hotel restaurants all enjoy a wide local following, and are too good to ignore. Despite their pricey menus, some of these establishments lose $10,000 to $20,000 a month. They aren't there so much to make money as to satisfy guests who expect a high level of cuisine. The rest of a hotel's operations essentially subsidize both the talent in the kitchen and the trained staff on the floor. These restaurants are, at their own level, bargains—and can be counted on to provide among the best prepared and presented meals the Islands have to offer.

The telephone area code for Hawaii is 808.

The Top of the Line
Of all the great hotel dining rooms in Waikiki, **Bagwells 2424** was given the least prepossessing location, a dull, dark room on the third floor of the Hyatt Regency Waikiki (2424 Kalakaua Avenue). The lobby of the Hyatt is spectacular, with its crashing three-story waterfall, but you will probably have to wander a little and perhaps even ask directions to find Bagwells.

Recently the hotel invested a great deal of money to lighten up the room, which now has blond wood furniture, vast expanses of etched glass, and its own 12-foot waterfall. But never mind, the food is what's important here. Executive chef Jeff Wind's cuisine is high-powered and expensive. There's a nightly six-course set menu that is always worth trying, but the regular menu includes such marvels as a salad with seared salmon, local prawns in black-bean sauce, and, perhaps Wind's masterpiece, lamb chops on a sauce of red bell peppers with caramelized garlic cloves.

You may not get past Wind's appetizers, however— tasty items like *opakapaka* (a much-prized local snapper) in a pocket of phyllo pastry on mango puree, or lobster won ton in an unsweetened vanilla sauce. If you like to make dinner out of a number of small courses, the wine bar at Bagwells serves many small dishes (including a small-scale version of the incredible lamb chops) on a "grazing" menu. The wine bar offers some excellent wines by the glass. In the dining room, the wine list is substantial, with special depth in California Cabernets and Chardonnays. Tel: 923-1234.

If Bagwells suffers from its unprepossessing location, **Bali by the Sea** gains a great deal from its setting. It's on the ocean at the Hilton Hawaiian Village (2005 Kalia Road). When you make a reservation, you might ask for a table along the open outside wall, where you can hear the surf. The furnishings, including the fussy white chairs, are a bit overdone, but the moonlight on the water makes up for it all.

The restaurant was named Bali years ago when it was an Indonesian *rijsttafel* restaurant. The name stuck, but the cuisine, under the direction of chef Yves Menoret, is now Continental, with a number of Island touches. *Opihi,* a strongly flavored Island limpet, is served on ice with oysters, clams, and prawns as an appetizer. Kaiwi Channel *opakapaka* comes in fresh basil sauce. Other noteworthy dishes include a coquille of shrimp and scallops, a red snapper soup topped with puff pastry, and tenderloin of beef with black peppercorns. The Bali's soufflés—sweet, light, and steaming—can round off a meal nicely. Wine steward Stephen Fuller is good about recommending good value from the wine list. Tel: 941-BALI.

Also at the Hilton is the **Golden Dragon**. Under normal circumstances it's absurd to eat Chinese food in Waikiki. Outside Waikiki, Honolulu is dotted with inexpensive, good to great Chinese eateries, and the established Chinese restaurants inside Waikiki (House of Hong, Lau Yee Chai) have been resting on their laurels for decades. But the Golden Dragon is not normal circumstances. It is a first-string restaurant that happens to have a Chinese chef, Dai Hoy Chang of Canton.

The black and red lacquered dining room, filled with Chinese antiques, is divided by pillars into small intimate areas, most with a view of the Hilton's artificial lagoon. The menu here may sound familiar—almond duck, lobster with black-bean sauce, imperial beggar's chicken—but the food and the presentation are out of the ordinary. The stir-fried lobster with curry sauce, *haupia* (a Hawaiian pudding), and raisins is not to be missed, and the grilled Szechwan beef starts as filet mignon. The service is unobtrusive, except for the tea lady, who after your meal brings a half dozen varieties of tea on an antique cart. She allows you to choose your own tea, brews it, and then tells your fortune. This is one of the few Chinese restaurants with an excellent wine list. Call 24 hours ahead if you would like to order Peking duck or beggar's chicken. Tel: 946-5336.

La Mer at the Halekulani (2199 Kalia Road) is the most formal restaurant in Hawaii. Men do not usually feel compelled to wear coat and tie to dinner in Hawaii, although the practice is not unknown. Still, La Mer and Michel's (see below) positively require jackets for gentlemen, but not—in deference to the climate—ties. La Mer is in an upstairs dining room, done in muted browns and tans, with a pleasant view of the ocean, and an open-air bar below.

Service is designed to be impeccable, with elaborate tableside presentation of each dish. The water in your water glass is Evian. The menu is French, designed by chef Philippe Padovani, who trained under the creative Philippe Chavent at La Tour Rose in Lyon. For the hungry, there is a nine-course feast; there are also four- and five-course offerings of elaborate fare: free-range chicken with foie gras mousse, lobster with squid ink pasta, Molokai venison with pineapple and sauce poivrade. Outside of a sea urchin mousse, which was promptly yanked off the menu, La Mer's kitchen has probably never produced a bad dish. This is a good place simply to trust the chef and follow the fixed-course dinners. You can order à la carte, but you should watch the expense. The wine list is heavily French, with California adequately represented. Tel: 923-2311.

Michel's at the Colony Surf Hotel (2895 Kalakaua Avenue) is the grande dame of Waikiki restaurants, aging perhaps, but still beautiful. Michel's is a well-appointed formal restaurant, saved from stuffiness because one wall opens directly on Sans Souci Beach, which is just east of Waikiki Beach, across Kapiolani Park, near Diamond Head. At lunch you can sometimes smell the coconut oil of the beach-goers lying on the sand a few feet away. At sunset the view over the water is spectacular.

Jackets are required for gentlemen after six; ties optional. The cuisine is somewhat staid, but the *onaga* (a local snapper) in black-bean and ginger sauce, sautéed *opakapaka* with a velvety hollandaise, and scalloped veal in Madeira sauce are all classics. Michel's has taken a new chef on board, Khamtan Tanhchaleun, who promises to add variety to the menu with some daily specials. But Michel's is likely to remain a place where you can always get onion soup, a Caesar salad, and Chateaubriand. The wine list, while not overpowering, is serviceable.

Alone among Waikiki's glittering dining rooms, Michel's also does breakfast, lunch, and Sunday brunch. If you enjoy ambience but are not quite up to dinner, one of the earlier meals is less expensive, and likely to be very good. The cool of morning is a particularly pleasant time to be dining at the beach. For reservations (call well ahead for weekends and Sunday brunch), Tel: 923-6552.

Of all Waikiki's haute cuisine restaurants, **The Third Floor** (Hawaiian Regent Hotel, 2552 Kalakaua Avenue) is the most comfortable. It's a local favorite for sentimental occasions such as anniversaries. No view here, but there's a towering ceiling and a large tiled carp pond in the center of the restaurant. High-back rattan chairs provide a pleasing sense of privacy for each diner in the vast room.

Service is excellent, though a bit informal. Your waiter may very well introduce himself by saying, "Hi, my name is———." Over the years, a Third Floor dinner has become heavily ritualized. It begins with warm East Indian *naan* bread and duck liver pâté and ends with ice-cream bonbons served with a chip of dry ice underneath, giving off theatrical billows of steam. The printed menu is conventional stuff; it is better to order from the long list of daily specials. Frogs' legs Provençale or in garlic butter are usually available, as either an entrée or an appetizer.

There are always a fresh fish or two and excellent veal dishes. You may be tempted by the vast appetizer bar buffet called Promising Start, but unless you're very hungry it's best skipped, because there's nothing *nouvelle* about the size of the portions here.

The wine list is particularly strong in German whites and French reds. Sommelier Richard Dean is one of the best (and least pretentious) in Hawaii; his advice is worth taking. Reservations a must; Tel: 922-6611.

Expensive to Moderate

In addition to the top-of-the-line restaurants, Waikiki has a mixed bag of other restaurants that have distinguished themselves. Most of these are also expensive. These usually are not hotel restaurants, although some are located in smaller hotels, from which they lease space. None has the extensive menu, the legions of sous chefs, or the deep wine lists of the hotel dining rooms, but they have found a niche in the market and fill it well.

Bon Appetit is located in the first floor of a towering condominium called Discovery Bay (1778 Ala Moana Boulevard). Under owner Guy Banal and chef Hervé Chabin, Bon Appetit has evolved into an unpretentious but comfortable eatery that specializes in French country cooking, especially from the South of France. Perhaps the signature dish here is *cassoulet au confit de canard,* rich with the taste of double-cooked duck, veal, and sausage. The food at Bon Appetit is rich: fresh goose liver with truffle sauce, baby chicken with morel mushrooms, and both steak and crab tartare. Each week there are four- or three-course dinner specials. The wine list includes about 50 wines, French with a sprinkling of California, ample enough for a small restaurant. Tel: 942-3837.

Both travellers and residents often get confused between Michel's at the Colony Surf Hotel (see above) and **Chez Michel** at Eaton Square, the tall, white buildings with the blue stripe at 444 Hobron Lane, a side street off Ala Moana Boulevard. Both were started by legendary Honolulu restaurateur Michel Martin, who established Michel's at the Colony Surf and then went out on his own with Chez Michel. (Martin is no longer with either restaurant; he's now running a commercial bakery.) Chez Michel, which for years has enjoyed an excellent reputation, was recently sold to Japanese investors. The restaurant still looks the same, open and airy with bright pink tablecloths and fresh flowers, and the menu seems the same, including the delicate vegetable soufflés, but who knows what the future will bring. Exercise caution. Tel: 955-7866.

There seem to be steak houses on every corner in Waikiki, but **Hy's Steak House** (2440 Kuhio Avenue) is the reigning red-meat champion—steaks of all cuts and varieties, wonderful rack of lamb or lamb Wellington, with, as you would expect, Caesar salad and flaming cherries jubilee on the menu as well. There are two dining rooms here: The Art Deco room is smaller and quieter than the large, wood-paneled, "library" room, which tends to get smoky from the grill in the corner. There is good attention to detail, both in the kitchen and on the restaurant floor. The wine list, not surprisingly, is especially deep in red wines, and the house Cabernet from California's Ridge Vineyards is a bargain. Tel: 922-5555.

For years **Matteo's** (364 Seaside Avenue, across from the Waikiki theaters) enjoyed a large local following; it used to be the only good Italian restaurant in town. That following has diminished, ironically, at a time when the restaurant, under new ownership, has improved greatly. Gone are the red-vinyl booths and tacky decor; they have been replaced by French brocade and koa wine cabinets outlined in tiny, white Tivoli lights. The restaurant branched out from its Italian roots and now includes such standard Continental items as rack of lamb. The wine list here puts many larger establishments to shame; if you are a devotee of Italian wine, no other place in Hawaii has a comparable cellar. A note, however: Matteo's is getting a reputation for making people wait an hour or so for a table. Tel: 922-5551.

It's usually a good idea to stay out of restaurants whose major asset is the view from the top of a tall building, but **Nicholas Nickolas** (410 Atkinson Drive, near Ala Moana Center) is an exception. It's perched atop the tallest building in the state, the 36-story Ramada Renaissance Ala Moana hotel, with a sweeping panoramic view of Waikiki, the Ala Wai Yacht Harbor, and the ocean. The room was designed so that the view is accessible from every seat—and, incidentally, so that it is easy to see and be seen by the other patrons. More a supper club than a dinner house, Nicholas Nickolas has a limited menu. But what it does, it does well, including several special salads, escargot, steak, lamb, and lobster. And—a rarity among Honolulu restaurants—you can get a late-night supper here seven nights a week, with live music (usually jazz) and a dance floor. Tel: 955-4466.

The dining room is dark and intimate at **Nick's Fish-market** (2070 Kalakaua Avenue; parking is on Kuhio Avenue), but the tempo for this dressy Waikiki night spot is set by the crowded cocktail lounge and dance floor. In his tiny kitchen, chef Eddie Fernandez accomplishes some marvels with fresh local fish and imported seafood, including live Maine lobster and green-lipped New Zealand mussels. The young, well-dressed waiters strive for elegant service; occasionally they overdo it and become obtrusive. Tel: 955-6333.

Orchids is the second-string dining room at the Halekulani (2199 Kalia Road), which also boasts the more formal La Mer (see above). But there's nothing really second-string about Orchids' open-air, oceanfront dining room. Ask for a table on the terrace if you can get it; over a little stretch of grass and a low concrete wall is Waikiki Beach. The food here is inventive—a light, open-faced lasagna with cilantro sauce, for instance, or carpaccio of venison with ginger. Orchids is less expensive than La Mer upstairs, but is far from inexpensive. The table d'hôte lunches and dinners are usually the best deal. Service—surprisingly, in this kind of establishment—has occasional lapses, perhaps because the dining room is so large. Orchids also serves breakfast and Sunday brunch. Tel: 923-2311.

Restaurant Suntory (Royal Hawaiian Shopping Center, Third Floor, 2233 Kalakaua Avenue) is owned by the Japanese whiskey company. Originally the most elegant of Waikiki's Japanese restaurants, Suntory has faded a little and needs some sprucing up, but it's still a pleasant setting. Displayed on lighted glass shelves in the lounge are customers' individual bottles of Suntory. In the elegant *shabu shabu* rooms you cook at the table by dipping items into a pot of hot broth. The real star here, though, is the *teppanyaki* room. Teppan cooking is almost a cliché in the United States because of the success of the Benihana chain, but this is *teppanyaki* as the Japanese themselves do it. And you will find Japanese travellers dropping by to enjoy the steaks and seafood. The adventurous should try the seaweed salad. Good, unobtrusive service. Tel: 922-5511.

In **Sergio's** (445 Nohonani Street) you might as well be on the Mainland—the small dining room is dark and windowless. Nevertheless, there's a nice, intimate feel here. The standard Italian menu is supplemented by some interesting pasta treatments—caviar, smoked salmon, wild mushrooms. The tortellini in cream sauce, when available, are richly satisfying. Service is usually friendly and attentive. Tel: 926-3388.

The Royal Hawaiian Hotel, opened in 1927, was the first of Hawaii's luxury resorts. And the **Surf Room** at the Royal Hawaiian (2259 Kalakaua Avenue) still has something of the unhurried elegance that marked the grand pink hotel in the old days. You can be comfortable in this beachfront restaurant, with its pink-and-white awnings and pink table-cloths, whether you're wearing a suit or more casual clothes. The emphasis here is not so much on culinary innovation as quality. The dinner menu is largely made up of classics—shrimp cocktail, onion and snapper soups, lobster tail and filet mignon, veal chops, and prawns in herb butter. But lunch, when the sun is glistening off the water and the beach is packed with bodies, may be the meal of choice here. A bountiful buffet is offered as well as lighter entrées such as tempura and a cold, poached chicken breast stuffed with herbs. The mai tai reached the peak of perfection at the Royal Hawaiian, and this is still the best place to drink one, complete with orchid, pineapple slice, and sliver of sugarcane, plus, of course, a healthy dose of rum. Tel: 923-7311.

The new proprietors of Matteo's (see above) also own **Trattoria** (2168 Kalia Road, across from the Outrigger Reef Hotel). Trattoria is a less formal restaurant than Matteo's, and serves a more traditional Italian menu, but shares the same excellent wine list. The tables are smaller at Trattoria, the dining room more crowded, the prices slightly lower. It's noisier here and perhaps more fun. The small cocktail lounge is beautiful, with some richly colored murals on the wall, well-done copies of some well-known Italian paintings. Tel: 923-8415.

Moderate to Inexpensive

Unfortunately, a good number of Waikiki restaurants that should be moderately priced are instead designed to turn travellers upside down and shake every last nickel out of their jeans, and without providing a decent meal in re-turn. But there are a few oases of sanity: restaurants that provide decent food at reasonable prices.

Perched on the edge of Waikiki (1837 Kapiolani Boule-vard) is the ninth outpost of that trendy international chain, the **Hard Rock Café**. Rock 'n' roll is foreground rather than background music here, there's a classic woody station wagon hanging over the bar, and the walls are hung with gold records, guitars, and other rock 'n' roll and surfing memorabilia. People stand in long lines outside to purchase tee-shirts and other merchandise emblazoned with the brown and yellow Hard Rock logo. All this brouhaha obscures the fact that the Hard Rock is a pretty good place to eat, with simple food from a limited menu: lime-grilled chicken, Texas ribs with watermelon barbecue sauce, fresh fish, burgers, fries, shakes, and hot fudge sundaes. House wine only, but several brands of beer. If you must buy a Hard Rock tee-shirt, please note: If you actually eat in the restaurant, you don't have to stand in the long merchandise line outside. Just ask your waitress for what you want; she'll add it to your check.

At the **Hau Tree Lanai** (New Otani Kaimana Beach Hotel, 2863 Kalakaua Avenue, a few doors from Michel's) the main attraction is the location. The Hau Tree Lanai is an open courtyard. It sits next to a stretch of Waikiki Beach called Sans Souci (the name comes from a 19th-century hotel that once occupied this spot). Robert Louis Stevenson, who spent hours sitting under the spreading *hau* tree that still graces that courtyard, wrote, "If anyone desires such old fashioned things as lovely scenery, quiet, pure air, clear sea water, good food and heavenly sunsets hung out before his eyes over the Pacific and the distant hills of Waianae, I recommend him cordially to the Sans Souci."

The Hau Tree Lanai is essentially the New Otani Kaimana Beach Hotel's coffee shop; it does three meals a day. The food is a cut above coffee-shop fare—a good, seared *ahi* (yellowfin tuna) with fresh tomato salsa, for instance. The service can be erratic, but that's not the point: This is a nice place to eat outdoors on the beach without spending a fortune. Tel: 923-1555.

Most Waikiki restaurants are dressy casual, but you can wear shorts and a tee-shirt to the **Shore Bird Beach Broiler** (2169 Kalia Road, at the back of the Outrigger Reef Hotel). About half of this large beachfront restaurant is taken up by the bar, which at 9:00 P.M. turns into a disco with a ten-foot video screen and a laser light show. But this is no flashy, high-tech dance parlor. The floors are wood planks, the interior decoration consists mainly of painted signs, and there are overhead fans and two power-boats parked in alcoves. The waitress will bring your order—steaks, chicken, fish, or hamburgers—uncooked; you do the honors yourself at a massive barbecue grill at the far end of the dining room. In addition, there's an unfancy, but substantial, salad bar where you can load up on chili, pasta, and rice as well as greens. The food is far from dazzling, but it's certainly adequate. The whole atmosphere says you're allowed to have fun here. If you could love a restaurant that holds weekly bikini contests, this one's for you.

—*John Heckathorn*

WAIKIKI NIGHTLIFE AND ENTERTAINMENT

Nightlife in Waikiki is like an aloha shirt: full on, gaudy, and hanging out everywhere. It's celebrated in sky-room restaurants, offshore on "booze-cruise" boats, over sundown mai tais under banyan trees, at Hawaii-style *pau hana* (which means "work over") street parties, on teak-railed fantails of sloops in Ala Wai Yacht Harbor, in dimly lighted bamboo-and-thatch bars like Tahitian Lanai, at rowdy Chinese restaurants, over tropical cocktails at Surfer's Corner, in Japanese *karaoke* (singalong) bars, by waterfalls at **Harry's Bar & Café** at the Hyatt Regency, inside Hula's Bar & Lei Stand, on top of the glass dance floor at the glitzy new Maharaja disco, with caviar and Dom Perignon at black-tie Ilikai penthouse parties, on luxury cruise ships gliding by Diamond Head.

The pursuit of earthly pleasure goes on nearly around the clock every night of the year. It commences about 3:00 every afternoon when luau vans pull away from hotel curbs, and ends shortly after 4:00 A.M. the next day, when the last disco closes. In that 13-hour span the Hawaiian night belongs to anyone with courage and cash enough to enjoy all the fine dining, good music, and live entertainment available here 365 days a year.

Hawaiian Music

Only New York City and Las Vegas have more square footage dedicated to fun than does Waikiki. Sadly, little is devoted to Hawaiian music, the steel-guitar, slack-key, and falsetto-voiced sound that originally attracted hundreds of thousands to Waikiki via Webley Edwards's "Hawaii Calls," the popular radio show of the 1940s, broadcast "live" from the banyan tree court of the Moana hotel on beautiful Waikiki Beach.

Hapa-haole music (those old pseudo-Hawaiian songs such as "Cockeyed Mayor of Kaunakakai") of that era may still be heard in Waikiki, but engagements by Hawaiian performers are limited, and anyone in search of the local sound must work to find it. Such great Hawaiian entertainers as Eddie Kamae and the Sons of Hawaii, and Makaha Sons of Niihau, Tony Conjugacion, Bla Pahinui and Bernard Kalua, Sonny Chillingworth, Moe Keale, Palani Vaughan, Jimmy Kaina, Mahi Beamer, and Haunani Apolonia, and steel-guitar virtuoso Jerry Byrd, and groups like Olomana, the Peter Moon Band, and Cecilio and Kapono seldom appear in Waikiki, and then only at special engagements. Even that grand old singer-composer Andy Cummings, who wrote the song "Wai-kiki," is relegated to a steak house a mile away (Buzz's Steak House, one block mauka from Beretania Street off University Avenue).

The lack of contemporary Hawaiian music in Waikiki is offset slightly by two Hawaiians, the Brothers Cazimero, who sing and play at the Royal Hawaiian Hotel's **Monarch Room**. The current darlings of Waikiki, Roland and Robert are accomplished musicians who write and compose their own versions of Hawaii-inspired songs. They are real brothers, too, sons of Bill Cazimero, a Big Island orchestra leader in the 1930s. The Cazimero brothers got their start as two-thirds of a trio called Sunday Manoa, with slack-key guitarist Peter Moon (more on him later), and in the summer of 1982 followed Hilo Hattie and Alfred Apaka to become Monarch Room headliners. The Caz, as they are affectionately known, have recorded 13 albums, including *Waikiki, My Castle by the Sea,* with the Ray Jerome Baker cover photo of Waikiki in the 1930s, when only the Royal Hawaiian and Moana hotels dominated the seascape.

Some of the best shows in Waikiki are free, or come with the price of a tropical cocktail. Under the *kiawe* tree of the **Halekulani's House Without a Key** lanai/lounge on certain nights at sundown, Sonny Kamahele, joined by Alan Akaka on steel guitar and Benny Kalama on ukulele, sings old Hawaiian favorites. This nostalgic trio, which calls itself the Sunset Serenaders, usually features hula dancer Kanoe Miller, a former Miss Hawaii, and if the music and hula don't give you goose bumps maybe you should have gone to Jamaica after all.

Waikiki Shell, the open-air Kapiolani Park bandstand, attracts the rock and jazz stars of the day—but, unfortunately, they must hang it up at 10:00 P.M., just as they start getting it on. Hiroshima, the Los Angeles–based jazz-fusion group, got fined for playing electric *koto* too loud. Curfew aside, the 3,257-seat bandstand is Waikiki's best outdoor club on warm tropical nights, and after the performance you can still go out for a late show somewhere else. But rock and jazz may not be the best reason to go to the Shell:

"Does the moon still dance to music at the Shell?" goes the local pop hit "Hello Honolulu." Yes, but only when slack-key guitar virtuoso Peter Moon hosts one of his "Blue Hawaiian Moonlight" shows, featuring the Islands' best Hawaiian music, including rare appearances by Niihau church choirs. (Bring an umbrella to *any* outdoor concert in case of a sudden shower.)

Hula

Tourist luaus should be avoided if you have any sensitivity to Hawaii's cultural past. Even at the best commercial luau the dinner is a thin imitation of a real Hawaiian meal (overcooked chunks of roast pig, a cup of salty salmon, no-fish entrée, a slice of macadamia-nut pie), served on paper plates while the announcer makes lewd remarks about hula "girls" (who look Filipino and dance a Tahitian *tamure,* not a hula at all).

Like Hawaiian music, the real hula takes some effort to see, for despite a comeback of sorts, the ancient, sensuous dance banned by missionaries is still almost an underground event, forbidden even at the Kamehameha Schools until the 1960s. The faux hula easily seen by tourists is show biz; it meets expectations and keeps thousands off the streets.

Those who want to see authentic hula should go to the **Kodak Hula Show** in Waikiki's Kapiolani Park, **Waimea Falls Park** at Waimea Bay on the North Shore, and—very best of all—the **Merrie Monarch Festival** in Hilo on the Big Island each year. Or look for a special appearance by a *hula halau* (school) like Mapanua De Silva's Halau Mohala Ilima, one of Hawaii's best.

Dinner Shows and Clubs

Jazz in Waikiki has always depended on who dropped in to cool out on the New York–Tokyo haul and blow a horn at Trappers, but since the Act Deco Hyatt Regency Waikiki jazz club dropped its "legends" series—which featured, among others, Stan Getz, Wynton Marsalis, Herbie Mann, Freddie Hubbard, Les McCann, and Richie Cole—in favor of a variety show, the night belongs to Jimmy Borges. The velvet-voiced crooner sings the standards in front of his jazz quartet at the Hilton Hawaiian Village's new **Paradise**

Lounge, a big, airy, casual, palm-filled room that is packed on weekends.

If Jimmy is king of the groove, then Andrea Young, the Hawaiian-born daughter of late, great jazz trombonist Trummy Young, is queen. A vocalist with echoes of Billie Holiday and Carmen McRae, this second-generation jazz artist should be declared a state treasure. She sings as if she wrote the songs; her rendition of "My Funny Valentine" takes over where Chet Baker left off. Don't leave Waikiki without catching Andrea, possibly at the **New Orleans Bistro**, a sidewalk café at 2139 Kuhio Avenue, between Lewers Street and Saratoga Avenue.

When Big Band leader Del Courtney swings at the **Royal Hawaiian Hotel's tea dances** on Sunday afternoons, with Diamond Head in the background and Waikiki at your feet, there's no more romantic spot for cheek-to-cheek dancing. Some of Honolulu's top players help make the big sound.

The undisputed king of Waikiki is **Don Ho**, a laid-back, Dean Martin–like singer who has camped his way through a 22-year show-biz career on the strength of his 1967 hit "Tiny Bubbles" and the old "Hawaii Calls" favorite, "Pearly Shells." Can you name any other Don Ho songs? It doesn't matter. His fans stand on line like teenagers hours before the doors open at the **Hilton Hawaiian Village Dome** to see this Waikiki legend.

A headliner since the 1960s, Ho opened at the Dome on December 26, 1981 (after Jim "Gomer Pyle" Nabors), and shows no sign of stopping. He continues to showcase young talent and squeeze grandmas onstage.

The steak dinner and show, which costs $39, features Ho mumble-singing all the Hawaiian songs he knows, backed by a peppy troupe of singers and dancers. For an extra $12 anyone can go backstage after the show and get a picture taken with Don. You'd be amazed at the queue. The 1,120-seat geodesic dome, the first public dome erected in the United States (it went up in 36 hours in 1959) is leaking and doomed, but the legendary Don Ho lives on. If you plan to see only one show in Waikiki, this is still it.

Al Harrington, the self-styled "South Pacific Man," sings love songs, delivers bits of Hawaiian history, and tells "good clean" jokes. His 16-member variety act captures the essence of Polynesia without hoking it up—twice nightly in the **Al Harrington Showroom** at the Outrigger Reef Towers Hotel, 227 Lewers Street.

In the **Tropics Surf Club** at the Hilton Hawaiian Village, Las Vegas headliner Charo, the aging "cuchi-cuchi girl" once wed to Brazilian bandleader Xavier Cugat, is as of this writing the latest "big-time" performer trying to fill the 250-seat, international showroom after John Rowles, New Zealand's Englebert Humperdinck, returned down under. She leads a game troupe on a merry chase.

Elvis lives on at **The Hula Hut** (286 Beach Walk on the mauka side of Kalakaua) in the person of Jonathan Von Brana, who moved his Presley act from Las Vegas to Waikiki—to the delight of graying Elvis fans. The King comes to life in The Hula Hut's theater-restaurant, along with the likes of Diana Ross and the Supremes and Tina Turner, thanks to other imitators. Performer Jim Owen out-Hanks Hank Williams.

On the last Sunday of each month the Hula hosts its "backyard bash," a low-key, Hawaiian-style, back-porch party. Nobody knows who may stop by to sing, play, or hula, and that down-homeness is what makes the Hula special.

The Waikiki pop club scene is dominated by **Wave Waikiki** (look for the mural of the Japanese snorkeler in red swimsuit and turquoise water at 1877 Kalakaua Avenue), which under impresario Jack Law has booked Grace Jones, George Thorogood and the Destroyers, Dave Valentin, The Boom Town Rats, Fleetwood Zoo (the garage band of Mick Fleetwood with Stevie Nicks), Cinderella Rockefella, Bronski Beat, and Bow Wow Wow.

The fledgling **Honolulu Comedy Club** is still open as of this writing, and while proprietor Eddie Sax isn't laughing all the way to the bank yet, he has managed to keep this lone comedy venue alive. This vaudeville club, at the top of the Ilikai, plays to a mid-20s to early-40s crowd.

No one gets more laughs in town than Waikiki's Frank DeLima, however, the freewheeling funnyman with the devilish mind who is Hawaii's reigning comic genius. A master of impression, DeLima makes good fun of everyone, from Japanese tourists to his own Portuguese folks. He voices the unspoken and gets away with it at **The Noodle Shop** (in the Waikiki Sand Villa Hotel at 2375 Ala Wai Boulevard). His Imelda Marcos is better than the original.

Evening Cruises

Waikiki's nightlife also goes on beyond the reef on some 26 booze- and dinner-cruise ships, some little more than barges tricked up like Disneyesque versions of Polynesian craft. They tack back and forth in front of Waikiki as if on underwater tracks while presenting ersatz luau-style entertainment, airline meals, and Hawaiian Punch drinks. The best thing about these little sea cruises, besides the view, is that they are soon over. If you want a cruise, go out on the **Leahi** at sunset (see the Waikiki narrative above). If you want booze, go to Murphy's Bar & Grill at the corner of Nuuanu Avenue and Merchant Street in Chinatown (see Honolulu Nightlife).

Gay Waikiki

Some of the most fun after dark occurs in the Tivoli-lighted gay quarter of Kuhio, named for Hawaii's last prince. The Kuhio district, a two-block area between Kuhio and Kalakaua avenues and Lewers and Kalaimoku streets, is Honolulu's Castro Street, a collection of gay men's shops, such as 80 Percent Straight and Down There, restaurants, and bars. **Hula's Bar & Lei Stand**, on the corner of Kuhio Avenue and Kalaimoku Street, across from the Kuhio Theater, is a gay disco with videos and an open-air courtyard that infrequently features Hawaiian singers. **Hamburger Mary's Organic Grill**, just around the corner on Kuhio Avenue, features what many believe are Hawaii's best hamburgers. A few steps farther down Kuhio you'll find **Surfer's Corner**, a palmy oasis amid high-rises, featuring *nouvelle tropicale* cuisine, French pastries, and Italian coffee. The nearby Honolulu Hotel is a small hotel that caters to gays.

Disco

The disco never died in Waikiki, and probably won't until the last person under 35 in North America and Japan has been to **Bobby McGee's Conglomeration**, the last bastion of old-time disco fever. At 2885 Kalakaua Avenue, near the entrance to the New Otani Kaimana Beach Hotel, Bobby McGee's is an arena-style dance hall inside a restaurant, where you can eat, drink, and boogie all in one place.

And just when you thought disco was history, the Japanese have reinvented the genre in Waikiki with **Maharaja**, a pull-out-all-the-stops, multi-million-dollar dance hall that is a candidate for *Ripley's "Believe It or Not"* and the *Guinness Book of Records*. There's nothing like the Maharaja, anywhere.

This 13,000-square-foot showplace covering much of the ground floor of the Waikiki Trade Center at Kuhio and

Seaside avenues combines Tokyo's latest high-tech sound and light wizardry with a glitzy European style, around a glass dance floor etched with optical designs that create the illusion that you're dancing on water. This architectural bazaar of sound and lights includes five bars, three restaurants, and an 80-seat glass-encased VIP lounge where the high-rev sound is reduced to a whisper. Maharaja is the first U.S. venture by Japan's Nova 21 Group, which has more than 100 clubs from Hokkaido to Okinawa and hopes to have the same from Honolulu to New York.

Cafés and Bars

Two cafés, the **Blue Water**, in the heart of Waikiki, at 2350 Kuhio Avenue, at Kaiulani, and the **Hard Rock**, on the edge (corner of Kalakaua Avenue and Kapiolani Boulevard), offer food, music, and self-serving tee-shirts. The more fun is the Blue Water, with live rock 'n' roll nightly, something the Hard Rock tried, but couldn't do, after condo neighbors complained of high decibel levels.

Waikiki's last neighborhood bar is long gone (try Smith's Union Bar at 19 North Hotel Street in Chinatown), but two unique bars are worth a visit: **Lewers Lounge** at the Halekulani, a leather-lined, Manhattan-like tavern with big comfortable chairs, gracious stewards, but no ocean view, is the perfect place to relax over a Bombay up. Evenings, the lounge features the soft, melodic voice of Melinda Caroll, who accompanies herself on acoustic guitar.

The **Tahitian Lanai**, a nostalgic South Seas–style bamboo-and-thatch bar and restaurant on the Waikikian's beachfront (between the Ilikai and the Hilton), is an old favorite for sipping mai tais and staring out to sea.

Up on the third floor of the Royal Hawaiian Shopping Center, that block-long merchandise mart, **Naniwa-ya** is an oasis in the midst of retail that makes you feel as if you're in Tokyo, especially late in the evening when the customers start singing *karaoke*.

Still out on the town? Swing by Hyatt Regency Waikiki's new "after-hours" club at **Trappers**, and Mai Tai Sing, Waikiki's first lady, might let you in—if she likes the cut of your jib.

After the fun, night owls, the post-disco crowd, and other insomniacs hurry to the all-night eatery **Eggs 'n' Things**, at 1911B Kalakaua Avenue, which opens at 11:00 P.M. Other red-eyed patrons wolf down all-you-can-eat pancakes, bacon, and eggs for $3.99 at the 24-hour **Wailana Coffee House** ("since 1941"), at 1860 Ala Moana Boulevard.

—Rick Carroll

SHOPS AND SHOPPING IN WAIKIKI

In the days before the Matson container ships changed Island consumerism, well-heeled Honolulu matrons sojourned at San Francisco or Los Angeles to replenish their fall wardrobes, or in Tokyo and Hong Kong for silks, jewelry, and furniture. Today, it seems, Rodeo Drive has come to Waikiki, treasures from the Orient are to be found in any number of shopping plazas, and fine collectibles from the past are abundant in downtown Honolulu antiques shops. The problem with shopping in Hawaii, as a matter of fact, is ferreting out the worthwhile from the schlock before your eyes glaze over and you quit looking because there's just too much stuff and it all looks the same.

In tee-shirts alone, the variety in Waikiki ranges from souvenir cotton tees for $2.50 (which might make you feel like a shrink-wrapped sausage after the first washing) to one-of-a-kind, $38 Chinese tees hand-painted with lavender orchids. Waikiki's open-air International Marketplace is like some overcrowded Asian emporium, with merchants hawking wares made in Taiwan, the Philippines, China, Japan, and maybe even Hawaii. Fine arts, crafts, jewelry, and resort wear *are* produced in the Islands; they're just not easily found among the jumble of plastic flower leis and aloha-stamped key chains, coffee mugs, and ashtrays sold from sidewalk stalls in Waikiki. On the other hand, the Royal Hawaiian Shopping Center on Waikiki's main street, Kalakaua Avenue, is home to the first Chanel boutique ever opened in the United States. Such prestigious and internationally known shops as Louis Vuitton, Polo/Ralph Lauren, Cartier, Benetton, and Lancel carry quality goods.

In general, stores and shopping centers open at 9:00 or 9:30 A.M., and many of those in Waikiki stay open until 9:00 P.M. or later.

In Waikiki, in addition to Liberty House and McInerney's department stores and 31 ABC Discount Stores (where you can find macadamia-nut products, Hawaiian perfumes, beach mats, tanning lotions, liquor, whatever) there are three types of shopping areas, each progressively more expensive: stalls, malls, and hotels. First, the stalls.

Stalls

You can buy gold chains by the inch from a street stall; the salesperson will tell you it's 14-karat gold mixed with silver and your satisfaction is guaranteed for a lifetime. Beware; by the time the golden glow is gone, most travellers have lost the receipt and the address for making any exchange. Buy it for fun, for the spur of the moment, and try not to pay full price. In stalls along **Duke's Lane** and in the adjacent **International Market Place** (2330 Kalakaua Avenue, across from the Surfrider Hotel), the gold-chain sellers often drop their prices as soon as you hesitate to buy, or their signs advertise 50 percent off. In the Market Place you don't even have to bargain. Merchants, many of them fairly recent Asian immigrants, face stiff competition, and, particularly on semiprecious jewelry like coral or ivory and even costume bracelets, necklaces, and earrings, their final price will be a third off the original when you declare, "I'm just looking." Other good buys in the Market Place are brightly colored beach towels and the ever-popular tee-shirt. Since its inception 30 years ago, the International Market Place, by the way, has grown from a laid-back little place where you could hear the birds chatter in the branches of the giant banyan tree to a crowded maze of stalls and kiosks. Yellow lines are painted on the cobbled and paved ground beneath your feet to lead you through.

Today the future of the Market Place is in question. Developers are planning to build a multistory convention center on the site, and promising to preserve something similar to the Market Place on the ground level. Public controversy is heated, but be sure to take in this famous shopping maze just in case it's gone the next time you're in Honolulu. Behind and adjacent to the Market Place is **Kuhio Mall** (2301 Kuhio Avenue), an additional two-story cluster of stalls selling tee-shirts, beach towels, and costume jewelry.

Malls

Excluding the International Market Place, Kuhio Mall, and the Rainbow Bazaar at the Hilton Hawaiian Village, there are three shopping malls of some size in Waikiki—King's Village, the Royal Hawaiian Shopping Center, and Waikiki Shopping Plaza—as well as a walkway through the **Waikiki Trade Center** (2255 Kuhio Avenue) that houses **C. June Shoes,** one of the best (and most expensive) shoe stores in the area, and **Town and Country Surf Shop,** for bathing suits, wet suits, surf wallets, and tank tops in the brands that are cool with honest-to-goodness local surfers. Be sure to investigate the upper reaches of all these multilevel malls, as often the most interesting little specialty shops are found on the upper-level, lower-overhead floors.

The **Royal Hawaiian Shopping Center** (2201 Kalakaua Avenue, in front of the Royal Hawaiian Hotel) is a three-story, three-building mall with a ten-story parking lot attached (merchants validate parking with purchases). On the ground level in Building A, a laser-disc information system called Info-Vision provides shoppers with detailed information on stores, restaurants, and activities at the touch of a button. Free hula, ukulele, Hawaiian quilting, and coconut-frond-weaving lessons are regularly offered, as is a minishow sponsored by the Polynesian Cultural Center, featuring music and dances of the South Pacific. Check out **Loewe** (fine leathers from Madrid) and **Hawaiian Heirloom Jewelry**, where beautiful 14-karat-gold engraved bracelets can be ordered in various widths, styles, and designs. Engraved plumeria flowers or *maile* vines are two popular designs that form the background for the wearer's name, usually engraved in Hawaiian in black enamel.

Then wander past the kiosks full of flowers and perfumes, kites and suntan lotion, to the glass-enclosed elevator next to Chanel in Building B. On the third level to the right of the elevator is **The Little Hawaiian Craft Shop.** Fifty or more local craftspeople are represented in this shop, and all the items are made by craftspeople in Hawaii or the South Pacific. A lady on Maui contributes sandalwood necklaces, but if you prefer to string your own you can buy sandalwood or coconut-shell beads and other polished nuts separately. This is a good place to purchase all those small gifts for people back home— maybe handmade bookmarks with pressed flowers for $1.95, or Christmas tree ornaments of tiny Hawaiian angels, miniature *ipu* (musical gourds), or woven *lau hala* birds for around $5. On the other end of the price range, the deftly stitched hatbands in brilliant red and yellow feathers or shimmering peacock feathers ($65 to $400) can add a rakish touch to a man's or woman's hat. The ultimate indulgence, rare Niihau-shell leis, will cost you from $26 to $7,000. The tiny shells are found only around the privately owned island of Niihau, and the creation of these delicate necklaces is becoming a dying art. Every true *kamaaina* (longtime resident) has a Niihau necklace tucked away for safekeeping, or else has aspirations of owning one. If Kauai is a scheduled stop on your itinerary, save this ultimate splurge for that island, which has the closest ties and location to Niihau. If you do buy a Niihau necklace on Oahu (either at the Little Hawaiian Craft Shop or in Honolulu at Hildgund), be sure to ask where you can have repairs made, and safeguard the address in case you ever break a shell.

On the second floor in Building A, **Boutique Marlo** features hand-painted and tie-dyed originals. Here are Artful Wear painted tee-shirts, light, floaty, tie-dyed voile dresses, cool and comfortable raw-silk outfits, and hand-woven skirts from Bali—all in natural fibers. Across the street at the five-story **Waikiki Shopping Plaza** (2250 Kalakaua Avenue; you can't miss it, it's got a fountain spraying in the trade winds just inside the entrance) you can watch the free hula show Monday through Saturday at 6:00 and 8:00 P.M., or, if you need a respite, simply browse through the coffee-table and history books about Hawaii at Waldenbooks. Again, stretch your investigating to the upper levels. On the third floor you'll find three shops for eel-skin wallets, key chains, purses, and shoes. (Buy wallets and purses that are cloth lined to prolong the life of credit cards; contact with the eel skin supposedly voids the information carried on the cards' magnetic strips.) Most of the fifth floor is occupied by jewelry retailers and wholesalers, but the bargains and the fantastic variety of necklaces, earrings, and bracelets at **Betty's Import and Export** make this a great place for inexpensive gift shopping. Perhaps the hottest stores for fashionable day and evening wear for women at the Waikiki Shopping Plaza are **Chocolates for Breakfast**, on the second floor, and, for the younger set, its sister shop, **Villa Roma**, on the first.

Amble toward Diamond Head along Kalakaua Avenue and turn left at Kaiulani Avenue to enter **King's Village** (131 Kaiulani Avenue). This charming low-rise mall has a cobblestone lane that wends upward past a colorful kiosk at the entrance with kites and wind socks called **Gone with the Wind**, past **Oahu Fabrics**, which carries the beautiful, locally made Alfred Shaheen prints for $10.98 a yard (Alfred Shaheen resort dresses in the shop at the entrance carry price tags averaging $100), past **Kitamura's of Kyoto** with cotton *yukata* (like those complimentary robes furnished in nicer resorts) for $15 to $25, to the funny little **Fossil Shop**, where fossils can run from $10 for a nondescript fish to $2,950 for an ancient impression of a stingray. Small plaques along the lane in King's Village describe incidents in Hawaiian history during the reign of the monarchy, and a changing-of-the-guard ceremony is staged at the entrance every evening at 6:15.

Many of the malls in Honolulu outside Waikiki—especially those along Ala Moana Boulevard, such as Ala Moana Center, Ward Centre, Ward Warehouse, and Restaurant Row—are easily accessible from Waikiki via TheBus (see Honolulu Shopping).

Hotels

The cream-of-the-crop shops in hotels are generally for the shopper with discriminating taste—and money to spare—but no one should hesitate to walk through any of the finest hotels. With Waikiki's casual dress code, even clerks in the most expensive jewelry stores and boutiques won't look down their noses; any prospective customer might turn out to be Bruce Springsteen or Bette Midler. As a matter of fact, **Bebe** in the Hawaiian Regent and Hilton Hawaiian Village (also at the Waikiki Trade Center) carries sparkle-studded leather bustiers that only someone with Bette Midler's chutzpah could get away with wearing. (Bebe also has great leather skirts and jackets.) The Hawaiian Regent and the Hilton Hawaiian Village also have **Nautilus of the Pacific**, shell shops with lovely and practical shell gifts, such as bowls and boxes of gleaming white capiz shells with pastel-painted orchid designs for $20 to $30.

Sometimes hotel shops carry merchandise you can't find anywhere else in Hawaii. At the Royal Hawaiian Hotel, **Kula Bay** carries "the world's finest Panama hats," Montecristi Fino, which take two to six months to make in Ecuador. **Chapman's** is another fine men's store at the Royal Hawaiian and other leading hotels. The Sheraton Waikiki Hotel's jewelry shop, called **Rachel's Chateau D'Or**, has jewelry to die for. The designs of lapis lazuli, emerald, sapphire, and red and black coral rings, necklaces, and bracelets are from their own factory. The Halekulani Hotel carries award-winning designs by Hawaii's Harry Haimoff at **Haimoff & Haimoff Creations in Gold**. The Kahala Hilton and other upscale hotels feature designer wear at **Collections**, an elite affiliate of Liberty House. Several hotels have branches of shops that you won't find elsewhere in Hawaii, but that you can find everywhere else in the world, such as the Jindo Fur Salon at the Hyatt Regency Waikiki and Tiffany's and Alfred Dunhill of London at the Sheraton Moana Surfrider.

The **Rainbow Bazaar** at the Hilton Hawaiian Village (2005 Kalia Road) is a self-contained shopping mall strung out in three separate theme villages. A large, round red gate marks the entrance to the Bazaar and to Hong Kong Alley; Imperial Japan has a Japanese farmhouse; and the South Pacific shops suggest a sugar plantation theme. Check out **Elephant Walk** for its limited edition prints of bromeliads and orchids by Ruth Glenn Little, from $35. Her serigraphs from original watercolors of plumerias and orchids are about $125. Here you'll also find such treasures as blown-glass unicorns and dolphins mounted on crystal rocks for $48 and up, and lovely ceramic colorscopes, similar to the old kaleidoscopes (made in Colorado, however), for $125 including the stand.

Other elegant, upscale shops are clustered at the new Alii Tower at the Hilton Hawaiian Village, where the plush hotel rooms even have miniature televisions in the bathrooms. At **Bernard Hurtig** there is wonderful faux jewelry to fool the eye—and the real stuff, too. **Lamonts Gift and Sundry Shop** carries scrimshaw (carved ivory) cribbage boards for $50 and little refrigerator magnets decorated with starfish and other colorful tropical friends for $2.50.

Art connoisseurs will find hotel and Ala Moana Center (see Honolulu Shopping) galleries stocked with delightful paintings by Maui's Guy Buffet, picture-perfect scenes by Gary Reed, and the surreal undersea world depicted by Robert Lyn Nelson. More than one of these leading painters, however, began his climb to fame by selling at the **Zoo Fence** on Monsarrat Avenue at the Diamond Head end of Waikiki. You just might discover an unknown talent among the many artists who display their work there every Friday and Saturday. You can find small original works for $25 and large oil paintings of oceans and mountains for $400.

If you've gone as far as the zoo, you might as well stop, on your return walk, at the **Zoo Gift Shop**, which carries original little remembrances with animal themes suitable for young nieces and nephews.

—Betty Fullard-Leo

OAHU OUTSIDE HONOLULU

By John W. Perry

John W. Perry, a contributor to several North American and Asia-Pacific magazines, is a longtime resident of the Pacific area. He lives in Honolulu and frequently travels throughout the South Pacific on assignment.

Charles Nordhoff, a 19th-century journalist (and grandfather of a co-author of the Bligh-Christian saga *Mutiny on the Bounty*), suggested in 1874 that a traveller exploring Oahu outside Honolulu take a pack mule, an English-speaking guide who could cook, and a daily stream bath. The scenic grandeur remains as Nordhoff saw it, but the mule is gone, replaced by a rental car, baths are taken in beach-park showers, and the guide's great-great-offsprings are riding the North Shore's big-wave surf. Now as then, though, a trip outside Honolulu can be a traveller's most rewarding experience on Oahu. An hour's drive from Waikiki, through sugarcane and pineapple fields, are shorelines where Hawaiian royalty vacationed and surfed. By tunnel (Highways 61 and 63) through the spine of a mountain range at the Pali is a landscape where legend is preserved in natural landmarks and in curious place-names filled with age-old meanings. Beside quiet bays on Oahu's Windward (eastern) side you can feel head on the trade winds that cooled the ancient god who created the first ancestor of all Hawaiians. On the North Shore, especially around Haleiwa on weekdays, it's difficult to remember that this is Hawaii's capital island, not Maui or Kauai, and that phone calls to Honolulu are local, not interisland. Along Kamehameha Highway fruit sellers beside make-shift stands hawk papayas and finger-sized bananas and may tell you, truthfully, that mom or pop grows them in their front yard. Always near as you traverse the island are mountains. The Koolau Range, the southern end of which looms over Honolulu, is the remains of an eroded shield volcano and site of the Nuuanu Pali Lookout; and the Waianae Mountains, at the western side of the island, are home to an Oahu guardian spirit, Kolekole, who, like American military personnel, awoke off guard in December 1941 to discover carrier-based Japanese aircraft violating Hawaiian airspace and attacking the U.S. Pacific Fleet's battleships moored along Battleship Row at Ford Island.

MAJOR INTEREST

Pearl Harbor
Arizona Memorial
USS *Bowfin* submarine tours

The Southeastern Coast
Whale-watching
Scenic grandeur
Hanauma Bay/Koko Head
Bodysurfing at Makapuu Beach
Sea Life Park oceanarium

The Pali Area
Queen Emma Summer Palace
Nuuanu Pali Lookout
Haiku Gardens

The Windward Coast
Cafés and restaurants
Kualoa Regional Park's rustic landscape
Polynesian Cultural Center
Eating freshwater prawns

The North Shore
Haleiwa's beaches and art galleries
Eating shave ice
Waimea Bay Beach surfing (world's largest ridable
    waves)
Full-moon walks in Waimea Falls Park
Sunset Beach surfing contests

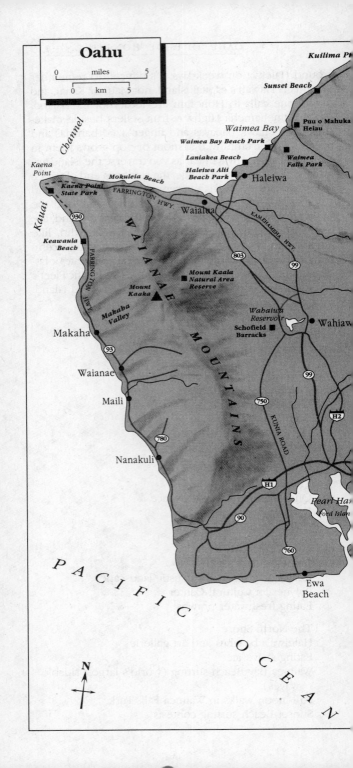

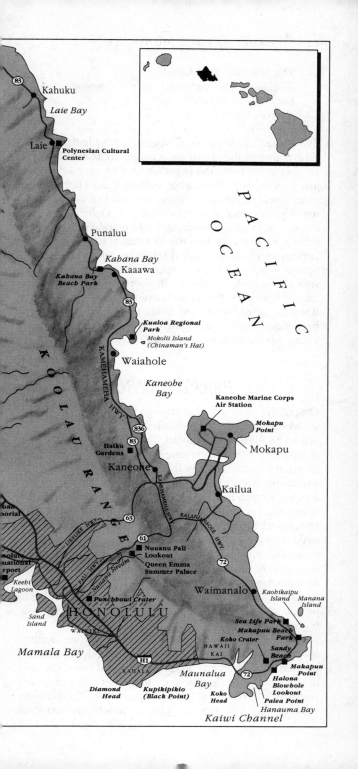

The Waianae West Coast
Wild West landscape and spirit
Kaena Point at land's end
Kaena's Ghosts' Leap

Exploring Oahu outside of Honolulu is a pleasant adventure, taking in the above six separate areas, which are all an easy drive from the city. Our tour by rental car starts just west of Honolulu. After visiting Pearl Harbor naval base, home of the best-known memorial of World War II, we skip east over Honolulu/Waikiki to Oahu's southeastern toe and visit a pristine bay and a marine park. Turning inland, we drive up into the mountains to the Pali, a cliff famous as a battleground in Hawaiian history, then travel up the Windward Coast to spend an evening at a Polynesian theme park. On the North Shore we stop at a botanical garden noted for its archaeological sites, and on the Waianea Coast, separated from the North Shore by a mountain range, we motor into the beautiful Makaha Valley, which shelters a backcountry resort.

PEARL HARBOR

One of the most dramatic trips to be made on any island anywhere is a morning or afternoon visit to Pearl Harbor's **USS *Arizona* Memorial**. The immediacy of the ship directly below you, the name list of the dead in the shrine room, the battleship flag flying at full mast can be overwhelming, even to those hardened to military sites. It is moving to watch handfuls of flower leis drop onto *Arizona* and, pulled by the outgoing tide, drift over the remains of the forward gun turret. War and its aftermath make strange bedfellows, and at Pearl Harbor two very dissimilar groups—Navy and National Park Service—act in unison to guide and transport visitors to this underwater cemetery inside an active military base. When naval warships fill the harbor, gunmetal gray and masculine in profile, the memorial, tiny and alone on Battleship Row, is an unforgettable sight.

The memorial and shoreside visitors' center, located about 10 miles west of Waikiki, are both on military property inside an important Pacific naval base. The center's grounds are open to the public, but other areas are restricted. To reach the visitors' center from Waikiki drive west on the H-1 freeway past Honolulu International

Airport, exit at the *Arizona* Memorial off-ramp onto Highway 99 (Kamehameha Highway), and drive west for a
mile; parking is free. The modern center, opened in 1980,
is an open-air facility with snack bar, bookshop, theater,
museum, and boat landing. At the information desk in the
entrance lobby, opposite a salvaged *Arizona* anchor, a
park ranger hands out tickets to a film and the boat trip to
the memorial.

As you might expect, *Arizona* is one of Hawaii's heavily
visited sites. The crowds are large with reason: The trip is
both patriotic (though some of the visitors are Japanese)
and free of charge. There's no best day to visit the memorial; every day is busy. The wait to see the 20-minute film
on the Pearl Harbor attack and then visit the memorial
can be as long as one to three hours, often longer than
the official hour-and-a-quarter tour itself, which is given
seven days a week from 8:00 A.M. to 3:00 P.M. Between
June and September, the busy summer season, arrive
early to avoid being turned away; tickets are first come,
first get. To alleviate the wait once ticket is in hand, stroll
through the exhibits at the visitors' center opposite the
theater and observe the stern-faced portraits of Admirals
Yamamoto and Nagumo, who planned and executed the
attack, then the harbor view from the center's south lawn
(the "back porch"), which faces toward the memorial and
its backdrop, Ford Island, green as parkland and housing
naval officers. Behind Ford are the distant Waianae Mountains, over which Nagumo's Zeroes flew. A boatswain's
whistle, followed by a tour number, calls visitors to their
queue.

Because *Arizona* is an aquatic graveyard, the approach
is by boat over the often murky waters of Pearl Harbor.
The ten-minute ride in a navy-operated shuttle named
Kukui or *Aloha* or *Nene* is itself worth the wait (no
civilians under 45 inches tall allowed). En route a sailor
describes the Pearl Harbor attack, speaking with military
precision about *Arizona* and her memorial, the type of
bombs dropped, the number of brothers killed, and the
fuel oil that has leaked from *Arizona* each day since the
attack at a rate of four drops per minute.

The slender memorial, spanning *Arizona* amidships
like a suspension bridge, is a work of art. Designed by
Alfred Preis, a Vienna-born architect, the sagging roofline
is symbolic, some believe, of America's post-attack depres-
sion, and the three rows of seven open-air windows each
is an eternal 21-gun salute. The reality is less romantic:

The sag distributes weight, and the openings, including the viewing well above *Arizona,* lighten the structure. Preis purposely omitted overtones of sadness to permit visitors to make their own personal responses, such as tossing flowers into the well onto waters where, in the words of Admiral Yamamoto (who opposed starting the war with the United States), Japan "awakened a sleeping giant and filled him with a terrible resolve."

The battleship that lies beneath the memorial, entombing more than one thousand officers and men in a metal sarcophagus, is unrecognizable as a warship. The superstructure is missing, and the deck guns were removed and converted to shore batteries to protect Oahu from further Japanese invasion. What is left is a naked, eerie hull mostly submerged in mud and encrusted with coral. Steel plating thicker than a human head failed to save *Arizona* from armor-piercing bombs, but tiny coral polyps, fragile as flower petals and as intricate in design as any warship, are entombing *Arizona* in a cocoon of calcareous skeletons and saving it from saltwater corrosion.

The park service tour is the only tour that allows you to *board* the memorial, but those who wish to see and not touch the memorial can take the Pearl Harbor Cruise's three-hour sight-seeing excursion. A private tour boat circles Ford Island, passes a target ship destroyed during the attack (USS *Utah*), and pauses near *Arizona* for a lei-dropping ceremony. Daily departures are at 9:15 A.M. and 1:15 P.M. from Fisherman's Wharf at Kewalo Basin, opposite Honolulu's Ward Warehouse shopping center; Tel: 536-3641.

To immerse yourself in more naval memorabilia of the World War II variety, walk from the *Arizona* Memorial's shoreside visitors' center to the nearby USS *Bowfin,* a retired combat submarine floating at harbor's edge. Unlike *Arizona,* destroyed in the first moments of conflict, *Bowfin* conducted nine war patrols and sank 44 ships. Speed is what visitors ask about: *Bowfin* went 21 knots surfaced, 10 submerged, the reverse of nuclear subs, which are faster submerged than surfaced. The walk through the brightly lit interior is a delightful experience, provided the carry-on headphones, activated as you enter each compartment, play the recorded message describing the sub's interior anatomy from torpedo room to captain's quarters. Because of the tightly confined space no one is allowed inside the conning tower—the brain of the sub's combat operations—but the conning tower of

Bowfin's sister sub, *Parche,* can be seen in nearby Bowfin Park (be sure to look through the periscope). Time spent on board *Bowfin* complements an *Arizona* visit by enabling you to see firsthand a naval vessel that fought a war denied *Arizona* and its crew.

The **Pacific Submarine Museum**, adjacent to *Bowfin,* is worth a walk through; most interesting are the cutaway models of modern subs and the hands-on displays of electrical devices used to locate enemy targets. The open-air snack area, surrounded by cigar-shaped torpedoes, is a shady spot to pause and reflect on naval history or simply drink a Coke. Along with *Bowfin,* the museum is a memorial to the 3,500 U.S. submariners who, like *Nautilus*'s Captain Nemo in Jules Verne's *Twenty Thousand Leagues under the Sea,* lie submerged forever in dark waters.

THE SOUTHEASTERN COAST

In dramatic contrast to Pearl Harbor's naval landscape are the beautiful oceanside parklands on the opposite side of Honolulu, east past Waikiki and Diamond Head along Kalanianaole Highway (Highway 72) as it rims Hanauma Bay, parallels a shore of lava cliffs, coral-sand beaches, and tiny coves, then curves past a picturesque red-topped lighthouse on Makapuu Point, Oahu's easternmost tip. The reward for exploring this shoreline is a sense of geographical wildness almost within rifle shot of Honolulu itself.

Hanauma Bay

A geographical oddity, Hanauma is a volcanic crater with a bay inside, formed when ocean waves eroded the crater's seaward rim and created an amphitheater of coral and sand. Because Hanauma is only seven miles east of Diamond Head (past Honolulu's exclusive Kahala district, Maunalua Bay, and Hawaii Kai Marina), it's very popular with residents and visitors alike, so arrive early for a choice beach spot. On holidays thousands descend into the crater, forcing lifeguards to cordon off their square of sand with conical traffic dividers. Historically you will be in good company, because in the old days royal daytrippers from Honolulu came to this beach, and King

Kamehameha V fished in the bay itself, now an underwater marine park.

Perhaps Hanauma's most striking feature from a beach sitter's point of view is **Koko Head**, towering above the bay's rim and forming a rugged backdrop for snorkelers on their downward trek from the parking lot. Even veteran lifeguards are awestruck by the topography, which is, without exaggeration, ethereal. Kohelepelepe, the old name for Koko Head's neighbor, **Koko Crater**, means labia minora, and the crater was once the site in myth where sensual bait was used to lure a rapist to southeast Oahu. If other place-name connotations interest you, try arm wrestling (a sport of ancient Hawaii) atop a picnic table here; Hanauma means "hand-wrestling bay."

Despite the bay's domesticated appearance, drownings do occur, about ten a year, most being Japanese snorkelers unfamiliar with bay water. Curiously, Hanauma's three best-known landmarks are the places where lifeguards most frequently find swimmers in trouble: Witches' Brew, where strong surf boils in caldronlike swirls; Toilet Bowl, a pool that flushes like a bathroom commode; and Keyhole, a swimming area where the reef is shaped like an Alice in Wonderland peephole. Keyhole is a popular fish-feeding area; frozen green peas are the best feed, not carrots, which the Moorish idols and Achilles tangs dislike. Stay within the bay to avoid the notorious Molokai Express, a strong current that will take you not to Molokai as the names implies but on a one-way trip to meet the god of waters.

Halona

The short and scenic drive from Hanauma east to Halona Cove is stunning, making it difficult to keep an eye on traffic. Overhead looms Koko Crater, and below Kaiwi Channel's incoming surf collides head on with a shoreline of ancient lava. During the breeding and calving season (December to April), pods of humpback whales blow and breach, some cruising near Hanauma Bay. On the horizon, beyond the farthest visible humpback, is a group of neighboring islands, Molokai, Lanai, and Maui. **Halona Blowhole Lookout**, though crowded between 9:00 and 11:00 A.M. with tour buses, tee-shirt hawkers, and Krishna devotees with vegetarian snacks and guru guidebooks, is an enjoyable stop. The name Halona means "peering place." The blowhole, an appropriate landmark on this whale-watching coast, expels sea spray with the same dramatic showmanship with which a whale exhales breath. Opposite the blowhole is Halona Cove, wedged between ocean-cut cliffs and capped with a white-sand beach. In this romantic spot, reached by a downward winding trail, filmmakers shot scenes for *From Here to Eternity.*

The Makapuu Point Area

Makapuu Beach Park, one of Oahu's best-known body-surfing beaches, is a pocket of sand alongside the high-way overlooked by a distant lighthouse. The surf's slow roll and excellent shorebreak is ideal for bodysurfing; the sport is so popular here that board surfing is prohibited. A red flag signals offshore risk; when it is posted ask a lifeguard for the safest place to swim. The two offshore islands are Kaohikaipu and Manana (the larger), which is nicknamed "Rabbit Island" because a plantation owner once raised rabbits here. Both are bird sanctuaries where thousands of seabirds nest and breed. Opposite Manana Island, high atop the Koolau Range's Kamehame Ridge, hang gliders launch from the awesome "Green Wall" and share the Makapuu and, to the north, **Waimanolo Beach** trade winds with black-winged frigate birds and white-tailed tropic birds.

If you visit the North Shore's Waimea Falls Park (see below) and wish to complement your resulting cache of botanical knowledge with insights into marine biology and whale ecology, Waimea's sister park, **Sea Life Park**, is within walking distance of Makapuu's beach, and is the main man-made attraction on this coast. Besides the usual oceanarium entertainment—splashing dolphins, sleeping turtles, waddling penguins—numerous informative lec-tures are scheduled throughout the day explaining the fascinating marine environment that surrounds Hawaii. A one-room museum devoted to the Pacific whaling era is next to the aptly named **Spouter Deck Bar**. The **Galley Restaurant** (dinner Thursdays, Fridays, and Sundays, with a view toward the sea lions' feeding pool) has Hawaiian victuals such as *kalua* pig, *lomilomi* salmon, and a local favorite, *poi* (taro), very edible and nutritious but disliked by many *haole,* including Mark Twain: "A villainous mix-ture, almost tasteless before it ferments and too sour for a luxury afterwards."

A worthwhile excursion is Sea Life's behind-the-scenes

tour, offered daily and limited to 16. The tour enters off-limits areas where dolphins reside, watched over by trainers carrying buckets of dead herring and smelt. The tour's top attraction is Kekaimalu (Peaceful Sea), a hybrid cross between an Atlantic bottle-nosed dolphin and a false killer whale. Called a wholphin, Kekaimalu, a *wahine* (female), has characteristics of both her dolphin mother and torpedo-shaped father. Circling in her tank, she frequently breaches to eye onlookers. The wholphin's training program is still infantile: fish-snack rewards for jumping and tail slapping.

A must see for fish lovers here is the aquarium: Descend three fathoms on a spiral ramp and view Hawaiian reef fish swimming behind acrylic windows. Undersea marine life, once Hawaii's best-kept secret, is no longer the exclusive domain of snorkelers and scuba divers; at Sea Life, landlubbers can view in comfort. The colorful *uhu* (parrot fish) swims here (old-time fishermen climbed the cliffs below Makapuu's lighthouse to make offerings to a stone image devoted to *uhu,* a fish favored by the gods). Primeval hammerhead sharks also circle the aquarium, eyeballs set at head's edge—a curious coincidence, as Makapuu means "bulging eye." (The mother of King Kamehameha I, when she was pregnant, had an appetite for raw sharks' eyes.)

Be sure also to look for Hawaii's state fish at the aquarium; its shape resembles a human nose, in particular that of Captain Cook, Hawaii's European discoverer. A pre–World War II song sung to tourists immortalized the triggerfish's name: "I want to go back to my little grass shack in Ke-ala-ke-kua Hawaii where the *humuhumu-nukunukuapuaa* go swimming by."

THE PALI LOOKOUT AREA

On the northern outskirts of Honolulu, past Punchbowl Crater and the Royal Mausoleum, the **Pali Highway** (61) on its upward journey into the Koolau Range parallels Nuuanu Stream, which flows seaward through dense rain forest, the last refuge of Oahu's endemic land birds. A right turn near Nuuanu Park leads to the **Queen Emma Summer Palace**, a wood-shuttered house with a wide veranda supported by six Doric columns erected on cleared rain forest as green as Maori jade. Here Emma Rooke, who married King Kamehameha IV in 1856, escaped from Honolulu's summer heat and enjoyed short reprieves from downtown court life that (by her design) resembled the court etiquette of Europe. Nowadays visitors to her cozy retreat are constantly confronted with visual reminders of monarchical Europe's strong influence on Hawaiian royalty, and especially on Emma, who named her son Albert after a prince of England.

A house tour offers a brief glimpse of Hawaii's own Victorian era. Knowledgeable Daughters of Hawaii, charmingly enthusiastic about Emma and her vanished world, guide you room to room, chatting about unusual vases, koa-wood furniture, and deceased kings and queens. Typical of Emma are the mementos she kept: her son's wooden cradle shaped like a canoe, her first piano, built in 1801, and gifts from European aristocrats, including Queen Victoria, whom she met in 1865 at Windsor Castle. A special keepsake is a locket bracelet containing a picture of the English queen and a lock of her hair. Outside the house are the stone remains of Emma's kitchen, carpeted by an overgrowth of vines. Viewed from the bench beneath a nearby rainbow shower tree, the ruins resemble a green Victorian hedge. The house is open daily from 9:00 A.M. to 4:00 P.M.

Nuuanu Pali Lookout

Returning to the Pali Highway: Oahu's landmark viewpoint, Nuuanu Pali Lookout, is only minutes away, reached by an uphill side road lined with ironwood trees. "The celebrated view," wrote Victorian traveller Isabella Bird, "burst on us with overwhelming effect." As Bird discovered, the view is unforgettable, the history more so. Over this thousand-foot precipice in 1795 tumbled an entire army of Oahu defenders, fighting with their faces toward present-day Honolulu Harbor and forced backward and upward by the warriors and European gunners of the invading Kamehameha, Hawaii's great warrior-king. Puiwa ("to startle"), a lane near Emma's palace, is a subtle reminder of the battle, the name describing the noise made by Kamehameha's cannon, fired by John Young, Emma's grandfather.

From the lookout over the Windward Coast you will see a peninsula jutting seaward, separating the twin towns of Kaneohe (left) and Kailua (right), each spread like aerial reconnaissance maps on the flatlands below. On the peninsula is Kaneohe Marine Corps Air Station, built on the site where Kane, one of Polynesia's most powerful gods, created the first Hawaiian.

The Haiku Gardens

A drive east, down past the lookout to **Haiku Gardens** restaurant on Haiku Road in Kaneohe, is a perfect conclusion to an over-the-*pali* excursion. The restaurant, which overlooks the garden, is open for lunch and dinner, but the garden, not the food, is the attraction. Though the place is well known to Oahuans, you will be certain that you have discovered a private oasis known only to bridal couples and botanists. Saturday is the best day to observe the weddings held in thatched-roof huts that are hidden in vegetation. Even if you don't eat at the restaurant, make the five-minute walk around the garden; the view from the dense foliage upward toward the Koolau Range is astonishing. The bright green breadfruit tree, nature's edible gift to the Polynesians, grows near the pond, sharing the garden's coolness with an over-the-water gazebo. The fruit has a texture like bread when baked or roasted (seedling breadfuit trees were the cargo carried on board William Bligh's ship HMS *Bounty*).

(The Haiku Gardens can also be a stop if you are driving from Honolulu to the Windward Coast on the coastal highway east around Makapuu Point.)

THE WINDWARD COAST

Viewed from the Nuuanu Pali Lookout, the distant Windward Coast headlands to the north of Kaneohe Bay appear both remote and mysterious, a place where legend pinpoints the birth of Oahu itself. The island's creation, the main event in the mythology of this eastern Oahu coastline—reached from Honolulu via the Likelike Highway (Highway 63) or, more roundabout, the Pali Highway (Highway 61; see also the Pali Lookout section, above) or the Kalanianaole Highway (discussed above in the Southeastern Coast section)—occurred long before the arrival of the first voyaging canoes from present-day French Polynesia: A brother and sister with magical hands locked fingers and united the Koolau and Waianae mountain ranges, creating Oahu and a shoreline of beaches and bays. Today, this coastline, still rich in legends, shelters the bays of Laie, Kahana, and Kaneohe, cooled by Windward Oahu's trademark, the incoming trade winds.

Kualoa Regional Park

An area with a special outdoor aura is Kaneohe Bay's Kualoa Regional Park, a favorite hangout of Hawaiians who prefer the simple amenities of fresh water, park toilets, picnic tables, and isolation from fast-food stops and gas stations. Mist clouds the nearby mountains, and "Local Boy" is likely to be tattooed on the arms of partying lads holding, against rules, cans of beer.

As you enter Kualoa on Kamehameha Highway coming up from Kaneohe to the south, notice the Hawaii Visitors Bureau's historical marker (a cloaked Hawaiian) calling attention to the beach from which the double-hulled canoe, *Hokulea,* was launched in 1976. When *Hokulea* (Star of Gladness) returned to Kualoa in 1987 after several successful Polynesian voyages, a Hawaiian chanter welcomed it ashore: "Arise and look to the faraway seas . . . here comes the worthy canoe." Because chiefs' children were taught beside the beach, canoes of yesteryear lowered their sails in reverence when passing.

The circular lava wall at the end of the parking lot protects an old-time fishpond, purposely camouflaged beneath trees to discourage human intrusion, much to the delight of songbirds nesting among the branches. Such ponds were filled with mullet and milkfish, favorite foods of Hawaiian chiefs, who believed guardian water spirits, called *moo* (MO-oh), inhabited fishponds and appeared as beautiful girls or mermaids combing their hair. In precontact times the open land around Kualoa was known as Apua, the fish basket.

Kualoa's most curious landmark, said to be the severed tail of a water dragon, is the offshore island of Mokolii (Little Dragon), which dominates the ocean view. In Hawaiian mythology, Hiiaka, a sister of Pele, killed a water dragon, cut off its tail, and cast it seaward, creating the island. The most popular non-Hawaiian name for this island, nonetheless, is **Chinaman's Hat**. Artist Dean Howell's painting of a gargantuan Chinese submerged beneath the island, his hat protruding above the waterline and humpback whales feeding from his rice bowl, colorfully visualizes Mokolii's nickname. A table beside Kualoa's Hokuleu Beach, facing Mokolii, is a perfect spot for a picnic.

As you leave Kualoa and drive north toward Kahana Bay, the surrounding landscape is called Kaaawa, named after a yellow reef fish in the family Labridae. Four roadside parks, one named after the bonefish, another of them after a marsh, flank the roadway, as does an elementary school. This is "night marcher" country, where, centuries before Halloween's ghosts and goblins captured Hawaii's fancy, processions of dead spirits walked at night, and human beings who happened to block their passage or addressed them without humility died before sunrise.

Disregard Nordhoff's outdated advice to travel with a cook outside Honolulu, and eat at the **Crouching Lion Inn**, four miles up the coast from Kualoa park, and named after a lion-faced rock on an overhead cliff. Formerly a family residence, the inn dates from 1927 and is built from U.S. West Coast timber shipped to Hawaii aboard one of the Islands' last lumber schooners. The Hawaiian-born *wahine* (woman) bartender has worked 30 years at the inn; a not-so-Hawaiian vodka sign behind the bar reads "Smirnoff loves Hawaii." Try the bar's Maui Lager, a fine beer brewed in Hawaii, or nibble the restaurant's "mile-high" coconut pie. Be warned that the crowd is not local—it's usually Japanese, American, and Canadian—and at noon a procession of tour buses and rental cars arrives. Nonetheless, there is decent food here at reasonable prices, friendly service, and an ocean view, which overshadow the heavy tourist trade. (Reservations are recommended for dinner; Tel: 237-8511.) A converted four-car garage houses a gift shop, selling Waikiki-style souvenirs—aloha shirts and non-Hawaiian handicrafts. Skip it and chat with the yardman or friendly neighbors who people-watch on the premises.

Kahana Bay

A lovely curve farther north along the highway brings you to **Kahana Bay Beach Park** on the shores of a cozy bay fronting an undeveloped state park. Immediately apparent is the coolness that engulfs your car, as if you were entering a rain forest. Kahana is a place to sit quietly on the beach and meditate about *akule* (big-eyed scad), one of Hawaii's most delicious fish, easily found in Honolulu's Farmer's Market or in supermarkets. The Hawaiians who once lived in the valley behind the beach netted *akule* from canoes and built fishing shrines on bluffs surrounding the bay. A dense thicket of ironwood trees—the same species seen in Honolulu's Kapiolani Park—shades the beach, making this a fine spot to read Jack London's short story "The Water Baby," in which London and a Hawaiian fisherman talk dreams while afloat in a canoe: "Perhaps it is that you are a dream," remarks London, "and that I and sky and sea and the iron-hard land are dreams, all dreams." Few visitors know that fishponds once flanked Kahana Bay and the remains of one, Huilua, can still be seen.

Country & western connoisseurs will wish to pause at the **Paniolo Café**, between Kahana Bay and Punaluu Beach Park, where beer is served in mason jars, brandy-laced coffee is named after Willie Nelson, and he-man hamburgers come with french fries that would please Gabby Hayes. The word *paniolo* means cowboy in Hawaiian, and boots and Stetsons are very welcome, though the noontime clientele is mostly the tour-van trade. The café's special is sometimes rattlesnake chili, a dish mainly for the "I tasted rattlesnake" set; it's rarely available because Texas rattlers hibernate in winter, thus avoiding the chili bowl. Tables outside the café are under a shade tree growing beside the bowsprit of a derelict schooner.

• The Polynesian Cultural Center

It's a seven-mile drive from the Paniolo's beer-filled mason jars past Punaluu Beach Park to Laie's sober Polynesian Cultural Center, a money-making theme park run by the Church of Jesus Christ of Latter-day Saints (familiarly, the Mormons). This is sanitized Polynesia, blemish free and highly manicured, yet exceptionally educational, even for veteran Pacific travellers weaned on Frederick O'Brien's *White Shadows in the South Seas* and *Atolls of the Sun*. More than a passing glimpse is demanded here, as the showcase is Polynesia-wide, containing seven re-created villages (six Polynesian, one Melanesian), each with its own cultural uniqueness. New for 1990 is an ultra-large movie screen featuring a South Pacific travelogue, *Polynesian Odyssey*, grander, the gods of Polynesia might think, than Odysseus's original Mediterranean voyage.

Despite a smorgasbord of dance extravaganzas, exotic-food tastings, and canoe rides (which can be shoulder to shoulder, sardine style), the cultural center's real Polynesian experience is simply walking from village to village, over waterways and bridges, observing the excellent thatch and wood craftsmanship of the dwellings, and listening to a Samoan, Tongan, or Hawaiian explain the foods and handicrafts native to his or her homeland. Some of the highlights are watching fire started by rubbing sticks, a Maori war canoe that was carved for King George V of England, and a paper mulberry tree, used to make *tapa* (bark cloth). Always popular is the Tahitian village, where dancers who fulfill the Western idea of South Seas beauty do the hip-shaking *tamure*. (One guidebook to Hawaii recently featured a Tahitian dancer on its title page.) Paul Gauguin, whose *Two Tahitian Women on the Beach* hangs in Honolulu's Academy of Arts, described Tahitian women as "possessing something that is indescribably penetrating and mysterious."

The Marquesan village will be of special interest to travellers familiar with Herman Melville's *Typee: A Peep at Polynesian Life,* which recounted his stay in the cannibalistic Marquesas in the 1840s. His island sweetheart is the enchanting Fayaway, who rides naked in the bow of his canoe, transforming her *kahu* (robe) into a sail—a literary scene that has bred generations of South Sea romantics. You won't find Fayaway in this re-created village, but elderly ladies weaving palm-leaf baskets near the tattooing hut will answer questions. Strangely, a blowup portrait of a tattooed Marquesan displayed inside the tattooing hut is not a Marquesan at all, but the French beachcomber Jean Baptise Cabri, whom the Marquesans tattooed on face as well as body. When Cabri returned to Europe, he performed Polynesian dances, exhibited his tattoos, and denied eating "long pig," a Marquesan hors d'oeuvre made from sliced human flesh wrapped in leaves and baked in earth ovens.

Set aside ample time to explore the cultural center's many attractions; a visit can quickly become an all-afternoon experience, continuing until sunset or even moonrise depending on the ticket chosen. (Gates open at 12:30 P.M., Mondays through Saturdays; closed Sundays; reservations required for some packages; Tel: 293-3333 or 800-367-7060.) An all-you-can-eat dinner is served at the **Gateway Restaurant,** a massive eatery with Maori birdman figures and replicas of Easter Island stone sculptures; or you can opt for a fancy luau with an *imu* (earth oven) ceremony, roast pig, Hawaiian music, and hula dancing, the evening ending with a 90-minute Polynesian revue with flashy stage effects. The downside of all this is the sheer tourist volume, and a *kapu* (taboo) on alcoholic beverages, including *kava,* the mouth-numbing elixir made from a pepper-plant root and renowned as the national drink of Polynesia and Melanesia. Of course you couldn't drive, or even find your car, after drinking from two or three kava-filled coconut shells; kava is notorious for encouraging the left leg to travel north while the right proceeds south.

Kahuku

Beyond the cultural center, where northernmost Oahu bends around to the west toward the North Shore's Sunset Beach, is the old sugar-plantation town of Kahuku. The town's charm is its atmosphere of remoteness, that far-from-the-freeway feeling worth its weight in traveller's checks. There are two reasons to stop here: to eat breakfast at Huevos and to buy Amorient Aquafarm shrimp and prawns.

Huevos, Spanish for eggs, is hidden in a cluster of wood-frame plantation houses and isn't your usual easy-to-find eatery: Turn right at the Huevos sign between the Kahuku Supermarket and the sugar mill; follow the dirt road, with potholes, into the "main camp" neighborhood and you're there. The owners (admirably) have shunned the tour-bus trade to protect the neighbors from overexposure to outsiders and gas fumes. An omelette made with Portuguese sausages is a popular breakfast with the *akamai kamaainas* (locals in the know) who eat here. At **Amorient Aquafarm,** the Island-grown shrimp (saltwater) and prawns (freshwater) come cooked or uncooked, fresh from the ponds. A small shrimp cocktail is served on the premises in a plastic cup. The roadside store, with a backdrop of aquaculture ponds and crustacean-stealing birds, is labeled "Royal Hawaiian Shrimp & Prawns," flies the U.S. and Hawaiian flags, and closes at 5:00 P.M. It's easy to find, on the outskirts of Kahuku. Outback Oahu? This is as close as it gets.

THE NORTH SHORE

The North Shore, the Windward Coast's neighboring shoreline, is beach, surf, and shave-ice country, where the surf rises in 30-foot "monster" waves, and where on weekends escapists from Honolulu come to enjoy the laid-back, suntanned atmosphere and "talk story" about the shore's choice surfing spots—Rocky Point, Off-the-Wall, the Banzai Pipeline. (To get to the North Shore direct from Honolulu take the H-1 to Pearl Harbor, the H-2 to Wahiawa, and Highway 99 northward.)

Haleiwa

The main village in this area is Haleiwa, a town of rustic charm struggling to cope with weekend crowds, its growing fame as Oahu's last historic town, and the difficult task of keeping the country in Haleiwa's country atmosphere. At sunrise, visitors departing from the Turtle Bay Hilton to the north, or early-bird arrivals from Honolulu, can hear roosters crow beside the Haleiwa post office, and can eat breakfast across the street at **Café Haleiwa**, an unpretentious place with handwritten breakfast specials thumb-tacked to the front door. A snapshot of a record-holding snow skier who stopped for pancakes decorates the wall; the windows look out on the west coast's Waianae Mountains. The conversation is surfing ("waves 10 to 12") and the breakfast large.

The town's heartland is the area around **Alii Beach Park**, with its well-known "Haleiwa" surf break. An hour can be spent simply watching the surf from shore or walking the black-rock jetty sprinkled with fishermen, where views of beach, surfers, and the Waianae Mountains fading seaward toward Kaena Point are superb. Between the park and Anahulu Bridge is the Seaview Haleiwa, serving swordfish steaks and offering almost no sea view. Historically, what's of interest here isn't the food or the view but real estate: The restaurant is built on the site of the long-demolished Haleiwa Hotel (1899 to 1928), which made the town's name famous. This was Oahu's first luxury accommodation, accessible by train from Honolulu on a railroad that circled Kaena Point. Nothing remains of the hotel except the name it gave to the area, Haleiwa, "house of the frigate bird." Nearby is **Jameson's by the Sea**, offering a menu of fish entrées, the frigate bird's favorite snack. Local fishermen provide the catch that includes *ulua* (crevalle; old-time Hawaiians preferred the liquid around the eyeballs), *opakapaka* (blue snapper, a deep-sea fish favored by foreigners), and *mahimahi* (dolphinfish). Hawaiians like this last fish because the male has a vertical head, like the bow of a sailing ship. The lanai (terrace) fronting the bar has an ocean view, and the colorful sunset, not listed among the entrées, is free.

Visiting Haleiwa and not eating shave ice is as criminal as touring Burgundy or Tuscany and refusing wine. Each day in quaint stores fronting the highway skilled shave-ice makers crush ice into finely shaved crystals, compress it into snowballs, and drench it with flavored syrup. Just about everyone goes for shave ice to **M. Matsúmoto Grocery Store**, in town since 1951, and king of North Shore shave ice. Inside are an antique-looking ice machine, a hand-pull adding machine, and old-fashioned, glass display cases filled with candy and sundries. On rainy days newspapers carpet the floor. Artist Guy Buffet, known for his whimsical watercolors, captures the charm of Matsumoto in a painting of the store's shave-ice clientele: surfers, tourists, and shark-jaw sellers. Try strawberry, a local favorite, or, for the more adventurous, shave ice with sweet *azuki* beans; be sure you ask for ice cream at the bottom of your shave ice.

Very close to Matsumoto is **Liliuokalani Protestant Church**, erected where the North Shore's first missionary church stood. Enter beneath the lava-rock archway leading into the churchyard and walk to the cemetery, where gravestones, some garlanded with wilted leis, some tumbledown, memorialize North Shore citizens who died as long ago as 1830. Inside the church—no shave ice allowed—is a clock presented in 1892 by Hawaii's last monarch, Queen Liliuokalani, who wrote the soft farewell "Aloha Oe." The clock's hours are represented by the 12 letters of her name, N minutes to K is five minutes to seven o'clock. Outside, look at the church's steeple: The metal bird atop the weather vane is a frigate bird.

Haleiwa is a growing art community, with plenty of galleries to occupy time off the beach. The tiny **Fettig Art Gallery**, specializing in Island scenes and housed in a former bank building (vault included), neighbors the Seaview Haleiwa. A two-minute walk away is the **Wyland Galleries of Hawaii**, opened in 1988 by Hawaiian muralpainter Wyland, opposite the Haleiwa Shopping Plaza. Wyland's themes are marine, and he is noted for his "whaling walls," three large, outdoor murals on Oahu. **The Pacific Island Arts Gallery**, near the town's only traffic signal, sells the work of a dozen or so local artists.

To discover your basic, down-home country bar and back-street, mom-and-pop grocery store, drive south to

Waialua, an old sugar-plantation town hidden in a sea of sugarcane. Daily, like clockwork, regulars assemble at the **Sugar Bar and Restaurant** inside a restored bank building shaded by monkeypod and *kukui* (candlenut) trees. One regular (known as "The King") has his own parking space and barstool, and like his fellow drinkers, likes to brag that the bar stores its brews in the bank's vault, safe from fantasied beer bandits. A grouchy-looking bust of Ludwig van Beethoven, the owner's favorite composer, stares out at the customers, who prefer country & western and Hawaiian music.

A few streets away, within smelling distance of a sugar mill that still sounds the old curfew whistle at 8:00 P.M., is **R. Fujioka & Sons Ltd.** grocery store, a family-run business with road dust on the canned beans and a church pew beside the doorway offering soda-pop drinkers a fine view of the twin gas pumps. Like native land birds, the mom-and-pop store is an endangered species on Oahu, and survivors such as Fujioka are state treasures, a world apart from Waikiki's convenience groceries.

Waimea

Returning to Haleiwa, cross the Anahulu Bridge, built around 1921, and continue east to a horseshoe bend in the road that surrounds **Waimea Bay Beach Park**, a small, intimate place where newlyweds smooch beneath coconut trees and, when the waves are high, Hawaii's best surfers challenge the world's largest ridable waves, the "cathedral peaks" of this sport. The beach and shorebreak are spectacular; once you've seen Waimea, you'll never forget it. Centuries ago no Hawaiians swam here, fearing the wrath of the gods; only the nocturnal *menehune,* mythical midgets, ventured onto the bay to fish (their night-lights are still visible to those area residents that believe strongly enough). The tan-colored landmark nearby is the bell tower of Saints Peter and Paul's Mission Church. The tower is a former storage bin for the gray-blue lava rocks quarried from the Waimea shoreline; inside are piles of stones left over from the tower's rock-crushing past. The mission's name is a volcanic tribute to apostles Peter and Paul, the "rocks" of Christianity.

Waimea Falls Park, tucked in the valley behind the bay, is an arboretum and botanical garden built around Hawaiian historical sites. Archaeologists, digging near floral gardens and meadows, probe temple foundations and the remains of chiefs' residences for clues to the North Shore's ancient past, while, nearby, visitors attend Hawaiian cultural performances and view endangered plant species—all within walking distance. Peacocks, show-offs not native to Oahu, strut the grounds in front of the **Proud Peacock Restaurant**. The restaurant, like the peacocks, has a somewhat captive clientele, and diners suffer few disappointments here. Hawaii's state flower, the hibiscus, grows in abundance here, and a fragrant garden has lei flowers from each island. Ask to see the yellow *ilima,* Oahu's official lei flower, once worn by Hawaiian royalty.

A must for an autumn itinerary is the annual **Makahiki Festival**, a two-day celebration with ancient-style hula, lei making, and Hawaiian games held the first weekend in October. Captain Cook first came to the island of Hawaii during a *makahiki* festival devoted to Lono, a fertility god who carried in his penis the sweet potato's sweetness. The park cultivates sweet potatoes, and there are reconstructed potato mounds (an old cultivation method) near a burial temple. Once they've checked into the Turtle Bay Hilton (see below) and dined, perhaps at the Proud Peacock, those visitors who enjoy moonbeams illuminating their skin in a tropical setting shouldn't miss the park's free, full-moon walk each month. Moonwalkers stroll past night-blooming plants, croaking frogs, and nocturnal birds on a one-hour safari to the park's waterfall, used in daytime for Acapulco-style diving shows. Two rules apply: no nude dancing in moonbeams and no skinny-dipping under the falls (there's no lifeguard). Crowds can be large, mosquitoes troublesome (take repellent), but the moonlight on the waterfall will delight the romantic and, of course, the lunatic.

Above the park, on a *pali* (cliff) behind the Peter and Paul tower, is **Puu o Mahuka Heiau** (Hill of Escape), Oahu's largest sacrificial *heiau* (temple). As meaningful to ancient Hawaiians as St. Peter's basilica in Rome is to modern Roman Catholics, this *heiau,* though now reduced to knee-high walls of rubble, remains an active spiritual center for many Hawaiians. To find the *heiau,* turn right off Kamehameha Highway onto Pupukea Road (beside the Foodland supermarket), drive the curved road to the *heiau* turnoff sign, and minutes later disembark at this sacred destination. The site affords a superb view of Waimea Beach, and there is a cliff-top listening post for voices of the sacrificial priests that, say Hawaiians, still haunt the countryside. In 1792 several British sea-men, captured while taking water from the Waimea River, died here, victims of sacrifice. The leaf-wrapped stones that you see scattered about the temple are *ti*-leaf offer-ings, made by Hawaiians and knowledgeable visitors. A small piece of temple rock is wrapped in a green *ti* leaf and placed on the walls' remains, bringing good fortune to the person to whom the offering is dedicated.

Sunset Beach

If you prefer sand, another fine surfing beach, Sunset Beach, is three miles up the coast northeast from the *heiau,* overlooked by a COMSAT satellite station and a stone that president-minded cartographers believe re-sembles a toothless George Washington. Like other big-wave beaches, happiness at Sunset is measured in surf footage and in the frequency with which surf champion-ships occur here, such as the Hard Rock Café's World Cup of Surfing, Marui Pipeline Masters, and Billabong Pro. At Sunset Beach, the precontact Hawaiians who invented surfing (they called it *hee nalu,* wave sliding) paddled seaward on huge koa-wood boards and risked their bodies in high water. Today a nearby chiropractic clinic (the sign has a life-size image of a man's back) cares for Sunset's victims. Even if you don't surf, ask a lifeguard about swimming conditions, which may be hazardous. These tower-sitting watermen are paid to protect you, and their main complaint is that people seldom ask for advice—or ignore it when it's offered. Also keep in mind that weekend traffic between Sunset Beach and Haleiwa is a growing problem, and on a crowded Saturday, with surfers' cars jammed along the roadside and Honolulu day-trippers escaping from the city, the Haleiwa to Waimea Bay to Sunset Beach drive can be frustratingly slow, even bumper-to-bumper dur-ing midday. A highway bypass is planned for the early 1990s to free Haleiwa of nontourist traffic. In the mean-time, unless you prefer the auto-congested atmosphere of weekends, the best time to visit is on weekdays.

Farther north of Sunset Beach is **Kuilima Point**, a finger of grass-covered lava that supports on its back, like a mythi-cal tortoise, the **Turtle Bay Hilton** (off the Kamehameha Highway), the only resort hotel on the North Shore.

There's nothing special architecturally about the hotel's three-wing main structure, but the location is remote— it's as far north as you can drive—and the isolated, yet still posh, environment is appealing to those who prefer a low-keyed, outback accommodation. A night or two here is an excellent way to explore the North Shore in detail, allowing for early morning drives to Haleiwa and the shore's beaches, or a leisurely afternoon visit to the Polynesian Cultural Center in Laie (see the Windward Coast section).

The hotel's **Palm Terrace** restaurant and Green Turtle Lounge are welcome retreats after a beach stroll at Kuilima Cove or a golf game played on a course approved by Arnold Palmer. The restaurant overlooks the bay and distant hills spiked with white propellers converting wind power into electricity. The lounge, beside the Palm Terrace, unfortunately has no view. Its reptilian namesake, *honu,* the green sea turtle, is an endangered species in Hawaii; should you see a bay-swimming *honu* consider yourself blessed by sea gods.

OAHU'S WEST: THE WAIANAE COAST

Dry and rocky, Oahu's west coast doesn't evoke love at first sight or dazzle the senses with postcard lushness. Unlike the North Shore, endearment to its benefits takes time.

The area stretches from Nanakuli to Makaha to Kaena Point and is reached from Honolulu by the H-1 freeway, which loops around Pearl Harbor and intersects Highway 93 (Farrington Highway) near Nanakuli. The key words to remember when travelling here are *makaha* (savage) and *kaena* (heat). As these ancient names indicate, the Waianae Coast is Oahu's "Wild West," the last bastion of the rough-and-ready spirit absent from Honolulu's more affluent areas such as Kahala and Hawaii Kai. While buses filled with luau-goers head for destinations here near an industrial park, and there are a profusion of army and navy installations in the area, independent travellers can golf, surf-watch, and simply tour by car. Because this *is* a rough-and-ready area, though, *haole* should proceed with caution. Only one major hotel serves the area, the Sheraton Makaha, but massive resort development, especially for golf courses, is planned south of Makaha, and already local land-use controversies have surfaced.

Makaha

Makaha is *the* beach here, though compared to the North Shore's most attractive beaches it appears rather ragged, and butts close against Farrington Highway. During winter months the beach suffers from erosion due to the heavy surf, but in summer the sand returns, rejuvenating the shoreline. For years Makaha hosted a big-wave surf contest, but that event faded, replaced by a community benefit called Buffalo's Big Board Surfing Classic, named for local surfer Richard "Buffalo" Keaulana, who crewed on *Hokulea,* the replica Polynesian voyaging canoe. The long-board competition is held in February or March, depending on surf conditions. This is a back-to-yesterday event, a fun affair replaying the era when long boards (ten feet plus) cruised the surf unleashed to ankles, and top surfers won waxes and boards, not prize money and photogenic kisses from bikini-clad models.

Directly behind the beach is Makaha Valley, its centuries-old rock walls sheltering the **Sheraton Makaha Resort** and surrounding golf course. The valley's name, which means "savage," comes from a community of bandits who preyed on west coast wayfarers. Lookouts shouted "High tide!" when travel groups too strong to rob approached and "Low tide!" for likely victims. Nowadays the valley's loudest shouts are golf warnings ("Fore!") and quacks from the ducks floating in the pond beside the hotel's driving range.

The hidden Sheraton Makaha, in contrast to Waianae's rustic coastline, is a sophisticated oasis of palm trees surrounding open-air pavilions and low-rise cottages with private lanais. The surrounding cliffs are a mountain watcher's delight—they may make you forget that planned drive to nearby Makaha Beach as you stroll the grounds with an eye toward the skyline.

For a quiet drink, share the lobby lounge with returning horseback riders fresh from trails circling the remains of a coffee plantation and *paniolo* (cowboy) ranch; for lunch try the **Pikake Café** beside the swimming pool; and for dinner the elegant **Kaala Room,** named after Waianae's highest mountain peak. Though the hotel is strong on tennis and horseback riding, guests are rather golfish, and café chitchat centers on tees and greens.

Kaena

A short drive north beyond Makaha leads to **Kaena Point State Park**, site of rustic **Keawaula Beach**, the last beachhead before land's end. Waikiki sand is far away, and your beach neighbors will mostly be locals. Elder Oahuans call this beach "Yokohama" after a railroad man who worked for the now-defunct Oahu Railroad, which looped Kaena from 1895 to 1947. Don't expect to ride a steam engine, cross the railroad tracks, or meet the switchman—all are gone. The point of land fading into the ocean is Oahu's western tip, Kaena Point. Standing on the beach facing the point, you can almost hear the words of a Hawaiian chant: "Kaena, salty and barren, now throbs with the blaze of the sun; the rocks are consumed by the heat." At point's end, a battery-powered light inside a miniature lighthouse sends an eight-mile beam into the night, searching, perhaps, for the souls of pre-Christian Hawaiians who departed from the rocky shore on an eternal voyage to the netherworld. The spot from which a soul exited Kaena is Leinaakauhane, Ghosts' Leap.

GETTING AROUND

A rental car is the most convenient transport outside Honolulu. Car travellers will find the *Oahu Drive Guide,* which comes in every rental car, valuable. For strong cartographic detail, James A. Bier's two-part reference map, *Oahu 1* and *Oahu 2,* is also recommended. These maps, available in most bookstores and in Waikiki shops, plus a rental car, put outback Oahu at your fingertips.

Daily public-bus service (number 20, always crowded) is available to the *Arizona* Memorial Visitors' Center from Waikiki (TheBus; Tel: 531-1611). Pearl Harbor Express (Tel: 923-2999) and Arizona Memorial Shuttle (Tel: 926-4747) provide round-trip transportation from Honolulu to the memorial's visitors' center.

A public beach bus runs between Waikiki and Hanauma Bay on weekends, and there are buses that circle the island, both clockwise and counterclockwise, leaving from Ala Moana Center (TheBus; same number as above). Bus information booklets are available in bookstores for those with the time and patience required.

For those driving, a profusion, and confusion, of Hawaiian highway names and route numbers clutter Oahu's highway maps. The Koolau Mountains are encircled by one roadway, with two over-the-*pali* (cliff) highways cut-

ting through the range's southern end. No road suitable
for rental cars circles the Waianae Mountains. All the
major regional areas outside of Honolulu, except the
Waianae Coast, can be reached by around-the-island driving, which means around the Koolau Mountains.

The section of the Windward Coast from Kualoa Regional Park to Kahuku, for example, can be reached by
four routes. The most direct is the over-the-*pali* Likelike
Highway (Highway 63), through the Wilson Tunnel into
Kaneohe, and onto northward-bound Kamehameha Highway (Highway 83); more roundabout is the Pali Highway
(Highway 61) past the Queen Emma Summer Palace and
Nuuanu Pali Lookout, joining the northbound Highway
83 in the Kailua-Kaneohe area. And by travelling either
clockwise or counterclockwise around the mountain
range you will, of course, also enter this coastal area.

The H-1 freeway eastbound from Honolulu, narrowing
into Kalanianaole Highway (Highway 72), is the traffic
artery leading to the Southeast Coast and Hanauma Bay,
while westbound, the H-1 is the departure point for Pearl
Harbor, the Waianae Coast, and, north of Pearl Harbor,
the northbound H-2 freeway to central Oahu and Kamehameha Highway leading to the North Shore.

ACCOMMODATIONS REFERENCE
*The rates given here are projections for winter 1989
through summer 1990. Unless otherwise indicated, rates
are for double room, double occupancy. Hawaii's telephone area code is 808.*

▶ **Sheraton Makaha Resort and Country Club.** 84-626
Makaha Valley Road, **Makaha**, HI 96792. Tel: 695-9511; elsewhere in U.S., (800) 325-3535. $95–$145; suites $200–$275.

▶ **Turtle Bay Hilton and Country Club.** P.O. Box 187,
Kahuku, HI 96731. Tel: 293-8811; elsewhere in U.S., (800)
HILTONS. Rooms $135–$235; suites $405–$950.

BED-AND-BREAKFASTS
*In recent years, a number of bed-and-breakfasts have
opened on Oahu and the Neighbor Islands.*

▶ **Bed and Breakfast Hawaii.** P.O. Box 449, **Kapaa**, HI
96746. Tel: 822-7771.

▶ **Bed & Breakfast Honolulu.** 3242 Kaohinani Drive,
Honolulu, HI 96817. Tel: 595-6170.

▶ **Pacific-Hawaii Bed and Breakfast.** 19 Kai Nani Place,
Kailua, HI 96743. Tel: 262-4848.

THE BIG ISLAND
HAWAII

By Linda Kephart

Linda Kephart, editor of Discover Hawaii *magazine for three years and associate editor of* Hawaii Business *magazine for two years before that, has contributed articles on Hawaii to such magazines as* Pleasant Hawaii *and* Manulani. *She lives and works in Honolulu.*

In the cool upper reaches of the island's center, *ti*-leaf offerings to the fire goddess Pele perch on the edge of a steaming live volcano. Miles away, young sunburned visitors from places like California and Australia drink a toast as they wait for the sun to set beside an oceanside bar. And on another distant patch of land in north Hawaii's Waimea, real Hawaiian cowboys—called *paniolo*—ride doggedly over the rolling green hills, rounding up the year's bumper crop of Polled Herefords, Brangus, and Black Angus for branding.

The Big Island of Hawaii, on more than 4,000 square miles of land, encompasses nearly every climatic zone in the world, from arid desert to arctic highland. This island—the southernmost land in the United States—has the state's highest peak and the only flowing lava. Mark Twain and Robert Louis Stevenson wrote of the place, comparing it to the world's wildest frontiers. Its history includes the birth of Hawaiian unity under the leadership of the Big Island warrior who became King Kamehameha.

Its diversity, and of course the mix of races and cultures, makes the Big Island so appealing. At the same time, it's what makes getting acquainted with it so frustrating: To do it justice takes time, energy, and persistence.

MAJOR INTEREST

Kailua and North Kona
Hulihee Palace and Hawaiian history
Fishing charters
Oceanfront eating and drinking

Holualoa
Artists' community
Galleries

South Kona
Puuhonua o Honaunau ancient Hawaiian site
Painted Church

The Kohala Coast
Lava fields
White-sand beaches
The luxury resorts
Petroglyph fields
Puukohola Heiau ancient Hawaiian sacrificial
   temple

Waimea and the Hamakua Coast
Dining
Shopping for crafts and artwork
Hawaiian cowboy country
Parker Ranch
Waipio Valley history and dramatic scenery
Tours to Mauna Kea's summit

Hilo
Hawaii Tropical Botanical Garden
Suisan fish auction
Lyman House Museum

Volcano area
Live volcano in Hawaii Volcanoes National Park
Volcano Art Center
Jaggar Museum (volcanology)
Volcanic scenery
Black-sand beaches

Kau
Mauna Loa volcano
Stark scenery
Green-sand beaches

There is a natural evolution that occurs on islands born of volcanoes. After the lava spews out, a gentle geological wearing down has its way with the resulting land and the coral that grows around it, until the island's interiors are a patchwork of rich greens and reddish browns, and its edges a thin skirting of sand.

On the Big Island of Hawaii, geologically the youngest in the chain, the transformation continues daily as the active volcano Kilauea creates new real estate in the southeast. The Big Island is already nearly twice the size of all the other Hawaiian islands put together, and in the process of making it even larger, Kilauea also acts as the island's prime visitor attraction.

The child of five volcanic centers, the Big Island first saw life above the ocean's surface about a million years ago when the now-extinct volcano Kohala exploded. Because of its youth, the Big Island's origins are still apparent in the lava clinging tenaciously to ridge after ridge. Moreover, its beaches are sparse and not as well developed as those of its sister islands.

Perhaps the Big Island's youth is partly to blame for the identity crisis it faces. Its real name is Hawaii, like the state, but to avoid confusion locals started calling it the Big Island. Not always satisfied with the moniker, islanders on occasion toy with more romantic nicknames, such as "The Volcano Isle" or "The Orchid Isle," then, still not convinced, go back to simply "The Big Island" once again.

The sparse population on the island is separated into two groups by the huge mountains running north-south down the center, further perpetuating the identity crisis. These two groups differ in character: The people of West Hawaii's Kona and Kohala coasts bring home the bacon for the island, but those of East Hawaii control the budget—a situation guaranteed to generate a few family rifts.

Sunny **West Hawaii** is where the island's tourism industry is located—at first an odd notion, since the land here is so stark and uninviting. But people are enterprising on this side of the Big Island, constantly hunting for the new restaurant, activity, or retailing gimmick that will be a surefire attraction. They're a friendly bunch, dealing as they do with nearly a million visitors each year, who travel to this coast for the endless sun and bone-dry days. In West Hawaii, some of the state's finest resorts have carved lush oases out of the lava fields of the southern Kohala Coast, establishing a niche in the market with their careful attention to service and amenities.

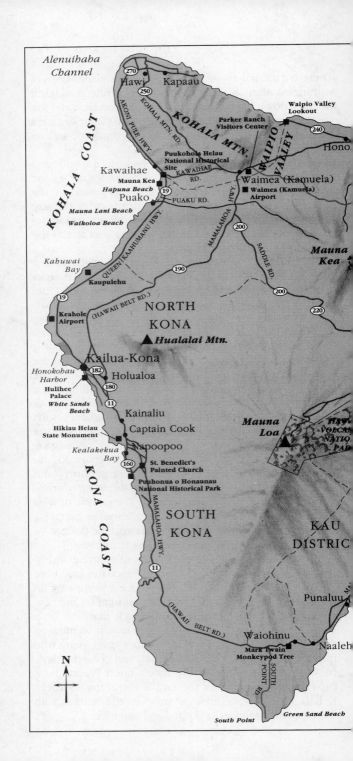

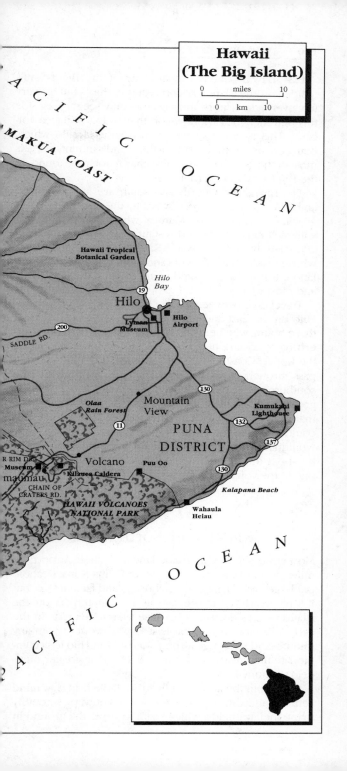

East Hawaii claims the majority of the Big Island's residents—the island's county seat is in Hilo—but has very few overnight visitors; most visitors only see the east side through their bus windows on their way to Kilauea volcano. This is unfortunate, because East Hawaii—which, being on the windward side of the island's mountains, gets most of the rain—has a tropical charm not to be found on the Big Island's western shores.

The Big Island's north and south are as different in ambience as east is from west. In the northern coast's growing community of **Waimea**, where cowboys mingle with rich kids, artists, and restaurateurs, the pace is easy and friendly. South Hawaii's **Kau** district, a rural outpost whose residents are farmers and pioneers, has little population. It is the least visited of any area on the Big Island, and most islanders would rather just leave it that way.

Travel time between the Big Island's two major cities— Hilo on the east and Kailua-Kona on the west—is about three hours, whether you travel on the northern or southern route. Going north from Kailua will take you along the Kohala Coast and up into Waimea. From there, you'll pass through the Hamakua Coast and on into Hilo. The southern route passes through the Kau district, with its green-sand beaches, its friendly farming residents, and many lava flows, including that in the volcano area. You could drive around the Big Island in a day, but you wouldn't want to. The minimum for a relaxed trip would be about three days, with one overnight in Waimea and one in the volcano area.

WEST HAWAII
Kailua and North Kona

Most visitors to the Big Island land at Keahole Airport, six miles north of the growing town of Kailua-Kona. Keahole is a large, new facility, as Neighbor Island facilities go, but it isn't nearly as impressive as its counterpart on the island's east side. That's because tourism experts in the early 1970s predicted that East Hawaii would boom any minute, and so a huge airport was built in Hilo to accommodate the crowds—who now flock in far greater numbers to sunny Kona.

Seen from the air as you fly in, Keahole brings to mind certain landscapes from *Star Wars*. Runways smoothly stripe the lava fields, which seem to cover the ground in every direction. On land, however, the scenery isn't quite so forbidding, as plumeria and red and yellow hibiscus crowd the gates. Hawaiian music filters in through strategically placed loudspeakers.

From the airport, some Big Island visitors simply continue north on the Queen Kaahumanu Highway (past messages written with white rocks—"Aloha visitors!" or "Bill loves Judy"—along the lava roadsides) to the toney resorts that line the North Kona and South Kohala coasts—from the Kona Village and Waikoloa beach resorts to the Mauna Lani and Mauna Kea resorts. Others prefer the action in **Kailua-Kona**, the island's tourism center, and opt to stay in one of the little condos, hotels, or guesthouses that have sprung up there.

West Hawaii's major metropolis is actually named Kailua, but because a more populated Honolulu suburb bears the same name, this little town of only 4,800 tacked on the name of its district, and is known as Kailua-Kona, or sometimes simply Kona. On the island itself, call it Kailua or Kailua Town.

Hawaii the island is packed with *heiau* (elaborate stone platforms that served as pre-Christian places of worship), old villages, and other remnants from the days before the unification. King Kamehameha I was born on the Big Island and undertook his plans to unify the Islands (through war) from here. During his later days he ruled Hawaii from his residence at **Kamakahonu,** now a national historic landmark next to the Hotel King Kamehameha at the head of Alii Drive in Kailua. It was also on this spot that the king, Hawaii's first royal, died in 1819. The **Ahuena Heiau,** a temple adjoining the king's residence, was restored by Amfac Resorts, the hotel's owner, and the state's leading Hawaiian conservator, the Bishop Museum.

There isn't much in the way of a beach scene in Kailua, but the ocean views are pretty good from a variety of locations. Many people are fond of perching on the seawall that borders one brief section of Alii Drive, just south of the Hotel King Kamehameha. This is where the famous Ironman Triathlon endurance event begins each October. The rest of the year it's a good vantage point for watching the boats that cruise in and out of Kailua, both sailboats and fishing vessels designed for bagging marlin or *ahi, mahimahi, aku,* or *ono* (local game fish). Kailua is unquestionably the best place in the state for deep-sea fishing; there are several dozen charter-boat companies in business here. Among the best of them are Kona

Activities Center (Tel: 329-3171), Billfisher II–Sport Fishing (Tel: 329-1973), and Kona Charter Skippers Association (Tel: 329-3600). You can find others listed in the free visitors' publications in streetside racks or in the Yellow Pages. The boats leave out of **Honokohau Harbor** about two miles north of Kailua.

At the seawall's end is the two-story palace with coral-and-lava-rock walls built in 1838 by Governor John Adams Kuakini. Now open to visitors each day, **Hulihee Palace** contains a collection of furniture and artifacts owned by Hawaiian royalty before Hawaii was territorialized in 1898. Hawaii's last king, Kalakaua, used the home for his summer palace. Hulihee is run by the Daughters of Hawaii, all of whom are at least part Hawaiian. Mokuaikaua Church, erected in 1823 and rebuilt in 1836 by the Island's first Christians, sits directly across Alii Drive.

Many of the town's residents end up viewing the sunset over the bay from the **Kona Inn,** an open-air eating and drinking establishment next door to the palace. Informal and boisterous, the servers and patrons here show an amazing proclivity for fast talking and, in the case of some paying guests, fast drinking. The Kona Inn is also the name of the shopping center here, where you can find a few interesting items, such as the rack of vintage "silkies"—old, colorful aloha shirts—in the back of the little shop **Brew-arama,** or cookies from **Mrs. Barry's,** named for a woman who won a local cooking contest several years back and put her expertise to good use. Just as popular as the Kona Inn bar is **Fisherman's Landing,** about a block south, another free-spirited place that attracts an active group looking for a sea breeze to accompany their greeting of the day's end. The **Old Kailua Cantina,** just opposite the seawall on Alii Drive, serves up the best margaritas in town.

A slightly more uptown crowd opts for drinking and dining at **Jameson's by the Sea,** a new oceanfront restaurant at White Sands Beach (also called Magic Sands, Vanishing Sands, or Disappearing Sands Beach for obvious reasons). Specializing in seafood, Jameson's is good for excellent eats in a quiet Polynesian-style setting. Also popular with those who have good dining in mind, the **Beach Club** is a word-of-mouth spot in a hard-to-find location in the Kona By The Sea condominium. Once those in the know have meandered their way through the covered parking "structure," they're rewarded with a tiny oceanfront restaurant serving steak, seafood, and pasta at about ten linen-covered tables (better reserve; Tel: 329-0290).

Hardly anyone who has been to the Big Island looks for lodgings in Kailua itself. Instead, repeat visitors often stay in the Keauhou resort area five miles to the south, most notably at the **Kona Surf Hotel**, the southernmost property on the strip of condos and hotels in the Kailua-Kona area. The Kona Surf's white stucco walls and interior courtyard filled with jungle plants such as ginger and *ti,* as well as a smattering of primitive and Pacific art throughout the building, provide a quiet environment. This hotel has run through a variety of owners recently, and the once-fine place has definitely lost its luster. There's no beach at the Kona Surf, but the ocean surrounds the saltwater pool rather dramatically on three sides.

Holualoa

Inland on the slopes just above Kailua Town is the little village of Holualoa, a gathering place for artists, especially so during the past several years with the opening of at least five art galleries along the town's main drag. The whole art movement really started here some 24 years ago when two California art teachers, Bob and Carol Rogers, bought the dilapidated Kona Coffee Mill and started offering classes there, calling it the **Kona Arts Center**. Two decades later the couple still gives lessons each day in their active and colorful Coffee Mill Workshop to groups of 20 or 30. Many of their students are "snowbirds" living in Kailua condos six months of the year; others are young mothers who haul their infants to class with them; and still others find out about the center during a brief vacation and sign up for a pottery class, a batik lesson, or instruction in basketry or painting. (For information write to: P.O. Box 272, Holualoa, HI 96725; or call the Rogerses at home, 322-2307).

About 15 years ago the Kona Arts Center negotiated a lease on an old church across the street and turned it into **The Little Gallery**, primarily for the artists who take classes and want to display and sell their work. It also has shows several times a year. This is the only place to find the detailed, Rockwellian Big Island scenes by Nannie Duncan Rogers, or the block prints by Claudia Suen.

More often than not you can walk across the street and meet the artists working on their next projects.

Soon other galleries started opening their doors in Holualoa. One of the Rogerses' former students, Hiroki Morinoue, specializes in contemporary watercolors and wood-block prints in his own gallery up the road, and also sells the pottery, paintings, and silk screenings of other Island artists.

Holualoa is also home to the lavish **Holualoa Inn**, a 12-year-old red-cedar mansion owned by the Twigg-Smith family of Honolulu. Thurston Twigg-Smith publishes one of Honolulu's two daily newspapers and is renowned for his patronage of the arts (he established an art museum in the Honolulu News Building and refurbished an estate to house the Contemporary Arts Museum in Honolulu). Initially Twigg-Smith built the Holualoa house as a vacation retreat, but when he found he didn't go there much he started letting artists hole up there in solitude. As a result, bright paintings, huge sculptures, and other monuments to creativity fill the home.

In splitting up some family property, Twigg-Smith's young nephew and his wife came up with the idea of opening a bed-and-breakfast in the 5,000-square-foot home. A journalist by trade, the nephew hired a staff and moved off the property. There are only four bedrooms available, but there is an expansive swimming pool and several living areas where guests (predominantly from Europe and North America's West Coast) can talk or play billiards. Breakfast comes with the room, but guests are on their own for other dining and drinking. The views at the inn are fabulous, spanning the entire Kona district from the airport south to Kealakekua Bay—and there is a rooftop gazebo to capitalize on them. The Hibiscus Suite's private Jacuzzi faces the same view. (Call the inn for driving directions.)

While the **Kona Hotel** in Holualoa was once popular with adventurous travellers who thought they had stumbled upon a bare-bones, back-roads experience, there are now far better ways to find the same thing (see the Manago Hotel, below). Nevertheless, you can't beat the Kona's rates ($12 for a single and $20 for a double), but you'll share a bathroom with construction workers, bargain-hunting Island families, and backpackers from around the world. Admittedly, the bathroom perched at the end of a long open catwalk boasts the best view of this type in the Islands.

South Kona

Folks who want local color of the Kona Hotel type but prefer digs a bit nicer opt for the **Manago Hotel** on Highway 11 in the town of Captain Cook, about eight miles south of Holualoa. Opened in 1917 by Kinzo and Osame Manago, the hotel has some standard dormitory-type rooms with a shared bath as well as individual accommodations in a newer wing. A third-floor room, dedicated to the hotel's founders, is the most comfortable. Japanese in decor, it is furnished with tatami mats, a deep *ofuro* for bathing, and a fluffy futon for sleeping. The hotel's dining room serves hearty home-style meals that attract crowds from around the island, while the hotel bar guarantees local yarn spinning.

Although small coffee farms dot the entire Kona Coast, the heaviest growing areas start around Captain Cook and stretch to the south. The only coffee cultivated in the United States, the famous Kona variety has flourished on this western slope of Mauna Loa for more than 150 years, the generally dry air and cool temperatures being kind to the delicate bean. Coffee isn't much fun to grow; the beans must be handpicked exactly when they're the right ripeness, and more beans ripen every day. Most coffee farmers on the Big Island do it part-time; they are families who inherited their tiny two- or three-acre spreads, or they do the work for the extra money. On a Saturday, you might see them out with their bags plucking the coffee and tending their fields.

About six miles south of Captain Cook is a road marked "Coffee Mill," veering to the right off Highway 11. While a working coffee mill does indeed sit at the bottom of the two-lane switchbacks that amble through the coffee orchards, what is open to the public is largely a tourist display and gift shop. It's of mild interest to see how the mill roasts and dries the coffee. Prices here—close to the source—are not any better than at anyplace else in the Kona district.

Continue from the mill toward the ocean and then south about 5 miles to find **Puuhonua o Honaunau National Historical Park**, one of the Big Island's most accessible and interesting pieces of cultural history. Puuhonua o Honaunau, which means "place of refuge at Honaunau," still looks much the way Hawaii did back before the advent of Western ways. This was a sort of no-tag zone for the ancient Hawaiians. Warriors who couldn't fight a battle could find sanctuary until the storm passed, or a woman could come here if she'd broken one of the sacred *kapu* (taboos) that governed so much of her behavior—eating with the men, for example, was strictly *kapu,* as was violating the space of a royal. The trick was that she had to get there first, often with others in hot pursuit. Upon reaching the *puuhonua,* any *kapu*-breaker could be absolved by a *kahuna* (priest).

What gave the puuhonua its power was the *heiau* (temple) that housed the royal bones (the ancient Hawaiians believed each person's spirit lived in his or her bones). Within the Puuhonua o Honaunau are two *heiau* built around 1550 and another that dates from about 1650. The newer one, which served as a temple and mausoleum until 1818, harbored the bones of at least 23 chiefs, giving this particular puuhonua power that went beyond any other. In 1820 King Kamehameha II abolished the *kapu* system and there was no more need for places of refuge; however, this puuhonua has been carefully rebuilt and maintained ever since as an important part of Hawaiian history. Hawaiian arts and crafts are sometimes exhibited on the grounds, which also contain several reconstructions of Hawaiian thatched huts, idols, and canoes.

The **Hikiau Heiau** lies a few miles north up the beach at Kealakekua Bay, the site where Captain James Cook was honored by the Hawaiians as their favorite god, Lono, when he arrived in 1779 during the *makahiki* festival—the most important celebration of the year—established, according to legend, by Lono himself. About a month later, forced back by foul weather, Cook returned to the bay, not knowing the *makahiki* had ended, but this time an argument broke out and he was killed.

In the other direction from Puuhonua o Honaunau is St. Benedict's, most affectionately called the **Painted Church**. A simple wooden structure, St. Benedict's interior was painted with Renaissance-style murals around 1900 by its priest, who wanted to show his congregation what Europe's grand and glorious cathedrals looked like—if only in a small way. Unfortunately, the church has been the target of vandalism in recent years, sometimes forcing its closure.

On Highway 11 back north toward Kailua again, there is more activity these days in the tiny town of **Kainaliu**, partly due to Alan Grodzinsky and his wife, Susan Garland, who bought the vintage 1932 Aloha Theater about eight years ago and opened the **Aloha Café**, serving up delicious homemade pastries, delicately flavored soups, fresh local fish, and wonderful sandwiches. The pair originally offered only breakfast and lunch, which most often attracted residents plugged into the grapevine and visitors who stumbled upon the restaurant. Now the Aloha Café also does a dinner that's every bit as healthy and wholesome, served not in the theater—used by the Kona Community Players—but either outside along one side of the building or in the old lobby.

The Kohala Coast

Lava no longer flows onto this upper-left-hand quadrant of the Big Island north of the Kona Coast, but the Kohala Coast wears its past on its sleeve, as ancient Hawaiian heiau, petroglyphs, and villages poke up unexpectedly here and there between fingers of hardened lava. Even more dramatic are the monuments to the present that earnestly began taking root amongst the lava fields in the early 1960s and now comprise one of the finest groups of luxury hotels in the world. Luxury is their only similarity; in other ways each is as different as the people who brought them into being.

Although technically south of Kohala in the North Kona district, the **Kona Village Resort** easily compares with its sister properties in South Kohala in terms of service and price. The village was the dream of Texas oilman Johnno Jackson and his wife, Helen, who sailed into Kahuwai Bay back in 1959 on their 42-foot schooner and came upon the abandoned Hawaiian settlement of Kaupulehu. Jackson visualized an escapist resort that would combine plush accommodations and primitive surroundings. Most people thought he was crazy trying to put a hotel on the lava—there wasn't even a road in at first—but succeed he did, with a passel of individual bungalows that remind some visitors of camping out, upscale and Hawaiian style. Although Jackson has since retired, general manager Fred Duerr carries on the same commitment to the roughing-it-in-style atmosphere. Jackson's schooner now serves as the poolside Shipwreck Bar.

Five miles north of the Keahole Airport off the Queen Kaahumanu Highway, Kona Village consistently opts for the understatement, starting with its thatched-hut security gate set back 50 feet from the road. There's no sign, no way for the uninformed to identify what lies beyond. The wealthy families who come back year after year for another dose of the Kona Village's restorative powers, the couples who start their Hawaiian vacation with oceanside matrimonials, then honeymoon in seclusion the rest of their time, and the harried execs and celebrities who know they'll get some peace at this outpost don't need any further advertisement. The likes of Lou Rawls, Goldie Hawn, and Katharine Ross simply want to sit unnoticed behind their sunglasses.

After a two-mile drive over one of the worst roads in the state, Kona Village guests find 100 individual *hale* (thatched bungalows), where they can hole up in privacy. No phones here, no televisions, no jackets or ties allowed. There's also no golf course, but visitors can play tennis, sail, scuba dive, or sign up for sportfishing. All meals at the village are included in the price, with dining choices in one of two charming establishments on the property. On Friday nights the hotel holds a luau, setting out *lomilomi* salmon, *kalua* pig, *haupia, tako,* and *opihi,* with the smiling staffers standing by with a handy description. Besides privacy, the Kona Village gives its visitors—if they wish—a forum to make lifelong friends, who often then plan successive Kona Village vacations together each year.

The southern Kohala Coast's newest luxury lodging has settled in another 10 miles north in the Waikoloa Beach resort area. The **Hyatt Regency Waikoloa** was the idea of Honolulu developer Christopher Hemmeter, who wanted to "create a fantasy," but this is a fantasy unlike what most folks in Hawaii would imagine for their islands. The hotel reportedly spent some $3.5 million on Asian and Pacific art, but it could have saved about $2.5 million and had a more tasteful hotel. Opened in September 1988, the 1,244-room property, one of the most unusual and exciting resorts in Hawaii—or anywhere—has drawn major convention groups and more than a few curious individual travellers—who have responded both positively and negatively. There's plenty of activity at the Hyatt, something the Kohala Coast frankly needed. Nightclubs, theme restaurants, vaporettos plying the waterways, and a monorail to journey between buildings are only some of the ways Hyatt has found to entertain its guests. One unique activity is the dolphin program. Once a day, about a dozen lucky guests can enter the lagoon and swim with the water-bound mammals. It's hard to tell who has the most fun here, the dolphins or the people.

When the Hyatt began taking reservations, there was only one other operating hotel in the Waikoloa resort area: the **Royal Waikoloan**. Not as well-endowed, exciting, or flashy as its neighbor, the Royal consistently attracts more low-keyed guests who want the relaxation of the Kohala Coast but prefer not to pay the steep prices charged by the other hotels here. The entire Waikoloa resort area sits amidst tide pools and ancient fishponds, and the Royal Waikoloan has done the better job of wrapping its hotel around the essential Hawaiianness of the geography.

Only five miles north, the Mauna Lani Resort, on some 2,300 acres of stark lava purchased back in 1972 by the Tokyu Group, is one of Hawaii's earliest examples of Japanese investment outside Waikiki. It was ten years before the company even broke ground on its first hotel, but when it did, the resulting **Mauna Lani Bay Hotel** was a stunner: white stucco with bougainvillaea tumbling from the balconies, a lavishly tropical courtyard that segues smoothly from the lush, open-air lobby.

For several years, occupancy was poor at the Mauna Lani while the hotel sought to establish its reputation. Although owned by Japanese—and famous for its Japanese attention to detail and presentation—the Mauna Lani hasn't turned out to be a haven for visitors from the East. North American businessmen on holiday with their families, many of them repeat visitors, favor the hotel. The restaurant **The Third Floor**, serving local fish and produce with a French touch, is one of the coast's finest restaurants, as is the less-formal **Gallery** at the resort's tennis club. Both welcome guests from other hotels (Tel: 885-6622 for reservations for both restaurants).

Mauna Lani faithfuls are partly drawn by the same qualities that appealed so much to the area's original inhabitants, the Hawaiians who fished the ancient ponds that cover part of the property. Around 1930, a noted Hawaiian businessman and sportsman, Francis Ii Brown, took title and built a compound fit for Hawaiian royalty: simple wood buildings and a spring-fed pond for his beloved, Winona. Brown would be the last individual owner of the Mauna Lani area, which Hawaiians called Kalahuipuaa. His nephew Kenneth, however, remains as president of Mauna Lani Resort, a move that indicated the developers' intent to preserve some semblance of Hawaiian spirit. One of Francis Brown's cottages has even been restored and is accessible to the public on a limited basis. Francis and Winona's pond is very hard to find, but the hotel's concierge will give semi-directions to guests whose looks he likes.

Some come back to the Mauna Lani because of the golf course, named for Francis Ii Brown, that is carved out of the surrounding lava. The 18 holes are among the most photographed in the golfing world, particularly the number 6 hole, which requires a duffer to drive the ball across more than 100 yards of raging ocean. The hazards along the course are of the natural variety: dozens of free-form lava mounds left as they were found. (Although this area hasn't seen volcanic activity since the mid-1850s, its results are abundant and obvious everywhere.)

Up the coast from the Mauna Lani, the tiny village of **Puako** keeps its own counsel as the quiet, seldom-visited site of one of the state's oldest and most extensive petroglyph fields, spared during the lava flows. At the turnoff from Queen Kaahumanu Highway, the standard green-and-white sign points down toward the water where the modern Puako has existed since the early 1950s. Once in town, archaeology buffs should look for the Hawaii Visitors Bureau's warrior path-marker, then walk down the path for nearly half an hour. At the site, carvings, mysterious even to the archaeologists who have studied them, crowd acres of lava.

Only two beaches away to the north, the Big Island's widest white-sand crescent lures swimmers, bodysurfers, and picnickers who find the appeal of beautiful **Hapuna Beach** much too hard to resist (but during the winter months there are dangerous undertows and riptides here). Most resort guests end up lounging at the beaches that front their hotels, so the Hapuna bunch often consists of people who live on the Big Island or those staying elsewhere who simply need a wet respite. Mauna Kea Properties, developers of the toney hotel next door, has plans to erect another hotel on this beach.

The **Mauna Kea Beach Hotel** (just off Highway 19) has been the doyenne of Kohala Coast resorts for a full quarter-century. Conceived and built by Laurance Rockefeller in the early 1960s, the property has been a faithful vacation home for those to whom Rockefeller most wanted to appeal: folks just like himself. Rockefeller determined that his Mauna Kea would be of classic, refined architecture, and to it he added a very valuable art collection, in what was one of the nation's first examples of a corporate art program. The twice-weekly art tours led by professor Don Aanavi have become one of the hotel's most unusual amenities. The art historian explains the subtleties of this Asian-Pacific collection, from the early 7th-century granite Indian Buddha to the late 19th-century Japanese garments, from the New Guinea ritual masks to the 30 Hawaiian quilts Rockefeller commissioned for the hotel's opening. Without the tour, the significance of the artworks might go unnoticed, because there are no ropes or signs (Rockefeller didn't want his place to look like a museum).

Hawaii's mistress of lei making, Barbara Meheula, is ensconced at the hotel. Meheula specializes in customizing each lei according to the occasion or the wearer's clothing or sensitivities, using Big Island plants and flowers as well as an occasional bloom from a Neighbor Island. Orders for Meheula's leis must be placed through the Mauna Kea.

Nearly three-quarters of those who take a room at the fairly formal hotel have been there before. Once the enclave of blue bloods who would take a three-month holiday during the winter, then check in again with the kids for the summer, the Mauna Kea is now heavily visited by those children, who have grown and are married themselves. That relatively younger crowd inspired the hotel to initiate more activity-oriented programs, such as a two-mile jogging path and an 18-station running and exercise course to complement a golf course annually rated as one of the best in the country by *Golf Digest,* and tennis courts that rate high with the pros. Rooms at the Mauna Kea are breezy affairs furnished in teak, cane, and colorful Thai cottons. The very formal **Batik Room**, one of five restaurants on the property, glows by candlelight and serves fine Continental cuisine. Right outside, the mood is more casual, as a Hawaiian trio lazily serenades those who stop for a romantic dance under the stars. Mauna Kea revelers often cap off the night with a stroll along the beachside path to view the massive manta rays that swim around an underwater light the hotel installed to attract smaller fish.

The Mauna Kea is within a short driving distance of some of the island's interesting historical sites. Only about two miles away, the **Puukohola Heiau**, a temple restored by Kamehameha in 1790–1791, before he was Hawaii's first king, welcomes visitors in a far friendlier fashion than its original owner did. It was at this site that Kamehameha eliminated the last chief standing in the way of his quest for power. Shortly after Kamehameha completed restoration of the heiau, his rival, Keoua Kuahuula, came to visit. Showing no hospitality whatsoever, Kamehameha had his enemy brought to the temple and sacrificed. An imposing structure, Puukohola Heiau is now a national historic site.

Another mile up the coast and you'll come to the small industrial town of Kawaihae, not a scenic spot, but home of the diner **Café Pesto**, at the only shopping center. Pizza lovers while away whole afternoons here, downing the gourmet Italian pies that roll out of the kitchen. They are so good that some of the Kohala Coast hotels have started filling their own pizza orders from Café Pesto.

Around the northern point of the North Kohala district, in the tiny town of Kapaau, is the workshop of master guitar-maker David Gomes. Although he learned his craft in Spain, Gomes has developed his own way of shaping and bending his guitars and ukuleles. Gomes takes orders from those truly interested in owning one of these prize instruments—a uke will cost its buyer nearly $500 and a classical guitar about $1,200, and delivery may take several months.

Waimea and the Hamakua Coast

If the Big Island's credo is diversity, then consider the scenic contrast between the Kohala Coast and the cowboy town of Waimea. Also called Kamuela to avoid confusion with the town called Waimea on Kauai, the Big Island's Waimea nestles in the saddle between the Kohala Mountains and Mauna Kea at an elevation of about 2,700 feet. In its entirety, Waimea sits on land owned by the Parker Ranch, the largest individually held spread in America. Waimea is green, with clouds hanging low in the Norfolk pines and views of Mauna Kea (snow-capped in winter) dominating the town.

The single heir to Parker Ranch is Richard Smart, the great-great-great-grandson of the ranch's founder, John Palmer Parker. A refined man in his 70s, Smart has a fondness for acting, art, and enjoying the finer things in life. Because Waimea is his town, it reflects that attention to culture. One of the state's most prestigious private schools, the Hawaii Preparatory Academy, brings students to Waimea from around the world. Some of their parents have moved in as well, shipping over their Rolls-Royces and furs, better to tame the wilds of the Big Island. Kahilu Theatre is Smart's nod to drama, and the patron himself often dons costume and stage makeup to act in a community production.

Parker Ranch also has something for the visitors who venture into its environs, having launched a visitors' center and small ranching museum in 1975. Ten years later Smart opened his century-old family home, Puuopelu, for tours, and in 1987 he installed the furnishings of patriarch Parker's home in a replica of the original structure next door. Puuopelu, the grander residence, showcases the wealthy landowner's art collection, while the simpler home beside it, Mana, houses a variety of the Parkers' historic photos. In 1988 Parker Ranch also began a tour that takes visitors up into the ranchlands to watch the *paniolo*—cowboys— at work. *Paniolo* is a local derivative of the word *Español,* the language spoken by the first cowboys brought from Mexican-owned California in 1832 to domesticate the wild cattle herds.

Another Parker descendant founded her own memorabilia repository, the **Kamuela Museum** (Highway 19 at the entrance to Waimea). If Parker inheritance traditions had worked slightly differently, Harriet Solomon might own a piece of Parker Ranch today. As it is, she and her husband, Albert, have made do with their own tribute to history, cramming their large home with some of the most curious stuff in Hawaii, thousands of items they've put together during the past 50 years from family collections, estate sales, private auctions, and dealers looking to unload their wares. Some of it is valuable: the only known ancient Hawaiian canoe buster (a weapon for destroying canoes), for example, and a five-foot-high wooden Hawaiian idol. But some is bizarre: ostrich eggs, a pen filled with black dirt inscribed "Mt. St. Helen's Ash May 18, 1980," a Czechoslovakian machine gun, and a stuffed black bear shot by Mrs. Gay Wilfong in British Columbia in 1965. There's no order in this museum, no rhyme or reason to the exhibits—simply meeting the eccentric Solomons is worth the admission.

Waimea's allure has also brought in several professional chefs who first moved into the area to commute to their jobs in the elegant Kohala Coast hotels, then went all the way, setting up their own kitchens in Kamuela. The first in this genre was former Mauna Kea chef Hans-Peter Hager, whose cozy **Edelweiss** restaurant on Waimea's main street has packed in eager diners for six years now. A little red-frame building in the middle of town, Edelweiss successfully blends cultural incongruities: Hawaiian

waitresses in German dirndls, Viennese waltzes for entertainment, and Big Island anthuriums and koa-wood walls
for decor. The food is similarly blended, Hawaiian fish
specialties such as *opakapaka* and *mahimahi* side-by-
side on the menu with schnitzel and pot roast. This is the
best restaurant in town, and a visit to Waimea won't be
complete without a stop.

Another Mauna Kea chef spent much of 1988 building
his dream eating establishment, which he opened to
paying clientele in early 1989. For 23 years Bernd Bree
held court at the Mauna Kea's illustrious Batik Room, but
now he slaves in the kitchen of his own **Bree Garden** (a
block off the main street, behind the 7–11). His menu is
Continental, his decor reflects a glowing comfortableness
that draws the well-dressed crowd that frequents his
place to come back for more. Also in Waimea, chef Peter
Merriman made his entrepreneurial foray early last year
with his restaurant **Merriman's** (on the main street), featuring regional Hawaiian cuisine. Only 33 years old,
Merriman was chef at the Mauna Lani's Gallery, and now
cooks with local products such as lamb from nearby
Kahua Ranch and fish from Kawaihae boats.

As these three chefs make food an art, so does Waimea
embrace other artistic pursuits. Some of the island's finest
galleries are here, displaying the work of painters, weav-
ers, and wood-carvers. Jane Curtis at **Topstitch Fiber Arts**
in Parker Square works directly with Hawaiian quilters to
commission the large appliquéd covers that take up to a
year to make and set interested buyers back about $3,000
to $4,000. Next door, the **Gallery of Great Things** special-
izes in the works of island artists. Their collection includes paintings and a selection of koa (a dark, rich
wood) and rare-wood furniture, rockers, desks, bowls,
and chairs crafted in Hawaii. They also have museum-
quality items from other Pacific islands, such as New
Hebrides, New Guinea, and the Philippines.

Most visitors to this part of the Big Island don't overnight here, mostly because until recently there simply
weren't many lodging choices. In 1988, however, rancher
Carolyn Cascavilla bought the once-dumpy **Kamuela Inn**,
on the north side of Highway 19, and renovated it in oak,
turn-of-the-century antiques, and calico fabrics. She
added on a sprightly first-floor room where she now
serves a Continental breakfast each morning and keeps a
pot of coffee on for the magazine readers who drop in
during the day. The au courant book the inn's third-floor

penthouse for its expansive views of Mauna Kea. Actually two suites that can be rented separately, the penthouse boasts several sleeping areas as well as a kitchen and wet bar outside. Edelweiss and Merriman's restaurants are within a two-minute walk down the forested path to the main road.

On the lively end of the peace-and-quiet spectrum is the exciting Waipio Valley tour, started in mid-1988 by Englishman Peter Tobin and his Maui-born wife, Makaala. **Waipio Valley** is a must see for Big Island explorers, because this north shore enclave was the seat of power for the island during the 14th through the 16th centuries. You can see the valley from a very accessible lookout past the town of Honokaa to the west at the end of Highway 240. Waterfalls cascade down the 2,000-foot wall opposite the scenic point, while taro fields grow in patchwork far below. Or you can opt for a drive down into the valley, one that must be made in a four-wheel-drive vehicle. Although several companies offer a Waipio tour, the Tobins' new business (Waipio Valley Wagon Tours; Tel: 775-9518) puts the adventurous into a mule-driven wagon at the bottom for a canter through the villages and riverbeds and onto the state's largest black-sand beach.

The land along the Hamakua Coast southeast to Hilo has huge fields of sugarcane that rise from the ocean up onto the slopes of Mauna Kea. In this condition, sugarcane looks like tall grass and makes a soft rustling sound in the wind. As for the mountain that gives it nourishment, **Mauna Kea** is largely inaccessible in its highest reaches. The preferred way to visit the summit is by four-wheel-drive vehicle with an official tour guide, because the Saddle Road is off limits to rental cars (some of whose drivers make the attempt anyway; if the car breaks down, however, they're on their own). Pat Wright (Paradise Safaris; Tel: 322-2366) will take small groups to the summit for stargazing, as will the Waipio Valley Shuttle (Tel: 775-7121).

EAST HAWAII

Hilo

Few people outside the 35,000 who call it home spend any time in Hilo; if they see it at all, it's during a quick drive through or a hurried stop for gas. The airport here is large, and largely empty, too. The tourist desertion is due in part to the weather: Curled around the bay where Mauna Kea meets Mauna Loa, Hilo is on the island's windward side, which means it gets the bulk of the island's rain. That extra precipitation gives this town its abundance of plant life. Orchids fill fields throughout the area, providing nearly all the blooms that grace pillows in Big Island hotels. The heart-shaped flowers called anthurium also find willing soil and rain on this side of the Big Island. About four miles north of Hilo off Highway 19, the **Hawaii Tropical Botanical Garden** produces a wild variety of flora planted in a 17-acre valley by Dan Lutkenhouse, a retired San Francisco businessman. Torch ginger, heliconia, hibiscus, and flowering bromeliads are only a few of the several thousand species the entrepreneur now has on parade.

Hilo itself has no pretensions about its attractiveness to tourists. Although residents were once optimistic about their town's ability to entice a paying clientele, those notions have pretty well vanished. Most of those who live in the Big Island county seat have been here all their lives, born to parents imported from Japan, China, or Portugal to work on the sugar plantations. These descendants often report each day to government offices, finding employment either with the county or state. A smaller residential contingent are the Mainland imports who have put in the artsy shops and galleries along **Keawe Street** or hang around in the nearby sidewalk coffee cantina called Bear's. Some attend the University of Hawaii at Hilo.

One small coterie from the outside purchased a seedy old bank building on Keawe Street in downtown Hilo five years ago, renovated it, and opened a French Creole restaurant, **Roussel's**. New Orleans natives Bert Roussel and brothers Andrew and Spencer Oliver drew a lot of laughter when they first announced this radical idea, but zealous gourmands now come from all over to sample the blackened fish, shrimp étouffé, and beignets. The high ceilings, graceful arches, and white linen tablecloths provide a sophisticated background for the young, well-dressed-for-Hilo crowd that comes here. Roussel's even offers private dining for two in the former bank's vault. The same trio also initiated Hilo's own Mardi Gras, an annual event that, admittedly, pales next to the real thing, but has kept residents laughing each February since 1987.

Some visitors who come to Hilo overnight like the **Hawaii Naniloa Hotel**, an oceanfront establishment with fabulous views of the harbor. The hotel has recently undergone some renovation; the best room in the house is the Prince Philip Suite, remodeled for a visit by the royal spouse himself. The Naniloa is only a short walk from a daily Hilo ritual: the **Suisan fish auction.** Each morning at seven, fishing boats pull into the harbor and the day's catch of *ahi, opakapaka,* and smaller reef fish is auctioned off to the highest bidders. It's a multilingual event and a good opportunity to catch some local color.

Others scouting for accommodations in Hilo have discovered the **Dolphin Bay Hotel,** on Iliahi Street across the Wailuku River, run by the affable John Alexander, who was a teenager when he helped his parents build the hotel in 1968. Most of his guests could *be* his parents, in fact, and have returned to the hotel many times. His 18 units—from studios to two bedrooms—all come with kitchenettes, ceiling fans, and black-and-white TVs. Guests can help themselves to papaya, breadfruit, and bananas from the garden out back.

During the Merrie Monarch Festival in Hilo, late March and early April, accommodations are difficult to find. The festival is one of the most popular hula competitions in Hawaii, with hula *halau* (schools) coming from around the world.

Near downtown Hilo, the **Lyman House Museum** (276 Haili Street) welcomes visitors into its missionary-era confines. This was the home of the Reverend David Belden Lyman and his wife, Sarah, missionaries from Boston who were sent to Hilo in 1832 to run a school for boys. In 1973, Lyman's great-great-grandson, Orlando Lyman, was named museum director. Thanks in part to him, visitors poking through the contemporary building adjoining the old home now find such displays as a complete Taoist shrine carried piecemeal to Hawaii in the luggage of Chinese immigrants around 1850; the Earth's Heritage Gallery, which explains volcanology; exhibits of cut glass, art glass, pressed glass, international ceramics, and Oriental teak furniture. The original house with period furniture is also open for guided tours.

The Volcano Area

The two districts most affected by current volcanic action, Puna and Kau, account for only about one-third of the Big Island's land mass, but if you know where to look, you can watch that mass expand. While it is possible to walk right up to a volcano that is fountaining, only a fool would actually risk life and limb to do it. There are better, and safer, ways to get volcanic thrills—such as opting instead for watching where the lava ends up.

Kilauea Caldera, the Big Island's most active volcano, has been spurting lava off and on since 1983. Quiet for a few days or weeks, or even months, the volcano then begins to rumble and erupt, without warning to anyone except the scientists who are monitoring it. As the red, semi-liquid lava travels from the active vent to the ocean, it starts to cool, and when it hits the water there's an awful hissing as steam fills the air. The coastline looks eerie, as other spectators' wraith-like figures appear unexpectedly out of the mist.

Of the two volcanic areas, the **Puna district** is the smaller, but the recipient of just about all the activity. Puna is that knob of land sticking out of the island's east side. The major road that once circled the area along the ocean (Highway 130/137) was partly covered by lava in 1987, making it impassable in one section. It is where the road comes to a dead end that much of the excitement occurs, as lava continues to take this path across the road and into the ocean. All along this coast, black-sand beaches attest to the district's bouts with lava.

As Highway 137 meanders down the coast, ancient trails and heiau also poke up from time to time, survivors of the flow of lava that somehow parted to leave them unharmed. Right before the road yields to the 1987 flow, the Big Island's most photographed black-sand beach, **Kalapana**, appears unexpectedly around one bend. At the road's end, Kilauea's active vent, **Puu Oo** (POO-oo OH-oh), is far up the slope to the right. When it's erupting, residents sometimes park along this road to watch the island's best entertainment.

Puu Oo is also just visible from Highway 11, which runs inland through the volcano area and ascends in about 30 minutes' driving time from sea level to 4,000 feet. Temperatures quickly drop as the air takes on a certain clarity and the jungle gives way to forest.

About 10 miles outside of Hilo on Highway 11, the **Mountain View Bakery** has become one of the Big Island's favorite excuses for *omiyagi,* the Island tradition from the Japanese culture that says you must take something home—preferably food—to those who couldn't make the trip. This little home-style establishment takes only about ten dozen stone cookies out of its ovens each morning, and they're soon snatched up. They're called stone cookies because they're hard and bland—but they grow on you. Some Hawaiian Islanders are so hooked on stone cookies that they can't make a trip to the Big Island without stopping at the Mountain View.

About 20 miles from Mountain View, the village of **Volcano** marks the entryway to Hawaii Volcanoes National Park. The gathering place in this mountain hamlet is the general store, which stocks all the essentials—and also fresh-cut tropical flowers such as orchid sprays, anthuriums, and the only calla lilies you can buy in the state, for $2.25 a dozen.

Volcano's residents include ceramicists, painters, and sculptors who happily live and work year round in this artists' community. Some have even opened their studios to visitors by appointment. For a peek inside the Volcano artistic life, there are the studios of famed ceramic-mask maker **Ira Ono**, whose popular Trash Face Collection is the rage in Mainland boutiques (Tel: 967-7261); photographer **Boone Morrison**, who makes the hula and the volcano come alive in his work (Tel: 967-7512); and fiber artist **Pam Barton** (Tel: 967-7247), who fashions natural Big Island materials into baskets, hangings, and sculpture.

Until a few years back, visitors wanting to stay at the volcano would opt for the **Volcano House**, the 1920s inn perched on the edge of Kilauea Caldera (crater) inside the national park. Back then, when the vent was more active, guests delighted in watching it steam while they sipped a cup of hot coffee near the stone fireplace. It tends to be cold at this elevation, and the Volcano House still heats its interior with geothermal energy from the volcano. The hotel also still rents rooms, but the grande dame has been surpassed in reputation—partly because of its fondness for the ubiquitous tour bus—by several establishments in the village proper. Although they are not on the volcano rim, these new lodgings are gaining clientele by offering higher quality.

Kilauea Lodge and Restaurant, one block off Highway 11 on Wright Road, is a former YMCA camp that was turned into a restaurant and four-room bed-and-breakfast inn by Lorna and Albert Jeyte. Recent arrivals, the couple moved to Volcano when Albert's job as a makeup artist on the popular TV series "Magnum, P.I." dried up in 1988. Their homey, 50-year-old lodge now serves three meals a day at tables set around the immense "fireplace of friendship," a constantly crackling hearth built of rocks donated by civic and youth organizations from 32 countries around the Pacific. In the kitchen, Albert puts his masterful touch on entrées such as veal Milanese and prawns Mauna Loa. Each of the four rooms available comes with a fireplace and skylighted bathroom. The savvy visitors who have discovered they can overnight pleasantly in Volcano are even more pleased by the full breakfast included in the lodge's reasonable rate.

The **Volcano Bed & Breakfast** was another well-received high-altitude alternative in mid-1988 when Jim and Sandy Pedersen turned their home into a haven for visitors who long to get off the beaten path. A few blocks from Highway 11 on Keonelehua Road, the Volcano B & B particularly attracts the kind of guests who want to get to know their hosts. A Big Island native, Sandy has a wealth of good advice on where to go and what to see during your visit, even supplying bicycles for the adventurous who want to explore the volcano under their own power. Jim, who runs his planning consultant business out of the couple's home, is also an affable host, with plenty of ideas about unusual ways to see the area. Their three-story, five-bedroom, country-furnished home provides a cozy backdrop to getting to know the island. The Pedersens even offer guests the use of their VCR and their stock of tapes, including some they filmed themselves of the Merrie Monarch hula festival as well as documentaries on the area. Although most of their guests have been Europeans accustomed to the B and B way of life, Americans have also been finding their way to the Volcano Bed & Breakfast.

Just down Highway 11 is the entrance to **Hawaii Volcanoes National Park**. If you take advantage of all the park service has to offer here, it's worth the five bucks admission. The visitors' center, within miles of the turnstile, should be the first stop. Here the park has complimentary maps and exhibits that explain the workings of the volcano. The most interesting display is the glass case filled with letters from repentant Big Island visitors who ignored the signs that warn against taking volcanic rocks. Legend has it that those who disobey Pele's anti-theft directive and lift pieces of her mountain will anger the volcano goddess and find themselves in a mess. The park service receives letters frequently from those disbelievers who tell of their medical problems, divorces, and other disasters—and who always enclose the stolen rocks.

Next door, the **Volcano Art Center** houses one of the island's largest collections of local art in a restored 1877 mountain lodge. This building was the original Volcano House, once hosting adventurous overnight visitors in its former rimside location. When the new hotel was erected back in 1921, this edition was moved into a field and left for scrap—until the park service and a group of local residents rescued it in the mid-1970s. Now it houses a potpourri of paintings and pottery, baskets and batik, photographs and fossil rubbings. Volcano artists sell their wares here; among the favorites are Dietrich Varez's brown-and-white, Hawaiian block prints, Marian Berger's watercolors depicting a range of Hawaiian wildlife, and Chiu Leong's dramatic *raku*-ware pottery. The art center also maintains an aggressive schedule of classes in all kinds of visual and performing media, as well as concerts, dance programs, writers' retreats, lecture series, and rotating exhibits. Like all the others in the upper reaches of the Volcano area, the art center's stone fireplace is often crackling and glowing, and flute or guitar music enhances the mystical mood for the art lovers who have wandered in.

Past the art center the pine trees give way to a scrubby desert. Scenic lookouts that encircle the caldera are terrific vantage points from which to view the huge hole that once bubbled and spurted lava. Now vents only puff sulfuric steam into the air. At the main stopping point, above Halemaumau—a crater within Kilauea Caldera that is known as "the fire pit" because it was the site of spectacular activity in the early 1900s—the fumes are particularly noxious, and warning signs advise that caution be exercised.

The **Thomas A. Jaggar Museum**, along the caldera rim about midway between the art center and Halemaumau, is a must. Only three years old, this park service museum, next door to the Volcano Observatory, brings the geological phenomenon to life with its display of Hawaiian volcanology. The museum gives a complete account of eruption history and forecasts for the Big Island, has exhibits on seismic activity, demonstrates data-gathering equipment, and offers volcanic landform models. There are also plenty of photos of previous eruptions, and a videotape keeps visitors up to date on the latest volcanic activity—sometimes the footage was shot as recently as that morning.

Because the park service wants to answer as many questions as it can, rangers lead several daily walks from the museum and give lectures to educate visitors further about the famous national park. Some hikes get close to current lava flows, while others focus on alien-looking plants and animals in the area.

You can circle the entire crater, stopping to stroll the boardwalk called Desolation Trail before ending up again at the visitors' center, and exit the park the way you came. Or you can make a right at the trail and drive down **Chain of Craters Road**, which eventually ends at the other, western side of the 1987 lava flow that blocked Highway 130/137. Chain of Craters Road is exactly what its name implies: little craters forced up by volcanic activity in what seems to be a meandering path to the ocean. Lua Manu Crater, Puhimau Crater, Kookoolau Crater, Hiiaka Crater, and others document flows from 1969, 1974, and 1982, among other years. The road winds its way efficiently through the geological bumps before making a straight shot through the black terrain to the ocean. The few cars that go this way often stop along this road, which is totally surrounded by lava, and their inhabitants pile out to take photographs or to study the two lava types: *aa,* which is jagged and rocky, or *pahoehoe,* which is smooth and ropy.

At the bottom of the hill the road runs along the ocean a few miles before ending at the Kamoamoa Campground, also operated by the national park. As the road hovers above the water, sea arches appear as part of the cliffside scenery, with ancient Hawaiian villages and petroglyphs hiding along the road's island side. The nearby Wahaula Heiau, an ancient Hawaiian temple built in 1275, is still accessible but is periodically threatened by the flow of lava.

Hikers love this region because it has trails that lead through the lava to secret coves and beaches. These are major forays, not day hikes, and you'd be better off saving this for another trip. Talk to the park service about trails and conditions (you are required to register with them if you go on certain trails) or consult Craig Chisholm's *Hawaiian Hiking Trails.* By car the only way out of this area is back the way you came, along Chain of Craters Road and around the Kilauea Caldera.

As for viewing the volcano really close up, the best way is with David Okita's Volcano Heli-Tours. Based at the Volcano Golf Course, only a few miles outside the park entrance, Okita takes passengers up in a Hughes 500-D several times each day for 45-minute flights over the active Puu Oo vent. There is no other way to get this close. Other companies offer volcano flyovers, but Okita's Volcano Heli-Tours is the best (Tel: 967-7578).

The Kau District

Only adventurers who can't leave a stone unturned continue on around the Big Island's southern half. This is the Kau (KAH-ooh) district, sometimes called the Kau Desert, although it's not really a desert in the sense that people from the southwestern United States might envision. Plants grow here, but not many people do. Of the two volcano areas, Kau is the far larger, encompassing the southern slopes of the gigantic **Mauna Loa**, a fitful volcano that last erupted in 1984. Charmingly rural Kau is usually bypassed because it has no dramatic visitor attractions. The Mark Twain Monkeypod Tree is only a tree on the side of the road that bears no evidence that Twain actually patted dirt over the seedling; the green-sand beach, comprised of volcanic olivine crystals and lava, is nearly impossible to find, and pretty bizarre once you do; and South Point is difficult to reach—drivers of rental cars are strongly cautioned against driving to it, and do so at their own risk.

The tiny communities that populate the southern section of Highway 11 were born in the plantation days when workers needed a place to live and owners gave them one "near the office." Scenery here remains much as it was in those heady plantation days—sagging storefronts and frame houses splashed with a hopeful coat of colorful paint. Rental-car explorers who dare to venture to **South Point**, or Ka Lae, as the locals say, find a bumpy 13-mile road that leads through stark pastureland right to the sea cliffs at land's end. A sizable band of fishermen operates there, dropping their wooden ladders to the surging water at the cliff base. And that green-sand beach, looking sort of dirty and unappealing in its tropical setting—not at all what you'd expect—awaits the determined traveller willing to hike about two miles to the east.

For years the area's most important sugar manufacturer has been C. Brewer & Company, which decided in the 1970s to take some of its vast land holdings out of sugar and put them into the resort business. That was when the company, once a member of the Big Five (the corporate quintet that ruled the Islands from the mid-1800s to the mid-1900s), opened **SeaMountain at Punaluu**, to serve as the hub of the area's low-keyed tourist activity. A 450-acre oasis, SeaMountain (on the south side of Highway 11) has only 76 condominiums in secluded low-rise buildings. The rolling 18-hole golf course is consistently packed with folks who winter at the resort, working to rid themselves of their Mainland pallor by shooting a round or two each day. Others find their way to the resort because of the Aspen Institute–Hawaii conference facility on the property, a cerebral center for humanistic professional, government, and business conclaves. A nearby black-sand crescent attracts a younger crowd that arrives from elsewhere by bus or rental car.

For Kau visitors who want a more rustic experience, the Shirakawa family hosts guests in its 13-room facility on the north side of Highway 11 in Waiohinu, near Naalehu. An old-fashioned country inn featuring simple furnishings, family-style breakfasts, and a lush atmosphere, the **Shirakawa Motel** includes the family homestead as well as a newer, motel-style addition on the 15-acre property. Authors finishing their latest novels seem to be popular guests at the Shirakawa, although the most attractive aspects of this little place are Takumi and Lenore Shirakawa themselves, a couple of friendly Japanese grandparents who are as likely to sit you down in the kitchen for milk and cookies as they are to enforce any house rules.

GETTING AROUND

United Airlines flies directly to the Big Island's Keahole Airport (at Kona) from San Francisco, and to Keahole via Honolulu from Los Angeles, Denver, Philadelphia, New York, Chicago, and most other major North American cities. Other airlines require a separate interisland flight.

From Honolulu, as well as from the Neighbor Islands, Hawaiian Airlines and Aloha Airlines fly to both Kona and Hilo airports on the Big Island about once every half hour. United has recently inaugurated interisland service for *local* travellers, but the flights are so few and far between (two or three a day) that you are better off just hopping on one of the local companies' flights, which leave with the regularity and ease of a shuttle bus. Aloha IslandAir flies to the upcountry Kohala town of Waimea (Kamuela). Interisland flights usually take 20 to 30 minutes—not nearly enough time to finish a drink, so you might as well wait until you land.

If you're staying at one of the big Kohala Coast resorts,

they can arrange for a shuttle to pick you up from the Keahole Airport in Kona. Once at the resort, you can usually rent a car from the hotel desk. Otherwise, it's best to reserve a car at whichever airport in advance and, once you've retrieved your luggage, proceed to the car-rental buildings across the road from the terminal at both major airports. All the big-name agencies, as well as some less-expensive, locally run companies, maintain operations on the Big Island—National and Tropical, among the most notable. The Waimea Airport has only one choice, Avis. Be sure to pick up the *Island of Hawaii Drive Guide,* which has a complete set of maps with close-ups of selected areas.

ACCOMMODATIONS REFERENCE

The rates given here are projections for winter 1989 through summer 1990. Unless otherwise indicated, rates are for double room, double occupancy. E.P.: European Plan; no meals included. M.A.P.: Modified American Plan; breakfast and dinner included. A.P.: Full American Plan: breakfast, lunch, and dinner included. Hawaii's telephone area code is 808.

▶ **Dolphin Bay Hotel.** 333 Iliahi Street, **Hilo**, HI 96720. Tel: 935-1466. $39–$69.

▶ **Hawaii Naniloa Hotel.** 93 Banyan Drive, **Hilo**, HI 96720. Tel: 969-3333; elsewhere in U.S., (800) 367-5360. $70–$100; suites $135–$175.

▶ **Holualoa Inn.** P.O. Box 222-D, **Holualoa**, HI 96725. Tel: 324-1121. $75–$125.

▶ **Hyatt Regency Waikoloa.** 1 Waikoloa Beach Drive, **Kohala Coast**, HI 96743. Tel: 885-1234; elsewhere in U.S., (800) 228-9000. $195–$360; suites start at $425.

▶ **Kamuela Inn.** P.O. Box 1994, **Kamuela**, HI 96743. Tel: 885-4243. $44–$55; suites $72; penthouse $118.

▶ **Kilauea Lodge.** P.O. Box 116, **Volcano**, HI 96785. Tel: 967-7366. $65 and up.

▶ **Kona Hotel.** P.O. Box 342, **Holualoa**, HI 96725. Tel: 324-1155. $12–$20.

▶ **Kona Surf Hotel.** 78-128 Ehukai Street, **Kailua-Kona**, HI 96740. Tel: 322-3411; elsewhere in U.S., (800) 367-8011. $95–$145.

▶ **Kona Village Resort.** P.O. Box 1299, **Kaupulehu-Kona**, HI 96745. Tel: 325-5555; elsewhere in U.S., (800) 367-5290. $330 and up, A.P.

▶ **Manago Hotel.** P.O. Box 145, **Captain Cook,** HI 96704. Tel: 323-2642. $29–$32.

▶ **Mauna Kea Beach Hotel.** P.O. Box 218, **Kohala Coast,** HI 96743-0218. Tel: 882-7222; elsewhere in U.S., (800) 228-3000. $336–$481, M.A.P. (other plans available).

▶ **Mauna Lani Bay Hotel.** P.O. Box 4000, **Kohala Coast,** HI 96743-4000. Tel: 885-6622; elsewhere in U.S., (800) 367-2323. $220, E.P. (other plans available).

▶ **Royal Waikoloan.** HCR2, P.O. Box 5000, **Kohala Coast,** HI 96743. Tel: 885-6789; elsewhere in U.S., (800) 537-9800. $140–$225.

▶ **SeaMountain at Punaluu** (Colony One Condominiums). P.O. Box 70, **Pahala,** HI 96777. Tel: 928-8301; elsewhere in U.S., (800) 367-8047, ext. 145. $73–$133.

▶ **Shirakawa Motel.** P.O. Box 467, **Naalehu,** HI 96772. Tel: 929-7462. $21–$30.

▶ **Volcano Bed & Breakfast.** P.O. Box 22, **Volcano,** HI 96785. Tel: 967-7779. $45.

▶ **Volcano House.** P.O. Box 53, **Hawaii Volcanoes National Park,** HI 96718. Tel: 967-7321. $57–$82.

BED-AND-BREAKFASTS
For information about other bed-and-breakfast accommodations in the Hawaiian Islands see Oahu Outside Honolulu Accommodations Reference.

MAUI

By Linda Kephart

humuhumunukunukuapuaʻa

People murmur "Maui" as if it is a mantra. With these two syllables they declare themselves trendy, hip, gone troppo. The Valley Isle, as Maui is known, has wormed its way into the hearts and minds of millions of travellers who swear by its magical properties—and make regular pilgrimages to prove it. Has Maui merely been the recipient of the modern roving hunger for the next new hot spot, or does Hawaii's second-largest island deserve all this attention?

Maui is like no other island. Tiny fishing villages where a few brown and weathered residents still head out each morning in their rickety boats to cast their nets are only a stone's throw from some of the most modish night spots in America. Red volcanic mountainsides spread with the gently waving green of sugarcane under a turquoise sky run smack-dab into sleazy storefronts hawking five tee-shirts for five bucks and the once-popular puka-bead necklaces (now imported from Taiwan). Maui is very Hawaiian in its passion for the native culture, but it is also Californian in its infatuation with what's new. With all this, Maui, a confident island, also has an unselfconscious way of knowing you're going to love it despite the few flaws it might admit to.

But Maui does have some problems. Although the Valley Isle first courted the upscale traveller—and continues to be a favorite destination for "beautiful people"—Maui's brilliant marketing strategies made it a household word among many other kinds of visitors looking for an exotic vacation. In fact, of all the Hawaiian islands, Maui was the first, if not the only, to succeed in promoting its name separately from the rest of Hawaii. So while some

Mainlanders may not have ever heard the name Oahu—
the island that is home to 75 percent of the state's
population—just about everyone knows about Maui. And
everyone wants to go there.

This has created a bit of a class system on Maui. The
visitors who can afford it tend to gather in the high-priced
resorts of Kaanapali, Kapalua, and Wailea, while those who
have bought the Maui mystique but have little to pay for it
end up in the Kihei condos. Travellers who go to Maui
aren't always sure why; they have a vague notion that a
spell will fall over them and grant them the perfect vacation. Like the other Hawaiian islands, Maui has its share of
historical sites and natural wonders, but many people
don't go to Maui for those reasons. It's the magic they
believe they'll find there amidst the flash and glamour—
and those expecting Nirvana are often disappointed by the
crowds they find on Maui.

MAJOR INTEREST

Lahaina
Historical sites
Nightlife
Restaurants
Whale-watching by boat
Day trips to Lanai
Sailing

West Maui outside Lahaina
Luxury resorts
Beaches
Whalers Museum
Shopping
Old Hawaiian fishing village at Kahakuloa

Central Maui
Historical Wailuku
Kepaniwai Park, site of Hawaiian battle and melting
    pot memorial
Iao Valley scenery

South Maui
Luxury resorts
Beaches
Whale-watching from shore

Haleakala/Upcountry
The volcano

Rural scenery
Hawaii's only winery
Protea farms
Cowboy town of Makawao

East Maui
Artists' studios and shops
Lush scenery
Hana town's quiet Hawaiian charm
Seven Pools

Maui could have been two islands. Gentle Puu Kukui was the first volcano to rise from the ocean, forming a group of peaks a couple of million years ago that now dominates the smaller, western side of the island. Several millennia later, Haleakala volcano emerged with far greater force and filled in the gap between the two, giving Maui its nickname, the Valley Isle. At 10,023 feet, Haleakala is nearly twice as high as the West Maui Mountains. As a national park, Haleakala plays host to hundreds of thousands of visitors each year.

Maui is a sophisticated resort destination, one that has expertly marketed its attributes. Maui, they say in the Islands, is *no ka oi,* indeed the best. But travellers bound for Maui should know they must pay for the best; it is the most expensive island in the Hawaiian chain. Maui boasts twice as many hotel rooms and condo units as the Big Island, but the Big Island has twice as many rooms renting for under $100 a night.

Developers on the Hawaiian Islands build their resorts on the dry leeward coasts, and Maui was blessed with two such sunny spots, West Maui and South Maui. Like its geography, **West Maui** as a tourist destination—Kaanapali, Kapalua—is the older, and so more developed, with more hotels, restaurants, activities, and people. It was a natural development, since the old West Maui port at Lahaina had been attracting visitors for years before the mass jet-travel boom.

West Maui is about an hour's drive from Kahului, site of Maui's major airport, where direct flights from the Mainland can land. Those who book a room in West Maui might find that flying into the Kapalua–West Maui Airport puts them closer to their hotel, but only interisland aircraft can land on the short runway, so it means a brief, 30-minute hop from Honolulu or from one of the other islands. The new Kapalua–West Maui facility has the best

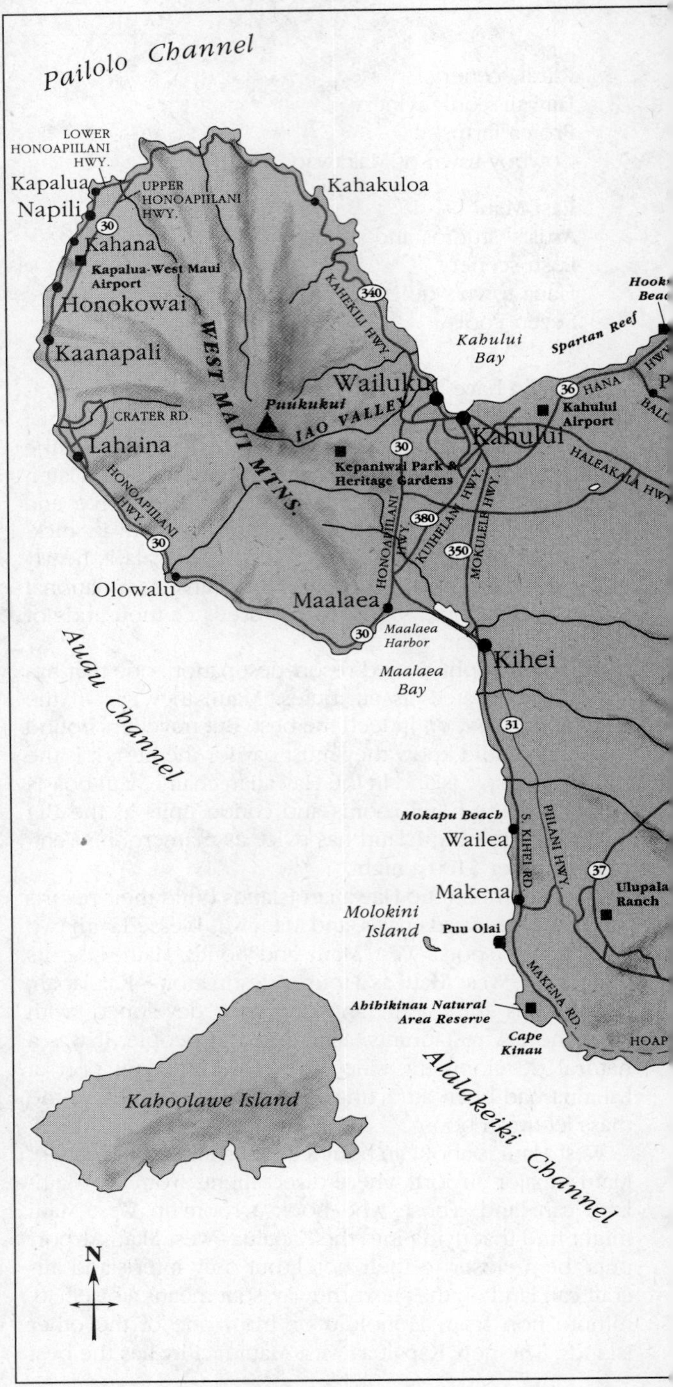
Pailolo Channel
LOWER HONOAPIILANI HWY.
Kapalua
Napili
UPPER HONOAPIILANI HWY.
Kahakuloa
30
Kahana
Kapalua-West Maui Airport
Honokowai
KAHEKILI HWY.
340
WEST MAUI MTNS.
Kaanapali
Kahului Bay
Spartan Reef
Hook
Beac
Wailuku
36
HANA HWY.
BALL
Puukukui
IAO VALLEY
Kahului Airport
CRATER RD.
Kahului
Lahaina
30
Kepaniwai Park & Heritage Gardens
HALEAKALA HWY.
HONOAPIILANI HWY.
HONOAPIILANI HWY.
KUIHELANI HWY.
MOKULELE HWY.
380
350
30
Olowalu
Maalaea
30
Maalaea Harbor
Kihei
Maalaea Bay
Auau Channel
31
Mokapu Beach
Wailea
S. KIHEI RD.
PIILANI HWY.
37
Ulupala Ranch
Makena
Molokini Island
Puu Olai
MAKENA RD.
Ahihikinau Natural Area Reserve
Cape Kinau
HOAP
Kahoolawe Island
Alalakeiki Channel
N

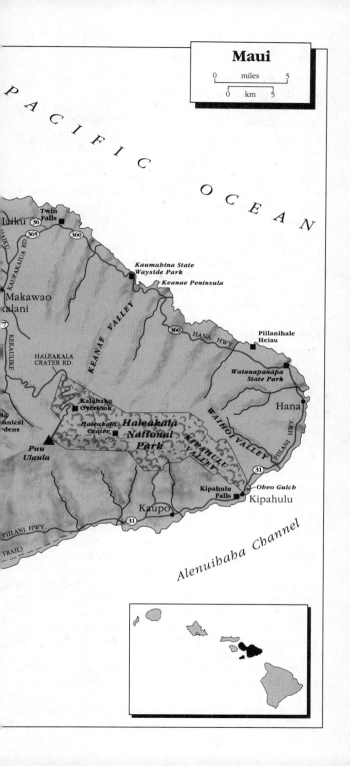

view of any airport in the state, as planes land high in the hills after coming in over acres of pineapple fields.

West Maui's counterpart, **South Maui**, has been quiet, reserved, and slower to develop. However, there is a building boom in both its Wailea and Makena resorts that may create activity—including rush-hour traffic—similar to that in West Maui. South Maui's advantage is the modern, four-lane Piilani Highway (Highway 31) between Kihei and Wailea, which makes the drive from Kahului (the airport) to Wailea only 20 minutes tops.

Ironically, not many visitors make it to the part of the Valley Isle that gave it its name, the **Central Valley**, because most arrive at the Kahului Airport, then head straight to one of the outlying resorts. That's partly because there are no places to lodge in Central Maui, aside from the few marginal hotels patronized mostly by interisland business people who need to stay close to clients, or by people who bought the cheapest package deal. Central Maui is home to most of Maui's residents and, as such, tends to cater to their needs rather than to those of the visitor. Kahului Airport itself is large and efficient, and a ten-year renovation begun in 1982 is making it even better.

Haleakala in **Upcountry Maui** attracts day-trippers who want to explore the rural atmosphere along the mountain's slopes. An increasing number of Mainlanders who first found West Maui to their tastes have built homes in the Upcountry area, enjoying the solitude, the country lifestyle, and the cooler weather there. In **East Maui**, the town of Hana, long famous for its difficult access, lures people brave enough to make the drive (or brave enough to sign up for the daylong van ride from West or Central Maui). Contrary to what you may have heard, the road to Hana (Highway 36) is smooth and well-maintained—but it *is* narrow, and twists and turns. Pros can go the distance from Kahului in under two hours; the average driver will need three to four hours. Along the way, the lush scenery along the northeastern coast more than makes up for the inconveniences of hundreds of hairpin turns and dozens of narrow bridges. And once you've arrived you'll find a Hawaiian town that will take you back to a simpler time in the island's history.

The ideal way to get around Maui is in a rental car, because there is no reliable island-wide public transportation. The roads are easy to use, even though most are only two lanes, and travel time between major towns is only an hour or two. While you could in theory see much of Maui in a day or two, you would probably want to allow twice or three times that amount for a more enjoyable visit.

WEST MAUI
Lahaina

West Maui is the vacation center for most Valley Isle visitors. The state's first capital city, Lahaina, dominates West Maui with its honky-tonk Front Street, bustling harbor, and eclectic mix of bronzed surfers, old salts, and sun worshipers clad in neon-bright bikinis. The old whaling port has a magnetic effect on most people, even those who try just to drive by. Throughout Lahaina's past, hardly anyone has been able to resist her charms.

Hawaiian royalty were perhaps the most important group to find Lahaina seductive, especially after 1810 when Kamehameha unified the Islands, naming himself king in the process, and made centrally located Lahaina his capital. He also built himself a brick palace—though he never lived in it—near the spot now occupied by the Pioneer Inn. The king was from the Big Island, but his favorite wife, Kaahumanu, and his most sacred wife, Keopuolani, were both Maui natives. Nevertheless, King Kamehameha and his 21 spouses soon moved to the more exciting town of Honolulu, although the capital stayed officially in Lahaina through two more kings.

Foreigners also loved Lahaina. After Captain James Cook came to Hawaii in 1778, more and more Europeans found their way to the Sandwich Islands, anchoring off Lahaina for a little R and R with the native women. By the early 1820s word of the Islands had spread to whalers, who began sailing toward Maui for its R and R possibilities. At about the same time, missionaries bent on educating the heathens also alighted in Lahaina. The resulting blend of hell-bent rowdies and savage-saving Christians gave everyone a reason to live, and set the town's character.

Lahaina later fell into disrepair, like so many Mainland towns whose residents can't quite remember the former significance of the ramshackle buildings that lean on every corner. In 1966, however, a 37-acre parcel of town land was declared a national historic landmark, and renovation then started in earnest through the efforts of the Lahaina Restoration Foundation. The foundation now publishes a free map and has installed signs pointing out the 31 stops on a self-guided walking tour of the town. The map is available at most site locations throughout Lahaina, in most West Maui hotels, or from the Hawaii Visitors Bureau.

Now open for viewing are the Baldwin Home Museum, where the Reverend Dwight Baldwin, a missionary and physician, and his family lived for 33 years; the **Fort on the Canal**, which was erected in 1831–1832 after whalers reacted with cannonballs to a law stating that native women could no longer swim out to meet the ships; and the U.S. Seamen's Hospital on Front Street, refuge for many diseased and disabled mariners in the mid-1800s, which now houses **Lahaina Printsellers**, the state's only dealer in authentic antique maps. Like the Seamen's Hospital, the renovated **Court House**, farther south on Front Street, also has a new function, as a gallery for several groups of Maui artists.

Part of Lahaina's charisma comes not from its past, but from its present. Nightlife runs through this old port's veins, just as demon rum was once the lifeblood of its sea dogs. Tucked in amongst Front Street's many altars to retailing are several choice joints in which to while away an evening or salute the setting sun. **Kimo's Restaurant** calls to a comfortable crowd that wants more than ocean-front: The bar places you right over the water. From Kimo's you can watch the sun sink quietly behind the Pineapple Island (Lanai) to the west.

There's nothing quiet about **Blackie's Bar**, the orange, six-sided beanery run by Blackie Gadarian and his wife, Sara. On the main highway above Blackie's Boatyard, the roadside bar's decor is nautical naughty, the eats are tacos, burgers, and beer, and the entertainment is live jazz Monday, Wednesday, Friday, and Sunday nights from 5:00 to 8:00 P.M.—in addition to Blackie himself, and his no-crap attitude. "Order something!" he might bark at an unsuspecting dawdler. "Get your feet off the chair. Can't you read the sign?" he's likely to tell another. The renegade proprietor can be downright docile to those who have manners, but his signs reveal his personality even when he doesn't (Metric Sucks, says one). On jazz nights, those ordering food net the best seats.

Those who want some authentic Hawaiian entertainment should head for the **Old Lahaina Luau** at the beach right off 505 Front Street. This, they say, was where the Hawaiian royals once partied, although from the evidence of the historical sites around Lahaina, the royals partied everywhere. At the Old Lahaina Luau, the four young men who founded the venture attend to details: all-you-can-eat Hawaiian fare such as *kalua* pork, long rice, *lomilomi* salmon, *haupia* cake, and fresh Island fruit. In keeping with the party mood, you also get all you can drink. The evening's entertainment includes hula, chanting, and singing. This luau is one of the best in the state, and it happens every night. Reservations are necessary; Tel: 667-1998.

Lahaina has also attracted its fair share of refined establishments, such as the trendy **Avalon Restaurant & Bar** in Mariner's Alley at 844 Front Street. Opened in 1988 by a California rock promoter and a partner who does the cooking, Avalon has drawn hordes of celebrities and other beautiful people to feast on the bistro's Pacific Rim menu, with dishes from California, Mexico, Indonesia, Thailand, Japan, Vietnam, and, of course, Hawaii. That range gives the chef, Mark Ellman, lots of license; his signature specials include a roast duck with plum sauce and Chinese steamed dumplings; guacamole made tableside; and Caramel Miranda, a dessert of fresh exotic fruits with caramel sauce, sour cream, and brown sugar. Designer-clad diners sup from fiestaware, music plays softly, and bold Hawaiian tropical prints à la the 1940s lend a suitable decor to the patio brasserie.

A few buildings northwest at 888 Front Street, **Longhi's** has practiced its kicky approach to dining since 1976. To start, there are no menus. Sun-bronzed waiters or waitresses simply pull up a chair and orally run down the day's selections, complete with prices. The restaurant keeps several full-time bakers and pasta makers busy whipping up the homemade pasta, bread, and desserts that have made Longhi's famous, while at least ten cases of oranges get squeezed into breakfast tumblers each morning. Longhi's is always packed—often with the proprietor's major-league football buddies.

More genteel gourmands take their evening meals at one of Lahaina's French restaurants. One of them, **La Bretagne Restaurant Français**, across the lane from the Maluuluolele baseball field (3 Mokuhina Place), looks like a vine-covered shack. The wood-frame building was actually built by the town's sheriff in 1920, but La Bretagne's chef and owner, Claude Gaty, has turned it into a cozy, candlelit, French-style country inn serving such delicacies as puff pastry, Maui onion soup, and other "nouvelle Hawaiian" meals to those looking for a touch of romance with dinner.

Likewise, **Gerard's Restaurant**, at 174 Lahainaluna Road, has captured an ardent following with chef Gerard Reversade's sumptuous menu, a bill of fare that includes such exquisite delectables as medallions of veal Normande, noisette of venison, and confit of duck. Set in the lobby and veranda of the Victorian-like Plantation Inn (a block and a half from the ocean on Lahainaluna Road), Gerard's milieu is as exquisite as the food: Rich oak walls, brass appointments, and crystal chandeliers provide a homey atmosphere for the tall, white wicker chairs and country-print linen that continue out the door and onto the breezy porch. Tables are close enough that diners find themselves exclaiming over the meal together, and even swapping stories and addresses.

Of course, some Gerard's revelers are guests of the **Plantation Inn,** the one truly decent hotel in Lahaina. With only nine rooms, the bed-and-breakfast inn was originally designed by owners of Lahaina's Central Pacific Divers, who had a brainstorm about building a place where scuba divers could lodge while they were getting underwater experiences from CPD. Soon after opening in 1987, however, the group discovered the crying need for attractive quarters in Lahaina, and now regularly book nondivers as well, including honeymooners and couples who love the inn's romantic atmosphere.

The Plantation Inn appears to be a renovated building, but in fact it's brand new—with modern plumbing, roomy closets, and lights and fans operated by remote control. Each room received special attention: One has a canopy bed set next to French double doors with gauzy curtains; another has a maple four-poster and a crewel-covered divan. There is a pool; breakfast is included; and guests get a 40 percent discount on dinner at Gerard's. The owners plan a look-alike building for another portion of the property, which will open up more rooms in the near future.

Lahaina's harbor provides plenty of opportunities to engage in water activities. You can take a whale-watching cruise between December and April, when the humpbacks journey to the Islands to calve. (Whale-watching boats also leave from Maalaea Harbor, about a 45-minute drive from Lahaina toward South Maui.) If you get lucky, your boat captain will know where to look for the behemoths—who are just as curious about you. They often spout and breach near the boats, which, by law, must keep their distance. **Captain Zodiac Raft Expeditions** (Tel: 667-5351) and **Seabird Cruises** (Tel: 661-3643) are probably the best Lahaina-based whale-watching companies. From Maalaea, try **Ocean Activities Center** (Tel: 879-4485).

Lahaina also provides anchorage for sailboats bound for other islands, such as Lanai immediately to the west, and is the jumping-off point for various interisland excursions. **Club Lanai** (Tel: 871-1144), for example, takes visitors from here to its private eight-acre beachfront retreat on Lanai for a day of sunning, bicycling, eating, and drinking from the open bar. This tiny piece of property is the only part of Lanai not owned by the Dole Corporation, which uses much of the rest of the island for growing the spiky fruit it cans in Honolulu. A more informative Lanai trip, but completely dry because the owners are Seventh-Day Adventists, is **Trilogy Excursions** (Tel: 661-4743). Once on the little island, Trilogy's sailing Coon family (which is how this lovable bunch actually bills itself) takes its charges on a tour of Lanai City, the island's only town, before snorkeling and lunch at Hulopoe Bay.

Other boating trips that leave from Lahaina include sunset sails, snorkeling, trips to Molokai on the *Maui Princess* ferry, and fishing excursions. You can find companies doing these trips listed in the Yellow Pages or in the free visitors' publications available throughout Lahaina. Or you can simply walk along Lahaina Harbor past the desks set up on the dock; the captains and crews will be more than happy to book you then and there.

Kaanapali

The **Kaanapali Beach Resort**, two miles north, is the state's oldest master-planned destination resort (Waikiki obviously had *no* plan). Now, more than 25 years later, the resort boasts flashy hotels, pricey condominiums, and toney boutiques. Nothing about Kaanapali will fit into an average budget, but most who stay here have made their peace with its cost—although some do roam the golf courses, beaches, and shops in what appears to be a daze. All told, Kaanapali's owner, Amfac Resorts Hawaii, lays claim to some 15,000 acres on Maui, but in the nearly three decades since this former Big Five company first went about the business of turning land unsuitable for agriculture into the Kaanapali resort only 600 acres have been incorporated into the West Maui enclave. Another 1,200 acres, however, are scheduled for development, including a northern counterpart of about the same size. This could make the West Maui traffic, which already backs up for miles during the day's commuting hours, even worse.

Within the confines of the Kaanapali resort as it now exists are six hotels and five condos. First out of the blocks was the **Sheraton Maui**, which opened amidst great fanfare in 1963 and continues to be a comfortable hotel (although it is in need of some redecorating). The construction that followed was mostly unremarkable until 1980, when Christopher Hemmeter took his Hyatt Regency Waikiki success story and applied it to the **Hyatt Regency Maui** hotel. In Waikiki, the young developer had installed a giant waterfall cascading into a shallow courtyard pool and decorated the walls and corners with tasteful selections of South Pacific art. In the Maui Hyatt, Hemmeter went for *nine* waterfalls and a 750,000-gallon swimming pool; stocked the grounds with peacocks and flamingos; and placed Asian bronze sculpture, granite statuary, and other *objets d'art* throughout the property. More recently, the Hyatt installed a telescope on the hotel's roof, and offers a nightly complimentary stargazing program.

Hemmeter had another shot at Kaanapali in 1984, when he bought the sagging Maui Surf hotel three doors down from the Hyatt Regency. In three short years he transformed it—with the aid of many tens of millions of bucks—into **The Westin Maui**. Waterfalls here are too numerous even to count; one begins its descent from a two-story, lava-rock cliff guarded by a lighted Buddha ensconced in a niche, then splashes into a palm-rimmed lagoon festooned with swans and mandarin ducks. Within the grounds are five interlocking swimming pools and gurgling streams overlooking the beach, while the collection of Oriental and European art prepares to star in its own lavish coffee-table book. The Westin doesn't look much like Hawaii, but it sure is something to see.

Kaanapali's friendliest hotel is the **Maui Marriott Resort**, a rose-colored medium high-rise next door to the Hyatt. The decor is low-key, the staff is helpful, and the junior suites are huge—with fine views. Its *teppanyaki* restaurant, **Nikko**, is so good that Japanese visitors come from around the island to eat here. Families staying in Kaanapali tend to choose the **Kaanapali Alii** condominium with its separate bedrooms and well-stocked kitchens, although the decor is much too uptown for sandy, wet kids after the beach—artwork, carpeting, and fine upholstery create a rather genteel beachside environment. The **Kaanapali Beach Hotel** is the budget member of the lineup, with a large contingent of its guests there on package deals, but the atmosphere is authentic, reflecting the intensive Hawaiian-values classes that the hotel's employees take. You won't find much that's fancy here, but what the KBH is is friendly.

Some visitors come to Kaanapali to play golf, especially after seeing the resort's two championship courses featured on nationally televised tournaments. Others find some of the 50 shops at **Whalers Village** more enticing, hunting down custom resort wear at Silks Kaanapali Ltd., Blue Ginger, and Foreign Intrigue Ltd. or perusing the boutique-size outlets that Esprit, Aca-Joe, and Benetton have opened on the Valley Isle.

Whalers Village also houses the **Whalers Village Museum,** a collection of memorabilia that illustrates the industry once so predominant in the area, with ship models, scrimshaw, and photographs as well as films and lectures. Still other visitors prefer to simply hang out on the beach, a wide, three-mile-long strip that is one of the best people-watching spots on Maui.

Just north of Kaanapali are more condos, and one new hotel that was planned to be the signature property for the North Kaanapali resort development. Opened in late 1988, the **Embassy Suites Resort** is an explosive, unrestrained pink structure that rises to the sky like an Egyptian pyramid. Designed by a Mexico City architect, the Embassy Suites evokes Acapulco; its bright turquoise, Art Deco umbrellas, lounge chairs covered in Hawaiian neon prints, glass elevators, and breezy flagstone walkways are flippant and fun. While guest rooms drop the ball on the tropical-hip theme—done, instead, in a sedate Blue Willow motif—they're large, with separate bedrooms, gigantic bathrooms, mini-kitchens, and televisions and VCRs. Because the Embassy Suites isn't within walking distance of the other Kaanapali hotels and restaurants, the rate includes a full breakfast each morning and a nightly cocktail hour—as well as complimentary scuba lessons twice a day in the pool. The hotel also has a restaurant and is on the beach.

Kapalua and Northwest Maui

The Lower Honoapiilani Highway (Highway 30) continues north from Kaanapali past the towns of Honokowai,
Kahana, and Napili, which lie along the lower beachside
road. This is condo city: nicely landscaped, but with buildings close together. One exception is the **Coconut Inn**,
away from the ocean on Hui Road F in Napili. The disad-
vantage of the Coconut Inn is that you'll have to schlepp
your Coppertone about a quarter of a mile to the beach,
but the property is charming, the people are friendly, and
the rates are reasonable. Once a dumpy apartment building, the Coconut Inn was renovated in 1986. Each day the
inn's pool draws a crowd who lounge around near the
dense foliage and get to know one another. A Continental
breakfast is included in the rate for the one-bedroom
apartments.

Past these little towns on the Upper Honoapiilani Highway (also called Highway 30), nearly at the end, the turnoff for the **Kapalua Bay Resort** beckons with its sedate
sign. Inside, the **Kapalua Bay Hotel and Villas** is West
Maui's most understated major accommodation, with
only 194 rooms, and first class all the way. Built in 1978 by
Colin Cameron, a descendant of missionaries (whose
company, Maui Land & Pineapple, also owns and operates
all the pineapple fields on Maui), Kapalua's elegant de-
meanor reflects its creator's personality: his love for art
and music, his ties to the Hawaiian culture, and a noncha-
lant acceptance of family wealth that's been around
longer than he has. (He sold the Bay Hotel to an em-
ployee and partners in 1986.)

Cameron had never been in the resort business before,
but he knew what he liked, so he ordered the plans to
include low-rise buildings of off-white stucco with polished wood and open views to the ocean. He had the place
heavily landscaped and filled the walls with wild, colorful
flower paintings by Maui artist Jan Kasprzycki. When the
hotel wasn't immediately successful, Cameron's company
started coming up with novel events that are now corner-
stones for the resort. Each summer, the **Kapalua Wine
Symposium** lures enthusiastic enophiles for two days of
tastings and lectures by some of the wine world's greats,
such as, for example, Robert Mondavi and Rodney Strong.
Some guests come for the summer **Kapalua Music Festival**, an event that has now become a working vacation for
musicians from the Juilliard music school and the Chicago

and New York philharmonics as well as the Tokyo and Israel symphonies. The widely televised **Kapalua International Championship of Golf** was started in the early 1980s.

Kapalua has become a favored hideaway for many who want the luxury and seclusion found in either the hotel proper or in one of the outlying condominium buildings. Many show-biz people are frequent guests in the spacious condominium units. Visitors to Kapalua with a car and $150 to spare who want to tour the Valley Isle have popularized **Guides of Maui** (Tel: 877-4042) and **Temptation Tours** (Tel: 878-2911) for personalized trips. Some who don't want to be bothered with going to one of the Kapalua Hotel's fine restaurants—**The Bay Club** and **The Plantation Veranda** both consistently win awards—call in the chic, personalized caterer Discriminating Taste Inc., whose chefs will prepare any meal they want (Tel: 871-7127). Like the guide services, the resort's dining options have also grown in popularity among other visitors to Maui.

Kapalua's shops have also gained a reputation, attracting many buyers who aren't even guests at the resort. The most interesting in the bunch is **Distant Drums A Cultural Art Gallery**, a mystical, cavelike boutique selling primitive masks and idols from the South Pacific, Balinese hand-carved ducks, Chinese bronze sculptures, South American artifacts, and Hawaiian wooden bowls. **Longhi Fine Clothing** stocks some of the trendiest silks, leathers, and ultra-suede in the Islands; **Windsurfer Kapalua** carries affordable cotton and rayon resort wear.

For years, Kapalua had planned on building a second lodging a few miles north of the current hotel. Work began in 1988 in preparation for a Ritz-Carlton, but was delayed when it was discovered that an important Hawaiian burial ground lay directly under the site. Kapalua resort owner Cameron agreed with Hawaiian activists that all bones should be returned to their original graves, but the expense in re-siting the Ritz was so great that it has delayed opening, probably for several years.

North and South of the Kapalua-to-Lahaina Area

Past Kapalua to the north, the road gets bad. Although it is passable, its chuckholes are wide and deep, matching the terrain, which is so steep it seems to drop away from the road in a vertical line. From here, there's a good view of Molokai (the Friendly Island). After about 15 miles of this vehicular torture, the tiny town of **Kahakuloa** appears on a hillside opposite. This old fishing village has only about ten families left, all Hawaiian, who earn their daily living with boats and nets. There's no store at Kahakuloa, and no gathering place except for the few churches that welcome travellers to their roadside locations. Visitors are watched carefully, but residents are friendly once they sense that a response in kind will come. Past Kahakuloa, the road continues until it reaches Wailuku (but car-rental agencies warn against taking this stretch of road).

Around the southern end of West Maui, going the other way, down Honoapiilani Highway (Highway 30) south from Kapalua and Lahaina toward Maalaea, as the mountains bend the road first toward the flat island of Kahoolawe and then into Maui's interior, there are plenty of places where drivers can stop to watch the whales that so often breach in these waters from December to April. The big black mammals love this protected bay, so if you spot one, pull over, because it's easy to lose track of the winding road. (For whale-watching cruises from Maalaea, see Lahaina, above.)

A wide spot in the road about five miles south of Lahaina is home to yet another of Maui's fine French restaurants. **Chez Paul French Restaurant**, in the tiny town of Olowalu, has been dishing up specialties such as scampi Olowalu, poisson buerre blanc, and veal à la Normande since 1975. Behind the small, curtained windows in the wooden storefront, Chez Paul appeals to an "in" crowd that doesn't mind dressing for dinner—in the casual chic style becoming popular among Maui's cognoscenti. With only 14 tables, Chez Paul seats diners twice nightly, at 6:30 and 8:30 (Tel: 661-3843).

CENTRAL MAUI

Many Maui visitors don't bother exploring the rather uninteresting central part of the Valley Isle, only passing through on their way to or from the airport in Kahului or to the heavily advertised **Maui Tropical Plantation**, in Waikapu, a few miles south of Wailuku on the Honoapiilani Highway (Highway 30). In only a few short years, the plantation has become Maui's most popular visitor attraction. However, the supposedly "free" attraction comprises only a huge gift shop and a few meager displays. Plantation visitors who want to see or do anything else—such as take a tram ride through the fields of tropical fruits and vegetables, see coconut-husking demonstrations, or get lei-making instructions—have to pay eight dollars apiece for the privilege.

Wailuku

Nearby, Maui's county seat (Maui County also includes Molokai, Lanai, and Kahoolawe) imparts an experience on the opposite end of the spectrum. Humble, historical Wailuku, on the north coast below the West Maui mountains, doesn't try to be anything it's not. A recently activated Main Street program has begun the tedious task of turning some of the town's old buildings into functional edifices along Vineyard and Market streets, while scrappy inhabitants like **Hazel's**, a local luncheonette serving up real Hawaiian-style home cooking, lend an air of reality to the whole procedure. Down the street, a Mexican beanery, La Familia, sends its mariachi music into the street. Around the corner on Market Street, **Siam Thai** dishes up nightly the island's best Thai cuisine. Robert Redford's autographed eight-by-ten glossy hanging on the wall may attest to that diner's impeccable tastes, as do the excited reports that Harrison Ford took his family there three times during one Valley Isle visit.

Wailuku's most photographed landmark, the pink **Iao Theater**, stands proudly at the head of Market Street, almost daring anyone who admires its Art Deco architecture to just try to get in. Built in 1927 as a movie house, the Iao is home to the Maui Community Theater—which only opens the theater when a play is running—until it moves to a more modern center in Kahului in late 1990. A new owner may then turn the theater into a more accessible visitor attraction.

Just down the street, a few intrepid shopkeepers selling antiques and unusual collectibles daily set out their signs. Joseph Ransburger calls his patchouli-scented establishment **Memory Lane**; he stocks a healthy collection of antique aloha shirts, old Hawaiian sheet music, and such oddities as Legalize Pot bumper stickers. Epes Sargent and Barry Infeld keep a huge Santa Claus statue dressed in a loud aloha suit outside their **Things From The Past**, while inside they've got dark, deeply grained koa furniture and delicate antique glassware. And Tye Hartall's **Traders of the Lost Art** sells the primitive wood sculpture, masks, rugs, and baskets he collects from trips to New Guinea and other exotic locales throughout Oceania. Hartall's shop is open only weekdays from noon to 5:00 P.M., or by appointment (Tel: 242-7753).

Some of Wailuku's edifices go back to the time of the missionaries who journeyed to the Sandwich Islands, and to one group in particular that settled in Central Maui. In 1833, the Reverend Jonathan Green first set foot on the Valley Isle, founding the Central Maui Mission Station on a choice piece of Wailuku land that Maui governor Hoapili had given to Green's employer, the American Board of Commissioners for Foreign Missions. The lush property was in the Wailuku foothills, at the entrance to Iao Valley, and had an expansive view all the way to Kahului Bay. In time Green established what is now **Kaahumanu Church** at the corner of Main and High streets, and what was then known as the Wailuku Female Seminary to train girls in the feminine arts.

In 1840, missionary Edward Bailey and his wife, Caroline, moved to Maui to teach at the Female Seminary and eventually moved into the Greens' home after the reverend left the board of commissioners when it wouldn't stop accepting funds from slave states. In time the home became known as the **Bailey House**, or Hale Hoikeike, and the Maui Historical Society now runs a museum in the old timber-and-stone home. The upper floors look much as they might have back in Bailey's day: A canopied bed dominates one room, while clothing from the period hangs in the closet. In the top-floor sitting room, a koa dining table made for President Ulysses Grant reminds visitors just how far away and distinct from the United States Hawaii once was: The president had to refuse the table, because he couldn't accept gifts from foreign nations.

Downstairs are Hawaiian artifacts from the days before the white man's arrival: Stone tools, dog-tooth necklaces, *tapa* (cloth made from bark), and fishing gear are only some of the items the society has displayed. In the basement, the museum's small shop stocks a good selection of Hawaiian gifts, from quilt kits to note cards to books on Hawaiian culture. The Bailey House grounds show that its proprietor also had commercial vision: Bailey was fascinated by sugar cultivation, perhaps suspecting he wouldn't always be principal of the Female Seminary that was, indeed, finally shut down. Sugar industry relics sit around the property as testimony to the missionary who had prepared himself to be the first manager of Wailuku Sugar Company.

Long before the Greens or the Baileys ever dreamed of Maui, the Wailuku area was the scene of a bloody battle that lives on in the minds of many Hawaiians. At the site of **Kepaniwai Park and Heritage Gardens** on Iao Valley Road a few miles west of Wailuku, Kamehameha and his troops engaged in a bloody battle for domination in 1790. When it was over bodies blocked the normally rushing Iao Stream, giving the village downstream its name: Wailuku means "water of destruction."

The Kepaniwai Park belies its past; the small pavilions that memorialize Maui's melting pot provide a peaceful setting for a picnic, a stroll, or a stop at the adjoining **Mark Edison**, an airy restaurant that serves hearty sandwiches and substantial lunches and dinners to the many Mauians who like to escape to the cooler climes for a meal. Within the state park, visitors follow paths that lead past an early Hawaiian thatched house and taro field; Japanese teahouse and gardens surrounded by ponds filled with *koi* (carp); a Portuguese villa fronted by arbors and a Madonna statue; and a white clapboard New England saltbox. The Chinese and Filipinos are also represented, as are present-day local folk, who often reserve one of the large picnic pavilions for a party. The neighboring **Iao Valley Lodge** has seven rooms for rent, and although they say Mark Twain thought enough of the place to stay here during a Maui visit, local folks sensitive to the battleground location and the spirits of the slain warriors—who they believe still rule the area—say the lodge has a spooky feeling. The rooms are rustic and sparsely furnished; a decent swimming pool is the main attraction. Some room rates include use of a car.

Just a few miles farther on you will see signs pointing you to a rock promontory called the John F. Kennedy Profile. Native Hawaiians' practice of looking for shapes in nature sometimes gets carried too far, but in this case the rocks really do look like our 35th president.

Right around the corner is **Iao Needle**, a stone spire rising dramatically some 1,200 feet from the valley floor. Erosion gave this outcropping its pointed shape, and when the mists roll in off the north shore they create an eerie effect. There are several easy hikes here in the **Iao Valley State Park**, originating in its parking lot. There are also more difficult ones, although frequent rains encourage walkers to stay on paved trails and out of the mud.

Central Maui cradles one other major town: **Kahului**. Except to residents, who love having the island's largest mall, the most movie theaters, the major airport, and a pivotal location, there's not much to recommend the town. Created by Alexander & Baldwin Inc. when its workers wanted to launch themselves into the happy state of home ownership, Kahului is still called "Dream City" by those who remember its beginnings as a company town.

One resident with a memory now runs **Alexander & Baldwin Sugar Museum** in a renovated plantation manager's home just outside Kahului. Although small, the museum, next door to the still-belching Hawaiian Commercial & Sugar Co. refinery in Puunene, captivates the crowds with such exhibits as a working model of a sugar mill. Already an absorbing presentation, the museum plans to unveil its restored locomotive sometime this year. Originally the number one engine on the Kahului Railroad, the vintage train is the oldest restored locomotive in the state and one of the oldest in the United States.

If you have some time to spare before boarding a plane you might want to check out **Artful Dodgers Feed 'N Read**, a charming coffeehouse-bookstore on Kaahumanu Avenue about a mile before the airport, where you can get sandwiches, desserts, and coffee—including cappuccino and espresso—and browse through the large collection of used books. Tables fill one side of the place, and you can peruse potential purchases while enjoying a snack. Work by local artists hangs on the walls on a rotating basis.

SOUTH MAUI

For a while, it was only West Maui that was booming. Now the shore that hugs Haleakala's western slopes is having its own construction explosion, particularly in its far southern reaches, where a battle rages for the upscale market. New hotels are going up at breakneck speed, creating competition for the all-important ocean view.

On the other hand, South Maui also contains the island's low-rent district. From the elbow where Maalaea Bay bends toward Highway 350 (Mokulele Highway), stretching to the south about 10 miles, the beach town of **Kihei** controls the coast with its hodgepodge of (mostly budget) condominiums. Determined travellers can find decent lodging in Kihei—clean and reasonably priced— but the overall atmosphere borders on the tacky. Strip shopping centers and fast-food joints have been given far too much rein.

Polli's on the Beach Mexican Restaurant is the gathering place for the trendiest group in the area, serving up meatless Mexican food and the island's best margaritas from its prime oceanside spot in far north Kihei. The best place to stay in Kihei is about three buildings before Wailea, the **Mana Kai Maui Resort**. This little hostelry looks out at the same beaches that you'll pay top dollar for down the road, and you can get studios or one- or two-bedroom units. Some rates even include a compact rental car. The decor isn't fancy, but the views are great and there's a decent restaurant on the premises.

Wailea

Both the South Kihei Road and the parallel Piilani Highway (Highway 31) farther inland lead down to the **Wailea Resort**. Wailea possesses stunning natural attributes: five crescent beaches, one right after another; good swimming in the protected bays; and the wild terrain of Ulupalakua Ranch ascending from the water, some of which has been sculpted into the resort's duo of golf courses, some allowed to go au naturel. For years there were only two hotels here, and a couple of extravagant condos and some large homes. In 1988, however, cranes began towering over the landscape, and at this writing are creating an 800-room Grand Hyatt, a 390-room Four Seasons, a 426-room Grand Champions, and a 451-room Embassy Suites. Wailea real-estate brokers have had some very good years.

When the **Maui Inter-Continental Wailea** opened in 1976, it was the first hotel for the resort, developed on a beautiful beach by sugar power Alexander & Baldwin and its partner, Northwestern Mutual Life. To this day the property remains Maui's stately dowager, refined and gracious, feeling no need to keep up with the Joneses' elaborate waterworks, ostentatious art collections, and other eye-popping diversions. A few nice shops, three swimming pools, and one of the island's best Continental restaurants, **La Perouse**, suit it just fine.

The IC, as the guests who come back year after year fondly call it, houses its clientele in an eight-floor "tower" and seven low-rise buildings that hug a central mall. In this breezy walkway, the IC holds the popular **Maui Marine Art Expo** for two full months each February and March, when schools of artists display their watercolors, sculptures, and textiles, all of which focus on marine life. The IC also brings in a series of lecturers, including admired ecologist Jean-Michel Cousteau, son of Jacques, as many times as he can make it.

Each Friday, the IC also welcomes aloha aficionados to its weekly **Aloha Mele Luncheon**. This is an authentic Hawaiian party, unlike any you'll find outside of Poi Thursdays, an old Hawaii-style celebration of food, song, hula, stories, and laughter at the Willows in Honolulu, or in private Hawaiian homes in the Islands. Smiling and gentle, "Auntie" Emma Sharpe presides over the Mele Lunch in her fragrant lei and colorful muumuu, assisted by popular entertainer Jesse Nakooka strumming his ukulele. After an hour-long Hawaiian arts and crafts demonstration, lunch begins at 11:30 A.M. Auntie Emma and Jesse sing songs, talk story, and dance the hula throughout lunch. Visitors who are not guests of the IC are welcome, but the hotel recommends reservations for everyone (Tel: 879-7227).

Two years after the IC began booking guests, the **Stouffer Wailea Beach Resort** hotel opened its 350 rooms (though it wasn't a Stouffer in those early years). The Stouffer hotel boasts the best beach on Maui—Mokapu—and has 26 detached, top-of-the-line units right on the water. There, at the exclusive Mokapu Beach Club, guests get breakfast in bed while they lounge in the hotel's plush robes.

Some Stouffer guests are taking advantage of vacation packages; other guests come just to tee off at one of Wailea's two golf courses, both named in numerous polls as being among Hawaii's finest. Tennis players love the resort's three grass courts, which have earned the moniker "Wimbledon West." The public areas are adorned with contemporary tapestries and colorful carpets, and the gardens contain exotic flowers, waterfalls, and reflecting ponds.

Stouffer's most elegant dining experience is at **Raffles'**, named for Sir Stamford Raffles, agent of the British East India Company who secured the transfer of Singapore to the Crown. Maui's Raffles' displays exquisite taste: dark wood, etched crystal, soft lighting, and dishes such as oyster cassolette with fresh sea urchin or broiled tiger prawns with fresh tarragon cream.

The Stouffer Wailea also emphasizes its Hawaiian heritage. Staffers offer Hawaiiana classes every day; guests can learn how to make leis or discover how pineapples are grown and selected. In addition, there are exercise classes, garden and reef tours, sunset cruises, and picnic sails as well as a weekly luau. The Sunday brunch requires guests to engage in an amazing feat of overindulgence at tables set in the breezy Palm Court restaurant. Next to the pool, in an intimate, trellised spot, the **Maui Onion** café serves up the world's best onion rings, made from Upcountry (Kula) onions.

Makena

Maui's baby resort lies south down the beach a piece from Wailea, over a winding road lined by scrubby *kiawe* trees (more commonly called mesquite on the Mainland). In fact, if it weren't for prodigious watering, the land all along Maui's southern coast would look like this, arid and rather unappealing. In the distance, finally, a three-story white hotel—the Maui Prince—appears in the vast field to the right. Beyond, the red cinder cone of the vent Puu Olai stands sentinel to this rural frontier, while offshore the crescent tip of Molokini, an underwater volcano, gives shelter to myriad snorkeling boats. And, past that, **Kahoolawe**, the uninhabited island used by the U.S. Navy for bombing practice, stops the eye from venturing any farther over the horizon.

Inside, the **Maui Prince Hotel** is mannerly, reflecting its Asian owner's ideas about hospitality: A Japanese rock garden fills the interior courtyard; a small stream ripples between the temple statuary and tiny, meticulously tended trees. Front-desk attendants graciously proffer hot washcloths at check-in so that guests can wipe away the dust of travel. And each evening three musicians dressed in symphony black set up their chairs and stringed instruments beside the brook to play classical selections.

Rooms at the Prince are simple, one prosaic painting per chamber. But the couples from California and the Japanese honeymooners who stroll the property in the evenings seem to like them just fine. They also show up for the lavish Sunday brunch, an all-you-can-eat affair featuring sideboards heaped with seafood and salads, and offering omelets cooked to order. Afterward, some head out for the nearby golf course that boasts Maui's lowest greens fees.

South of Makena

On the coast road exactly one mile south of the Maui Prince turnoff is the first of several unmarked rights-of-way to the huge sand expanse lovingly called **Big Beach**. At the far north end of Big Beach—to the right as you face the water—a trail leads over a rock embankment to what's even more lovingly called **Little Beach**, the favorite strand for locals who'd rather go suitless. Big Beach is frequented by families, as well as some guests of the Maui Prince who prefer the more ample acreage they find here. Some 3,000 feet long and 100 feet deep, Big Beach rarely looks crowded, even with kids darting between ocean and sand structures. Little Beach is probably the better-maintained of the two, however, since a group of regulars police the area, keeping the place clean and monitoring rowdy behavior. Officially, Hawaii outlaws nude sunbathing, so locals try to be extra careful about the comings and goings on this beach.

Beyond the beaches, Makena Road soon becomes the Hoapili, or **King's Trail**. A paved path for the ancient Hawaiians, who used it to travel around the island's southern shore to Hana, the extremely rough road now goes through—and sometimes under—Maui's last lava flow. Back in 1790 Haleakala spit out her last lava, forming the fields that covered portions of the trail and some ancient *heiau* (temples). Eventually, the trail joins the Piilani Highway and continues the journey east to Hana along Maui's southern coast on extremely bad "roads."

HALEAKALA CRATER

One trip was all it took for Mark Twain, who, years after his 1866 visit, wrote to a friend, "If the house would only burn down, we would move to the isles of the blest, and shut ourselves up in the healing solitudes of Haleakala." More than a century later, Haleakala still inspires such praise, from the people who visit and the people who take up residence on its lower slopes.

In its entirety, Haleakala stands 10,023 feet tall. The volcano, which filled in the sea gap between itself and the

West Maui Mountains, is not extinct, only dormant. She hasn't spewed lava in 200 years, but scientists are never really sure of these things; she may just change her mind without warning. On a good day, clouds wait until a bit before noon, then cover the mountain's upper half. On a bad day, Haleakala goes completely into hiding, giving a shock when she finally does appear to visitors who arrived when she was invisible. Bad days on Haleakala are better left for exploring Maui's other environs, because visibility downward is just as impossible as visibility upward.

In any event, it's best to start the drive up to Haleakala's summit early in the morning. Take a jacket or sweater; it stays chilly up there. Those who have done it swear that sunrise from the peak should rank as one of the natural wonders of the world—but that requires launching yourself into the car and onto the Crater Road (off Haleakala Highway/Highway 37) by about 4:00 A.M. Serious sunrise worshipers don't stop until they reach the **Puu Ulaula Overlook**, the highest lookout, a glass enclosure that perches right at the pinnacle and offers stunning 360-degree views. It's open 24 hours a day, so there's no problem getting past assertive park rangers. In fact, every morning at 9:30, 10:30, and 11:30 at the top, rangers give brief, informative talks on park geology and natural history.

Rangers are invaluable throughout the 27,284-acre national park, which was dedicated in 1961 to preserve Haleakala's natural resources. At the Hosmer Grove Campground a few miles before park headquarters, national park employees lead a two-and-a-half-hour hike each Monday, Thursday, and Friday morning at 9:00, pointing out native Hawaiian birds and plants along the way. Park headquarters itself traces Haleakala's volcanic origins and eruption history through a series of exhibits and lectures. And at the summit of Haleakala rangers take hikers on a descent into the crater along the **Sliding Sands Trail**. This two-and-a-half-hour stroll starts at 10:00 A.M. Saturdays, Sundays, and Tuesdays. The landscape in the crater probably rivals the scene witnessed by Neil Armstrong back in 1969: moonlike in its barren, pockmarked geology.

Between park headquarters at about 7,000 feet elevation and the summit there are plenty of lookouts for viewing and trails for self-guided walks. At the **Leleiwi Overlook** on the Crater Road the **Halemauu Trail** begins a two-mile descent on switchbacks that eventually reach the crater floor. Some people are lucky enough to see the phenomenon known as the Brocken specter at Leleiwi, an optical illusion that sometimes occurs if you are between the sun and a mass of clouds, when the right tricks of light project your much enlarged reflection, sometimes surrounded by rainbow colors, onto the clouds.

At about 9,000 feet, the **Kalahaku Overlook** is home to the silversword, a rare plant that grows only in craters in Hawaii, and whose spiked flowers match the surrounding environment's bizarre appearance. Eight hundred feet higher, the Haleakala Visitor Center has a few exhibits, and from there it is an easy walk to **White Hill** with its small crater. From White Hill there is a good view of Haleakala that reveals the volcano's geological structure.

UPCOUNTRY

The habitable, western side of Haleakala is called "Upcountry" for obvious reasons. Here, as the elevation progresses ever upward, the air cools and the trees grow tall and strong. In its higher reaches, Upcountry gives haven to those who need solitude and have chosen one of the long, winding roads for their hideaway estates. Farmers are busy in the fields, nurturing such diverse crops as carnations, onions, and grapes. Hawaii's only winery cultivates and ferments its harvest on Ulupalakua Ranch land on the southern end of the Kula Highway (Highway 37).

Tedeschi Vineyards was founded in 1974 when the Tedeschi family joined the Erdmans of Ulupalakua in testing California and European grapes. The climate and soil were found to be suitable, and soon the winery was in business, producing both still and sparkling wines from grapes, as well as a dry wine from pineapples grown on the island. Now open daily, the winery's tasting room was built by James Makee, who called his spread Rose Ranch when he founded it back in the 1850s. He raised cattle, but kept himself busy importing as many varieties of the blooming beauties as he could get his hands on. Vineyard staffers give behind-the-scenes tours of the wine-making equipment, and also lead a stroll around the grounds, which still have their original landscaping, including a 100-year-old camphor tree and a healthy stand of Norfolk Island pine.

Gardeners should visit the **Kula Botanical Gardens** on Upper Kula Road about 10 miles from the winery, and the

University of Hawaii's **Kula Experiment Station** on Mauna Place, easily reached just off the Kula Highway on Copp Road. The KBG features a relaxed 30-minute walk beside koa and *kukui* trees, ginger and orchid blooms, and the exotic protea shrub. Protea, whose immense blossoms seem straight off the set of *Cocoon* (but actually come from Australia), were first introduced to Hawaii at the University of Hawaii station. More than 300 varieties grow here, in colors from blushing pink to fireball red to flaming orange, and with fanciful names to match: Sunburst Pincushion, Pink Mink, and Hawaii Gold. Several nurseries in the area will pack protea for shipping to the Mainland.

Down the road, the **Kula Lodge and Restaurant** looks out over the protea fields and on to the valley below. Both a restaurant and an inn, the lodge has become a favorite breakfast spot for trekkers to the Haleakala summit for the sunrise, in need of sustenance on their way back down the mountain. The eggs Benedict melt in your mouth, and the view is especially great for those who can't quite tear themselves away from the urge to merge with nature. Tables sit next to huge banks of windows, and on misty days when there is a fire in the fireplace it could be heaven. The lodge also serves lunch and dinner. At the bottom of a winding, stone stairway, the lodge's **Curtis Wilson Cost Gallery**, with its pastoral oils and ethereal music, adds to the effect.

Residents of other islands, as well as rugged visitors who really love Upcountry Maui, use the lodge for longer stays. A quaint and cozy hostelry, the lodge has only five chalets, three with their own fireplaces and lofts. Several also boast the same view as the restaurant, and the lucky inhabitants of those units often sit simply staring from their lanai. By early 1990 the lodge—60 years old but recently renovated—expects to open ten more chalets, all with fireplaces.

Other pockets of Upcountry Maui are also appealing. The little town of **Makawao**, between Haleakala and Kahului, was once a typical western burg, its sagging storefronts along the lone main thoroughfare offering serious staples such as saddles, hard tack, and *palaka*-print work shirts (*palaka* is a plaid popularized by Island plantation workers). Settled by Portuguese immigrants who took up working the nearby ranches after their sugar plantation contracts ran out, Makawao was the Maui version of the Old West. Now, the once rough-and-tumble cowboy hangout is having flutters of gentrification, as a few art galleries, boutiques, and cafés have quietly opened their doors.

Glassman Galleries is the extrovert of the bunch, run by Barbara Glassman, who first published *Maui Art & Creative People,* then created Maui Art Tours (Tel: 572-8374) to put the public together with Maui artists. Her gallery now brings the work of her favorite Valley Isle artists to visitors driving through Makawao.

Makawao's cowpokes probably don't shop at the town's tiny clothing and knickknack emporiums anymore, but the buildings, both inside and out, remain true to their origins. In a breezy, tin-roofed dwelling, **Collections** has been importing unusual baskets, colorful woven rugs, clothes from places like Cyprus and Guam, and delightful jewelry for more than a decade. **Coconut Classics** has stuffed its wood-frame store with antique aloha shirts, old books, and oddball Hawaiian collectibles—including a chartreuse grass skirt. And the simply named **Maui Child Toys & Books** is perhaps one of Hawaii's finest toy stores, with quality playthings and a healthy selection of beautifully illustrated reading material.

But Makawao has not given up its roots: The centerpiece for this wide spot in the road is still the venerable general store called **T. Komoda Store & Bakery**, where a six-decade tradition continues. Each morning, a crew of Japanese-American women bake the pastries—the cream puffs are especially popular—that have made Komoda's an Upcountry favorite. Although baked goods get the most attention, Komoda's also stocks an assortment of fabric and other necessities.

Down the street, Norman and Patty Diego run **Tack 'N Things** for the diehard cowboys who still need bridles and stirrups, many of whom also compete in the annual **Makawao Rodeo**. Held each Fourth of July, the riding and roping event draws thousands to the Upcountry fairgrounds. For entertainment of a more everyday sort, Makawaoans head on over to the **Makawao Steak & Fish House**, a darkly paneled restaurant that serves up thick slabs of expertly grilled beef. A livelier crowd opts for **Polli's Mexican Restaurant**—big sister to Polli's on the Beach in Kihei—where proprietor Polli Smith perfected her veggie Mexican recipes and her margaritas. **Casanova Italian Deli** has killer pasta; many patrons drive from Maui's lower elevations just for the ravioli or rigatoni.

As Baldwin Avenue winds down from Makawao toward the beachside town of Paia, it gives shelter on a gentle curve to the **Hui Noeau Visual Arts Center**, set back off the road behind a simple stone gate. The pink, tile-roofed, Mediterranean mansion was once the home of Ethel Baldwin, who founded the Hui—the Hawaiian word for "group"—in 1934, holding meetings and ceramics classes at the estate she and her husband called Kaluanui. About 13 years ago, descendant Colin Cameron (of Kapalua Bay Resort) gave the home to the Hui, and the association now holds workshops here, open to the public, in a wide range of subjects, including drawing, photography, ceramics, and design. Each spring the Hui also opens its grounds to **Art Maui**, the Valley Isle's only juried art show. Some 250 artists participate in the event, even donating their time to lead tours through the exhibits.

Some of the area's artists hang out at Beverly Gannon's **Haliimaile General Store** off Baldwin Avenue on Haliimaile Road, as do some of her husband's pals (Joe Gannon is a Hollywood producer). Once a market for workers from the pineapple plantation that surrounds it, the Gannon's reincarnation is a hip restaurant, its peach, green, and white exterior a stylish anomaly to its out-in-the-middle-of-nowhere location. Inside, the Gannons employ a casually elegant decor—pastels, woods, and large paintings decorating expansive walls—while the menu, which changes every two weeks, includes such staples as barbecued ribs, smoked chicken, and duck with different sauces. A long deli case lining one wall serves as a reminder of the Gannons' success story. Bev was running a little catering company, cooking for a few clients in addition to her husband's colleagues. She decided to open a deli in the old general store, put in eight tables and some shelves offering fiestaware, baskets, and cooking gear for sale. One week later, she had 32 packed tables, then 60, then 80. It is easy to taste why.

EAST MAUI

Some like to exclaim over the **Hana Highway** (Highway 360) as if it were the Coney Island rollercoaster, wearing cartoony "I Survived the Hana Highway" tee-shirts just to prove their bravery. Others laugh that anyone would even call it a highway, with its 600 hairpin curves and 65 narrow bridges challenging even the most careful driver to stay focused on the ribbon ahead. But no one should let this put the brakes on a Hana Highway adventure. And if you think the Hana Highway is bad, try the southern route along the South Maui coast to Hana—here, pavement is a foreign word.

True, the road that traverses the distance from Kahului east to Hana along Maui's north coast demands attention, but no more than the scenery that surrounds it. East Maui is the wet, windward side of the island, and the Hana Highway route is characterized by an abundance of waterfalls, tropical rain forests, and secluded trails. Along its entire 55-mile length the highway to Hana is well-paved. Drivers are more likely to pull over to snap a quick photo than to stop from exhaustion. And when it rains, the resulting rivulets that blanket the coast convince most sightseers that they're about to have an ecstatic out-of-body experience.

Hana does have an airport of sorts, but only those who plan to spend their entire vacation in Hana opt to use it. Far more visitors drive out on the Hana Highway, taking a leisurely day to make the round trip (starting pretty early in the morning).

Paia

Many think of Paia as the last outpost before the road really begins. There, a stop at **Picnics** is a must for snacking along the way. Picnics packs simple lunches that include sandwiches, fresh fruit, cookies, and drinks, or you can go all out on the Executive Picnic: slices of ham, beef, turkey, and a split *kiawe* (mesquite)-roasted chicken, along with cheeses, wheat buns, chips, fresh fruit, nut bread, drinks, and condiments. This hole-in-the-wall spot on Baldwin Avenue also lets you combine your own favorite picnic foods, and provides ice chests and tablecloths.

Paia has come a long way since its early days as the retailing headquarters for an Alexander & Baldwin sugar operation. During World War II, marines pitched their tents nearby, and for a while the town really boomed, but they soon left. A & B also decided that its unprofitable Paia operation should come to an end. Many Paia residents took advantage of the opportunity to buy their own homes in Kahului, the town created by A & B in Central Maui, which further depleted the population.

In the 1960s, Paia was psychedelic; hippies hung out in the little town, running funky shops and organic restaurants. Windsurfers became the predominant group in the late 1970s, with the discovery that **Hookipa**, a bay a mile past town, is one of the best-winded places in the world. Artists and craftspeople also like Paia. Thirty of them founded the **Maui Crafts Guild** here in an old green building at the entrance to town, where visitors can poke through original Maui work: unusual baskets woven from twigs, leaves, and boughs; mystical *raku* pottery subtly featuring the female form; and tie-dyed *pareu* (sarongs) suitable for wearing. The artists staff the guild, so ask the person behind the desk to point out his or her work.

Artist **Eddie Flotte** will talk about his precise watercolors if you find him at his studio. He's often out on location painting, but his girlfriend, Sandy Cotton, is a loquacious hostess who can describe the process better than he can. Flotte paints Maui scenes—interesting storefronts, expressive old faces, and weather-worn boats—in a painstaking style that captures every detail. He also has a healthy collection of subjects he painted in Greece and France, and plans to release limited-edition prints of selected works sometime this year. You can find Flotte's studio by heading down the alley between **Exotic Maui Woods** and Dillon's, or ask at EMW for Sandy, who runs that store, which carries an excellent sampling of work by 30 woodworkers, from delicately turned bowls to massive conference tables.

As for other studio visits: Painter **Piero Resta**'s studio is an art lover's delight, and the Italian painter loves to show it off to anyone who calls first (Tel: 575-2203). Set in the old Pauwala Cannery in Haiku (about five miles beyond Paia, then up Haiku Road), Resta's workplace vibrates with gracious creativity. While Piero and his son Luigi might point out the artist's latest extraordinary piece— large canvases abandoned to color that reflect Piero's travels around the world—Piero's wife, Gail, might pour a glass of wine for the visitor, or crank up the espresso machine if it's a cold day. Once a restaurateur, Resta still has the inviting hospitality of someone who wants you to come in, have a seat, and rest your feet.

Farther along the Hana Highway you can stop at places like **Twin Falls**, an easy, 450-foot hike just past mile marker 2, where there is a great swimming hole in addition to the freshwater falls. Right after mile marker 12, the **Kaumahina State Wayside Park** provides a lovely look at the rugged Hana coastline, with Keanae peninsula and its old village in the distance marking the halfway point to Hana. Kaumahina also has restrooms. If you need some exercise, the **Keanae Arboretum** just past mile marker 16 has several trails that will challenge a hardy hiker. **Uncle Harry's** is at the halfway spot, marker 20, selling fresh fruit, home-baked breads, and the requisite souvenirs.

Hana

Hana itself sneaks up on you. First-time visitors might wonder if they've even reached the place. Indeed, it has to be said that in terms of excitement the drive to Hana is more than half the fun. But Hana does have a quiet charm, the kind that requires guests to adapt to its pace. Some slow down by stopping at **Helani Gardens**, the creation of Hana native Howard Cooper. Set on a 60-acre plot right before town, Helani Gardens is a simple stroll among all kinds of tropical plants, laboriously labeled by Cooper, who's added his delightful witticisms and interpretations at every turn. Cooper's wife, Nora, is editor of the daily *Maui News,* and the couple commutes between Hana and Kahului, but if he's at the gardens he's usually happy to talk the day away with receptive gardeners.

Hana itself is heavily Hawaiian, and meeting the people who determinedly live in this rural outpost ranks as the area's best activity. Some Hana people are natives, such as Tiny Maleikini—his size is anything but—who owns and operates **Tiny's Tours** out of his brightly painted van. Tiny also works at the Hotel Hana Maui, and offers his sightseeing tours on an as-needed basis (book them through the hotel). The big Hawaiian man with a manner as open as the Hana sky above has a handle on the history of the area, and a friendly way of teaching interested passengers about his culture. Some Hana people worth meeting aren't natives. Richard Pryor often wanders Hana streets dressed as an itinerant worker, and Jim Nabors has a macadamia nut farm right outside town.

Fusae Nakamura runs **Aloha Cottages**, a four-room hostelry that's basic, clean, and inexpensive. Mrs. Nakamura offers the fruit off her trees, and has been known to watch her guests' laundry so they can see the sites around Hana. The **Hasegawa General Store**, a nearby market, is crammed full of essential items.

It is the graceful **Hotel Hana Maui** that seems to come up a lot in conversation here, however, and that's because it isn't just in the center of town, it *is* the center of town, both geographically and emotionally. If there's anything you need or want to know in Hana, just ask at the hotel—they will be more than happy to oblige you. Low-rise and low-key, the small hotel was recently renovated by Caroline Hunt's Rosewood Hotels (the same company that runs the Bel-Air Hotel in Los Angeles, the Remington on Post Oak in Houston, and Dallas's Mansion on Turtle Creek and Crescent Court). By the time Hunt's company purchased the Hana hotel and the 7,000-acre ranch that surrounds it in 1986, the property had been operating for 30 years. True, it was run-down, but it employed about a third of Hana's 700 residents—many of them related to one another. There was natural suspicion about an outsider taking over the hotel.

But Hana's family-style atmosphere has blended well with the Rosewood dedication to running the finest lodgings in the world, providing a most memorable vacation for those who seek out the secluded hostelry. People who enjoy the Hotel Hana Maui most are those who want to relax and entertain themselves. The Hotel Hana Maui is not on the ocean, it has no golf course, and there is no nightlife here to speak of, but the hotel has come up with a wide range of things to do, from ranch tours to beach shuttles to country barbecues to packing picnics for parties who want to set out on their own.

The most interesting picnic destination in Hana is the **Piilanihale Heiau**, a 15th-century Hawaiian temple. You can walk up to the top of the stacked-rock structure—it is the largest *heiau* in the state—and try to imagine how long it was in construction and even what it was used for, since no one really knows. The hotel not only packs the picnic for this excursion, but unlocks the gate that allows admittance.

The monied guests who had been coming to the Hotel Hana for years—often two or three months at a time each winter since its beginning—were particularly happy with the renovation job Rosewood bestowed on the hotel. White stucco walls, shake-shingled roofs, and trellised patios dominate on the outside, while bleached wood floors, overstuffed furniture, and soft earth tones take over on the inside. Impeccably decorated throughout with natural woods and fabrics, subtle Hawaiian art, and tropical landscaping, the hotel is pleasant and hospitable. The rate includes all meals, and the chefs are some of the island's best.

Back when sugar dominated the Hana lifestyle the town was far larger. But the last plantation finally went sour in the 1940s, and many people left in search of new jobs. When Rosewood decided to add some new guest accommodations about two years back, its executives looked to the town's sweeter days, and erected 24 duplex buildings on land where one of the town's last plantation housing camps had been. Moreover, they had their architect research the style of those old buildings and duplicate their simple shapes: post-and-beam structures with tin roofs and generous decks. Then they painted the outside in the once-pervasive "plantation green," the color favored by plantation owners, probably because it was cheap and easy to get. Rosewood also declined to enhance the landscaping, so the new Sea Ranch Cottages look as if they've been there for years, set among the native Hawaiian plants and wind-whipped sea grass.

The cottages' exteriors also belie their interiors, for once you go inside you find the same understated decor as in the rooms throughout the rest of the hotel. A distinct advantage of the cottages, however, is the views: The retreats perch near a cliff with the ocean broiling and crashing against the rock outcroppings below. Some of the units have hot tubs, some have living rooms, and all have pampering in mind.

Hana travellers who can't afford the steep rates at the Hotel Hana Maui often check in at Mrs. Nakamura's place or at the comfortable condominium **Hana Kai-Maui Resort Condominium**, the only Hana accommodation that's actually on the oceanfront. A few cabins at the **Waianapanapa State Park** are also near the ocean, and they're downright livable as well. Several miles before Hana Town, Waianapanapa's rustic setting appeals to those who want to get back to nature but don't want to rough it totally. Cabins are spacious and come with linens and kitchen gear, available from the state, at ten dollars per person a night. The park has a beautiful black-sand beach, swimming coves, and trails that lead past old Hawaiian burial sites. There are also 60 campsites available at Waianapanapa.

Just south of Hana the highway becomes rough. Many *heiau* were built by ancient Hawaiians in this area, but they are difficult to spot because there are few roads crossing the private land here. The traffic traversing the 10 miles from Hana to Oheo Gulch can get heavy in spite of the difficulty in making the passage. Most people are on their way to **Seven Pools** at Oheo Gulch (sometimes called Seven Sacred Pools). No one is quite sure how the pools acquired their revered status; Hawaiian mythology does not consider them sacred. It is commonly believed that overzealous tourism promoters probably made the whole thing up, and it sounded too good to change. Anyway, Seven Pools (there are actually nearly two dozen pools along the cascade down the hill to the ocean) is a delightful place to swim, sun, and picnic on the rock ledges that seem tailor-made for lounging.

One of Hana's most revered residents lies in the small Hoomau Congregational Church graveyard about a mile past Oheo Gulch. Charles Lindbergh and his wife, Anne Morrow Lindbergh, loved Hana, and built a home there so Charles could spend his last years in the secluded village. When he died in 1974 he was buried in Hana, just as he had requested. The dirt road to the church is narrow and unmarked, leading toward the ocean through a grove of trees. County officials and residents are protective of Lindbergh's grave, which is understandable after vandals left the site in a shambles several times. As a result, they took down the sign that once directed visitors to the site. Unless you know somebody, you can ask five residents for directions and you'll get five different answers—and they'll all be evasive.

Beyond the Hoomau Church, Kipahulu Falls mark the opening to one of Maui's most beautiful—and rarely visited—valleys, the **Kipahulu**. You must find someone knowledgeable to take you back into the wilds; the trails are rough, and most easily traversed on horseback. There are no organized tours into Kipahulu Valley, but if you are interested you might try asking at the Hotel Hana Maui (see above) for Carl Lindquist, the hotel's former managing director—if anyone can help you out, Carl can.

Along the coast road farther west are numerous *heiau* and the 1859 Huialoha Church, renovated in the early 1970s. The village of Kaupo comes up shortly, with another of Hawaii's venerable general stores. Eventually this road, the Piilani Highway (Highway 31), comes out in South Maui at Ulupalakua Ranch near Makena. This route, however, is Maui's greatest driving challenge, particularly if you do not have a four-wheel-drive vehicle. For the most part, it's best not to attempt this route.

GETTING AROUND
Only Kahului Airport gets direct flights from the U.S. Mainland. United Airlines flies nonstop each day from Los Angeles, Chicago, and San Francisco, with service via Honolulu from Denver and Philadelphia. Delta Airlines flies daily to Kahului via Honolulu from Atlanta, Dallas,

Salt Lake City, and nonstop from Los Angeles. American Airlines lands in Kahului via Honolulu from Newark, Chicago, Detroit, Montreal, Houston, Dallas, and Los Angeles. The interisland flight from Honolulu or from one of the other islands is a short, 20- to 30-minute hop. Hawaiian Airlines, Aloha Airlines, Aloha IslandAir, and Air Molokai all fly to Kahului.

If you want to touch down at the Kapalua–West Maui Airport you must fly on either Hawaiian Airlines or Aloha IslandAir. This route uses smaller, slower, noisier planes, but you can't beat the convenience if you're staying in West Maui. All interisland flights arrive and depart about every 30 minutes at Maui's two main airports.

Hana Airport is only serviced by Aloha IslandAir. There are relatively few flights per day, only four from Honolulu.

If you're staying at the Kaanapali or Kapalua resorts, you can catch a free car/van shuttle to your hotel or condominium from the Kapalua–West Maui Airport, or you can rent a car from one of the companies with desks at the airports. At Kahului Airport, car-rental companies are stationed across the road from the terminal. All the big-name agencies maintain operations at Kahului, as well as some less-expensive, locally run companies— Tropical is the best of those. Be sure to pick up a *Maui Drive Guide,* which will give you a complete set of maps with close-ups of selected areas.

If you're staying at the Hotel Hana Maui and land at the Hana Airport, the hotel will pick you up. Or you can reserve a car ahead of time with Dollar Rent A Car, or try to call Dollar when you get there (Tel: 808-248-8237). There are no car-rental desks at Hana Airport.

ACCOMMODATIONS REFERENCE
The rate ranges given here are projections for winter 1989 through summer 1990. Unless otherwise indicated, rates are for double room, double occupancy. Hawaii's telephone area code is 808.

▶ **Aloha Cottages**. Just north of the Hotel Hana Maui (see below); P.O. Box 205, **Hana**, HI 96713. Tel: 248-8420. $40–$78. Call for directions.

▶ **Coconut Inn**. 181 Hui Road F, **Napili**, HI 96761. Tel: 669-5712; elsewhere in U.S., (800) 367-8006. $69–$99 (from April 1 to December 20), $79–$109 (from December 21 to March 31).

▶ **Embassy Suites Resort**. 104 Kaanapali Shores Place,

Lahaina, HI 96761. Tel: 661-2000; elsewhere in U.S., (800) 462-6284; in Canada, (800) 458-5848. $175–$450, including breakfast and evening cocktails.

▶ **Hana Kai-Maui Resort Condominium.** Hana, HI 96713. Tel: 248-8426/7742; elsewhere in U.S., (800) 548-0478. $75–$90.

▶ **Hotel Hana Maui.** Highway 360, P.O. Box 8, Hana, HI 96713. Tel: 248-8211; elsewhere in U.S., (800) 321-HANA. $455–$555, A.P.; Sea Ranch Cottages $625–$855. Call for directions.

▶ **Hyatt Regency Maui.** 200 Nohea Kai Drive, Lahaina, HI 96761. Tel: 667-7474; elsewhere in U.S., (800) 228-9000. $195–$355.

▶ **Iao Valley Lodge.** Located on Iao Valley Road; for reservations, contact: Maui Accommodations, 34 North Church Street, Suite 204, Wailuku, HI 96793. Tel: 244-9551; elsewhere in U.S., (800) 252-MAUI. $65–$120.

▶ **Kaanapali Alii.** 50 Nohea Kai Drive, Lahaina, HI 96761. Tel: 667-1400; elsewhere in U.S., (800) 642-MAUI. $195–$245 for one bedroom; $215–$500 for two bedrooms.

▶ **The Kaanapali Beach Hotel.** 2525 Kaanapali Parkway, Lahaina, HI 96761. Tel: 661-0011; interisland, (800) 227-4700; elsewhere in U.S. and in Canada, (800) 657-7701. $115–$210.

▶ **Kapalua Bay Hotel and Villas.** One Bay Drive, Lahaina, HI 96761. Tel: 669-5656; elsewhere in U.S., (800) 367-8000. $185–$345; one-bedroom villas $250–$335; two-bedroom villas $330–$435 (low season rates).

▶ **Kula Lodge.** Highway 377, RR 1, Box 475, Kula, HI 96790. Tel: 878-1535. $87–$136. Call for directions.

▶ **Mana Kai Maui Resort.** 2960 South Kihei Road, Kihei, HI 96753. Tel: 879-1561; elsewhere in U.S., (800) 525-2025. $67–$147.

▶ **Maui Inter-Continental Wailea.** 3700 Wailea Alanui Drive, P.O. Box 779, Wailea, HI 96753. Tel: 879-1922; elsewhere in U.S., (800) 33-AGAIN. $175–$275.

▶ **Maui Marriott Resort.** 100 Nohea Kai Drive, Lahaina, HI 96761. Tel: 667-1200; elsewhere in U.S., (800) 228-9290. $195–$280; suites $425–$1,000.

▶ **Maui Prince Hotel.** 5400 Makena Alanui, Kihei, HI 96753. Tel: 874-1111; elsewhere in U.S., (800) 321-MAUI. $180–$280; suites $350–$600.

▶ **Plantation Inn.** 174 Lahainaluna Road, Lahaina, HI 96761. Tel: 667-9225; elsewhere in U.S., (800) 443-6815. $95–$140.

▶ **Sheraton Maui.** 2605 Kaanapali Parkway, **Lahaina,** HI 96761. Tel: 661-0031; elsewhere in U.S., (800) 325-3535. $185–$275; suites $400–$750.

▶ **Stouffer Wailea Beach Resort.** 3550 Wailea Alanui Drive, **Wailea,** HI 96753. Tel: 879-4900; elsewhere in U.S., (800) 9-WAILEA; in Canada, (800) HOTELS-1. $185–$350; suites $475–$1,200.

▶ **Waianapanapa State Park Cabins.** To reserve a cabin, write several months in advance to the Division of State Parks, P.O. Box 1049, **Wailuku,** HI 96793. $10 per person per night.

▶ **The Westin Maui.** 2365 Kaanapali Parkway, **Lahaina,** HI 96761. Tel: 667-2525; elsewhere in U.S., (800) 228-3000. $175–$350; suites $500–$1,500.

BED-AND-BREAKFASTS

▶ **Bed and Breakfast Maui Style.** P.O. Box 886, **Kihei,** HI 96753. Tel: 879-7865.

For information about other bed-and-breakfast accommodations on the Hawaiian Islands see Oahu Outside Honolulu Accommodations Reference.

MOLOKAI

By *Thelma Chang*

Thelma Chang is a Honolulu-based writer specializing in travel and human-interest stories. Her articles have appeared in such publications as Westways, Essence, *and the Smithsonian's* Air and Space *magazine.*

Molokai may be only a 15-minute flight east of Honolulu's hustle and bustle toward Maui, but it is one of the few places in the Islands that remains steeped in the spirituality of its Polynesian past.

It's no wonder that "The Friendly Isle" is a favorite weekend retreat for many refugees from Honolulu seeking escape from Oahu's crowds and traffic jams. On this narrow island—38 miles long from east to west, and only 10 miles wide—such modern trappings as fancy stores, movie theaters, elevators, and high-rises don't exist. Instead, you'll see acres of open plains and rolling hills. You'll also discover that a large number of Molokai's 6,500 residents are native Hawaiians who like their traditional, close-to-nature lifestyle. There is physical and psychological balm in the easygoing pace of an island that discourages complicated lists of "things to do." Yet Molokai unfolds its beauty in a complicated way.

The central plain connects Molokai's two major land masses, volcanic mountains that rose from sea depths about 1.5 million years ago, one in the west—the volcanic mountain here is called Maunaloa—and one in the east. Over time, streams carved huge canyons on the east side of Molokai, marine erosion created high sea cliffs on the island's windward, northeastern coast, and a subsequent, smaller eruption produced Kalaupapa (or Makanalua) Peninsula.

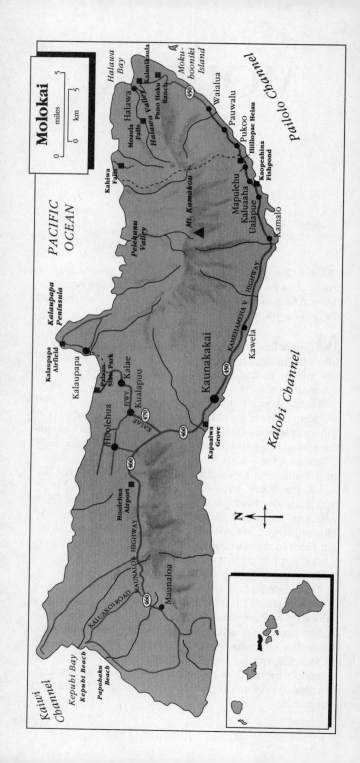

On the west side, giraffes and other exotic creatures roam a wildlife park that borders a resort complex. A bit farther to the east, the fertile plains of Hoolehua (also the location of Molokai's airport) bloom with fields of watermelons, sweet potatoes, onions, and bell peppers—reflecting the people's hope that diversified agriculture will balance tourism as the pineapple industry leaves the island.

The island's main town, Kaunakakai, sitting by the southern central shoreline, is home to quaint shops, local-style eateries, and people who gather to "talk story." The island east of Kaunakakai is a potpourri of spiritually powerful vistas: ancient fishponds, a well-preserved *heiau* (ancient place of worship), coconut groves, tiny churches, country scenes, and unexpected small sandy beaches.

On the North Shore, also known as the "back side," rough seas and sheer cliffs border the hauntingly beautiful area of Kalaupapa (the flat plain).

This last site is one facet of the dramatic past of the island, long known as "Molokai Puleoo," place of powerful prayer. Precontact Molokai was once the center of ancient learning and the bastion of *kahuna* (priests) who protected the island from invasion, partly through spiritual prestige. Later, in one of the saddest chapters of Island history, Molokai became synonymous with its Hansen's disease (then called leprosy) colony at Kalaupapa. Torn from their families, leprosy patients of the 1800s were dumped at this isolated spot to suffer their pain in loneliness under very harsh conditions. Their despair was eventually alleviated somewhat by the care of many Samaritans, the best known of whom was Father Damien de Veuster. The carpenter-priest dressed open sores, buried the dead, and built shelters, churches, and coffins until he, too, was ravaged by the disease.

MAJOR INTEREST

The West Side
The relaxed atmosphere of Kaluakoi Resort
Sandy beaches
Molokai Ranch Wildlife Safari
Maunaloa town

Kaunakakai
Molokai's charming "trading post" town

The East Side
The dramatic and spiritual beauty of ancient fish-
    ponds, the Iliiliopae Heiau, and the east Molokai
    mountains
Pristine bays and beaches
Lush Halawa Valley and Moaula Falls

Kalaupapa
A beautiful site with a tragic history

THE WEST SIDE

About 12 miles west of Molokai's Hoolehua Airport lies the
6,800-acre resort–residential community of **Kaluakoi**. This
oasis includes the luxury, 288-room **Kaluakoi Hotel & Golf
Club** on Kepuhi Beach, two fully equipped condominium
apartments available to visitors (the **Paniolo Hale** and the
Ke Nani Kai), and a championship, 18-hole golf course.

The Kaluakoi Hotel has a wide range of accommodations, from modest-sized rooms to suites and cottages
with kitchenettes and marvelous views of the ocean and
the golf course. The hotel also offers tennis courts that
are lit at night, a good restaurant, and other amenities.
(No need for air-conditioning here; the wind can sometimes come roaring through your room.) The hotel fronts
Kepuhi Beach, a wonderful stretch of white sand. (If you
walk the beach on a clear night you will see the bright
lights of Oahu, 25 miles away.)

South of the hotel is Hawaii's largest white-sand beach,
Papohaku, and a 10-acre beach park complete with showers and picnic spots. Papohaku's often turbulent sea and
pounding waves are tricky, however, and it is wise to stay
away from them.

Weather permitting, contact the hotel's travel reservations desk to join the **Molokai Ranch Wildlife Safari**. It's
an exciting way to see and photograph zebras, giraffes,
axis deer, and many other resident animals, numbering
1,000, who greet the tour director for "snacks." It's also a
way to see part of the 52,000-acre Molokai Ranch, the
island's largest private landholder.

From the resort, a ten-minute drive up Kaluakoi Road,
then west on the Maunaloa Highway (Highway 460), will
take you to **Maunaloa**, a former pineapple-plantation
town that is home today to just a few stores and homes,
and a restaurant. One of the most intriguing shops here is

the **Big Wind Kite Factory**, filled with international kites of all sizes, shapes, and colors.

If you feel you're being stared at, you are; on the ceiling huge kites in the shapes of bats, butterflies, and other exotica peer down at you. They share their space with knickknacks galore, from jewelry and local handcrafts to Indonesian fabric and cute wooden animals from Bali.

KAUNAKAKAI

Between the airport at Hoolehua and Kaunakakai, watch for **Kapuaiwa Coconut Grove**, once ten oceanside acres, now greatly reduced in size, that King Kamehameha V planted with a thousand coconut trees in the 1860s. Keep alert for falling coconuts, and try to find the freshwater spring bubbling at the ocean's edge.

Kaunakakai itself resembles a trading post straight out of an Old West movie set. Cowboys (*paniolo*) and fishermen join grandmas, grandpas, dogs, and store proprietors at wooden false-front buildings for the latest news. The town is a wonderful place to mingle with the people, learn about Molokai—stop by the **Molokai Fish & Dive** shop and ask about snorkeling or sailing cruises from Kaunakakai Wharf—and taste some local fare. **Kanemitsu Bakery** is one of the island's oldest establishments and the source of the popular Molokai bread as well as fresh-baked cookies. Hungry islanders often head for grilled fresh fish at the **Mid Nite Inn**, Chinese food at **Hop Inn**, and Filipino dishes at **Oviedo's**.

Kaunakakai's shoreline is graced by two cottage-style hotels—the **Pau Hana Inn** and the **Hotel Molokai**—comfortable, no-frills havens with lots of Island atmosphere. There are also fully equipped vacation apartments at the oceanfront **Molokai Shores**, which is surrounded by tropical gardens.

Like a lifelong friend, the Pau Hana Inn, Molokai's oldest existing hotel, is a popular end-of-day gathering spot for fun-loving islanders, who unwind at the hotel's outdoor bar under the benevolence of a century-old banyan tree (*pau hana* means "finished with work"). For oceanside dining try the **Holoholo Kai Restaurant** at the Hotel Molokai, where you can enjoy a (daylight) view of Lanai across the sea.

THE EAST SIDE

A 30-mile stretch along the Kamehameha V Highway (Highway 450) leads east from Kaunakakai to lush Halawa Valley. Pack a snack, check your gas tank, and allow at least half a lazy day for a round trip that takes in much scenic and spiritual beauty. The road hugs a southern shore fringed with ancient Hawaiian fishponds that deserve more than passing mention.

Conceived in the 1400s, the fishponds were a natural yet sophisticated kind of aquaculture. Like other early Hawaiian inventions they illustrate the people's intelligent and sensitive approach to gathering sustenance for survival from their environment.

Typically, the Hawaiians built the fishponds by constructing an encircling wall of stone or coral or by connecting two points of land with a wall. Wooden grates were placed at strategic points in the ponds to ensure circulation—and the entrance of young fish, which eventually grew too fat to escape. Some ponds remain, while others have been destroyed by silt, tidal action, and people.

Another dimension of Hawaiian history can be seen at **Kawela** (the heat of battle), the site of the crumbling walls of a *puuhonua* (place of refuge). Near Kawela is a battleground where in the 1790s Hawaii's King Kamehameha I won the victory that placed Molokai under his reign. (No doubt part of the king's overall military success in placing the Islands under one chief was his acquisition of weapons brought by Westerners, including the cannon.)

Western impact can also be seen farther east at **Kamalo**, where Father Damien erected St. Joseph's Church, a tiny chapel with a tall steeple, one of three surviving churches the priest built on Molokai. From the church, look toward the East Molokai Mountains and the pristine beauty and waterfalls of Mount Kamakou, the island's highest elevation—a dreamlike sight that has inspired numerous oil and watercolor artists.

Images of local life—and some oddities—are probably the most enchanting part about the drive to and from Halawa Valley. Chickens, ducks, and roosters scamper alongside the road, pecking at the dirt. A horse munches on grass; an egret sits contentedly. Old and new houses in east Molokai reflect the subtle changes taking place. At one turn, there's a series of ramshackle wooden homes in need of paint and fixing up; at the next, modern, almost luxurious, beach houses loom into view. And all along, pockets of sandy beach dot the shoreline.

If you wish to stay on the east side you may rent vacation apartments at the **Wavecrest** in **Ualapue**, a short distance east of Kamalo. Just past Ualapue, at Kaluaaha, there's another church Damien built, Our Lady of Seven Sorrows. Across the way is Kaopeahina, a well-preserved fishpond.

The spiritual presence of early Hawaiians can also be felt at Mapulehu, site of the magnificent, 13th-century **Iliiliopae Heiau**. You can get there by means of the **Molokai Wagon Ride**, a horse-and-wagon journey that bumps and grinds through bramble bushes and the Mapulehu Mango Grove. Wear comfortable clothing and footwear, because the trip involves a short hike and the crossing of a streambed. If you really want to be prepared, bring a raincoat or umbrella.

Conducted by lifelong Molokai residents, the tour also includes a freshly prepared picnic lunch at a lovely beach and a chance to chat with people who love their island. Larry Helm and his partners in the tour operation regale you with song, dance, laughter, and island-style cooking. Tel: 558-8380.

Still farther along the coast, The Neighborhood Store in Pukoo, in front of an interesting array of painted rocks and statues, is the last stop for refreshments, snacks, and restrooms before you get to the eastern end of the island.

Past Pukoo is a real get-away-from-it-all rental opportunity: **Pukoo Vacation Rental**, the second floor of Diane and Larry Swenson's beachfront home, complete with kitchen and views of the ocean and Maui island.

The road then twists and climbs to **Puu-O-Hoku Ranch** (hill of stars). The top of this bluff boasts gorgeous views of west Maui and turtle-shaped Mokuhooniki Island, the latter used for bombing practice by the U.S. military during World War II. Past the ranch's entrance, on private property, is Kalanikaula, a sacred *kukui* (candlenut) grove that once surrounded the home of a powerful *kahuna* whose *mana* (spiritual force) continues to be respected; the grove is one of the most sacred places in Hawaii.

A few more zigzags on the road and **Halawa Valley**—the oldest recorded inhabited area on Molokai—unfolds its beauty like a "Bali Hai" movie set. Far below, two bays front the grassy plains of this valley, which is home to only a few people. Inland, the thick, tropical jungle with waterfalls is visited only by the hikers who come to this place for its utter seclusion.

The three-mile descent into the valley on a narrow road can be a hairy one, most people honking their horns when they hit blind curves. Still, the valley is popular with picnickers and nature lovers, who sometimes trek into the jungle—take mosquito repellent—to see the 250-foot-high **Moaula Falls**, legendary home of a giant sea dragon. It's a complicated trail that requires the crossing of a stream or two that can be waist or shoulder high after a rain, so it's best first to inquire locally about safety conditions. (In any case, let people at your hotel know about any plans for going off the beaten track.)

Beyond Halawa Valley lies the **North Shore** and some of the most spectacular, hidden parts of Molokai: awesome 3,300-foot sea cliffs (recorded as the world's highest in the *Guinness Book of World Records*), and wilderness areas that may be seen only by prearranged helicopter or kayak tours. The seas here are so rough that even kayaks are restricted to summer months, and even then only when weather permits. Kalaupapa is the only place on the North Shore that may be visited throughout the year (see Getting Around for all these destinations).

KALAUPAPA

The history of this lovely, lonely peninsula at the bottom of rugged sea cliffs in the middle of the North Shore sparked strong emotion in author James Michener: "In the previous history of the world no such hellish spot had ever stood in such heavenly surroundings."

In this "heavenly surrounding," Hansen's disease devastated the lives of more than 8,000 people who had been separated from their families and brought here in the mid-1800s and early 1900s. Afflicted native Hawaiians, who had historically lived in a communal culture of extended families, could not understand the imposed Western value of isolation. Lonely and lacking adequate food or shelter, the first patients died quickly from despair and the harsh elements. (The powerful, howling winds at Kalaupapa can move people and make flying missiles out of objects.)

Mercifully, improvements came with such caretakers as Father Damien, Mother Marianne Cope, and Brother Joseph Dutton, who fought the bureaucracy and worked tirelessly for their patients. (The Roman Catholic church has placed Father Damien in its canonization process.) Today, more than 100 years after the first ships dumped their patients here, Kalaupapa looks like the pristine paradise it was meant to be.

From "topside" Molokai ("topside" is local parlance for the top part of the island) there are several ways to visit Kalaupapa Peninsula, which is located at the bottom of steep cliffs: by air, foot, or mule. No matter which method you choose, there's only one tour of the peninsula itself daily—it starts in the morning and will take most of the day—so coordinate your plans with Richard Marks at Damien Molokai Tours (see Getting Around).

For a spectacular bird's-eye view of what's entailed if you traverse by foot or mule, drive to **Kalaupapa Overlook**, about 20 minutes from Kaunakakai. Go west on Highway 450, then north at a juncture on Highway 470, the road to Kalae. You'll pass Kualapuu, a former pineapple plantation town. Past Kalae (where the mule stables are located), the road leads to Palaau State Park and the parking lot at the end of the highway. The trail to the north reaches the 1,600-foot-high overlook and a sight to behold: the North Shore, its 3,000-foot cliffs, and, a tiny dot below, Kalaupapa town.

Weather permitting (we don't recommend the hike or mule if it's rainy), the **Molokai Mule Ride** down into Kalaupapa is an unforgettable experience. From the topside corral on Highway 470 near Kalae, surefooted mules led by experienced guides meander down **Kalaupapa Trail** more than three miles and 26 switchbacks to the settlement below. The trail cuts through rain forest and sharp drop-offs, but your nerves are soothed with vistas of the distant peninsula and the Pacific Ocean—fabulous scenery as far as the eye can see.

At the bottom, you're likely to join others who've hiked down or taken the three-minute topside-to-Kalaupapa flight on Air Molokai or Aloha IslandAir.

The bumpy daily bus tour of the peninsula treks through the tiny town of Kalaupapa, beautiful rain forest, and green valleys. Nearly 11,000 acres of the area, including three valleys, were declared a national historic park in 1980.

Certainly a highlight is a visit to the windy and rocky east side, Kalawao, where crashing waves serve as a background to Father Damien's newly restored church, St. Philomena, the only structure left from the settlement's early days. Throughout the tour, marked and unmarked grave sites remind you of Kalaupapa's grim past.

Although Kalaupapa's remaining 95 patients are free to come and go—sulfone drugs cured and arrested the disease in the 1940s—most are old and choose to spend their later years in this quiet village.

GETTING AROUND

Molokai is served by Hawaiian Airlines, Air Molokai, and Aloha IslandAir, with frequent daily flights from Oahu and Maui. The latter two airlines also fly between "topside" Molokai and Kalaupapa.

There's no bus service on Molokai, but there is Molokai Taxi. The island deserves a leisurely pace, so it's advisable to rent a car. There are several auto rentals on Molokai, including Tropical Rent-a-Car, at Molokai Airport, Hoolehua, Molokai; Tel: 567-6118; from the Hawaiian Islands, (800) 352-3923; elsewhere in U.S., (800) 367-5140. Note: Most gas stations on Molokai are closed on Sundays.

For information about the **Molokai Wagon Ride**, contact Larry Helm, P.O. Box 56, Hoolehua, Molokai 96729; Tel: 558-8380. The tour leaves at noon from a spot along Highway 450, 15 miles east of Kaunakakai, marked by their sign.

Kayaking treks to Molokai's North Shore may be arranged with several experienced island firms: Go Bananas, 740 Kapahulu Avenue, Honolulu, HI 96816, Tel: 737-9514; Kayak Kauai, P.O. Box 508, Hanalei (Kauai), HI 96714, Tel: 826-9844; Adventure Kayaking International, P.O. Box 61609, Honolulu, HI 96839, Tel: 988-3913. A larger vessel, the 25-foot, twin-engine *Mahealani* makes summertime trips to the North Shore; write Glenn Davis, Hokupaa Ocean Adventures, P.O. Box 141, Kualapuu (Molokai), HI 96757 (no telephone). If you wish to see Molokai's North Shore by air, contact Papillon Hawaiian Helicopters, 421 Aowena Place, Honolulu, HI 96819, Tel: 836-1566; elsewhere in U.S., (800) 367-8047, ext. 142. Papillon offers North Shore tours from Oahu and Maui. (At this time Molokai has no island-based helicopter service.)

Some restrictions apply if you go to Kalaupapa. Visitors must be over 16 and all tours of the area must be escorted. Cameras are permitted, but pictures of residents are not allowed. Since there are no overnight accommodations at Kalaupapa, it is advisable to have confirmed departure reservations if you plan to leave by air. Mule rides are limited to physically fit persons weighing no more than 220 pounds and not too elderly. For more particulars about the mule ride contact Molokai Mule Ride, P.O. Box 200, Kualapuu, HI 96757; Tel: 567-6088; elsewhere in U.S., (800) 843-5978. For other Kalaupapa excursions contact tour operator Richard Marks at Damien Molokai Tours, P.O. Box 1, Kalaupapa, HI 96742, Tel: 567-6171.

ACCOMMODATIONS REFERENCE
The rate ranges given here are projections for winter 1989 through summer 1990. Unless otherwise indicated, rates are for double room, double occupancy. Hawaii's telephone area code is 808.

▶ **Kaluakoi Hotel & Golf Club.** P.O. Box 1977, **Maunaloa**, HI 96770. Tel: 552-2555; elsewhere in U.S., (800) 367-6046. $79–$165.

▶ **Ke Nani Kai.** P.O. Box 126, **Maunaloa**, HI 96770. Tel: 552-2761; elsewhere in U.S., (800) 888-2791. $75–$105; $95–$125 after December 20.

▶ **Hotel Molokai.** P.O. Box 546, **Kaunakakai**, HI 96748. Tel: 553-5347; elsewhere in U.S., (800) 423-6656. $55–$105.

▶ **Molokai Shores.** P.O. Box 1037, **Kaunakakai**, HI 96748. Tel: 553-5954; elsewhere in U.S., (800) 367-7042. $68–$95.

▶ **Paniolo Hale.** P.O. Box 146, **Maunaloa**, HI 96770. Tel: 552-2731; elsewhere in U.S., (800) 367-2984. $75–$155.

▶ **Pau Hana Inn.** P.O. Box 860, **Kaunakakai**, HI 96748. Tel: 553-5342; elsewhere in U.S., (800) 423-6656. $39–$79.

▶ **Pukoo Vacation Rental.** Diane and Larry Swenson, Swenson Construction and Real Estate, Star Route 279, **Kaunakakai**, HI 96748. Tel: 558-8394. $50.

▶ **Wavecrest Resort.** Star Route 155, **Kaunakakai**, HI 96748. Tel: 558-8101; elsewhere in U.S., (800) 367-2980. $56–$66.

BED-AND-BREAKFASTS
For information about bed-and-breakfast accommodations on the Hawaiian Islands see Oahu Outside Honolulu Accommodations Reference.

LANAI

By Thelma Chang

Peaceful Lanai is one of those get-away-from-it-all islands
that stands on the brink of being "discovered" at several
different levels—physically, emotionally, spiritually.

It's easy to see why this kidney-shaped island—just 17
miles long and 13 miles wide—is called the "Pineapple
Isle." Pineapples have dominated the island's plantation
economy since the early 1900s, when Boston businessman James Dole bought virtually all of the island from
missionaries, imported workers (mainly from the Philippines), and changed the face of Lanai.

However, Lanai is more complex than its visible face.
The island unfolds its landscape like a movie of interesting and sometimes bizarre contrasts, especially when
seen from the rain forest of Lanaihale, the island's highest
point. At one moment, there are only fields of pineapple;
at another, dusty trails and rocky, barren surfaces that give
way to stunning vistas of steep cliffs, eroded canyons,
shimmering bays, and a beautiful sandy beach. A turbulent ocean borders the east side where Lanai keeps its
secrets of the past—a *heiau,* a deserted village, and a
windswept beach.

Lanai, located about eight miles south of Molokai and
west of Maui, has long been the focus of different percep-
tions. Polynesians avoided the island for centuries, fearing it was inhabited by ghosts. Only when Lanai was
deemed safe did Hawaiians migrate to the island, probably in the 1400s. In the late 1700s a European ship circled
the island but chose not to land. In ancient chants the
place was called "Red Lanai," referring to the red dirt that
flies in the wind and tints everything it touches. Today
residents sometimes witness a thick, ghostly mist that

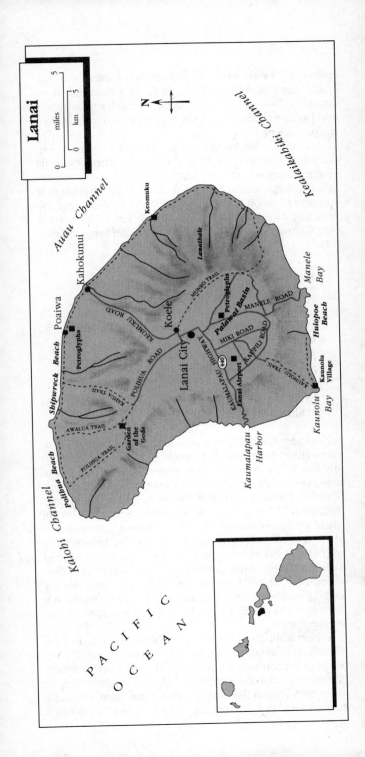

covers the fields in **Palawai Basin**, an extinct volcanic crater that is Lanai's best farmland. "It's beautiful in an eerie way," says a lifelong resident of the basin, which is also home to rock formations engraved with early Hawaiian petroglyphs.

Lanai's red dirt, rough terrain, and cool evening temperatures (particularly from November through April) demand common sense, practical clothing, a four-wheel-drive vehicle, and specific directions from old-timers if you plan to go off the beaten track. Vehicle rentals may be arranged directly with Bob Oshiro or Lanai City Service (see Getting Around) or through the Hotel Lanai in Lanai City.

MAJOR INTEREST

Relaxed, friendly atmosphere
Small-town Lanai City
Kaumalapau Harbor
Kaunolu village historic ruins
Hulopoe Beach and Manele Bay small-boat harbor
Lanaihale's summit and sweeping views of neighboring islands
Dramatic historical settings at Keomuku village and Shipwreck Beach

For decades the only guest stop in Lanai has been the ten-room **Hotel Lanai**, nestled among pine trees on a hill in tiny Lanai City. It's a pleasant, unpretentious, plantation-style house without television or telephones in its rooms, but with a front porch that invites neighbors to sit and "talk story." There you'll likely see a microcosm of the island's 2,200 residents: Hawaiians, Asians, Caucasians, a black, and a few Portuguese. And often you'll see visitors with sturdy boots or snorkeling gear, ready for rugged trails and some of the clearest waters Hawaii has to offer.

For now, Hotel Lanai is the main spot in town for lodging and food. Breakfast and lunch may be found at a few small eateries in Lanai City, but business hours there are flexible.

A short walk down the hill from the hotel leads into the island's only town, **Lanai City**, where most of the island's people live in plantation housing—modest wooden homes erected in the early 1900s. Graced by giant Norfolk pines, they border the large, grassy town square, a friendly get-together spot for people who frequent Lanai City's small eateries and markets, read the bulletin board at the post office, and share business news at Dole headquarters. Blink and you'll pass Lanai's diminutive police station, courtroom, and jail, a sign that Lanai so far enjoys a low crime rate.

The town itself serves as a handy reference point, since the island's estimated 30 miles of paved road branch from Lanai City to the coast in three main directions: southwest, to the working port of Kaumalapau Harbor; south, to Hulopoe Beach; and east, to Shipwreck Beach.

Lanai's busiest—if a few trucks on the road can be considered "busy"—road (Highway 440) leads to **Kaumalapau Harbor**, where millions of pineapples are loaded on boats for shipment to Honolulu's canneries 60 miles away. Off the highway and around the airport, a jolting drive down bumpy trails takes you to Kaunolu Bay and into Hawaii's past. The ruins of **Kaunolu Village**, King Kamehameha's summer home, offers a complete archaeological site: an abandoned village, house platforms, and gravestones. Locals respect such cultural sites; stories abound of people who disturbed certain spots, experienced unexplainable events, and quickly returned such "souvenirs" as rocks and plants by air mail.

While the very surefooted could walk east about five miles along the coast to **Hulopoe Bay** from Kaunolu, a 9-mile drive on Manele Road south from Lanai City is quicker. At the end of a ride through pineapple fields—here and there fields of morning glory flowers pop up unexpectedly—you'll be rewarded by lovely **Hulopoe Beach** and a park complete with picnic tables and barbecue pits. Snorkel fans will find some of the clearest waters around.

At nearby **Manele Bay**, small leisure sailboats bob about, where once only the fishing boats of Lanai's families were moored. This scene is more than symbolic; change is in the air, and it leaves some residents worried about the survival of their cooperative, sharing lifestyle.

David Murdock's conglomerate Castle & Cooke, Lanai's major landowner since 1961, when C & C acquired Dole Corporation, is scaling down its pineapple operation and looking instead toward tourism. Sometime in 1990 the Hotel Lanai will be joined by the luxury 250-room **Manele Bay Hotel** and the European-style, 102-room **Lodge at Koele** just north of Lanai City.

These changes and much more can be seen from **Lanaihale**, Lanai's highest ridge at 3,370 feet, and a knock-your-socks-off experience of rain forest and gorgeous views. You get there by means of the Munro Trail, named after a naturalist who planted pine trees along the ridge-line in 1910, creating a Colorado-like atmosphere. The trees serve as natural windbreaks around Lanai City, col-lect moisture from passing clouds, and so enhance the island's water supply.

It's wise to allow about a half a day (more if you plan to hike) for a leisurely and bumpy ride to and from Lanai-hale's summit. From Lanai City, head north on Lanai Avenue, past the golf course and the Lodge at Koele. At about the point where you see a graveyard to the right, take the middle fork—the Munro Trail—which leads to flat terrain at the top. On your way up, stay on well-travelled track. You'll pass Hookio Ridge, where Lanai's warriors unsuccessfully fought invading forces from the Big Island of Hawaii in 1778. However, it's at the top that you turn your motor off, unwind, and enjoy a dramatic feast for the eyes. The views of the major islands (*all* of them, except Niihau and Kauai) resemble dreamlike paintings—so beautiful you can't take your eyes away. No wonder people often come here at sunrise or sunset, with a snack, coffee, and their thoughts—and the silent rain forest for company.

Windward Lanai

From the ridge you can also see Lanai's east, or wind-ward, side, which includes the ruins of Keomuku village and Shipwreck Beach, both requiring at least an hour's travel time from Lanai City. Lanai Avenue takes you north to Koele and connects with Keomuku Road, which leads to a fork near the coastline.

The left fork takes you to the stark beauty of **Shipwreck Beach,** where powerful trade winds swept wooden ships and steamers toward Lanai's reef. The beach has also been used as a convenient dumping ground, where old ships were purposely beached and abandoned. The dra-matic setting has a haunting feeling to it.

A right at the fork leads to the ghost town of **Keomuku** and a bit of Lanai history. The site was once home to a sugar mill and its Asian workers. Hawaiians believe unfortunate events occurred because some stones were removed by *haole* (Westerners) so that a railroad could be built: Not long after the disturbance, the mill's sweet water turned salty, and a plague devastated the population. Before the sugar mill, Keomuku had been inhabited by native Hawaiians, who left behind, among other things, a *heiau* (temple), and it seems to have been this *heiau* that had been disturbed.

All over Lanai, such strong spiritual "presence" is what many Lanai residents wish to respect and protect as they face the ever increasing pressures of commercial development.

GETTING AROUND
Just 20 minutes flying time from Honolulu, Lanai is served by Air Molokai, Hawaiian Airlines, and Aloha IslandAir. Hotel Lanai guests receive complimentary transit service for the five-mile trek from the Lanai Airport to Lanai City. Direct arrangements for vans, trucks, jeeps, and four-wheel-drive vehicles may be made with Oshiro's Service & U-Drive (Tel: 565-6952) or Lanai City Service & U-Drive (Tel: 565-7227). Serious hikers on Lanai may want to read Craig Chisholm's 1985 guide *Hawaiian Hiking Trails*, Fernglen Press, Lake Oswego, Oregon.

ACCOMMODATIONS REFERENCE
The rate ranges given here are projections for winter 1989 through summer 1990. Unless otherwise indicated, rates are for double room, double occupancy. Hawaii's telephone area code is 808.

► **The Hotel Lanai.** P.O. Box A-119, **Lanai City**, HI 96763. Tel: 565-7211; elsewhere in U.S., (800) 624-8849. Double rooms $58. There is a nine-hole golf course nearby in Koele.

For up-to-date information about the **Manele Bay Hotel** and the **Lodge at Koele**, contact Oceanic Properties, Inc., 650 Iwilei Road, Honolulu, HI 96817; Tel: 548-4811.

BED-AND-BREAKFASTS
For information about bed-and-breakfast accommodations on the Hawaiian Islands see Oahu Outside Honolulu Accommodations Reference.

KAUAI

By John W. Perry

A Pacific historian partial to Kauai labeled it "a separate kingdom" in recognition of the island's long history of linguistic and cultural separation from the rest of the Hawaiian Islands. Even an attempted invasion from Oahu by Kamehameha the Great failed because of canoe-destroying winds in the channel separating the two islands, and that same geographic isolation—Kauai is Hawaii's northernmost landfall, and with tiny Niihau stands alone far to the west of Oahu—deflected much of the decimation the post-contact era inflicted on Hawaii's other islands. In many respects Kauai has retained a separateness of spirit, not just place, and, though aptly nicknamed the "Garden Isle," is remembered at journey's end as an island apart, a special port of call outside of Hawaii's mainstream destinations—Oahu, Maui, and the Big Island's Kohala and Kona coasts.

Kauai's physical beauty is stunning, taking a back seat to no other island, not even to Polynesia's "Island of Love" (Tahiti), Micronesia's "Garden Isle" (Pohnpei), or Melanesia's Aoba, fiction's Bali Hai. A popular misconception is that Kauai's major attraction is resorts, when the truth is the reverse: The island is preeminent, not the resorts. Even Kauai's often maligned trademark, *paka ua* (raindrops), the gentle waters that grow the "garden" in the Garden Isle, has a special significance in Hawaii, having passed into the language as a proverbial saying: *ka ua loku o Hana-lei*, "the pouring rain of Hanalei" (Hanalei being a town on Kauai's north coast). Travelwise, a typical island-wide weather report is "mostly sunny after morning rains," and umbrellas as well as swimsuits and bikinis are appropriate gifts for Kauai-bound visitors.

Those who love rain, a tropical landscape, and an island wilderness that is still *wilderness* will like Kauai.

MAJOR INTEREST

White-sand beaches
Lush, tropical scenery

Lihue and Environs
Kilohana plantation

Poipu and Koloa
Sunny-side resorts
Old Koloa Town restoration

The Waimea Area and the West Coast
Country towns
Waimea Plantation Cottages
High-country state parks
The spectacular scenery of the Na Pali Coast from
    Kalalau Lookout

Wailua and the Coconut Coast
Coco Palms Resort
Hawaiian legends and history along the Wailua
    River

The North Shore
Kilauea Point lighthouse wildlife refuge
Princeville's scenic resorts (golf)
Hanalei bayside town
Lumahai Beach
Kalalau foot trail to the Na Pali

A traveller's mental map of Kauai, drawn from the east coast county seat of **Lihue** (which is the site of the main airport), is, like the island itself, almost circular. The **Poipu-Koloa** area, destination of most new arrivals because of its plentiful sun, accommodations, and beach activities, lies to the southwest; the coastline west of Koloa is a thoroughfare for cars en route to the **Wilderness**, the high-country parkland above Waimea that delivers evergreen forests, peaceful hiking, rustic cabins, and magnificent views. Those who make the trek west will be charmed along the way by small rural towns like Hanapepe and Waimea, and pleasantly surprised by the expansive, largely undiscovered beaches they'll find on the **West Coast**.

North of Lihue is the **Wailua-Kapaa** Coconut Coast region, a way station for those on their way to **Hanalei** and

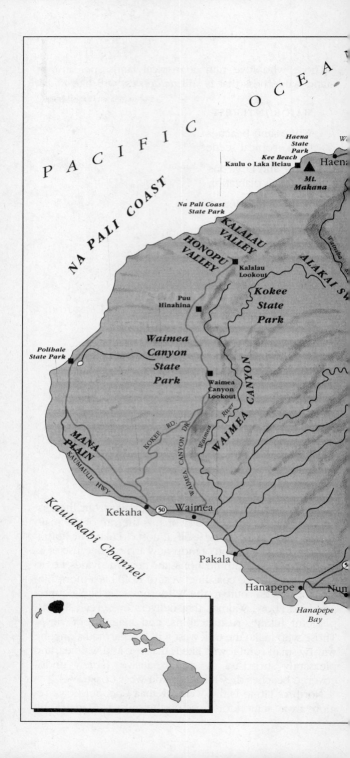

PACIFIC OCEAN

NA PALI COAST

Haena State Park
Kee Beach
Kaulu o Laka Heiau
Haena
Mt. Makana

Na Pali Coast State Park

KALALAU VALLEY

HONOPU VALLEY

Kalalau Lookout

ALAKAI SW

Kokee State Park

Puu Hinahina

Waimea Canyon State Park

Polihale State Park

Waimea Canyon Lookout

WAIMEA CANYON

Waimea River

KOKEE RD.
WAIMEA CANYON DR.

MANA PLAIN

KAUMUALII HWY

Kekaha
50
Waimea

Kaulakahi Channel

Pakala

Hanapepe
Nun

Hanapepe Bay

the wet **North Coast**, or a pleasant stop for those in search of a simpler, local experience (or the Wailua River). The drive to Hanalei and the North Shore, with its Princeville Resort, passes through peaceful small towns, lush, green, undeveloped countryside, and along some of the most beautiful coastline in Hawaii.

The around-the-island coastal roads end at the south at Polihale State Park, west of Waimea, at the north at Haena State Park, west of Hanalei, and inland in Kokee State Park, north of Waimea; between these road ends is the **Na Pali Coast**, reached by backpack, tour boat, or helicopter. Even more remote is the island's center, topped by Mount Waialeale (rippling water), which has a yearly rainfall of over 450 inches, earning it the cartographic label "The Wettest Area on Earth." Atop Waialeale's cloud-covered summit is an ancient altar devoted to Kane, the greatest of Hawaii's gods and, not surprisingly, the deity of rainwater.

LIHUE AND ENVIRONS

A traveller passing through Lihue in 1840 saw only a tiny Christian church, a few banana plants, and a chief's thatched *hale* (house), which he called a "straw palace." When the first hotel opened in the 1890s, featuring an oceanside annex for "sea-bathers," a dentist pulled teeth in his room, and the island's sheriff rented a bed. Now an airport here accepts DC-9s, streets are designed for cars, not horses, and the harbor is an anchorage for cruise ships, not sailing canoes—all reinforcing Lihue's relative big-town mystique on this country island. Despite the commercial scars inflicted by nondescript shopping centers—so visible when concrete and steel replace tin roofs and wood—and despite a connotation of coolness in the town's name (it means "cold chill"), a friendly atmosphere still prevails here, where the biggest official claim to fame is longevity: The Kauai County Building is the oldest continuously occupied county building in the state.

The best introduction to Kauai in "urban" Lihue is the **Kauai Museum** on Rice Street, a simple repository of artifacts reflecting the island's unpretentious lifestyle. Housed inside a distinctive stone structure with a faded, blue-tile roof is a large collection of Hawaiiana that provides a visual, though rather textbookish, history of Kauai from its volcanic origin six million years ago to the sugar plantation era of modern times. Those who admire trees, and artwork made from trees, will treasure the collection of hand-carved *kou*-wood calabashes used to hold *poi* (pounded taro) and fish. *Kou,* today extremely scarce, was a reddish-brown wood preferred by ancient Hawaiians, who transformed bowl making into an art form still used here by modern-day craftsmen. Small calabashes made for Hawaiians' favorite children became family heirlooms—a bright mind, bowl makers said, was like a food-filled *kou* bowl. Another curious wooden exhibit, though hardly a collector's item, is the corner of an old sugarcane plantation house.

On the outskirts of Lihue, beside a cove fronting Kalapaki Beach on Nawiliwili Bay, is **The Westin Kauai,** a so-called fantasy resort (the public-relations term) catering to travellers who wish to surround themselves with posh decor and *fresh* water. The Westin, with 847 rooms, is a new genre of resort for Kauai, strong on rich appointments and "international" charm—a tropical hybrid somewhere between a private estate and a water-spouting theme park. A herd of marble horses bathed by spraying fountains prances in the open-air reflecting pool, and any moment you expect to see Antony and Cleopatra appear on a golden barge, drinking from silver goblets. In keeping with its water theme, the high-rise hotel is built around a scallop-shaped swimming pool—Ray Charles has sung the blues at water's edge—that is reminiscent of the Hearst Castle pool in San Simeon. (In curious contrast to this man-made Versailles-by-the-bay sits nearby **Kalapaki Beach,** a simple, and lovely, white-sand beach.)

Despite the ersatz paradise environment, the Westin is, because of its location, ideal for day trips to the Poipu resort area and the state parks of western Kauai, or, in the opposite direction, to Hanalei and the North Coast. For those who prefer ready-made fantasies laced with marble sculptures, or simply an elegant address within minutes of downtown Lihue, the Westin would be Shangri-La on Kauai.

The most expensive dining under one roof on Kauai is also within the Westin's make-believe utopia. There is elegant dining in **The Masters** (jackets required), where the menu is based on that of a Michelin four-star restaurant in La Napoule, France. Another Westin restaurant, **Inn on the Cliffs,** created for seafood and pasta gourmets, has a 200-degree ocean view. The restaurants are reached by three modes of transportation: ancient Hawaiian (that is, on foot), horse-drawn carriage pulled by Clydesdale, Belgian, or Percheron breeds, and mahogany taxi-boat—touches of Disneyland.

A contrast to the high-class eateries and cocktail lounges at the Westin are the small restaurants and taverns in and around Lihue where locals eat and drink, rubbing elbows with an occasional visitor. A meal on simple plates, not museum-quality calabashes or handmade china, is served in an heirloom atmosphere at **Ma's Family, Inc.**, on Halenani Street, a back street a short drive from the Kauai Museum. If Ma is on duty and business is slow she will tell you about the old days when she had only one regular customer for breakfast, a *haole* (white foreigner) who ate eggs and toast—for less than a buck. Never mind that Ma's place isn't included on any travel magazine lists of the top 50 restaurants in Hawaii; you eat at Ma's because, like Hawaii's vanishing mom-and-pop grocery stores, someday (perhaps soon) the Mas of Kauai will be extinct, replaced by fast-food joints and star-rated resort restaurants.

For *saimin* (a noodle soup), walk around the corner to **Hamura Saimin Stand**, a longtime favorite among Lihue's noodle eaters and bubble-gum chewers, who are asked not to stick gum under the tables. No-frills canned beer is on ice at **Hap's Hideaway** on Ewalu Street, site of Kauai's first compact-disk jukebox, which is often played by the bartender. More crowded, especially when interisland cruise ships dock at Nawiliwili Harbor, is the **Oar House Saloon**, between the Westin Kauai and the new Anchor Cove shopping complex. The crowd is mixed—cruise shippers and locals—with blue-jean-clad waitresses shuffling between poolroom and bar carrying trays of long-neck beer-bottles.

Following Kaumualii Highway (Highway 50) south and west for two miles brings you to **Kilohana** (Hawaiian for "best," "superior"), a restored plantation home visible from the highway. Plantation owner Gaylord Wilcox lived here in lordly fashion during the 1930s, when agriculture was the island's major business, aloha shirts were fashionable, and lei reached to the bottom of a gentleman's double-breasted coat. Once the most expensive home ever built on Kauai, Kilohana became the center of Garden Isle business and social life. Modern restoration has created from it a chic museum that recalls the heyday of sugar. Posh shops with catchy names such as Cane Field Clothing and Half Moon Trading Company occupy converted rooms, and the master bedroom is a gallery of works by Hawaiian artists. Throughout the home are furnishings from the 1930s—a piano, for example, and floor-to-ceiling beveled mirrors—and out back are the simple houses of the workers who labored in Kilohana's cane fields.

Kilohana's gastronomic centerpiece is **Gaylord's**, a regal restaurant built around a covered courtyard, using, wisely, the museum's furnished interior as a backdrop. On the horizon is Kilohana Crater, where ancient bird hunters captured dark-rumped petrels, an *aumakua* (ancestral spirit) sacred to bird-loving families. In season, vegetables and fruits are picked from Kilohana's gardens, adding a homegrown taste to Gaylord's salads and sandwiches. Lihue business people like to lunch at Gaylord's, as do vacationing Hollywood celebs. A special treat is the Sunday brunch, with a menu that includes cheese blintzes with Kauai Portuguese sausage. (Reservations required; Tel: 245-9593.)

If you have an unhurried schedule, a countrified side trip that will complement Kilohana is one to **Grove Farm Homestead**, a plantation-life museum also associated with the Wilcox clan. The farm is located off Lihue's Nawiliwili Road (Highway 58), near the Kukui Grove Commercial Village. Compared to Kilohana, Grove Farm is delightfully rural and homespun. Lazy guided strolls take you through a guest cottage, the Wilcoxes' main house and library, and poultry pens with authentic chicken manure smells. In the farm's antique-looking business office, furnished with a picturesque safe topped with a cannonball, guides show old photos of Wilcox family members, talk about farm life, and tell visitors how the safe's long-lost, but recently discovered, combination (b-a-l-l) explains the cannonball's significance. Listen for the name Miss Mable, Grove Farm founder George Wilcox's niece, who in 1971 helped convert the farm into a museum; to some of the tour guides, she's an icon, and "before Miss Mabel left us" is a melancholy comment often heard beside the chicken coop or the antique rain gage. Tours are given Mondays, Wednesdays, and Thursdays at 10:00 A.M. and 1:00 P.M. (but not on rainy days); reservations are required (Tel: 245-3202). After the tour, tea and cookies are served in the homestead's quaint kitchen. A copy of Miss Mabel's icebox cookies recipe—they are made with raw sugar—is available on request. Your cookies will be good, promises the farm, but not as good as those baked in the homestead's wood stove.

The **Kauai Hilton & Beach Villas**, on Kauai Beach Drive north of Lihue Airport, has no icebox cookies or poultry pens, but compared to the Westin Kauai it has a relaxed, bring-the-family atmosphere that also suits hand-holding honeymooners. Located on not-so-scenic flatlands between Kuhio Highway and Kawailoa (Hawaiian for "long water") Bay, the hotel stands rather forlornly on the landscape, flanked by a cluster of multistoried beach-villa condominiums, one owned by a Japanese movie star. A pool surrounded by rock caves and waterfalls is the Hilton's outdoor centerpiece, almost a child's wading pool compared to the Westin Kauai's pool. The beach that fronts the bay is a rambling coastline of sand, rugged and wild, not the soft, crescent-shaped beach pictured on Hawaiian postcards. Long, lazy, beachcombing walks, not beach sitting, is the main activity. The draws here are the cheerful restaurants, the nightclub—**Gilligan's**—and the hotel's proximity to Lihue Airport.

POIPU AND KOLOA

Sixteen miles southwest of Lihue Airport, reached by Kaumualii Highway (Highway 50) and Maluhia Road, is an old sugarcane coast now famous for its more profitable stepchild, **Poipu**, Kauai's Waikiki—but one without fast-food stores, traffic jams, and overly crowded beaches. The area's heartland consists of clusters of hotels and condominium resorts sandwiched between the seashore and the parallel Poipu Road, stretching from Makahuena Point (Kauai's southernmost tip, meaning "eyes overflowing with heat") to Koloa Landing, a 19th-century whaleship anchorage. The attraction here is a coastline of beaches—Poipu Beach Park, Waiohai, Brennecke's Beach—and *sunny* weather on a rainy island. (The annual rainfall at Poipu is only eight inches more than at Waikiki.)

Though still low-keyed and unhurried compared to Waikiki, Poipu is determined to become a major Hawaiian tourist destination. The 605-room Hyatt Regency Kauai is under construction here, and will open in 1991. The Hyatt's architects promise a style reminiscent of pre–World War II Hawaii, but no one, not even Hyatt, can turn back the clock to an era when only a handful of family-owned vacation cottages serviced these undiscovered shores.

The Poipu-Koloa Landing area is the birthplace of Prince Jonah Kuhio Kalanianaole, honored every March on Kuhio Day for his achievements as Hawaii's second territorial delegate to the U.S. Congress. A trace of Kuhio's Kauai can still be seen at **Poipu Beach Park**, where fishermen mend their nets and talk about goatfish and sharks.

Poipu's most upscale, eyebrow-raising address is the **Stouffer Waiohai Beach Resort**, beside the beach park. The W-shaped Waiohai is low-rise and shaded by palms, in keeping with a Poipu ordinance limiting all buildings to the height of a coconut tree, four stories. Guests are greeted with lei in the open-air lobby and escorted to their rattan-furnished rooms by a concierge dressed in a white Hawaiian gown. Quiet suppers with local and international culinary offerings are available in **The Tamarind**, where, by candlelight, you can eat Molokai venison or Kona abalone and drink a distinctive European wine. A fine Sunday Champagne brunch is served in the Waiohai's open-air Waiohai Terrace, overlooking the beach. An Island-grown treat is *lilikoi* (passion fruit) hollandaise, served with unlimited pours of Champagne. At the Waiohai, that familiar face seen in the lobby may be a TV actor or a Hollywood star.

An essential ingredient in a fine hotel is its sense of place and history, and apart from the glitter of restaurants and accommodations, two curious geographic features accent the Waiohai's tie to the landscape. A restored *heiau* (temple), built from lava rocks in 1600 and dedicated to fishing and agricultural deities, is at beachside; and nestled amid the hotel's foliage is a freshwater spring that fed a long-gone *ohai* (monkeypod tree), the key to understanding Waiohai's place-name, which means "the *ohai* bush near the fresh water."

Next door to the Waiohai is another Stouffer property, the **Stouffer Poipu Beach Resort**, casual, family-type accommodations right on the beach. Each room has a kitchenette.

The **Sheraton Kauai**, though rather staid compared to the Waiohai, has an attractive beach bordering a tiny peninsula of lava rocks that makes a handsome shore front for any hotel. The guest rooms near the beach are in two- and four-story units; the rest of the hotel's four-story units are set in gardens across Hoonani Road.

The Sheraton's most pleasant beachside attraction is the **Outrigger Room**. As you enter the restaurant, examine the room's namesake, a *waa*, or outrigger sailing canoe. The room's beach view is toward the Waiohai's *heiau* (temple), and this proximity of canoe and temple, two of old-time Hawaii's most important creations, adds a special Hawaiian flavor to the restaurant's Continental cuisine. At low tide, Hawaiians hunt among the shore rocks for the edible *opihi,* a mollusk with a tent-shaped shell that inspired the triangular designs on bark cloth made in Poipu centuries before resort clothing stores arrived. A seafood buffet is served on Friday nights, but don't expect *opihi* among the offerings, because, being handpicked, it's too expensive.

Poipu's most attractive, almost parklike, condominium resort, **Kiahuna Plantation**, lies camouflaged in tropical foliage between the Sheraton Kauai and the Stouffer Waiohai. The Kiahuna's two- and three-story "plantation-style" units are dispersed over a large acreage and sit on land once part of the Territory of Hawaii's oldest sugarcane plantation. Inside the lushness of Kiahuna's greenery is the **Plantation Gardens**, a cozy restaurant in a home given as a wedding gift to Alexandra Moir in 1933 by her sugar-growing dad. (Open for dinner only; Tel: 742-1695.) The open-air restaurant serves local seafood amidst antique furnishings and a botanically inspiring view that overlooks the gardens Alexandra and her husband created over a 35-year period. Paths amble among palm trees, African tulips, monkeypod trees, ferns, and bamboo, and—on Kauai, believe it or not—a cactus garden. The secluded gardens are popular with young couples who marry amid the shrubbery, then honeymoon at the resort. Older couples—the resort calls them "second-timers"—come here to sniff the flowers and marry, too, preferring a romantic setting and a private ceremony for their second (or maybe third) matrimonial fling. "The Hawaiian Wedding Song" is the popular accompaniment.

Away from condominium and hotel turf, two Poipu restaurants feed beachgoers sophisticated food. **Keoki's Paradise** in Kiahuna Shopping Village, near the Plantation Gardens, defines "paradise" on its menu as fresh local fish eaten in a tropical setting. Ask your waiter for the seafood special of the day, which may be *ono,* a game fish whose Hawaiian name means "good to eat" (how can you go wrong?), or *au* (swordfish), once placed with tiger sharks on sacrificial altars in ancient Hawaii. Keoki's prefers Napa Valley wine, especially Cabernet. **Brennecke's Beach Broiler**, near the Stouffer Waiohai and Poipu Beach Park, is a popular lunch spot with beachgoers. The management favors the *mahimahi* (dolphin*fish*—not dolphin), famed for its bright color changes, and has made this sport fish the restaurant's symbol, selling as many Brennecke's mahimahi tee-shirts as Bikini Island salads.

Koloa

Dating back to 1835, when the first sugar mill crushed sugarcane with koa logs, and owners paid workers in scrip redeemable at the mill's grocery store, **Old Koloa Town** is less than three miles inland, north of Poipu Beach Park, by way of the Poipu Road. "Koloa is, and has always been, a delightful place," said a local historian in 1935, when the old town depended on long-jointed sugarcane for its economic livelihood. Now the *new* old town—bright paint over weathered timber—thrives on tourism generated by the Poipu resorts, and despite the proliferation of tourists' dollars, remains a delightful road stop. Travellers driving from Lihue to Poipu pass through Koloa; most continue on to their hotels, then return a day or two later to eat and, after dark, explore the well-lit shops. Today, as in 1935, Koloa's enjoyment is taken slow.

The heart of tiny Old Koloa Town is at the intersection of Koloa and Maluhia roads, where there are several eateries. **The Koloa Broiler,** noted for baked beans and broil-your-own steaks, flanks a wooden walkway beside windows that allow passersby to spy on customers seated at the bar. For Italian snacks there is **Fez's Pizza,** built around a planked porch beside a tiny garden, and which has a Wurlitzer jukebox. **Lappert's Aloha Ice Cream,** the brainchild of a former liquor distiller, is headquarters for local and visiting *aikalima* (ice cream) epicureans. Highly recommended here are mango, passion fruit, and guava cheesecake ice cream, as well as Kauai pie, made from Kona-coffee ice cream, fudge, shredded coconut, and Kauai-grown macadamia nuts.

Koloa also houses a Crazy Shirts outlet that sells high-quality tee-shirts in a restored mom-and-pop store, where for years Koloa schoolchildren stopped to buy dried abalone and coconut candy and watch the gasoline inside the "visible gas" pump. The store, beside a huge monkeypod tree growing from Waikomo Stream, is still a Koloa landmark.

In contrast to Poipu's resort life, a very different place to stay in the Hoary Head Range north of Koloa is **Hale-**

manu (birdhouse), a mountain retreat providing a taste of rustic country living without those rustic workaday chores. Time turns back a century when you step inside Halemanu, a large cabin moved to Koloa from Kokee, Kauai's western wilderness. Built in 1867 from *lehua* wood, a tree rich in Hawaiian legends, the original cabin, once a private residence, is divided into four units, each with private bath. The so-called Grandma's Room is especially cozy and comfortable, and looks out on Waita Reservoir, which is noted for bass fishing. The old-fashioned dining room serves guests (a maximum of ten) a home-made breakfast. Artists and writers enjoy Halemanu's seclusion, where the only intrusion is a *pueo* (Hawaiian short-eared owl) that circles the premises hunting for lunch. To reach Halemanu from Koloa, drive north past the town's fire station on Maluhia Road to a fenced green water tank at the roadside, where you turn onto a cinder road leading northward through the sugarcane fields to the hills beyond.

Koloa's two most visible landmarks are the **Tree Tunnel** and St. Raphael's Church. The mile-long "tunnel" of trees, near the intersection of Highway 50 and Maluhia Road, is a familiar landmark on the Lihue-to-Poipu drive; visitors often receive the directions "Turn left at the Tree Tunnel." These eucalyptus trees, also called swamp mahogany, were planted in 1911 by a fruit-and-land company with leftover saplings that, surprisingly, survived the hazards of roadside residence. St. Raphael's, reached from Koloa by way of a road with stoplights for sugarcane trucks, is Kauai's oldest Roman Catholic church (1856). The church's walls, built from lava rock that unfortunately is now painted an unattractive white, are three feet thick. Plantation workers and their families are buried in the church's graveyard; one grave ("Child Walter") has a plumeria tree growing from its center, the blossoms falling on the aged tombstone like fragrant snowflakes. (Plumeria blossoms, which make a cheap lei, are nicknamed "cemetery flowers.")

North of Koloa is the **Kahili Mountain Park**, at the end of a sugarcane field. Operated by the Seventh-Day Adventist Church, the park offers accommodations to campers-at-heart who nonetheless prefer cabins, and to "persons oriented to outdoor activities." Each rustic cabin has a private bathroom (toilet) and outdoor shower. These accommodations are heavily booked, and advance reservations are a must.

THE WAIMEA AREA AND THE WEST COAST

West of the Poipu resort area, Kaumualii Highway (Highway 50) cuts through the country towns of Lawai, Kalaheo, and Hanapepe en route to Waimea (reddish water), a favorite place-name of ancient Hawaiians. This historic region, first seen by Europeans in 1778 when the ubiquitous Captain Cook arrived, has no fancy resorts or ritzy hotels, only enclaves of workaday Hawaiians living in a landscape blessed with rivers and streams flowing to the ocean. An aura of rebellion and individualism lingers here, for the last battle fought on Kauai occurred near Hanapepe—a revolt against rule by the Kamehameha dynasty—and the rebel island of Niihau, a privately owned domain and last stronghold of Hawaiian-speaking natives, rises forbiddingly on the horizon across the water.

The garden lushness that is endemic to Kauai is readily seen about three miles west of Koloa on the way to Waimea, at Lawai's **National Tropical Botanical Garden**, home of the beautiful **Allerton Estate**. Those with ethnobotanical interests, or simply a curiosity about Island flora, can see plants of medicinal value to ancient (and modern) Hawaiians, as well as species that are rare and endangered. The trek into the garden estate (created by philanthropist Robert Allerton and his son John) is a gentle safari into a landscape resembling a private sanctuary. A special spot is the Diana Fountain, where a replica of Canova's *Diana* stands beside a pavilion and reflecting pool.

Near the Allerton house, where the estate's gardener now lives, is Queen Emma's Summer Cottage, destination of many royalty-minded visitors. Emma, like modern visitors to the garden, seldom escaped the rain: "It has rained all day," wrote a minister in 1871, "but the natives still ride four miles to visit the Queen." Nowadays the walk to her cottage is shorter and the plants more exotic. There's even a Queen Emma lily, *Crinum augustum*.

Be sure to visit the garden on a day when tours of the Allerton Estate are given; they are not offered on weekends and not offered at all when film crews have reserved the area. Weekday tours are at 9:00 A.M. and 1:00 P.M., departing from the garden's visitors' center at the end of Hailima Road, south of the town of Lawai; Tel: 332-7361.

(Maps still read Pacific Tropical Botanical Gardens, but the name has been changed to National Tropical Botanical Gardens because of the organization's ownership of other gardens outside the Pacific area.)

Chicken, a sacrificial offering that always pleased Hawaii's ancient gods, is available in Kalaheo, west of Lawai, at the **Camp House Grill**, located at roadside in a brightly colored, plantation-style camp house. *Hulihuli* (barbecued) chicken is the house specialty, and chicken eaters from Lawai to Waimea come to nibble on drumsticks. The grill's camp-house look re-creates a bygone time when simple wood-frame camp houses were an integral part of the Kalaheo landscape. Artist James Hoyle, who has a gallery in Hanapepe, between Kalaheo and Waimea, finds artistic expression in the old camp houses and succeeds in preserving them on canvas.

A motorist speeding westward to Waimea after ingesting *hulihuli* chicken might easily bypass Hanapepe, though an hour's detour to the town's center, perhaps lunch at the **Green Garden Restaurant** and a stroll through downtown, is a worthwhile stop if you want to see a rustic, west coast Kauai town where the big seller is nuts and bolts at the hardware store. The family-managed Green Garden, opened in 1948, is a converted five-bedroom home decorated with orchids and hanging plants. Tour-vans arrive around noon, but the service is still friendly even when the place gets crowded. Be sure to try the homemade pies.

Tourism is taking a toehold in **Waimea**, once the proverbial one-horse town, and more and more rental cars are seen parked near **Wrangler's Restaurant**, a midtown eatery in a restored building between a Chevron gas station and the wood-frame Waimea Hawaiian Church, built about 1870. Western antiques, saddles, and old hand-held lanterns surround diners. The beef is raised on Kalaheo hillsides and is served as "macho-cut" sirloins. With your knife in hand and steak on plate, you might expect to see old-time TV characters such as Miss Kitty and Marshall Dillon of "Gunsmoke" hobnobbing at a corner table. Not far away, on a wooden pier extending into the ocean, fishermen drink beer and pass the time of day. (A pier sign reads: "Two crab nets per person, no reserving of space.") Walk on the pier and ask for a crab recipe—the people are friendly here. And remember, in Waimea you may have to step over horse manure on the sidewalk to reach Wrangler's or the pier.

Waimea Plantation Cottages, a half block west of Waimea Canyon Drive, a short way from Wrangler's, is the most unusual accommodation on Kauai. Each house is an example of sugar plantation architecture, restored and fitted with modern amenities. Cottages take the name of the plantation worker who once lived in them, such as Samio, Alfredo B., Locy, and Cuaresma. No hotel accommodation can duplicate the warm, plantation-era atmosphere that pervades here. Ceiling fans and period furniture of mahogany and wicker are standard fixtures. The cottages border the Waimea shoreline, where Hawaiian kings once lived, and on the premises is a cluster of sugar-camp houses still occupied by Hawaiians and called "our living museum" by the Cottages' staff. Veteran Kauai travellers stay for weeks, telling only their closest friends about the cottages and hoping no one else discovers them. Reservations are booked months in advance, but cancellations do occur and an on-the-scene traveller may find a vacancy.

The Wilderness

"I can feel the spirit of its woodland solitudes," said Mark Twain, "and I can hear the splash of its brooks." Though Twain's 1866 Hawaiian travels didn't include Kauai, his observation about the Islands' outdoors is vintage Twain and aptly describes Kauai's wilderness areas.

Three high-country state parks that are interlocked geographically but dissimilar in terrain—canyon, mountain woodlands, coastal valley—form the backcountry's awesome *wao nahele* (wilderness), where a Hawaiian god partial to mortal travellers slew the frightful *akua,* forest spirits that molested intruders. Two roads forming an upside-down Y rise from the coastal Kaumualii Highway (Highway 50) and feed traffic upland to the parks: Kokee Road in Kekaha, the official gateway, and Waimea Canyon Drive in Waimea. The more scenic, and less travelled, is the Waimea Canyon Drive, which intersects the coastal highway near Waimea Plantation Cottages; the drive is an off-the-beaten-path route that complements this magic area.

Those who revere the Colorado River's Grand Canyon will find Kauai's more modest version, **Waimea Canyon**, nicknamed the "Grand Canyon of the Pacific," lilliputian in comparison, but from an Islander's point of view its beauty and vastness are matchless. The park that bears the canyon's name begins where the Waimea Canyon Drive merges into Kokee Road. The northward drive then leads to two viewpoints, Waimea Canyon Lookout and Puu Hinahina, both off-road stops with excellent vistas of the mile-wide canyon, helicopters on tour, and the Waimea River, which for a million years has carried water from Mount Waialeale to sculpt this intriguing landscape. A careful observer can see white-tailed tropical birds riding the airways (their tail feathers were once used to decorate sailors' hats). Unknown to most visitors, a golden eagle once lived in the canyon, harassing the tourist-filled helicopters. The mystery of the bird's origin—eagles are not native to Hawaii—and why it hated helicopters still lingers. Sadly, in 1984 it dive-bombed into the blades of a touring copter, leaving its golden feathers as souvenirs.

Kokee State Park is the final destination of all visitors to Kauai's high country. Within its boundaries are hiking trails, streams, and dense forest seemingly still unexplored. Rare birds, once hunted by Hawaiian bird catchers to feather royal capes, take refuge deep in the woodlands, camouflaged in *mokihana* and *maile* plants, which are used to make lei. July in Kokee is the plum harvest season, which in its heyday became so popular that hundreds of jam makers and jelly-heads eagerly awaited the annual shotgun blast that opened the pickings. August and September is fishing season for the rainbow trout that swim in the park's brooks, Hawaii's only trout-fishing area; the fingerlings are raised on Oahu and carried into Kokee in backpacks.

The hairy, black wild pigs that roam the woods are significant in Hawaiian history as food, friend, and, along with humans, sacrificial offerings. Ancient Hawaiians who carried pork after dark risked attack from hungry ghosts, and travellers in Kokee are advised to forget about aluminum foil and wrap ham or bacon picnic sandwiches in *ti* leaves, a traditional anti-ghost protection for *puaa* (pig) meat. Ironically, both the park's fish and plum are imported attractions, not native to Kokee's forest, and the original Polynesian pig exists only in archaeological evidence, having interbred itself out of existence long ago with introduced species.

Despite the high prices and not-so-exciting reputations of lodges within state and national parks throughout the United States, Kokee's only accommodation, **Kokee Lodge**, has a special charm—and price—that makes it a popular year-round hideaway with locals and visitors alike. The cabins sleep three to seven persons, and are equipped with basic housekeeping items. The first cabins were built in 1952, constructed from lumber salvaged from the U.S. Army. The restaurant, originally a country store, is open to the public and serves breakfast and lunch daily, and dinner Fridays and Saturdays. (Non-guests and guests are both welcome in the restaurant.) The kitchen's fresh-baked corn bread is a backwoods treat; the bar, topped with a slab of koa wood cut from a tree felled by a hurricane, is near the fireplace, a comfortable hangout after a forest walk. In ancient times, canoe builders ventured into Kokee to cut koa (Hawaiian mahogany) for double-hulled voyaging canoes.

Kalalau Lookout, among the island's most spectacular viewpoints, is easily reached by car from the lodge and overlooks **Na Pali Coast State Park**, which is accessible by foot from Haena State Park on Kauai's North Shore at the western end of Kuhio Highway (Highway 56) to the east of Na Pali. The lookout peers into distant **Kalalau Valley**, fronted by a shoreline that can be explored by Zodiacs (the crafts Jacques Cousteau uses) and twin-hulled catamarans departing from Hanalei, also on the North Coast. This beautiful valley holds a tragic tale. A century ago a leper named Koolau refused to be deported to the leper settlement on Molokai. Rifle in hand, he hid in Kalalau, firing at policemen and resisting arrest until his disease killed him. Koolau's tragedy appealed to Jack London, whose short story "Koolau the Leper" glorifies both man and valley.

The valley next to Kalalau, though not part of the state park, is **Honopu**, the so-called Valley of the Lost Tribe. The discovery years ago of human bones in Honopu led to speculation that the remains of a theretofore undiscovered Hawaiian kingdom had been found. All that is known for certain is that in Hawaiian mythology a tribe of "little people" lived in Honopu and stole campers' food.

These two valleys are only part of the famed Na Pali coastline, noted for its breathtaking beauty. The isolated, rocky crags appear from a helicopter as rugged skyscrapers walling off valley from valley and beach from beach. At Waiahuakua and Alealau the cliffs, sculpted by millions of years of erosion, rise to over 3,800 feet, and at Kalalau to 4,100. When you approach Na Pali by boat, the nearness of the sea, relentlessly pounding against the shoreline and splashing into mysterious sea caves, adds a chill of excitement to a high-rise landscape of cascading waterfalls and misty peaks, scenery so exotic that Dino De Laurentiis's 1976 remake of *King Kong* featured a Na Pali valley as the giant ape's kingdom. (Na Pali means "the cliffs.")

WAILUA
AND THE COCONUT COAST

Like Kauai's wilderness parks, the Coconut Coast, on the eastern, opposite side of the island, north of Lihue, is rich in mythology, especially the landscape around the Coco Palms Resort at Wailua, six miles from Lihue, where Kuhio Highway (Highway 56) intersects Kuamoo Road beside the Wailua River. Extending for ten miles along Kauai's eastern side, from Lihue to Kapaa, the Coconut Coast takes its name from the coconut groves at the Coco Palms Resort, an area once reserved for Hawaiian royalty. According to legend, on the shores of Wailua Bay where the Wailua River meets the sea, the first *alii* (royalty) from Tahiti beached their double-hulled voyaging canoes, planted *kapu* sticks—no trespassers allowed—and established them-selves as masters of Kauai. The area was considered the island's most desirable land, and the river's headwaters and banks became sacred ground, covered with temples and the residences of chiefs, whose *mana* (spiritual power) was second only to that of the gods. Even the beach became a place apart, reserved as a playground for the elite, and *kapu* (taboo) to commoners.

Beside the river, and now open to commoners and kings alike, is the venerable **Coco Palms Resort**, which rightly considers itself the *kupuna* (respected elder) among Kauai's resort destinations. At first glance the row of multistoried units paralleling Kuhio Highway is alarm-ingly unattractive, but on the premises a lush landscape of coconut groves and fishponds (called "lagoons") reveals itself. Especially charming are the thatched-roof cottages around the ponds. Though beachgoers may find the unro-mantic amputation of the hotel from nearby Wailua Beach a hardship—you have to cross the highway to get to the beach—it is the coconut grove and the ponds, not the beach, that are the outdoor attractions here; the best room views face inland toward the grove.

In the 1840s Deborah Kapule, widow of Kauai's last

king, lived here beneath the cluster of palms, filling the surrounding ponds with fish and feeding them to her distinguished overnight guests. Kauai's early Protestant missionaries, travelling between Waimea and Hanalei, stayed with Kapule, as did the island's first Catholic priest. A canoe carried the visitors across the river while their horses swam behind.

Highly touted is the hotel's nightly torch-lighting ceremony, recalling a bygone century when Kapule's guests dined on mullet at her royal table near the torchlit fishponds. After the wail of a conch shell, muscular Hawaiians in red loincloths swinging flaming torches light row after row of torches, the flames brightening the grove, and, on occasion, the smoke wafting into the faces of startled onlookers. The ceremony begins around sunset, so go early: The best tables in the Lagoon Dining Room and Lagoon Terrace Lounge fill rapidly.

The Coco Palms' grounds, popular with honeymooners, are steeped in TV and movie trivia, a curious fate for an area known to ancient Hawaiians as "Great Sacred Wailua." On this hallowed earth, Elvis Presley crooned "The Hawaiian Wedding Song" to Joan Blackman in *Blue Hawaii,* and Mr. Roark (Ricardo Montalban) welcomed deplaning travellers to "Fantasy Island" from a bridge that spans a fishpond. Surprisingly, the most appealing structure in the palm grove is the wedding chapel constructed by Columbia Pictures for Rita Hayworth's film *Sadie Thompson.* The book to read in the chapel is Somerset Maugham's *The Trembling of a Leaf,* which contains the short story "Rain," made into several film versions, one of which was *Sadie Thompson.* Inside are wooden pews and an altar holding red, valentine-shaped anthuriums; the chapel is cooled by a wood-bladed ceiling fan.

Within view of the Coco Palms, and unknown to most visitors, are two royal birthstones wedged between the river and Kuamoo Road, at **Holoholoku Heiau.** The stones, easily mistaken for tumbledown boulders from the cliff above, were believed to possess great *mana* to aid in childbirth, and against them rested chiefesses as they gave life to Kauai's royalty. After birth, the child's umbilical cord was hidden nearby. Mothers seeking good luck for their offspring also hid cords in Captain Cook's ships, thinking them godlike floating islands.

An economical alternative to the more luxurious Coco Palms Resort is **Islander on the Beach,** located at beach-

side on Wailua Bay, off Kuhio Highway. Recently renovated, the Islander has new paint, new wallpaper, but
retains its family-style atmosphere.

Farther inland, on Kuamoo Road, you will come to
Opaekaa Falls, where, on the road's opposite side, the
Wailua River curves upstream toward its mountain source,
Waialeale, disappearing beneath the trees. The curious-
looking collection of huts along the riverbank, reached by
a downward-sloping roadway, is **Kamokila Hawaiian Village**, a re-creation of an old-time Kauai settlement run by a
local family. This is not Hawaii resurrected in the overly
sophisticated style of Oahu's Polynesian Cultural Center,
but rather a Hawaiian family's dream come true: a collection of thatched dwellings, a sacrificial oracle tower, and
Hawaiian lifestyle demonstrations housed on the banks of
Kauai's most historic river. A few nails, but very few, hold
the village together. Visitors can see a dryland taro patch,
banana trees, *noni* (a medicinal tree)—all in a homely
environment. What is missing are pigs without pens, common in old-time village life. At first the idea of free-
roaming pigs appealed to Kamokila's managers, but the
state health department, for sanitary reasons, pooh-
poohed the pigs. Closed Sundays ("We go to church on
Sunday," says the owner).

Kapaa

Wailua's neighboring town, Kapaa, despite its city-size
appearance, shoreline location, and weather-beaten rooftops, is mainly a food stop for those travelling to and from
Kauai's North Coast. A mainstay for fish is the **Kapaa Fish
and Chowder House**, with fishnet and nautical-gear decor and a local chowder served in a copper pot. For
prime rib, try **The Bull Shed**, located beside the ocean
near a seawall, where wall-crashing waves are visible
from the window tables. The prime clientele at **Ono
Family Restaurant** are moms, pops, and kids partial to the
excellent lemonade and the friendly though unhurried
service.

THE NORTH SHORE

The drive from Lihue or Wailua to Kauai's North Shore
on Kuhio Highway (Highway 56) is a relaxing excursion
through green, undulating countryside where cattle

egrets—a ubiquitous white bird seen in fields—prowl the landscape looking for insects, and Garden Isle produce is sold at Banana Joe's roadside fruit stand near Kilauea. The mental restlessness of not quite yet being in the Kauai of your imagination, detectable in Lihue and even Poipu, fades away as you approach this coast, where most longtime residents will shake their heads in sympathy when you say that you must return south, to the Westin Kauai or a Poipu resort, or to an even more alien destination such as Honolulu. The coastal area's heartland begins at Kilauea and continues along Kuhio Highway (Highway 56) west to Princeville, Hanalei, and Kee Beach at (literally) road's end. This is a landscape rich in scenic grandeur, Hawaiian mythology, rainfall, avian wildlife, and, at Princeville, resorts.

The island's best bird-watching is in **Kilauea Point National Wildlife Refuge** atop steep cliffs a mile north of Kilauea, reached by Kolo and Kilauea roads. The sanctuary is home to large colonies of wedge-tailed shearwaters and red-footed boobies. The sight of a frigate bird—its V-shaped wing tips a favorite tattoo design of yesteryear's Pacific Islanders—riding cushions of air high above the coastline *below* onlookers is unforgettable. Visitors from November through June can also observe the bill-clacking, head-bobbing courtship displays of the Laysan albatross, nicknamed the "gooney bird" during World War II. The refuge's lighthouse, built in 1913, was, by accident, the first Hawaii landfall—"the light of last resort," said a pilot—for the first transpacific flight from California to Oahu in 1927, which almost missed the Islands entirely. The pilot's three-engine monoplane was aptly named *Bird of Paradise*. Now obsolete, the lighthouse serves in retirement as a picturesque landmark welcoming migrating sea birds and bird watchers.

Princeville

From Kilauea, the route westward on Kuhio Highway leads to one of Kauai's most spectacular viewpoints: not a roadside lookout or a mountain watchtower, but, surprisingly, a resort-studded tableland overlooking Hanalei Bay. This is Princeville.

Although the name sounds like a developer's dream, it is rooted in authentic Hawaiian history, being a place-name dating to 1860, when Kamehameha IV and his son, Prince Albert, visited the area. First a sugar plantation, then a cattle ranch, and now a resort community, Prince-ville has its own airport and its own shopping center, a spic-and-span "plantation-style" complex with supermar-ket, art galleries, boutiques, restaurants, and a post office. The resorts behind the shopping center encircle the **Princeville Makai Golf Course**, which has a reputation for being hard on scorecards. Survivors of this course delight in talking about how the cannibalistic fairways digest golf balls.

A name you will often hear in Princeville is Bali Hai. Though romantic in sound, it has no traditional Hawaiian connection, being a fictional place-name in James A. Mich-ener's *Tales of the South Pacific*. The real Bali Hai is Aoba, a small island near Espíritu Santo in the Melanesian na-tion of Vanuatu, where Michener served as a naval officer in World War II. In 1957 Hollywood filmed *South Pacific,* a musical based on Michener's book, on Kauai. The film immortalized such North Shore locales as Mount Makana, cast as the mysterious Bali Hai, and Lumahai Beach: Both are across Hanalei Bay from Princeville.

Perhaps Princeville's most eye-catching view of the bay and the "Bali Hai mountains" is from the **Bali Hai Restau-rant** at **Hanalei Bay Resort**. Even employees from other Princeville resorts come here to breathe in the scenery. Princeville, said a landowner in the 1850s, is "the most beautiful spot in Hawaii," and seated at the restaurant, with its wraparound lanai overlooking the bay, you will find that observation difficult to refute. If you stay at this condominium resort, bring your tennis racket: The ram-bling collection of guest units is erected beside tennis courts. The clientele here is likewise tennis oriented, and even the courts have nice views. No one seems to mind the downslope walk to the beach.

The **Sheraton Mirage Princeville**, built on the slopes of Princeville's Puu Poa Point in three descending terraces, is the ritziest, and most expensive, place to stay in Princeville. In 1989, after steady criticism of the lack of views of Hanalei Bay from within the hotel's lobby, and determined to make itself even more luxurious (and expensive), it closed for renovations, and will reopen in March 1990, with, hopefully, better views of Hanalei Bay—what the hotel calls "the zillion-dollar view." The Mirage's kingly restaurant, **Nobles**, named after Hawaii's House of Nobles under Kings Kamehameha III and IV, will also be remodeled and, perhaps, renamed. The newer, even ritzier "SMP" will certainly please Hawaii's gossip columnists, who like such snazzy places where aides-de-camp to the rich and famous arrive under the noms de plume of Felix the Cat and Rambo Rex.

More low-keyed are the two sister condominium resorts sharing the hillside north of the Sheraton, the **Puu Poa** and the **Pali Ke Kua** (both on Princeville's Ka Haku Road). Named for the point of land on which it sits, the Puu Poa's cluster of concrete buildings is designed for those preferring plenty of living space—the luxury of two bedrooms with an expansive lanai and atrium. The more homely Pali Ke Kua has one-bedroom, wood-frame units that can accommodate those travelling without an aide-de-camp or royal entourage. At the Puu Poa a secluded beach is a short walk downhill, and at the Pali Ke Kua an abundance of ground space invites lazy evening walks and dinner at the resort's popular **Beamreach**, a nautical-theme restaurant with photos of yacht races on the walls. The outdoor view from both resorts is, of course, breathtaking.

Hanalei

If you are staying in Princeville, or are just visiting for the views, see Hanalei as well, just minutes away southwest across the steel-covered Hanalei Bridge. This one-lane bridge, built in 1913, serves as a barrier to large, air-conditioned tour buses and heavy construction vehicles. "When the bridge goes, Hanalei goes," say some locals. The village itself is a hodgepodge of shops, eateries, and residences wedged between Kuhio Highway and Hanalei Bay. The bay, which is shaped like a half-moon (the name means "crescent bay"), is rimmed by Hanalei Beach Park and Waioli Beach Park. The village takes its name from the bay, as does the beautiful valley and the Hanalei River, which waters the weeping willows. The Hanalei willows trace their roots to Napoleon's island of exile, Saint Helena, where a 19th-century seaman stole cuttings and carried them to Kauai potted in his shaving mug. The village has no real downtown, but Ching Young Village Shopping Center, a rather nondescript plaza, is where most visitors park.

A popular activity in Hanalei is eating. Early arrivers from Princeville or Wailua can extinguish breakfast appetites at the **Shell House** or the **West of the Moon Café**, both small and pleasant. The **Black Pot Luau Hut**, as the word *luau* indicates, has Hawaiian food. Farther afield, near the Hanalei Bridge, is the **Hanalei Dolphin**, supper only, noted for seafood and *haole* (white) chicken breasts—*haole* is the word for white-skinned traveller. Still farther from town, westward toward Haena, is **Charo's**, whose owner honeymooned on Kauai, fell in love with the scenery, and returned to sell wayfarers stuffed papayas and macadamia-nut fried shrimp at this flashy on-the-beach night spot. There is a dinner show nightly, with Latin and Hawaiian music (reservations: Tel: 826-6422).

Hanalei also has a well-known bar and luau restaurant drafted from the pages of Somerset Maugham. Even those squeamish about frequenting rustic-looking taverns will treasure an hour spent loitering inside **Tahiti Nui Bar**, where the down-home philosophy is, "What the hell, it's the Tahiti Nui!" Managed for years by Louise Marston ("Hanalei's First Lady of Tahiti"), the weather-beaten exterior and thatched-wall interior remind you of the type of tropical-style wateringhole a bearded beachcomber might enjoy. If Paul Gauguin lived in Hanalei he would drink here. Twice a week, on Wednesdays and Fridays at 6:30 P.M., Marston opens the luau with the theme song "Tahiti Nui," putting to shame the highly polished resort shows. The fruit and plumeria lei come from her farm near Kilauea. No connoisseur of Pacific bars can resist the Tahiti Nui. (Luau reservations; Tel: 826-6277.)

On the opposite end of the town, attracting a more conservative congregation than the Tahiti Nui and fronting rain-soaked mountains that sprout falls of "splashing, singing water" (*waioli*), sits **Waioli Mission House Museum**, the residence of American Protestant missionaries between 1837 and 1869. The attractive wood-frame house with a chimney and a second-story lanai is one of the first American-style houses built on Kauai. Friendly docents, sharp on missionary history, conduct a chatty walk through the living room and bedrooms filled with the artifacts of missionary life, such as a bookshelf of bedtime readings (*Annals of the American Pulpit,* for example) and a walking cane with a whale-tooth knob. The secluded mission house is behind Waioli Huiia Church, a Hanalei landmark itself, nicknamed the "Green Church." To park, turn beside the schoolhouse and drive into the dense grove of trees. Waioli Mission House is open Tuesdays, Thursdays, and Saturdays until 3:00 P.M.. Ring the ship's bell on the porch to announce your arrival.

Because the Hanalei area is so wet, the resulting multitude of streams between Hanalei and Kee Beach to the west—

road's end—necessitated a series of one-lane bridges. These turn-of-the-century bridges, considered an insult to technological progress by some road builders, are over-the-water treasures acting as traffic dams, slowing movement to the low-keyed pace of North Coast life. Cars must queue to cross each bridge, good news for the aesthetic-minded driver, bad news for the impatient.

Following these bridges westward will bring you to **Lumahai Beach,** which, thanks to the film *South Pacific,* is the North Shore's best-known seashore. Located on Wai-koko Bay, the beach by the nature of its terrain is divided into a western and eastern section; the western end is easily reached by car, with off-road parking in a sandy parking area, but the eastern end, site of the Bali Hai scenes in *South Pacific* (the nurses' beach), is sandwiched between rocky bluffs and is reached only via a downward trek through dense foliage from the roadway. No signs point to this section of the beach, which begins a half mile from the third bridge crossed after leaving Hanalei—the adventure is finding it. To avoid a traffic ticket, be sure to park in the direction of traffic. Lumahai activities on either the western or eastern end tend to include such quiet pastimes as postcard writing, beach walking, and wave watching.

A dramatic conclusion to any North Shore visit is the short, uphill hike to **Kaulu o Laka Heiau,** sacred to Laka, goddess of the hula. The climb to the *heiau*'s hula platform is not difficult. A trail on the *mauka* (inland) side of Kee Beach, where the roadway ends, west from Lumahai and Hanalei—and near where the **Kalalau foot trail** to the **Na Pali** begins—leads to this dance-inspiring location, once the most important hula site in all Hawaii. Watch your language; crude talk was forbidden here. On special occasions Kauai's hula students still use this platform, where high on this hill of rain, hula masters of ancient Kauai chanted their devotion to a deity of dance: "Dwelling in the source of the mists, Laka, mistress of the hula; woman, who by strife gained rank in heaven."

Shops and Shopping

In old-time Hawaii the possession of Western trading-ship goods added great prestige to the owner. Especially prized were such contraptions as clocks and spyglasses. Kamehameha the Great was Hawaii's first passionate shopper, paying for foreign goods with island-grown sandalwood, a fragrant wood exported by Westerners to China. Kamehameha liked guns and gentlemen's clothes; he posed for his best-known portrait wearing a red European vest. Nowadays shopping history has reversed itself, and it is travellers from outside Hawaii who want island-made arts, crafts, and products. To go shopping, *kuai hele* in Hawaiian, still adds to one's prestige, even when purchases are made on credit, *kuai hoaie*.

Niihau shell leis. These leis are not simply beautiful shell jewelry, but an art form native to Niihau. The refined art of making shell leis has passed from generation to generation on Niihau, Kauai's neighboring island, and today Niihau leis are a local status symbol among women of fashion in Hawaii. Three types of tiny beach shells are used: *momi* ("pearl"), the most commonly used shell, with 20 different variants; *laiki,* shells that resemble grains of rice; and *kahelelani,* the smallest and most difficult to collect, thus used to make the most expensive leis. The most stately and romantic place on Kauai to buy Niihau-made leis is **The Hawaiian Collection Room** at Kilohana, the restored sugar-plantation estate two miles south of Lihue. They have a beautiful lei collection and provide knowledgeable, detailed guidance in lei selection and appreciation; a home-display box made of Hawaii wood is also available to exhibit and protect the lei that, in time, will become a treasured family heirloom— the essence of Hawaii itself.

Contemporary art galleries. **The Gallery at Waiohai,** inside the Stouffer Waiohai hotel in Poipu, has acrylic scenes of the Old Sugar Coast, fine ocean seascapes, and other Hawaiiana by local artists. **Kilohana Galleries,** in an elegantly restored bedroom at Kilohana, has selected contemporary art by many talented artists working in watercolors and mixed media. The beauty of Kauai's North Shore in oils and acrylics is on canvas at **Montage Galleries** in the Princeville Shopping Center; especially delightful are the colorful sea- and landscapes of Hanalei and the Na Pali Coast.

Arts and crafts. **Artisans' Guild of Kauai,** upstairs in the Old Ching Young Store in Hanalei's shopping center, is a cooperative of Kauai artists and craftsmen and has a diverse collection of artwork, including *kapa* (bark cloth) paintings. Would-be beachcombers looking for sandals will find **Kauai Sandalworks** in the Market Place at Coconut Plantation in Kapaa a "treat for da feet," where even sandals for big guys (size 14) are available. Contemporary scrimshaw for beginner and connoisseur collectors can be seen at **The Ship Store Gallery** in Kiahuna Shopping Village in Poipu and at **Ye Olde Ship Store** in the Market Place at Coconut Plantation in Kapaa. (Scrimshaw is a bone-engraving art form created by the 19th-century whalemen who passed through Hawaii in pursuit of sperm whales.) **Elephant Walk**, a gift gallery at the Westin Kauai in Lihue, has limited-edition jewelry pieces and hand-blown glass gifts, while Hawaii volcanic-glass jewelry—made from volcanic material from the Big Island's Kilauea volcano—is available at **Tideline Gallery** in Kiahuna Shopping Village in Poipu.

Island fruits. Roadside produce shopping is a Kauai tradition and a fun way for visitors to meet island residents. **Farm Fresh Fruit Stand** (4-1345 Kuhio Highway) in Kapaa has papayas and local jams and will deliver pineapples to the airport. **Banana Joe's Tropical Fruit Farm**, between Kilauea and Kalihi Wai on Kuhio Highway, specializes in dehydrated tropical fruits, and the owner also makes coconut-leaf baskets and hats. Papayas are always a good buy; pick a yellow and green papaya with a smooth skin and that shows no signs of shriveling. Pineapples are popular, of course, though most come from Oahu. To select the best pineapple examine the "eyes," the diamond-shaped figures on the outside. Look for a consistency of size: large, even eye-patterns, from bottom to top, indicate a mature pineapple.

Leis and plants. When you place a lei around your neck, remember that Hawaiian children were often called *lei* because their arms encircled their mother's neck like a necklace, or lei. **Pua & Kawika's Flowers & Gifts** in the Old Ching Young Store in Hanalei's shopping center has leis made of `ilima,* a delicate flower whose juice was once used to make a mild laxative for babies. For those preferring a lei steeped in mythology, leis made of *maile,* a periwinkle favored by Laka, goddess of the hula, are made at **Marina Flowers** at Wailua Marina in Wailua, across the river from the Coco Palms Resort. Shoppers with botanical interests who want Kauai plants "to go" can buy U.S. government-approved flowers and seeds at **Kauai Certified Tropicals** at Kilohana, where a popular take-home item is a miniature plant grown in Hawaii's lava rock.

Unusual shops. For those tired of mailing picture postcards of romantic sunsets, Georgio's Coconuts has personalized, hand-painted "cocograms" (whole coconuts) that will astonish the postman and the recipient alike; the artists at work can be seen at the **Old Hawaiian Trading Post** at the corner of Route 50 and Koloa Road in Lawai, on the road to Waimea. A good selection of books on Hawaiian myths and culture is at **Hawaiian Art Museum and Bookstore** (2488 Kolo Road) in Kilauea, a charming North Shore shop with *lau hala* (pandanus leaf) walls inside the town's former post office and general store. Near Lihue, **Stones of Kilohana,** housed in a 1910 guest cottage behind Kilohana's main house, has beautifully designed handworks collected from craftspeople throughout Polynesia.

GETTING AROUND

There are two airports on Kauai, one at Lihue, served by Hawaiian Airlines and Aloha Airlines, and a second, smaller one, near Princeville. Flight time from Honolulu to Lihue is 27 minutes. If you begin or end your stay in a Princeville resort, Aloha IslandAir (on Oahu, Tel: 808-833-3219) has scheduled interisland flights from Honolulu Airport to Princeville Airport on 18-passenger, twin-engine aircraft. Flight time is 50 minutes.

There is no public bus service on Kauai, and only on Niihau, 17 miles offshore, is real *horse*-powered transport available. The mode here is today's workhorse, the rental car. For the glove compartment, the best map is James A. Bier's *Kauai,* which provides a good overview of the island; it is available in most Kauai bookstores. Because of the rugged terrain, distances and driving times vary dramatically. The Lihue-to-Poipu drive, for instance, is a 16-mile, half-hour excursion; the 50-mile drive from Lihue to Kalalau Lookout in Kokee State Park takes about two hours; and Poipu to Hanalei (54 miles) takes an hour and a half.

A profusion of helicopter and tour-boat operators offers wilderness-area adventures. Bali Hai Helicopters in Hanapepe on the South Coast (Tel: 808-332-7331) flies over both the Waimea Canyon and the Na Pali Coast. Niihau Helicopters (Tel: 808-335-3500) departs from Port Allen on a flexible schedule for a two-hour flight with two stops on Niihau for $185 per person (four to seven passengers). Captain Zodiac Raft Expeditions in Hanalei (Tel: 808-826-9371) has year-round Na Pali Coast raft trips, plus whale-watching excursions from January to April, when the humpbacks, singing their strange songs, pass through Kauai waters.

A reminder: Binoculars are useful for enjoying Kauai's spectacular lookouts and wildlife areas.

ACCOMMODATIONS REFERENCE

The rate ranges given here are projections for winter 1989 through summer 1990. Unless otherwise indicated, rates are for double room, double occupancy. Hawaii's telephone area code is 808.

▶ **Coco Palms Resort.** In Waipouli, near the Wailua River. P.O. Box 631, **Lihue**, HI 96766. Tel: 822-4921. $105–$145; suites $150–$375.

▶ **Halemanu.** Located above the Waita Reservoir. Rates include breakfast. P.O. Box 729, **Koloa**, HI 96756. Tel: 742-1288. $85–$125 (cash or checks only—no credit cards).

▶ **Hanalei Bay Resort.** 5380 Honoiki Street, P.O. Box 220, **Hanalei**, HI 96714. Tel: 826-6522; interisland, (800) 221-6061; elsewhere in U.S., (800) 657-7922. $80–$435; suites $500–$1,000.

▶ **Islander on the Beach.** 484 Kuhio Highway, **Kapaa**, HI 96746. Tel: 822-7414; elsewhere in U.S., (800) 367-7052. $78–$99 (low season); $88–$109, suites $125–$145 (high season).

▶ **Kahili Mountain Park.** P.O. Box 298, **Koloa**, HI 96756. Tel: 742-9921. $32.

▶ **Kauai Hilton & Beach Villas.** 4331 Kauai Beach Drive, **Lihue**, HI 96766. Tel: 245--1955; elsewhere in U.S., (800) HILTONS. $125–$175; villas $140–$200.

▶ **Kiahuna Plantation.** 2253 Poipu Road, **Koloa**, HI 96756. Tel: 742–6411; elsewhere in U.S., (800) 367-7052. $130–$390.

▶ **Kokee Lodge.** P.O. Box 819, **Waimea**, Kauai, HI 96796. Tel: 335-6061. Cabins $35–$45.

▶ **Pali Ke Kua.** P.O. Box 899, **Hanalei**, HI 96714. Tel: 826-9066; elsewhere in U.S., (800) 367-7042. $90–$125.

▶ **Puu Poa.** P.O. Box 1185, **Hanalei**, HI 96714. Tel: 826-9066; elsewhere in U.S., (800) 367-7042. $135–$185.

▶ **Sheraton Kauai.** 2440 Hoonani Road, **Poipu**, HI 96756. Tel: 742-1661; elsewhere in U.S., (800) 325-3535. $140–$250; suites $330–$1,000.

▶ **Sheraton Mirage Princeville.** 5520 Kahaku Road, P.O. Box 3069, **Princeville**, HI 96722. Tel: 826-9644; elsewhere in U.S., (800) 325-3535. $240–$450; suites $750–$2,100.

▶ **Stouffer Poipu Beach Resort.** 2251 Poipu Road, **Poipu**

Beach, HI 96756. Tel: 742-1681; elsewhere in U.S., (800) 468-3571 or (800) 426-4122. $85–$140.

▶ **Stouffer Waiohai Beach Resort**. 2249 Poipu Road, **Poipu Beach**, HI 96756. Tel: 742-9511; elsewhere in U.S., (800) HOTELS-1. $135–$280; suites $375–$1,200.

▶ **Waimea Plantation Cottages**. 9600 Kaumualii Highway, P.O. Box 367, **Waimea**, Kauai, HI 96796. Tel: 338-1625; elsewhere in U.S., (800) 9-WAIMEA. $65–$120 (three-night minimum); $385–$770 for seven-day stay.

▶ **Westin Kauai**. Kalapaki Beach, **Lihue**, HI 96766. Tel: 245-5050; elsewhere in U.S., (800) 228-3000. $185–$385; suites $475–$1,500.

BED-AND-BREAKFASTS

For information about bed-and-breakfast accommodations in the Hawaiian Islands, see Oahu Outside Hawaii Accommodations Reference.

NIIHAU
THE FORBIDDEN ISLAND

By John W. Perry

The cartographic profile of Niihau looks like an upraised seal peering toward Kauai's western coast, 17 miles away across Kaulakahi Channel. Along the seal's spine, isolated from public Hawaii, is a small, Hawaiian-speaking community of native Hawaiians who live and work on the state's only privately owned island. Most of Niihau is restricted in access to tourists as well as longtime Kauai residents. The closest a visitor can get to Niihan is a helicopter tour above the island and a landing in a secluded, unpopulated area. Because of its history of being *kapu* (forbidden) for the most part to outsiders, Niihau (pronounced knee-ee-how) is nicknamed the "Forbidden Island," and has for decades retained an aura of seclusion akin to xenophobia. Viewed through rain from a high-country lookout atop Kauai's Waimea Canyon, Niihau—as mysterious to outsiders as King Arthur's fabled Avalon—appears and disappears in the mist, unhurried, seldom visited.

In a state where development is considered by some to be almost divine, many residents and tourists alike shake their heads in disbelief at Niihau's withdrawal from the modern world. The electorate there even voted against statehood, the only precinct to do so. Yet Niihau's isolated lifestyle is considered a blessing, not a hardship. Charcoal is made from *kiawe* (mesquite) trees and honey is collected. Horseback is a favored mode of transportation, used to herd cattle and chase pigs. There is no garbage collection, no telephones, no jails. Nothing is done on Sundays except going to church and reading a wish book from Honolulu: the Sears catalog.

A Scottish family bought the island from King Kamehameha V in 1864 for $10,000 in gold, and the descendants, the Robinson family, continue to keep it an offshore miracle where the original language is preserved and the tenet Limited Tourist Access is rigorously enforced.

Niihau's most famous unwelcome guest crash landed in a Zero fighter in December 1941, only hours after the Japanese attack on Pearl Harbor. The bizarre occurrence, known as the Niihau Incident, ended in bloody combat when the pilot shot and wounded a Niihauan. Still conscious, the injured man, used to manhandling sheep, grabbed the pilot, dashed him against a stone wall, and cut his throat with a hunting knife. The pilot's death inspired the patriotic song "They Couldn't Take Niihau Nohow."

Shell enthusiasts should know that the best necklaces in Hawaii are exported from here, and make meaningful—but expensive—souvenirs. Unlike flower leis, which wilt, the multihued necklaces are permanent mementos. On Niihau itself the shells are revered as "island flowers," collected by women from the seashore and strung through natural or man-made holes. Old-time hula dancers decorated themselves with these leis, and in the official photographic portraits of Queen Kapiolani and Queen Emma both are wearing ivory-colored Niihau leis to complement their Victorian-style dress.

Niihau Helicopter (Tel: 808-335-3500) departs from Kauai's Port Allen Airport daily at 9:00 A.M., 12:00 P.M., and 3:00 P.M. for a two-hour flight with two stops on Niihau. The cost is $185 per person, with a minimum of four passengers required, and a maximum of eight. The flight is on a two-engine copter used to provide emergency medical service for the island, and the air fares help to finance the copter's cost. It lands for half an hour on the island's remote north end, avoiding the main village of Puuwai. Visitors are allowed to walk around on a Forbidden Isle beach, becoming, for a moment, Niihau's only nonresident beachcombers.

You can also fly above and around the island on an aerial tour that includes a Kauai flyover. The 50-minute, narrated excursion, flown by Panorama Air (office on Oahu; Tel: 808-836-2122), departs from Kauai's Lihue Airport daily at 2:30 P.M. A minimum of four passengers is required.

CHRONOLOGY OF THE HISTORY OF HAWAII

Precontact Period

Centuries before the first European explorer sighted Hawaii, the Islanders had evolved a remarkable civilization that embraced a strong seafaring heritage, a pantheon of gods that rivaled that of the Greeks and Romans—Pele (volcanoes), Lono (harvest), Ku (war)—and a strict legal system (*kapu*) that kept order and punished *kapu*-breakers by roasting them in earth ovens until "the body grease dripped." Tribal leaders (*alii*) ruled the common laborers and fishermen, and the *kahuna* (priest) oversaw the religious aspects of daily life. The early Hawaiians were avid surfers, game players, and, like other Polynesians, tellers of tales. Their ancient lifestyle resembled feudal Europe, ancestral homeland of the white foreigners (*haole*) whose arrival in the closing years of the 18th century changed Hawaii forever.

Contact and After

- **1778**: English explorer James Cook, commander of HMS *Resolution* and HMS *Discovery,* sights Oahu, Kauai, and Niihau in January. Though Spanish navigators piloting the treasure-laden Manila galleons may have sighted Hawaii centuries earlier, Cook retains his fame as Hawaii's "discoverer."
- **1779**: In Kona, Cook unwittingly provokes the Hawaiians at Kealakekua Bay and is killed at water's edge. The Hawaiians, under coercion, return part of his hand to the ship's crew.

- **1795**: The Kohala-born warrior Kamehameha conquers Maui, Lanai, Molokai, and Oahu. His 1796 attempt to invade and conquer Kauai fails, but in 1810 he wins the island by diplomacy, unifying all Hawaii under a single ruler.
- **1819**: Kamehameha I dies in Kona and is buried in a cave beside the seashore. The burial site—"known only to the Morning Star"—has never been discovered. His son and successor, Kamehameha II, overthrows the traditional Hawaiian religion by ordering the destruction of *heiau* (temples) and an end to the *kapu* system. The first New England whaleships arrive in September.
- **1820**: The first shipload of American missionaries arrives at Kailua, Hawaii, on the brig *Thaddeus*. Protestant evangelism in Hawaii begins.
- **1824**: The Christian convert Kapiolani stands beside Halemaumau, the fiery pit within Kilauea's crater, and repudiates Pele (god of volcanoes), winning a victory for the Protestant missionaries. As an act of sacrilege she eats a handful of sacred *ohelo* berries.
- **1832**: Death of Kaahumanu, Kamehameha I's favorite wife, and Hawaii's first regent. Between 1819 and 1832 she virtually ruled Hawaii, with her stepson, Kamehameha II.
- **1842**: U.S. President John Tyler, in a subtle diplomatic move, recognizes the Kingdom of Hawaii by invoking the Monroe Doctrine to discourage intervention by European powers.
- **1845**: The Hawaiian capital is moved from the whaling port of Lahaina, Maui, to Honolulu, with its fine harbor.
- **1846–1855**: Decade of the Great Mahele, a land division among the king, his chiefs, Hawaiian commoners, and foreigners that converted native-owned lands to fee-simple title, following the tradition of Western property practices; in short, the long-term disfranchisement of Hawaiians from their lands in favor of whites.
- **1850**: First permanent Mormon missionaries arrive.
- **1852**: First Chinese contract workers arrive.
- **1856**: The first flush toilet in Honolulu installed in

King Kamehameha IV's home on the grounds of the modern-day Iolani Place.

- **1866**: First leprosy patients taken to the Kalaupapa Peninsula on Molokai.
- **1868**: First Japanese contract laborers arrive. (The Meiji Restoration, signaling the end of feudalism in Japan and the country's entry into the "modern" world, took place in 1867.)
- **1873**: Father Damien de Veuster, a Belgian priest, arrives on Molokai to aid leprosy victims; he dies in 1889 of leprosy.
- **1883**: King Kalakaua (The Merrie Monarch) holds a coronation ceremony nine years after his ascension to the throne. The event, held at Kalakaua's newly built residence, Iolani Palace, revives the hula.
- **1889**: Disgruntled Hawaiians, opposed to both Kalakaua and the growing numbers of anti-monarchists and reformers, attempt a coup d'etat, which is squashed, leaving several dead. Robert Louis Stevenson, author of *Treasure Island,* arrives in Honolulu and befriends the ill-fated Princess Kaiulani, who dies at the age of 23.
- **1891**: King Kalakaua dies in San Francisco while on a whirlwind tour of the West Coast. Prior to his death he complains that California weather is too cold compared to Hawaii's eternal summer.
- **1893**: Queen Liliuokalani, the last monarch of Hawaii, is deposed by annexationists seeking to further American sugar interests.
- **1894**: The Republic of Hawaii, with Sanford Dole as president, is proclaimed on July 4; U.S. president Grover Cleveland sends a letter of recognition to the new government.
- **1900**: The Territory of Hawaii is inaugurated in the United States in June, following President William McKinley's signing of the Organic Act, which defined the status of the territory and provided for its framework of government; many native-born Hawaiians are appalled.
- **1901**: The Moana Hotel, the first large tourist hotel in Waikiki, opens at beachside as a four-story highrise; two additional stories and wings are added in 1918. In 1987–1988 the hotel undergoes

restoration to re-create the bygone era of the early 1900s when the Moana reigned as "The First Lady of Waikiki." James Dole, future pineapple king, organizes the Hawaiian Pineapple Company.

- **1907**: The College of Agriculture and Mechanic Arts (today the University of Hawaii) begins with 12 faculty and 5 students.
- **1908**: Construction of Pearl Harbor begins, disturbing the shark goddess Kaahupahau, who is said to proctect the harbor by killing intruders. (In 1913, a dry dock collapses and a *kahuna,* a sorcerer, appeases the goddess with ceremonial blessings.)
- **1912**: Duke Kahanamoku, one of Hawaii's all-time surfing greats, wins a gold medal in the 100-meter freestyle swim at the Olympic Games in Sweden.
- **1927**: The Royal Hawaiian Hotel, one of the early luxury resorts, opens on Waikiki Beach.
- **1927**: First successful nonstop flight from U.S. Mainland to Hawaiian Islands.
- **1935**: Hawaii-based army aircraft drop 600-pound TNT bombs on a Mauna Loa lava flow to divert its course and protect Hilo from incineration.
- **1941**: On December 7 (President Roosevelt calls it a day of "infamy") Pearl Harbor is attacked by Japan, plunging the United States into World War II. A Japanese pilot sends the message *"Tora! Tora! Tora!"*—code words (*tora* means tiger) to indicate surprise attack achieved.
- **1959**: In March, Hawaii is admitted to the United States as the fiftieth state. In August, William Quinn takes office as first state governor. The first Boeing lands in Honolulu, cutting air travel to California to four and a half hours.
- **1960**: East-West Center founded in Honolulu.
- **1962**: The USS *Arizona* Memorial is dedicated on Memorial Day at Pearl Harbor.
- **1976**: *Hokulea,* a double-hulled voyaging canoe, departs from Hawaii for Tahiti, renewing interest in Hawaii's Polynesian heritage by retracing the ancient canoe routes between the two island groups.
- **1982**: Hurricane Iwa, strongest hurricane to strike the Islands in recorded times, decimates Kauai (the name Iwa is said to mean frigate bird, a harbinger of storms when seen over land).

- **1984**: Hawaii's silver jubilee of statehood is celebrated.
- **1986**: John Waihee, first elected governor of Hawaiian ancestry, takes office in December as the fourth governor.
- **1989**: Research continues on a deep-water cable to transmit volcanic geothermal energy; King Kalakaua originally proposed the idea to inventor Thomas Edison in 1881.

—John W. Perry

INDEX

WHEN TRAVELLING, PACK

PENGUIN TRAVEL GUIDES

All the Penguin Travel Guides offer you the selective and up-to-date information you need to plan and enjoy your vacations. Written by travel writers who really know the areas they cover, the Penguin Travel Guides are lively, reliable, and easy to use. So remember, when travelling, pack a Penguin.

☐ *The Penguin Guide to Australia 1990*
0-14-019911-X $11.95

☐ *The Penguin Guide to Canada 1990*
0-14-019918-7 $14.95
(available February 1990)

☐ *The Penguin Guide to the Caribbean 1990*
0-14-019908-X $10.95

☐ *The Penguin Guide to England & Wales 1990*
0-14-019912-8 $13.95

☐ *The Penguin Guide to France 1990*
0-14-019914-4 $14.95

☐ *The Penguin Guide to Germany 1990*
0-14-019922-5 $14.95
(available March 1990)

☐ *The Penguin Guide to Greece 1990*
0-14-019921-7 $13.95
(available March 1990)

☐ *The Penguin Guide to Hawaii 1990*
0-14-019909-8 $9.95

WHEN TRAVELLING, PACK

PENGUIN TRAVEL GUIDES

☐ *The Penguin Guide to Ireland 1990*
0-14-019917-9 $10.95
(available February 1990)

☐ *The Penguin Guide to Italy 1990*
0-14-019916-0 $14.95
(available February 1990)

☐ *The Penguin Guide to Mexico 1990*
0-14-019913-6 $13.95

☐ *The Penguin Guide to New York City 1990*
0-14-019919-5 $12.95
(available March 1990)

☐ *The Penguin Guide to Portugal 1990*
0-14-019920-9 $12.95
(available February 1990)

☐ *The Penguin Guide to Spain 1990*
0-14-019915-2 $13.95
(available February 1990)